Broken

by Nicola Haken

Cover Design by Reese Dante

http://www.reesedante.com

Edited by E. Adams

ISBN-13: 978-1523706723
ISBN-10: 1523706724

This book contains scenes and references that may pose as a trigger, or be uncomfortable to read, for some people. If you're struggling, you are not alone. Don't give up. Don't be afraid to ask for help. You are important.

www.mind.org.uk

http://www.mentalhealthamerica.net

For anyone who's ever felt a little broken. Keep
going – one breath at a time.
You are important.

Contents

Preface	1
Chapter One	3
Chapter Two	25
Chapter Three	41
Chapter Four	65
Chapter Five	79
Chapter Six	108
Chapter Seven	134
Chapter Eight	174
Chapter Nine	204
Chapter Ten	238
Chapter Eleven	278
Chapter Twelve	323
Chapter Thirteen	352
Epilogue	380

Acknowledgements 391

About the Author 394

Preface

Pain is inevitable, suffering is optional. I heard that somewhere once and it stuck in my mind, haunting me, ever since. I often toyed with its interpretation and, now, I have the answer.

The pain is there. It never leaves. Sometimes it's bearable, but it's *always* there. It's pecked away at my soul all my life and, finally, it's won.

I surrender.

It's taken everything. I am nothing more than a hollow shell. There are no more pieces left to try and put back together. I have nothing else to fight with.

I'm exhausted.

Pain is inevitable, suffering is optional.

Today, I opt to end the suffering. Today, I welcome the pain as it slices into my wrist, knowing it will be the last time. As I watch my tormented life seep from my body in thick, red spirals, a small smile crawls onto my lips.

It's over.

I'm free.

My body starts to tremble and I lie back in the bathtub, closing my eyes. A rush of peace, contentment, washes over my dying body, cleansing my soul as I drift into the serene darkness, embracing the shadow for the first time in my life.

Forgive me.

Chapter One

~Theo~

Beads of nerves roll around in my stomach as I walk into Holden House, the tallest building in the centre of Manchester. The first day in any new job is always daunting, but stepping into my first role in a publishing house pushes a further stab of pressure into my gut.

I'm met with a curious glance by a young, impeccably dressed, woman behind the long reception desk as I pass through the revolving glass doors. I walk over, holding up the I.D. card that dangles from my lanyard.

Her eyes hone in on it, squinting as she reads. "Good morning, Mr Davenport. Marketing is on the thirteenth floor."

"Thanks," I mutter, although I know where I'm going after my induction last week.

I fiddle with my collar as I ride the lift, eyeing myself up in the mirror on the back wall. My last job, managing a mobile phone shop, didn't require me to wear a suit and I can't help feeling uncomfortable. Restricted.

The lift pings and the doors peel apart. I step out onto the office floor, surveying my surroundings. A small lump forms in my throat as I wonder who to approach first, although you wouldn't know by looking at me. I am a swan as I make my way to the middle of the floor; kicking and struggling beneath the surface, poised and confident above.

A hand lands on my shoulder, startling me. "You're the new kid, right?"

I force a smile but inside I want to punch the fucker for calling me a kid. I'm twenty-seven years old; too old, in some people's opinion, to be taking a job as an office junior. But working in this industry has been my goal since I was ten years old. Unfortunately, life got in the way, until now. I was kicked out of college for showing up drunk on more than one occasion and ended up working tedious jobs until I got bored and found something else. Perhaps things would've turned out differently if I'd chosen my own path, but I applied to study biology at college with the aim of becoming a doctor, because that's what my brother did, my father, *and* my grandfather. It was kind of expected of me, but I just didn't care enough about the subject to bother putting the effort in.

I saw the opening here by accident while surfing the Job Centre website and dismissed it at first, but it stayed in my head until I eventually convinced myself I'm not too old to go after a career rather than just a job.

I'm not just a reader, or a writer; I inhale written words like they're my oxygen. It's not a hobby. It's a *passion.* People intrigue me. *Life* intrigues me. I see a story behind every set of eyes I meet, history in every voice. I'll see someone wearing a smile and wonder what put it there. Words allow me to immerse myself in a whole other world. I get to become a different person.

So, *that's* the reason I took this job. I want to see behind the scenes, learn the process of bringing someone's imagination, someone's *dreams* to life. I don't expect to make a name for myself with my own writing. I do it for no other reason than I love it. I do it to stop my mind exploding. I do it because while I have a pen in my hand, I can be anyone I want to be.

This job is a more realistic version of my dream. I will complete the menial tasks. I will fetch coffee, stuff envelopes. I will learn. Grow. I will work my way up, and I will achieve a successful career helping *others* to accomplish *their* dreams.

"I'm Mike. Section manager," the owner of the hand on my shoulder says.

I proffer my hand for him to shake and he accepts. "Theo," I say, nodding.

"Let me show you to your station."

Again, I nod, and trail behind Mike as he leads the way. My lips turn up a little as my gaze unashamedly hones in on his arse. I approve. *Utterly squeezable*, I think, before being dragged back into the room when he turns around.

"This is your desk. My colleague, Stacey…" He pauses to point at a smartly dressed woman, with a brown bob and thick-rimmed glasses, at the other side of the room. "…Will come and talk you through a few things shortly. But first, let's see what you're made of." My eyes widen and my ears prick up, eager to get stuck in. "Coffee machine's down the hall. White. One sugar."

I fight the urge to scowl and nod instead. Mike claps my back and walks away, disappearing into one of the large, private offices. I don't like him already.

I spend the rest of the day making coffee, filing documents, and being taken on a tour of the gigantic building by Stacey, who I've decided I like a *lot* more than Mike the Moron.

The rest of the week plays out pretty much the same, only now, on Friday, I recognise some faces and am no longer sitting alone in the cafeteria. Ripping open a sachet of salt, I sprinkle it over my chips and toss one in my mouth. I listen to the conversation around the table, not knowing enough about the topic to join in. They're discussing the mysterious James Holden, CEO of Holden House, one of the biggest publishing houses on this side of the world. He's someone I've yet to even see, let alone be introduced to.

"I heard he's called a meeting for next Tuesday," a guy called Edward says. I like Ed. He's a junior, like me, although he's four years younger and has been here for six months. I don't know him well, but he has the potential to become a good friend.

"He creeps me out," Katie, a supervisor from the design floor, replies. "I swear, I was discussing a client with him once, before he made CEO, and he looked straight through me like…well like he's not all there if you know what I mean. He's weird."

"He was probably just uninterested," Ed counters with an expression I can't quite decipher. "He pays other people to do the work for him."

Katie must notice the strange look on his face too because she jerks her neck back. "You've slept with him haven't you?" Her voice is high, almost a squeal.

What the… I keep listening, shovelling chips into my mouth like popcorn.

"*Shh,*" Ed snaps, scanning his immediate surroundings. "Keep it down." He looks flustered as he drops his half eaten sandwich onto his plate. "I have *not* slept with him."

"You so have. It's common knowledge the guy fucks his way through the juniors during their first year. Didn't think you'd be stupid enough to be one of them, though," she says, her tone almost disgusted.

"That's not true," Ed says, but his pursed eyebrows tell me he's not convinced.

He actually looks a little hurt, so I cut in, feeling uncomfortable with the direction of the conversation. "Anyone fancy grabbing a few drinks after work?"

"Can't," Katie says. "I have a date."

"Count me in," Ed pipes up at the exact same time as Stacey. Stacey has been in charge of showing me the ropes. She's a manager, but doesn't appear to be on the same power trip as the others. I like her.

"I'm going home to change first," I say. "Probably pick up my friend and head out to Canal Street. Meet at eight in Velvet?"

"I've never been to Canal Street," Stacey answers, and my jaw drops open a little.

People travel from all over the country, maybe even the world, to visit Manchester's famous gay village. "You live in Manchester and you've *never* been to the village?"

She shrugs. "I'm not gay."

"Don't worry," I say. "You don't need to pay by drinking from the furry cup. They accept cash like everywhere else."

"Funny," she mutters, only she isn't laughing. "I'll be there. Haven't had a night out in ages."

I rub my hands together and smile. My night is planned. Dancing, alcohol, and lots of laughter with friends, new and old.

Perfect Friday night.

* * *

"Yeah, he's totally screwed him," Tess says after I repeat the conversation from the cafeteria earlier. I met Tess when I worked at a bar here in the village to support myself through college. She'd been working there for several months already and took it upon herself to help me settle in. We've been best friends ever since.

"Hmm. I dunno. It can't be true. I'm not buying that *every* member of junior staff is gay so he can't possibly have fucked them *all*."

"Unless he's bi. I'll let you know if I meet him."

"Oh yeah? How you gonna do that?"

"I have built in Bi-Fi," she says, tapping the side of her head. "Or maybe he's a Christian Grey and stalks all potential employees beforehand and only employs the queers."

"I haven't read it so I wouldn't know."

"Neither have I. Didn't stop my auntie Michelle telling me all about it in excruciating detail though," she explains, shuddering at the memory.

"Well, even if that were true he won't be fucking *me*. I have self respect."

Beer in hand, I stretch out on the ornate chair shaped like a throne, glad to be out of my suit and in a more comfortable jeans and t-shirt ensemble. When I spot Ed and Stacey walking through the doors opposite the bar, I stand up and wave them over. Ed's still in his work clothes whereas Stacey looks every shade of hot in a tight red dress and matching shoes.

Placing my hand on the top of her arm when she reaches me, I peck her cheek with my lips. "If I was straight I'd be totally hard for you right now," I say, grinning as I pull back.

When I turn, I notice Tess has sucked her bottom lip between her teeth. "If I had a dick, so would I."

Stacey appears a little stunned by Tess' forwardness and an awkward smile tugs at her mouth. The thing is with Tess, she *has* a filter, but more often than not she chooses not to use it.

I introduce Tess to my colleagues, who I'm already starting to think of as friends, and we decide to stay here for a quiet drink before heading on to G.A.Y., a club designed for thumping music and dancing rather than conversation. Tess leaves the table to get a round of drinks and I nip to the bathroom. While I'm in there I take a moment to tease the strands of my short, fair hair that have fallen out of style back into place, stopping when my gaze lands on a guy in the mirror who's just stepped out of one of the stalls behind me.

He stops right next to me, looking into the same mirror as he adjusts the collar of his crisp, white shirt. My pulse quickens and it makes no sense to me. I've seen hot guys before. But this guy is *more* than hot. He's stunning. So beautiful I feel self-conscious in his presence. Ironing out imaginary creases in my shirt with flattened hands, I study the stranger's eyes in the mirror, searching for his story. There's a power behind them. An arrogance. He's a top, for sure. Something about the way he holds himself tells me he'd never allow anyone to have any kind of control over him.

"Like what you see?" he asks, running his fingers through his cropped, black hair. His accent is clearly northern, but there's a forced poshness, like he's taught himself to be *better* than everyone else.

Heat pools in my cheeks as I rip my gaze away, my mouth too dry to reply. Immediately, I wash away the sticky residue on my fingers from fiddling with my gelled hair, and then get the hell out.

Well that *was weird.*

Stacey and Ed have their backs to me when I arrive back at the table.

"I just don't get why they'd sleep with a woman who looks like a man. Why not just sleep with an *actual* man?" I overhear Stacey say.

I don't know if she's referring to Tess, or just androgynous -dressing lesbians in general, but I lower my mouth to her ear. "I think the lack of cock has something to do with it."

Stacey snaps her head around to face me, her cheeks clashing with her red dress. "S-sorry," she stutters. "I didn't mean anything bad by it."

I smile and settle down into my chair. "Don't worry. I don't understand their aversion to dick either." I wink and Stacey visibly relaxes.

"I have to say, I was surprised to find out you were gay. I mean, I suspected it when you suggested a night out here, but I didn't know for sure until you complimented me on my dress. You don't *look* gay."

I raise my eyebrow and notice Ed laughing beside her. "My fault. I'm always leaving my damn rainbow at home."

Stacey throws a hand over her face. "I've done it again, haven't I?" she mutters, her voice low, embarrassed. "I didn't mean to offend you."

"You didn't," I assure, raising my hands off the table to make room for the tray of drinks Tess has just appeared with.

"Well, *I'm* offended," Ed cuts in. "You didn't sound surprised when you found out *I* was gay."

"You have, you know, the *walk*. It was obvious with you."

Before Ed can reply Tess hands out our drinks, staring at me while wearing pursed eyebrows and a contemplative pout. "You're flustered," she notes. "You look like you've just had sex."

Stacey coughs, almost choking on the wine she's just sipped.

"I have *not* just had sex," I say, knowing she's joking because she knows *me*, knows I'm not into impromptu fucks against bathroom walls. "I *did* just make an arse out of myself though. I bumped into the hottest guy I've ever seen in the toilet and just stared at him like some kind of moron. Think David Gandy but younger."

Tess scrunches her nose. "My auntie fancies David Gandy."

"Your aunt has good taste," Stacey joins in, finally relaxing into our company.

David Gandy remains the topic of conversation for almost half an hour. Ed's never heard of him so Stacey pulls up Google on her phone and searches for images. Ed fails to see the appeal, comparing him to his granddad. We continue to chat, getting to know each other outside a formal work environment, and end up staying in Velvet for another three drinks. When we eventually head outside, my mum calls as we walk along the cobbled street.

I excuse myself and make my way over to the stone wall to answer, staring down to the canal. "Hey, Mum," I answer, shooing my friends with a wave of my hand, silently telling them I'll catch up in a few minutes.

"Where are you? You sound outside?"

"I'm with some friends."

"Oh sorry, honey. I didn't mean to interrupt, I just wanted to see if you're settled into your new job."

Her concern makes me smile. "So far, so good. I've made a couple of friends and have got the coffee machine down to a fine art."

She sighs down the line and I know she's debating whether to give me the *you're worth so much more than a brew boy* speech. "And the new flat? Have you finished unpacking?"

"Just about. Why don't you come over next week and I'll give you the grand tour?"

"Hmm."

"I'll pick you up," I offer, knowing her hesitation is due to the fact she's scared to drive on the motorway. With me being in Manchester, she won't use the roads either because she believes big cities are full of maniac drivers. "Or get Tom to bring you."

Tom is my older brother, by two years. By day he's an emergency doctor in St Andrew's hospital's A&E department and by night he's a loud, over-opinionated wanker. But he's my brother so I'm genetically programmed to love him and put up with his bullshit.

"I'll call him tomorrow," my mum agrees. "See when he's free."

"Great. Look, Mum, I need to go. My friends are waiting, but I'll see you on Sunday."

Sunday is mandatory family day, where my mum cooks a roast dinner with all the trimmings for me and my brother, and in latter years, Tess too. We haven't missed a single afternoon since my dad passed away four years ago. Losing a family member, especially a parent, makes you realise how important spending time together is. I still feel guilty that, before then, I took my family for granted. When you're young you want to go off on your own, find new adventures, party, have fun, all the while assuming your family will still be there when you get back.

Until one day one of them isn't.

"Okay, honey. Stay safe tonight and don't forget to text me when you get home."

"Sure," I say. I know the drill. "Love you."

"Love you too, baby boy."

I can't help cringe when she calls me that. It takes me right back to high school when I was ribbed for six months after she said it in front of my friends. It was hard enough trying to hide the fact I was gay without getting the piss ripped out of me on a daily basis for being a mummy's boy.

Tucking my phone into my jeans pocket, I jog the rest of the way to G.A.Y. I can't see my friends when I arrive so assume they've gone in without me. I know where to find them though. Tess and I have designated meeting spots in almost all of the bars and clubs around here, so after getting in, I head to the second floor bar, spotting them as soon as I reach the top stair.

As I make my way over to Tess, I see Ed pulling on Stacey's arm, trying to drag her out onto the dance floor. She protests weakly, giggling, but soon gives in and sashays away in rhythm with the beat of the music.

Tess leans into my ear. "Your friend is hot," she says, straining her voice so I can hear her.

"She's also very straight," I tell her, laughing as I grab the bottle of lager in her hand. "Dance?"

Tess nods and takes my hand. We weave through the crowd of people dancing and eating each other's faces, into the middle of the floor and show the club what we're made of. She grinds her arse against my crotch, making me laugh, and we stay that way for a couple of hours, grinding and singing out of tune, only stopping to buy more drinks.

By midnight, I'm lagging and feeling a little dizzy. "Piss break!" I call out, too drunk to feel embarrassed by the fact I'm stumbling on unsteady feet as I make my way to the bathroom.

I spend five minutes trying to remember how to undo the button on my jeans before taking a piss, all the while supporting myself with one hand on the wall because I feel like I'm going to fall over. Turning away from the urinal, I dance towards the sinks singing *Maybe Tomorrow* by the Stereophonics at the top of my voice.

"Simon Cowell would come in his pants if he heard you, mate," a guy I've never seen before jokes, clapping my shoulder on his way out of the bathroom.

He so fucking would, I think, and then carry on singing. I'm about to break into the second verse when hands appear on my hips from behind, stopping me dead in my tracks.

"I've been hard since I saw you earlier."

I know that voice. That's David Gandy's voice. Its owner's face is breathing heavily into my neck. I don't know if it's because I'm so drunk, or because I'm so stunned, but I can't speak. As I turn around to face the voice all I can think about is the fact if I don't breathe soon I'm going to pass out.

When I see his face it forces a rush of air into my lungs. I'm flustered, and he knows it. One side of his mouth twists into a smirk and he kisses along the rough stubble on my jaw.

"I want to fuck you," he whispers in my ear and I can't figure out why I haven't punched him in his beautiful face yet. Instead, all I can focus on is how gravelly and delicious his voice sounds. "You want it," he adds, cupping my dick through my jeans.

I'm hard. So hard it's almost painful. I've no idea what's going on with my body. Inside I'm yelling, asking myself what the fuck I'm playing at, but my dick is betraying me. I still haven't uttered a single word yet I'm allowing myself to be pushed backwards into a cubicle. David, as I seem to have named him in my head, pins me against the wall, raking his rich brown eyes up and down my body as he blindly reaches out and locks the stall door.

His mouth lands on mine as he fumbles with my zipper. He tastes of whiskey and tobacco and my eyes roll into the back of my head like he's physically intoxicating me. I tell myself not to, but I ignore it and arch my back, pushing my groin into him and allowing him to roll my jeans over my arse and push them down my legs. My cock springs free, hitting the material covering his crotch and all rationale and reason evaporates from my mind.

I grab his hair and drive my tongue between his lips while he reaches between our bodies and roughly tugs at my dick. I can't breathe. I can't even think. He releases my mouth, grinning wickedly, and my head falls back, hitting the wall as I groan into the air.

"Holy shit," I cry out, and I don't care if anyone hears me.

I bite my lip in an effort to stifle the intense moans and I know I'm only seconds away from exploding into his strong hand. His grip is so tight. He's pumping me so fast. *Too* fast. I can't hold off. My balls ache and my cock starts to weep as I reach for his shoulder to steady myself.

"Oh *fuck* I'm…" It's too late. I buck my hips, forcing my dick deeper into his palm as jets of hot cum burst from my tip, coating his fingers.

"My turn," he growls in my ear and I'm too breathless to protest as he spins me around and bends me over the toilet. "I'm going to fuck you so hard you won't be able to walk for a week without remembering this night."

Oh my God…

I hear him unbuckle his belt, followed by the sound of a condom wrapper being torn open, and right now I don't know who I am anymore. This isn't me. I don't fuck strangers in bathrooms. I've never even had a one-night stand. But I can't stop it. I don't *want* to.

I gasp at the sensation of cold lube being rubbed between my arse cheeks and take a deep breath. Without a word, he pushes inside me. Hard. Fast. I'm not ready and the burn takes my breath away as he slams into me over and over again, holding me down with one hand on the small of my back and the other gripping my hip.

"You're so fucking tight," he says and his voice sends shivers down my spine.

He's stretching me and it's only just bearable but I don't want him to stop.

"Holy shit," I whimper, my body trembling as I struggle to support my weight with one hand on the wall in front of me and the other locked onto to the cistern.

"Fuck yes," he breathes. "Take that dick."

I think he's close because his speed increases. All I can hear is ragged breaths and slapping flesh and my cock is already starting to swell again.

"Ah *fuck*," he chokes out, driving into me one last time, so forcefully I lose my grip on the wall and almost collapse.

I'm still panting when he pulls out of me and I rise to my feet slowly, feeling dizzy. When I find the courage to turn around, the stranger I've just let fuck me senseless is fastening the button on his pants. He reaches behind me and lifts the toilet seat, tossing the used condom inside before flushing it away. I can't look him in the eye as a rush of shame floods my veins. Instead, I focus on the discarded condom and lube sachets on the floor.

I see his fingers approach my face and he curls them around the back of my neck and pulls my heated face to his. I'm paralysed as I let him kiss my lips, and then he backs away.

"Thanks," he says….

And then he's gone.

Jeans still gathered around my ankles, I stumble back until I hit the wall.

What the fuck just happened?

I take a few minutes to compose my erratic thoughts and steady my breathing before pulling up my pants. Bending down, I pick up the torn sachets and throw them in the bin before leaving the bathroom in a daze. I'm instantly sober, no longer wobbly on my feet.

Tess is by the bar, chatting up some chick with long blonde hair. She leaves her behind, rushing over to me, the second I meet her gaze.

"What happened to you? You've been gone ages. I was just about to send Jimmy in to check on you."

I don't know who Jimmy is and, right now, I don't particularly care. "I, um…" I squeeze my eyes closed and rub my face to make sure I haven't dreamt it. "I just got fucked by David Gandy."

* * *

Tess crashed at my place last night. We left the club soon after my irresponsible encounter with the hot as hell stranger, while Ed and Stacey stayed behind, on course to drink themselves into oblivion.

This morning I've woken up with a hangover plucked straight from the pits of hell. My mouth is dry and tastes altogether disgusting, so I get up, stumbling from the head rush, and make brushing my teeth my first priority.

Tess must hear me get out of bed because she calls to me from the living room. "I made you a brew!" Her voice sounds like a freight train pummelling into my ears.

I can't summon enough energy to reply, so I carry on taking a piss and then turn to the sink to wash my hands and face. "Ugh," I mutter to my reflection in the mirror. I look like shit. My eyes are dark, sunken. My hair is a mess and my skin is dry. My highlights need touching up, too, and I make a mental note to ask Tess to do them at weekend. I refuse to look at my sorry arse any longer so I stare at my hands while I clean them, instead.

When I venture out into the small living room I find little comfort in the fact Tess doesn't look much better. Her hair is shorter than mine and it's currently sticking out in a thousand different directions. She's sitting on the laminate floor with her legs crossed, wearing a pair of my boxers and one of my hoodies.

"You need a fucking sofa," she whines, pointing to a mug of coffee on the floor in front of her.

I sit down next to her and take an eager sip from the chipped mug. "Do you know how little I'm earning right now? Think yourself lucky I can afford that coffee you're drinking."

"That's what this is? Tastes like piss."

I laugh at her dramatics. "I'll splash out on a jar of the good stuff on payday. Just for you."

Tess studies my face as she drinks the cheap coffee. I look away because I know she's about to probe me about last night and embarrassment creeps onto my cheeks. *What the hell was I thinking?*

"Stop looking so ashamed," she says. "You're not the only guy to have a one-night stand. In fact, you're probably one of the few who hasn't. Well, until last night, but you know what I mean. It's about time you got some. You haven't had a good shag since Stinky Steve."

Oh God. Stinky Steve. I've only had two relationships in my life, each lasting six weeks, and the last being with Steve. I've never been interested in casual, which makes serious relationships difficult when most other people in their twenties live to have fun and fuck around. He didn't smell *that* bad, and he was a good guy…until I caught him in bed with the lad who lived next door to him.

Maybe that's why I write romance. I'm a dreamer at heart. If I can't have it in real life, I'll live it on paper instead.

"I can't help it. I feel like a slut."

"You used protection, right?"

"He did. I shot it elsewhere."

Tess' face morphs into a revolted expression. "See, this is why I like girls. Less messy."

We stay quiet for a while and I decide I need painkillers before my brain detonates inside my skull. I haul myself up and walk the four steps to the kitchen area, plucking a box of aspirin from the cabinet.

Tess follows and puts our empty mugs in the sink with a clatter that makes me wince from the pain in my head. "Put it behind you and move on. You'll probably never see him again anyway."

The words stab into my chest and it aches more than it should. I hadn't finished looking for his story, too distracted by the unfathomable power he had over me. But I can't stop thinking about those eyes. They held a level of pain I'd never witnessed before. Pain so intense I couldn't even begin to unravel the tale behind it in the short space of time I had with him. Now, I never will, and I find myself filled with a bizarre sense of regret.

"We'll stop at the lake on the way to my mum's tomorrow," I say, forcing a subject change.

The only thing I really miss about living in Rochdale is my regular two and a half mile run around Hollingworth Lake. I still try to do it once a month before going to my mum's for Sunday dinner, though. If it were up to me I'd go every week but it's not worth the earache from Tess. It's a stunning place. There's a path which winds right around the water and takes you through a trail of trees and breath taking scenery. I need that right now. I need to focus on a different kind of beauty than the man whose face won't leave my head. I need to run until all I can focus on is the burn in my lungs rather than the sting in my arse I feel today. It's uncomfortable, and worse than that, it's a constant reminder of the night I want to forget.

"Ugh. Please don't make me," Tess grumbles. "I still haven't recovered from last time."

"That's even more reason to run tomorrow. You need to keep it up and each time will get easier."

"You've been saying that for the last three years."

"And for three years you've got over your bad mood and done it, just like you will tomorrow."

Tess scowls at me. "I hope you choke on your aspirin," she says as I swish the soluble tablets around in a glass of water.

Wincing at the bitter taste, I drink them down in three gulps and slam the empty glass down on the counter. "I'm going back to bed."

And I don't plan on crawling back out of it until tomorrow.

Chapter Two

~James~

When three AM rolls around, I close the word doc. I'm working on and decide to check the emails I've been ignoring for over a week. Amidst the four hundred, or so, business correspondences I see several from my older brother, Max. They contain nothing important, just general nonsense about his day. It's his not so subtle way of checking up on me to make sure I'm coping with the death of our father three months ago. I'm doing just fine. I have no choice since taking over his position as the head of Holden House. I don't have time to grieve when I have a staff of over three hundred people relying on me.

I close his emails and move on to the others. I can't reply to Max at this time of the night. If he finds out I've not been sleeping lately he'll be on my arse faster than a fly on shit. I work through the others for the next couple of hours and finish by composing an email to Helen, my PA, asking her to make the necessary arrangements to bring Tuesday's meeting forward to this afternoon.

We've recently acquired a new contract with one of the biggest selling magazines in Europe. Predominantly a fiction publishing house, this could be a huge game changer for us and I'm planning a complete restructure of my employees as well as extending the building and employing a team of new recruits. I expect some opposition, but my father trusted me to keep the business that's been in our family for four generations alive, to help it grow, and the only way to do that is to take risks and diversify.

I'm grateful when I hear my seven AM alarm sound on my mobile. It means I can finally stop pacing my vast living room and get ready for work. I like being alone, life is easier that way, but when it's coupled with phases of insomnia the nights seem longer and insanely boring.

Stepping in the shower, I take extra time to lather the soap into my heavily tattooed arms, and then shave the scruff off my face that has appeared during the night. I think I've passed an hour but as I walk out of the bathroom, naked and running a towel through my dark hair, I see on the clock it's only been twenty minutes.

Fuck it, I think. I will just go into work early. Heading into my bedroom, I dress quickly, fixing my father's cufflinks in place on my white shirt before shrugging into one of my tailored black jackets. I grab my suitcase and keys on the way out of my apartment and don't remember I haven't eaten breakfast until I'm already in my car. I consider stopping somewhere to pick up food but decide I'm not hungry and turn on the radio instead.

A small smile teases my lips when my ears meet the sound of *Maybe Tomorrow* by the Stereophonics blasting through the speakers, so loud, my seat vibrates. I think back to the cute guy who sang an almost unintelligible version of it on Friday night before I fucked him over a toilet. I don't usually give my shags a second thought, but this one has stuck. There was an intensity in his stare that I can't seem to forget, almost as if he saw deeper than what I was offering. Like, somehow, he saw *me*.

I shake my head at the ridiculous notion. He was a random fuck in a long line of many and I need to stop reading into it. Ideally, by plunging my dick into another eager arse as soon as possible.

After pulling into the nearest car park, a few streets away from my building, I pull out my phone and listen to my voicemails as I walk the rest of the way.

"Oh for fuck's sake," I say to no one while listening to a message from Helen, telling me her daughter is sick and she can't come into work. Thanks to the law protecting working parents, there's sod all I can do about it except scowl at every person I walk past as I near Holden House.

The building is all steel and glass and I walk inside without bothering to give my usual 'Good morning,' to the security guy on the door. I'm in a bad mood. The kind that balloons in your stomach and makes you feel nauseous from the amount of hatred you feel for the whole damn world.

I see a guy with red hair waiting by the lifts and it surprises me that I'm not the first person here. He has his back to me but he's vaguely familiar. The lift opens and he steps inside, and when he turns around I'm pretty sure I've fucked him before. In my office, if I remember correctly.

I follow him inside and he offers a nervous smile before staring down at his feet. I chew on the corner of my lip, trying to remember his name, but it's nowhere to be found. "How are you with emails?" The question rolls off my tongue without my permission.

He looks up at me with a confused expression and my eyes zoom in on his I.D. badge. *Edward Walsh.* I don't recognise the name and decide I probably wasn't interested enough to ask when I bent him over my desk.

"Um…" He draws his eyebrows together. "I know how to email. Doesn't everybody?"

Straightening my tie, I look straight ahead, refusing eye-contact with him. "Good. You're my PA for the rest of the day."

"Um…"

"Is that a problem?"

"N-no," he stutters.

I get the feeling I'm intimidating him. I like that. It means he'll do whatever I ask. "Be in my office in twenty minutes."

The doors open on the marketing floor and Edward steps out without looking back. I carry on up to the top floor and make my way straight to my desk where I pull up my emails and reply to my brother. I type out an insincere apology, tell him I've been busy securing the new contract, and that I'll visit him and his family soon. I've been saying that for two months now and it makes me sigh when I hit send, knowing I can't put it off much longer.

Edward's knock sounds on my door fifteen minutes later. He's early. Again, I like that.

"Come in," I call, proffering my hand towards the leather chair on the opposite side of my walnut desk when he enters. "Here are Helen's access codes," I say, sliding a brown document pouch over to him. "I need you to draw up an email and circulate it to every department head right away. You'll find instructions from me in Helen's inbox."

"Okay," he mutters, running a finger along the inside of his collar. He's flustered, causing a rush of heat to gather around his neck.

I let my eyes roam down his body and they hover over the bulge in his crotch. He must notice because he shifts nervously in his seat, clearing his throat. If he performs well today, I might just thank him with a little performance of my own later.

“Run along,” I say with a shoo of my hand. I’m a patronising arsehole but I love how easy it is to make this guy blush.

Scooping the document wallet from the desk, Edward stands and scurries out of the room. My dick is already twitching at the thought of being buried in his tight little arse as I watch him walk away, and I hope the day passes quickly so I can reward him.

Several hours later my meeting plays out pretty much like I expected. I see a few anxious faces and hear some opposition from people unwilling to move departments. I need to find out where I stand legally before I can tell them to either suck it up or resign so, after dismissing my team, I tell Edward to arrange an appointment with my solicitor and a union rep.

He’s done well today. He’s impressed me repeatedly, especially with the PowerPoint presentation he created for the meeting without being asked. His initiative definitely deserves praise, and as I hand him my Dictaphone containing letters I need typing up, I brush my hand against his arse in a way that can be explained as accidental if I see any hint of a sexual harassment complaint flicker in his eyes. When he bites his lip, I take it as a green light and give him a taste of what’s to come, moulding my palm to his arse cheek and squeezing firmly.

My PA’s office is adjoined to mine, separated by a glass wall with vertical blinds. I’ve left them open today to keep an eye on Edward, and a little while later, I'm on the phone to HR dealing with the first of likely many complaints about today's announcement, when, for the first time in my life, my breath catches in my throat.

"I'll call you back," I say into the receiver, slamming it down without waiting for a reply.

He's here. The guy responsible for massacring one of my favourite Stereophonics tracks. The guy who didn't utter a single word while I wanked him off against a bathroom wall. The guy I can't get out of my damn mind. The guy whose eyes chipped the iron walls of my soul. He's here. In Edward's office, talking to him like he knows him.

Does he work for me? I think, just as my phone starts ringing. Edward has his phone against his ear so I suspect it's him. "Yes?"

"I have a contract here for JD Simmons. Shall I bring it through now?"

"You have work to do. Send in your friend." As soon as I finish speaking I wonder why I've said it. I want to see this man again and it confuses me.

I watch with intrigue as Edward passes on my message and the guy I can't forget shrugs before strolling over to the shared door between our offices, clearly unaware of who he's about to meet. His disinterested gaze disappears the moment he lifts his head and his eyes lock onto my face.

For a moment, he just stares, his stubbled jaw slightly agape, and all I can think about is driving my tongue into the gap between his lips.

"I, um, I was told to give this to you," he says, his voice low, barely there. He hands me a folder and I hold it between my fingers, lingering for just a second, connecting me to him. "Apparently the author only deals with you."

"What's your name?" I ask, ignoring him as I take the file. I make a point of angling my arm so my wrist brushes against his knuckles and I feel it all the way to my dick. My brain tells me to look at his I.D. badge but my eyes refuse to leave his face.

He's a stunning man; brown hair with soft highlights that I suspect come from a bottle, vivid green eyes, and just enough stubble on his face to drive me insane as I imagine it grating against my balls while I fuck his mouth.

"I assume you have one?" I press, after several seconds of silence.

"Theodore Davenport. My friends call me Theo. *You* can call me Theodore."

So he does *have a voice?* A sarcastic one at that. It turns me the hell on. "Like the chipmunk?" I say with an amused smile.

I get the reaction I'm pushing for – a delicious scowl. "Original," he mutters, thoroughly unimpressed.

"And which department do you work in, *Theodore?*"

"I'm an office junior down in marketing. Just started last week." His voice gains more confidence with every word.

"A junior? How old are you?"

"Old enough to know I don't need to answer your questions unless they're business related."

It's like we're children in a staring contest, and as with any challenge, I accept, and I win. Eventually he gives in first and blinks, holding his eyes closed for a little longer than necessary.

"You weren't this fiery on Friday," I say, purposely goading him for no other reason than I'm an arse.

"I was drunk," he says, his pink cheeks betraying his conviction. "That won't happen again."

It will. "Of course. Anything else I can help you with?" *Like maybe the erection you're sporting?*

"No. That's it," he says, yet he's still standing in front of me.

"If you're waiting for me to open the door for you, I'm not that much of a gentleman."

He turns a whole new shade of red as he coughs into his fist and turns sharply on his heels. I stare after him until the door closes, with a smile on my face that I just can't seem to wipe away. It's unusual for me to be so attracted to a guy and I decide it must be because I didn't savour him for long enough. One more night, in a bed, taking my time, will erase my fascination with him I'm sure.

I stand by my floor to ceiling window, looking out onto the city while I wait for the business to finish shutting down for the day. I'm the head of this building, responsible for hundreds of people, yet I feel so small up here, watching the world go by beneath me. I mean nothing to a single one of the thousands of people hurrying along the pavements below. Sometimes I wonder if I mean anything to anybody. If I do, I shouldn't. I'm a selfish bastard.

I turn at the sound of a knock on my door, followed immediately by Edward strolling straight into my office without permission.

It riles me and my expression surely shows it. "I'm busy," I snap, feeling a small stab of guilt when Edward's gaze drops to the floor.

"Oh," he all but whispers. "I just thought, I mean everyone's left so…never mind."

I sigh deeply through my nose, annoyed with myself for being an unnecessary twat. "I have a headache," I lie. It's the nearest to an apology I can muster. "But I'll see you tomorrow. Helen needs a few extra days before she can come back."

A twinkle of hope glistens in his eyes and it makes me wonder if I should find someone else to assist me tomorrow.

"Sure. See you tomorrow." He smiles as he walks away and I try to return it but the muscles in my face seem to have broken.

Once alone, I switch off the lights to the top floor and lock up my office, briefcase in hand, before beginning the five-minute walk to my car. I see Theodore standing next to a Ford Fiesta, that's probably older than he is, as I approach the car park. That inexplicable tightening occurs in my throat again at the sight of him, but I force myself to ignore it and climb into my Mercedes.

It's an effort not to stare at him, but I manage it. Tossing my keys into the drawer beneath the stereo, I press the keyless ignition button and reverse out of my space. It's only when I drive past Theodore and catch a glimpse of him kicking his tyre in my rear-view mirror that I back up and open my window.

Clearly, fate wants me to talk to this guy again, so who am I to argue? "Car trouble?" I call out, leaning over the centre console.

Theodore huffs and kicks the clapped-out car once more. "Won't start." He sounds angry and I don't know if it's because of the car, or because he's talking to me.

Probably a little bit of both, I decide, feeling smugger than I should that I'm able to provoke such a reaction from him. "Have you called the AA?"

"I don't have roadside cover. Just go. I'll sort something."

"Do you need a ride home?"

"No," he says, refusing to look at me as he pulls out his phone and makes a call.

I'm intrigued as to why he has such an attitude towards me. So we fucked? Big deal. He didn't say *no*. In fact I'm sure I remember him saying yes, God yes, *fuck* yes, more than once.

After holding the phone to his ear for a minute or so, he huffs and starts tapping the screen again. He makes another call, and nobody answers that one either.

"You sure you don't want that ride?"

He rolls his eyes and I smile because I know I've won. Tucking his phone back into his jacket, he gives his car one last kick before approaching mine with his head down.

"Where do you live?" I ask as he slides into the passenger seat. He takes hold of his seatbelt and guides it over his taut chest. Suddenly, I'm glad I brought my car today. I walk to work most days because I usually spend the weekdays at my apartment in the city, but I spent the weekend at my place in Alderley Edge and came straight from there.

"Ancoats."

It's out of my way but I don't tell him that. Pulling out of the car park, I turn in the opposite direction of where I live. Theodore gapes out of his window, his hands drumming nervously against his knees.

"Where are you from?" I ask. I don't know why I'm interested, but I can't help wanting to know more about him.

"Rochdale."

Hmm. "You don't have the broad accent."

"Sorry," he mutters, sarcasm dripping from his voice.

"Brothers and sisters?"

"Brother."

"*Boyfriend*?" I ask because I'm wondering if that's why he's so pissed off that we had sex.

"No."

"Do you always stick to one word answers?"

"Not to people I like."

A wicked grin pulls on one side of my mouth. "Well that was *five* words. Guess you *do* like me after all."

"Whatever."

Whatever? Seriously? What is he, twelve? I find it oddly adorable.

I give up on trying to make conversation…for now. Using my thumb, I activate the stereo with the buttons on my steering wheel. It connects automatically to my iPhone and *Hey There Delilah* by the Plain White T's floods the car. I crank up the volume, expecting a reaction from Theodore but he doesn't even flinch. So I start singing, belting the words with as much power as my lungs will allow.

Still, I get nothing. Not even a sideways glance in my direction. So, I do something he can't possibly ignore. Fiddling with the controls, I skip through the tracks until I land on *Maybe Tomorrow* by the Stereophonics, and then turn it up even louder.

"I *know* you know this one," I yell over the music before breaking out into the first verse. Risking a glance to my left, I notice he's shifted in his seat, turning away from me. It's not the reaction I'm pushing for, but it's a reaction nonetheless and I take it with a proud smile.

When the song begins to die down, I turn off the stereo. "You weren't too shy to sing on Friday night."

"Stop comparing me to that night!" he snaps, finally looking at me. "That wasn't me."

His answer forces my brow to furrow. I feel like he's punched a hole in my chest. "You sure look like him. Maybe I should take another look at your dick to make sure."

"Next left," he says, pointing to the turning I need to take, ignoring me completely.

I don't understand this man at all. I shouldn't even give a shit, but I do, and it's frustrating me. "Do you want me to apologise for fucking you?"

"Don't be ridiculous."

"Then why are you being so hostile towards me? I'm doing you a favour here, and you're being an arsehole."

Eyes focused on the road, I can't see his expression, but I hear him sigh through his nose. "Look," he begins, his tone relaxed for the first time. "I know about your reputation and I don't want any part of it. If I'd known who you were on Friday I never would've-"

"My reputation?" I interrupt, curious and slightly amused.

"That you have a thing for fucking your way through the office juniors. Well, I'm not going to be one of them." He sighs again, sounding flustered. "Not *again*, anyway."

"It's not true," I say. His knees fall towards the middle of the car and I feel his gaze burning into my cheek. "I don't discriminate. I'm happy to fuck management, too."

I see him shake his head in the corner of my eye and, as a result, we're back to single word answers again. "Sure."

As told, I turn left and wait for his next command. Presumably, I've blown any chance of deeper conversation. At least, I *try* to keep quiet, but I just can't seem to help myself. "Were you a virgin?" I ask, wondering if *that's* why he's so uptight about what happened.

"No!" he barks, sounding almost offended. The fervency of his voice makes me believe him. "Please," he adds, his tone begging. "Can we just forget about Friday?"

I don't want to, and I won't. "If that's what you want."

"It is." He points to the windscreen. "It's those flats over there."

I make the effort not to scrunch my nose at the unsavoury surroundings. I hit the accelerator a little harder, jumping the amber traffic light before it turns red. If I were to pause in this part of the city for too long, my alloys would be gone before I could yell thief.

Theodore clicks off his seatbelt as the car starts to slow, jumping out the very second it stops. He goes to close the door but hesitates, holding on to the handle as he bends down so I can see his face. "Um, thanks," he mutters, hardly convincing. "See you around."

Oh, you can be sure of that. Before I can say my thoughts aloud, the door is slammed closed and he's jogging away from me. Gripping the wheel, I tip my head back and wait for my erratic pulse to calm. This guy is going to be a tough one to crack, but I *will* succeed. I have to. Only then, will this bewildering curiosity subside so I can move onto the next.

Damn you, Theodore Davenport.

Chapter Three

~Theo~

Slamming the door to my flat closed behind me, I slide down against it until my arse hits the floor. Drawing my knees up into my chest, I throw my head into my hands. I hate him. James Holden. I *detest* him, and I don't even know why.

"Hey, what's wrong?"

My heart flies into my mouth and I almost snap the bones in my neck when I look up to find Tess hovering over me. "Jesus, Tess! You scared the living shit out of me! What are you doing here?"

"Naomi's got her boyfriend over," she explains, referring to her roommate. "If I wanted to hear a guy panting and moaning I wouldn't be a lesbian."

I manage a small smile and Tess joins me on the floor, propping herself up on her hands while she stretches her legs out in front of her. "Bad day?"

A humourless laugh flies from my throat. "You know the guy I never have to see again? The one who stole my morals and turned me into a raging slut just by looking at me?"

"David Gandy?"

I nod. "Turns out David Gandy is, in fact, James Holden. My boss. Not just *my* boss, but *everyone's* boss. The fucking boss of all the bosses."

Tess gasps, and then pisses me the hell off by giggling. "No way!"

"It's not funny, Tess."

"Kinda is. I'd say you couldn't make that shit up, but I think you already did in one of your books."

She's right. I have three self-published titles under my belt and in my first novel, Lost and Found, the main characters find themselves in a situation not dissimilar to the one I'm facing right now. The difference, however, is this is real life and James and I aren't going to drive off into the sunset together. The real life version ends with me dreading going to work every single day because I can't bear to face my arsehole boss with an ego the size of China.

Tess' hand appears on my knee and I stack one of mine on top of it. "So you've slept with your boss. Big deal. I'm sure you're not the first."

"I'm not if the rumours are true." The thought makes me queasy.

"I meant in general, but whatever. If he's the CEO you probably won't have to deal with him anyway. Don't CEO's just sit around on their arse, smoking cigars all day, while everyone else does the work?"

I shrug, so many thoughts, scenarios, and emotions running through my head it feels like my brain is about to splatter all over the wall. "He's persistent."

"So you've already spoken to him again?"

She says *again*, but today is actually the first time, given the fact the feel of him on my skin last week rendered me completely speechless. "He gave me a lift home. My car's knackered and I didn't have another choice seeing as neither *you* nor Tom would answer your damn phones." I can't help scowling at her like it's all her fault I've just had the most uncomfortable car journey of my life.

She pulls her lips into a firm, guilty line, exposing her teeth. "I've got this new phone case and it knocks the silent switch every time I take it out to charge. *But*...you could've gotten the bus."

Yes. Yes I could. Why the hell didn't I think of that? Oh yeah, because I can't think of fucking *anything* when James Holden is around.

"So, I'm guessing, by the foul mood you're in, that he's a bellend?"

I open my mouth to say the only reasonable answer. *Yes*. Except it's *not* reasonable, so I close it again. "He's..." Hell, I don't even know what he is, or why he's crawled so far under my skin I'm not sure I'll ever be able to get him out. "He's not actually done anything wrong," I admit, but it doesn't stop a sour taste bubbling on the surface of my tongue. "I just hate him."

"Now, do you *really?* Or are you just mad at yourself for sleeping with a stranger?"

"No. It's him," I spit, refusing to acknowledge the alternative. I'm being petulant and I know it. I *am* mad with myself. Some people don't see an issue with casual sex and I don't judge anyone for living that way, but it's not for me. At least, it wasn't before Friday night and I can't shake the feeling that I've let myself down.

"Seriously, Theo, I think you just need to pull that stick out of your arse and move the fuck on." I can always rely on Tess to give it to me straight, and whether it pisses me off or not, I know she's right. "I bet he's not wasting his time thinking about it. Probably got his dick in another hole as we speak. You can't change it, so just forget it instead."

A part of me that I don't understand doesn't want to forget, and for that reason alone I wish I could kick myself in the balls. "You're right," I agree, forcing conviction into my voice as I slap my knees. "I'm starving. What d'you fancy?"

"Real chips and egg?" By 'real' chips, she means homemade and deep-fried.

I'm already salivating at the thought. "You peel the spuds and I'll butter the muffins."

I raise my hand and she gives me a high-five. "Deal."

* * *

This morning, I'm glad that Tess stayed over last night. A Netflix marathon and two bottles of cheap wine were just what I needed to get my stupid boss out of my head. I *may* have wanked off to the image of him in my mind this morning but I refuse to read too much into that. I wank off to Stephen Amell all the time but I don't go to sleep worrying about our future together.

I'm drinking coffee when Tess comes barrelling out of the bathroom, pulling on her trainers at the same time.

"Coffee?"

"That cheap shit isn't worth me being late for," she says, grabbing her jacket from the floor and swinging it over her shoulder. "I've already had a verbal warning."

Tess isn't the best timekeeper. Something I'm sure her boss at the sportswear shop doesn't appreciate.

"Will you be here tonight?" I ask as her hand reaches for the door handle. "I'll pick up a takeaway on the way home if you are."

"I'll text you when I know what Naomi's plans are. In a bit, little shit."

"Sure," I reply, but she's already gone.

Sliding my finger under the sleeve of my grey jacket, I check the time on my watch and huff. I need to get a move on if I'm going to make it to work on time. Buses are unreliable on a good day. I haven't been on public transport since I was in college but I imagine it's still over-crowded and smells like piss and sweat.

I drain my coffee, silently agreeing with Tess that it does indeed taste like shit, and then fix a knot in the silver tie draped loosely around my neck. I'm out the door and jogging down the stairwell, as usual the lift is out of order, just seconds later. Outside, I stop in my tracks, knitting my eyebrows together, sure I've just walked past an all too familiar car. I dismiss it, certain I'm going fucking crazy, and carry on walking.

"Need a ride?"

"Oh for fuck's sake," I mutter under my breath before begrudgingly turning around. Seemingly, I'm *not* going crazy, I'm being fucking stalked.

"I'm fine with the bus," I say, feeling rather proud of myself for not giving into him…*again.*

The confident arse cocks his head and then leans over to open the passenger door. "My leather seats won't leave you smelling like stale piss all day."

I don't want to, yet I'm walking towards him. It's almost as if he severed the connection between my brain and my muscles when he fucked me last week because I seem to have lost all control over my body. That pride I felt just seconds ago? Yeah, that disappears the second I slide into his pretentious car. It's all silver and black leather with more gadgets and technology than bloody NASA. If I didn't know better, I'd assume he was over compensating for a tiny dick.

But I know he's far from tiny and my arse clenches at the mere memory. I need to stop thinking about that before my cock swells any further, so I reach out and switch on the stereo to distract myself. It works, until his hand lands on the back of my seat, supporting him as he turns to the rear window while reversing out of his space. His skin is so close to my face. It's the same hand he had wrapped around my dick and I can't stop thinking about it, remembering how good it felt.

He returns his hand to the wheel and I spot flashes of colour on his wrist where the cuff of his jacket has rolled up slightly. It surprises me that he has tattoos. He's so refined and business-like. Suddenly, I want to know if he has more, if he has a full sleeve, *two* full sleeves. Does he have them on his chest, his back, his legs…

"If you keep staring at me like that I might start believing you don't hate me as much as you want to."

Shit. I rip my gaze away from his arm and shift in my seat so I can't see him, even by accident out of the corner of my eye. He's so fucking arrogant and it makes me scowl out of the window. *Why the hell am I in his car? Again!* I decide I'm going to have to practise saying 'Fuck off, you condescending, cocky bastard,' in the mirror when I get home.

We drive in silence, only interrupted by the small puff of humourless laughter that pushes through my nose when *Creep* by Radiohead starts trickling through the speakers.

"You think I'm a creep?" he asks, amusement tickling his tone.

Among other things. "You have to admit it's a bit weird waiting outside my flat like that. You don't even know me."

"You work for me. I take care of my employees."

"That's not why you did it." The words come out like an accusation and a tiny part of me wants him to agree.

"So why do *you* think I did it?"

I can't see his face, I won't let myself, but I can imagine the smug expression he's wearing.

"Because you want to screw me again."

"And that makes you mad?"

No. But I want it to. "Yes."

"Well you can relax. I'm not a rapist. It won't happen until you want it to."

"It won't happen, full stop."

"Because I'm your boss?"

"No. Yes. Partly." I'm flustered and it makes me hate him even more. He's wearing me down and I can't even begin to comprehend how the hell he does it.

"Partly because I'm your boss," he repeats. "And the other part?"

"Because…because…" *Jesus Christ, Theo, pull yourself together.*

"Because?"

"Because of comments like *that!* You're an arrogant, cocky, pretentious, self-important, patronising, arrogant ars-"

"You've already said arrogant."

I'm seething so vehemently my blood vibrates in my veins, and seemingly, I revert to being a child, huffing as I fold my arms across my chest.

I plan to stay silent the rest of the way, the rest of my *life* when he's around, but curiosity overpowers me when he veers onto a road that doesn't lead to Holden House.

"Where are you going?"

"Costa. I need caffeine to sustain this level of arrogance. Want one?"

Twat. "No."

Shrugging, James pulls onto a side street and parks against the curb. He gets out and walks off without another word and I drag some much-needed oxygen into my lungs. All weekend I dreamt about those damn eyes of his, the story they told, the demons they possessed…but now I can't even bring myself to look at them, because every time I do I forget how to function like a normal human being.

When I see James returning to the car I seize the opportunity to take another deep breath, knowing in a few seconds the art of breathing will become a luxury I'm not privileged enough to possess. My eyes roll at the sight of two tall cups in his hands. It's as if his sole purpose in life is to annoy me.

He balances one cup in the crook of his arm while he opens the door and then holds it out to me. "Caramel latte."

"I said I didn't want one," I spit, staring at the cup. I don't intend to take it out of pure childishness but James doesn't move and I suspect he won't until it's in my hand. So, as fucking usual, I give in and take the cup.

He slides into his seat and I refuse to look at the smile on his face but I know it's there. "But you do *really*. You were just being stubborn."

He's right, but he shouldn't be. He shouldn't be able to read me so well when he doesn't even know me. It frustrates me. *He* frustrates me.

The feeling dies down just slightly as I sip on the first decent coffee I've had in weeks, but then he ruins it by opening his mouth. "So what made you decide to move into the publishing industry?"

I shrug. "Curiosity. Passion," I say, forcing nonchalance into my tone.

"You like to read?"

"And write." *Shit!* Why did I tell him that? No doubt he thinks I only took the job to try and further my career. That's not even my biggest concern. I don't particularly care what he thinks, at least that's what I tell myself, but I don't want him to know *anything* about me. He'll only use it to his own advantage. He already has some kind of unfathomable power over me and I don't want to give him any more leverage.

"Have you published anything?"

"Three novels so far." *Fucking hell, stop talking, dickhead!* "I'm only self-published though."

"You say that like it devalues your achievement. Writing takes strength, commitment, a unique mind that has the ability to see the world differently and put that vision into words. Don't ever undersell yourself, Theodore."

His voice sounds so genuine that I break the vow I made to myself and look at him. I can't help it. His eyes are on the road but they hold something that intrigues me, compels me to look deeper. I think I see a vulnerability, a darkness, but I force myself to ignore it. I don't know this man and I never will. He pisses me off too much. I feel like he'd make a good character, that maybe I could write about him, but he'd end up getting a happy ever after and he's too much of a tosser to deserve one.

"They could be a bag of shite for all you know," I say. I'm feeling a little too content in his presence and I rectify that by being a prick.

"I doubt that."

"You haven't read them."

"I don't need to. I can see your passion. I *feel* it. I saw it the first time I met you, the way you looked at me."

"I don't remember," I blatantly lie. "I was drunk."

"You do," he says with that unrelenting confidence that makes me want to punch him in the face. There's no point arguing. Not only is he right, I *do* remember and I don't think I'll ever forget, but we've arrived in the car park.

"Your car is still here," he notes, nodding over to it.

"Perceptive as well as arrogant. That's a talent."

"Do you want me to call a garage to come and pick it up?"

"I'm not a moron," I snap, and it instantly sparks a twinge of guilt in my stomach. He's being nice and I'm behaving like a mammoth dick. "I've already sorted it." Except I haven't. I can't afford to right now. Hopefully, my brother will lend me the money to have it towed back to my flat this afternoon and I'll get it repaired on payday.

James' phone rings in his pocket as we get out of the car and I'm grateful for the interruption. He answers with a curt, "Holden," and continues to talk throughout our walk to the building. I don't listen to what he says, too busy trying to make sense of the unsettling emotion swimming in my chest.

Still on the phone when we step inside Holden House, James offers a brief wave before carrying on without me towards the lifts. I still have half my coffee but, feeling tense, I toss it in the bin before taking the stairs to my floor two at a time. I don't run as much as I used to and I need to burn off some of the energy that takes over my body whenever James fucking Holden is close.

I head straight to my desk and bring up my first task of the day on the computer. I need to type up a pitch to several distributors for Mike the Moron's newest client and get them emailed out before lunch.

Speaking of Mike… "I need these taking down to admin when you have a minute," he says, placing a tray of sealed envelopes on my desk.

"Sure," I reply with a fake smile.

I expect him to turn away, but instead he stares at me through narrowed eyes.

"Have I done something wrong?" I ask, trying to remember if I photocopied the documents he told me to yesterday. I did. I'm sure.

"You can't skip rungs to get to the top of the ladder here. You have to work for it like everyone else."

"Um…" I'm confused. "I'm sorry, I don't-"

"I saw you getting out of Holden's car this morning. You should know he doesn't return *favours* with promotion."

What the… "My car broke down. That's all there is to it." My tone is acidic, my expression disgusted. Who the hell does he think he is?

"Whatever you say."

My fist itches to knock the smarmy grin off his face. What is it with this place? I'm starting to wonder if you need a degree in arseholery to progress here. My mood is set for the rest of the day. I complete my work with a permanent scowl etched onto my face and don't bother speaking to anyone unless asked a direct question. It only gets worse when my computer crashes and I have to stay late while I wait for the technician to arrive.

Alone, bar the company of a handful of cleaners dotted throughout the building, I kick back in my swivel chair and prop my feet up on my desk.

After texting Tess to tell her I'll be late home, I pull up the Facebook app on my phone and tap out a quick status update about my bad mood. Switching to my author page app, my stomach flips when I notice I've reached the two thousand likes milestone. I doubt half of them have read my books but I don't care. If my stories have only reached one of them I consider it a success. I type a *thank you* status from my alter ego TS Roberts and then move on to Twitter.

"You're still here?" My eyes dart toward the sound of James' voice and find him standing a couple of stations away from me. "It's almost seven."

It surprises me that I'm actually pleased to see him. He's still an arsehole, but Mike is worse, and I'm grateful for a break from the boredom of my own company.

"My computer went down. I'm waiting for tech to arrive."

"You've waited long enough. Go home. It'll still be broken in the morning, they'll have to come back."

I consider it for a moment but decide against it. "I don't mind waiting." It's an excuse rather than a lie. "I don't need to give Mike any more reasons to chew my arse off." *Damn. Why'd you tell him that?*

"You've messed up?" he asks. I expect him to gloat or make fun of me but he doesn't. He walks over to my desk and perches on the edge of it, his thigh brushing against my ankle.

I almost gasp, but disguise it with a forced yawn. "No," I say. *Unless you count the fact I rode in your car this morning.* "Just don't think he likes me."

"I wouldn't worry. The only person he likes is his reflection in the mirror." There's a playfulness in his voice that makes me smile and, for the first time, I feel relaxed in his presence. "Get tech on the phone for me."

I pick up the phone and dial, but I don't know what he hopes to achieve. I've rang them four times already. "They're waiting for one of their guys to finish up in Middleton. They can't get here before nine."

He winks and it sends a rush of heat surging through my body. *Fuck me, he's beautiful.* He's still an arse, but a damn gorgeous one.

"This is James Holden, CEO of Holden House. A member of my staff requested technical support several hours ago and I find your response time utterly unacceptable. I want assistance in my building within twenty minutes or I'll take my business elsewhere." There's a brief pause while James gives the poor sod on the other end of the line a chance to speak, and then he puts the phone back in its cradle. "They're on their way."

Wow. "Impressive." I'm more than impressed. I'm actually a little turned on. I won't give him the pleasure of knowing that, of course. He's still a twat.

James shrugs. "I don't pay good money for bad service."

Damn, he's so close to me. There's no way I can bring my legs down from the table without touching him, so I don't try, even though I'm getting cramp in my calves. I assume he'll leave soon. There's no reason for him to stay.

"Is your car in the garage?"

"It's being picked up in the morning. My brother sorted it." I arranged it with Tom a few hours ago and he offered to cover the repair costs, too, until I get paid.

"How old is your brother?"

My brow wrinkles in confusion. "Twenty-nine."

"And you're the youngest?"

"Um, yeah." *Where is this going?* "Why?"

"Just trying to work out how old you are. It's not business related, so I can't ask you directly, right?" A sly smile dances on his lips and I want to slap it straight off the beautiful bastard.

"You mean you haven't looked it up on my file?"

"That's too easy. I prefer a challenge."

"Unfortunately for you, so do I."

I don't know what's changed but I have no problem staring at him right now. His intense gaze pierces mine and I allow it. I have no choice. I don't think I could look away even if I wanted to.

"So why did *you* get into publishing?" I probe, and realise it's the first time I've actually asked him a question of any significance.

"It was expected of me," he says, and I think I hear a hint of sadness in his voice. "This business has been in my family since the early nineteen-hundreds. I took over from my father just before he passed away."

"I'm sorry." I wonder if that's where the pain in his eyes stems from. "My dad died, too."

"We were close." His voice is low as he stares down at his knees. "He saw something in me that no one else does. Even *me*."

I don't know how to respond, so I don't. Weirdly, I want to touch him, maybe even *hold* him, but I don't do that either. Instead, I freeze, my eyes refusing to abandon his troubled face.

After several seconds that feel like hours, he looks at me, forcing a smile that doesn't reach his cheeks. "Sorry. Bit heavy for a Tuesday night, eh?"

I want to agree, but I can't. I can't seem to do anything but stare at him.

"I should get going," he says, standing up and turning immediately away from me. "Let me know if the tech guy doesn't show. I don't want you waiting around all night."

"I…" I pause while I remember how to breathe. "I don't have your number."

James stops next to the desk in front of mine, pulls what looks like a business card out of the hidden pocket inside his jacket and then scribbles something on the back of it. He takes a few steps towards me and holds out the card. Swinging my legs down from the desk, I take it from him, my thumb brushing against his. The contact sends a shiver down my spine that I can't ignore, but thankfully I manage to stop it reaching my expression.

"That's my personal number. Don't share it."

"Sure," I think I say, but my mouth is dry and there's every possibility I imagined it.

I watch him walk away and I'm unable to make sense of how I'm feeling. I didn't *want* him to give me a lift home but I must've subconsciously assumed he would because I'm surprised he's gone. Will he pick me up in the morning? Or is this, whatever *this* is, over now? The thought should make me happy. It's what I've wanted since the moment he walked out of the bathroom last Friday – to forget him. I don't *want* him to talk to me again. I don't want him to even *look* at me, and I certainly don't want to ride in his fucking posh car.

So why do I feel so deflated?

I make it home a couple of hours later. Tess is fast asleep in my bed and, after showering and slipping into some fresh underwear, I climb in next to her. I don't sleep well, and not just because Tess spreads herself out like a starfish. My brain won't switch off. I think about *him*…at work, in his car, but mostly I remember how good it felt when he fucked me in that damn bathroom.

Eventually, I drift into a restless sleep, but I'm awake again before the alarm sounds.

Tess grumbles at the noise and kicks me in the shin. "Make it stop," she mumbles, clamping a pillow over her head. "It's my day off."

"Well it's not mine," I say, smiling at her dramatics. She's never been a morning person.

I silence the alarm and crawl out of bed, feeling ninety years old as I stumble to the bathroom. I'm exhausted and unexpectedly nauseous. There's an anxious feeling in my stomach, similar to that twinge you get when you know you've forgotten something important but can't remember what it is. I search my mind for the answer while I get ready for work but by the time I reach the stairwell, leaving Tess in bed, I'm none the wiser.

Only when I spot James' car waiting outside my building, making the sickly sensation dissolve, does it hit me. I'd been nervous that he wouldn't show. Ludicrous, given the fact I hate him.

I stride straight over and slip into the passenger seat. With one hand on the wheel and the other on the back of my headrest in preparation to reverse, he raises an eyebrow. "No opposition this morning?"

His hand is too near my face. He smells of spicy aftershave and cigarettes. It's intoxicating and my thoughts become blurry, so I turn away before I say something stupid. Plus, he looks hot in his expensive fucking suit. *Why does he have to be so damn gorgeous?* It just makes it harder for me to dislike him.

"What time did you leave last night?" he asks as the car starts to move.

"Just after nine."

"Be sure to let admin know. You'll be paid double time for the extra hours."

That's unexpected and it brings a smile to my face. The ensuing silence seems awkward and I consider turning on the radio but I don't feel as bold as yesterday.

"So," James begins. "Are you working on anything right now?"

"Um… you mean a book?"

He nods, keeping his eyes straight ahead. "Yes."

My tongue sticks to the roof of my mouth. I'm not used to discussing my writing. No one ever asks except Tess. My family know, but in all honesty I'm sure they think I'm wasting my time on an unrealistic fantasy. They don't understand. It's not about fame and bestseller lists. I write because I enjoy it. Other people reading my work is a bonus, not a necessity. "I'm taking a little break. I started something new last month but I'm not quite connecting with it yet."

"Ah, you're in the dating phase. You're still getting to know your characters."

"You write?" I ask, studying his face as he drives. He's said a couple of things since we met that makes me think he understands life behind the pen.

"No," he says, making eye contact with me for a brief second before looking back to the road. "But I've been in this business a long time. You pick things up."

This morning I don't question it when he takes the 'wrong' turning. I assume stopping for coffee is part of his daily routine.

"Coffee?" he offers as he slows to a stop on the street behind Costa.

"Please," I answer, reaching into my wallet and removing a fiver. He tries to push my hand away but I grab his arm and force the note into his fist. After a few seconds, he grins at me and I realise it's because I'm still holding his wrist. Embarrassed, I snatch my grip away and stare down at my knees. *What a bellend.*

When I see James return holding coffee cups *and* two paper bags, I roll my eyes. I didn't give him enough cash for food and I decide he's done it on purpose just to piss me off.

When he opens the door, I take the bag from him but I can't prevent the scowl that appears on my face. "I'm not hungry."

"Ah, there's the Theodore I know," he says, sniggering as he slides into his seat. "Thought I'd lost you there for a little while."

Sarcastic bastard.

"If it makes you feel better, I used my loyalty points. Didn't cost me anything."

It doesn't. Presumptuous twat.

I don't speak the rest of the way. Instead, I listen to James sing along to *Run* by Snow Patrol. I tell myself it's annoying and that he can't sing for shit, but truthfully he's actually pretty good. His tone is deep, soothing.

I still hate him.

As we walk to the office I purposely lag behind a few steps, not wanting to give Mike any more ammunition. When James reaches the lift, I notice Ed scurry towards him, looking up at him with eager puppy-eyes while handing him a file. I guess this means James' PA is still absent. It frustrates me. I miss having Ed around. It means I have to work doubly hard and make twice as many coffees.

I run into Mike as soon as I exit the stairs. It's hard to believe I thought he had a nice arse just ten days ago. Now, I'm struggling to find a single redeeming quality about him. "I need you to make a reservation at Paulo's for one o'clock. Eight people. Secluded spot."

Good morning to you, too. "Sure," I say, carrying on toward my desk.

"I have a meeting in my office at ten. Make sure you're there to provide refreshments."

"No problem."

"And Carol in editing has some files for me. I need you to collect those beforehand."

Anything else? Want me to stick a broom up my arse and sweep the floors as I go? "Yep."

"Oh, and arrange a meeting with Holden. I need to talk to him about a client."

"Sure."

Mike starts to walk away and I sigh in relief, pulling out my chair.

"Before you sit down," he calls, turning back.

Oh for fuck's sake.

"Go to his office. He'll only fob you off on the phone. While you're there tell him I need Walsh back here this afternoon. I want him to join me at the lunch meeting. Do it now."

"Sure," I agree *again*, although I'm pretty certain you don't *tell* James Holden to do anything.

Huffing, I shove my chair back under my desk and make my way to the top floor. *This isn't turning out to be such a dream job after all.*

* * *

I have *no* idea how it's become routine, but I've climbed into James' car every morning and afternoon this week. I'm trying so hard not to like him, but he's not making it easy. One minute he's irritating the hell out of me, the next he makes me laugh. Then he gets smug because he's put a smile on my face and I'm right back to hating him again.

James is singing to *Rhythm of Love* by the Plain White T's when he veers into the small car park next to my block of flats and it's hard not to feel uplifted by the juvenile, carefree expression on his face. He throws his all into the words, pulling faces and twisting his body as if he's on stage.

"Oh come on," he says, turning the music down. "How can you *not* sing to this song?"

You've heard my singing voice. It's not pretty. "Quite easily," I reply, my expression stoic. I get out of the car without saying 'See you tomorrow,' because, as always, I'm not planning to accept another lift to work in the morning, even though I know I will.

I start walking down the concrete path to my building when I hear his car door close. *Is he following me?* I think, but I don't turn around. Then he carries on singing the lyrics to *Rhythm of Love*, his hand appearing on my shoulder and spinning me around.

"Dance with me," he says, positioning my arms into a tango position.

He sways me from side to side, still singing, still smiling, and as much as I don't want to, I give in and laugh. "What's gotten into you? People will stare at us!"

"So?"

He twirls me around and grinds our hips together, in the middle of a public car park in broad frigging daylight…and I let him, because it's fun. Until two teenage girls walk past, pointing and giggling like we've just escaped from an asylum.

Pulling back, unable to stop smiling, I shake my head. "I'll see you tomorrow."

James grins, that smug half-smile that annoys me so much. "That's all I wanted from you."

Seriously? He did all that because I didn't say I'd see him tomorrow? It frustrates me that I've given him exactly what he wants. "You're such a wanker."

"A wanker who'll see you at eight AM sharp." He winks and it makes me feel giddy. I don't let it show, or so I think before the smarmy twat smiles even wider. "Good night, Theodore."

Don't reply. Don't reply. "Good night, James."

For fuck's sake.

Chapter

Four

~James~

Ten days later…

I'm in a foul mood. I don't know if it's because I've been in my office since four AM, or because Theodore got his car back two days ago. I'd enjoyed bringing him to and from work. It broke up the monotony of the mornings and put me in a good mood for the rest of the day.

I miss it.

My initial goal was to soften him enough to get back in his pants, yet weirdly, I feel an even greater sense of satisfaction from the fact he no longer looks at me like he wants to ram his knuckles into my face. Each day, he's become a little more willing to answer my questions. He's stopped hesitating. He's fun, and that's a new experience for me. I want, *need* more, even if that makes me the most selfish guy on the planet.

The only thing I miss is that he doesn't blush as easily anymore. I need to work on that.

The building is deserted on a Saturday and I'm enjoying the calm. I'm easily distracted of late, making concentrating difficult, so I use the quiet of the weekend to catch up on all the loose ends left over from last week.

I'm reading through the contract my solicitor has drawn up for the new magazine deal when there's an unexpected knock on my door. My brother, Max, walks in before I can answer. He's only three years older than me but he dresses like an old man. Today, he looks like he's off to the golf course, dressed in an argyle jumper and beige trousers. The funny thing is he's never picked up a club in his life. "The bald guy on reception let me in," he explains. "What are you doing here on a Saturday? And why aren't you answering your phone?"

I resist the urge to roll my eyes and stuff the contract back in its envelope. "I had a backlog to clear. Saturday's the perfect time. No interruptions."

"On your birthday?" Max produces the hand he's been hiding behind his back and passes me a small box wrapped in silver paper with a card taped to the top.

"Thanks," I say, forcing a smile as I take it from him. I put it on my desk, knowing it contains my annual bottle of Armani aftershave without needing to open it.

"If you're not doing anything to celebrate, Laura and I would love to have you over for dinner."

"Sorry, Max. I'm going out with some friends." He knows I'm lying. I'm not a 'friends' kind of man. "Another time, though," I add. I doubt he believes that either.

"Isobel misses you."

It's a low blow, playing the niece card. She's only three. I'm not sure a child that age is even capable of missing someone.

"I'll come over, I promise." I take a deep breath and force myself to say it before I change my mind. "Next Friday. I'll come round after I've finished here."

Max smiles but doesn't look altogether convinced. I can't blame him for being sceptical, but I *will* stick to my word, if only to keep him off my back for a couple of months.

"I'll let Laura know. I'll invite Mum, too."

"Sure." I start replying to an email that can really wait until Monday, but it makes me look busy and I hope Max will take the hint and leave. He's a great brother, and I love him, I'm just not in the mood for him today. For *anyone*.

"I can see you're busy. I'll get going."

"Sorry." I'm really not. "I have to get things finished here."

"No problem. Don't spend all day here though, eh? You should be enjoying today."

Why? It's no different to all the other days of my fucked-up existence. "I will. Just later."

Max turns for the door, pausing when he reaches it. "And don't forget to call Mum. She tried this morning but couldn't reach you either."

"Will do." And I *will*, but again, later. I'm grateful she's staying with a friend in London this weekend so I don't have to see her. I don't celebrate my birthday and my mum is just another person I need to pretend for.

"You look tired. You sure you're okay?"

I'm not tired. I'm bored. Despite surviving on two hours sleep a night for the last several weeks, I haven't had so much energy in a long time. If I had to choose one emotion to describe how I feel about not being able to sleep it would be gratitude. *Relief.* It's terrifying to close your eyes and not know if you'll be okay when you wake up. Because that's how fast the switch can flip. "I'm fine, Max," I say, my tone frustrated.

"Don't be like that. You know I'm only looking out for you."

My mouth turns down into a guilty frown. "I know. Sorry. I got up early to come here, but I'm okay. Promise."

Max doesn't understand the sheer magnitude of my responsibilities here. He never took an interest in this business and is happy working a management post, nine-to-five in a call centre.

"Good. I'll call you in the week to remind you about Friday."

I nod and offer a brief wave before continuing to type out the unimportant email. I close it again, shutting down the system, as soon as Max is out of sight.

"Fuck this," I say to no one, sliding out from my desk. Sick of the boredom, I grab my jacket and toss it over my shoulder. I leave the office not knowing what I plan to do next, hoping it will come to me while I drive.

The further away I get from Holden House the more energy bubbles up in my stomach. Cranking up the stereo, I press a little harder on the accelerator and head back to my city apartment to change. I need to move. Run. Exercise until my lungs burn. If I don't corrode some of this excess energy I will combust.

So, after changing into some jogging pants and a white vest, I pull on my trainers and set off, on foot, to Heaton Park. I jog at a steady pace for just under an hour until I reach the north entrance. Once I'm through the gates, I attach my iPhone to the band around my upper arm and plug my earphones into my ears. Hitting shuffle, I set off into a fast run.

Radioactive by Imagine Dragons blasts into my ears as I veer onto the grass, cutting through some trees to avoid the crowded play park and public areas. There's a chill in the air, whipping my cheeks, but it does nothing to stifle the beads of sweat rolling down my back. I focus on my breathing, keeping it even, as I increase my speed.

After twenty minutes the muscles in my legs begin to burn and I keep going, embracing the pain. I'm so hyped up I feel like I could run for days without needing a break. There's another jogger in the distance. He's fast, but I'm faster, and I challenge myself to overtake him. I do it with ease and carry on going until I reach Heaton Hall. I rest for a moment, admiring the rolling hills in the distance while I stretch my limbs. They ache, but not enough, so I turn back and sprint the same distance again.

Some days, by this point, I call a cab to take me home, but not today. Today, I *need* this. I need both the exertion *and* the pain it brings. That's why I make my way home on foot, stretching my journey even further by using hidden pathways and side streets.

The burn in my lungs I've been chasing only appears when I see my apartment building, in the centre of Spinningfields, ahead. I relish it, panting through the throb in my chest as I jog towards it.

Back in my penthouse apartment, I head straight to the fridge and pluck out a bottle of spring water. My throat welcomes the coolness and I drink every drop without pausing to take a breath. I toss the empty plastic into the bin and brace myself on the kitchen counter, my head sagging.

Now what?

My foot taps impatiently against the tiled floor and I scan my surroundings as if they'll give me the answer. I check my watch, pleased to discover my run has made four hours pass. It's still too early to hit the village, but decide that's my plan once I've had a bath and a snack. A few drinks and a good fuck is what I need.

Happy fucking birthday.

* * *

I ended up taking a shower, unable to summon enough patience to wait for the bath to fill. I skipped the snack for the same reason. Now, I'm in the village, dressed in casual jeans and a smart black shirt, drinking alone in the corner of a bar. I'm bored out of my skull but as I sip the scotch I know I shouldn't be drinking, I see some entertainment walking towards the bathrooms. I drain my glass, wincing as it stings my throat, and follow him.

He looks pretty young but that doesn't bother me. He's by the sink when I reach him, washing his hands. I make eye contact with him in the mirror and I can't tell if he's going to be the eager type, which is unusual for me. I take a chance anyway, cupping his arse through his jeans.

I'm about to whisper in his ear but he spins around and shoves me away. "Get fucked," he spits, and walks straight out of the bathroom.

Well, shit. It must be years since I was last rejected. It pisses me off. Not because I'm not drilling his hot little arse right now, but because I can't shake this fucking boredom. Huffing, I head back to the bar. Maybe if I drink enough I'll forget that I'm bored. It's worth a shot, so I start ordering doubles. I know I shouldn't, but it's my fucking birthday. One night won't hurt.

Four doubles down, and I need to go someplace lively, so I walk out onto the street and hit up a club instead. The throb of the music beneath my feet uplifts me instantly and, after another couple of drinks, I find myself dancing on one of the podiums with some twink in a leather harness. He grinds his arse against my crotch but I'm barely paying attention. My arms are raised high above my head as I jump up and down in time with the beat. I can't be sure through the flashing lights, but I think I spot the redhead apprentice from marketing on the dance-floor below.

Bingo. I scan my murky brain for his name but only manage to come up with a memory of him kneeling on my office floor while I rammed my dick down his throat. Whatever his name is, he's a done deal already. If I remember rightly, I owe him a fuck anyway, so I jump down from the podium, stumbling when my feet hit the floor and losing sight of the redhead in the process.

Fuck. I feel dizzy. Sick. I look around and the dancing bodies surrounding me have blurred into fuzzy blocks of colour. I need some air, maybe a smoke, so I weave my way through the crowd until I see the orange glow of a streetlight shining through an open door. I knock into several people as I make my way outside. They yell at me, but I don't hear what they say.

My legs feel weak, wobbling under the weight of my body, so I cross the cobbled street and use the wall guarding the canal for support. Grabbing it with both hands, I tip my head back and relish the cold air that blankets my flushed face. It feels good. I close my eyes, concentrating on the direction of the breeze. Although lightheaded, I feel fucking amazing. A rush of ideas for the business flood my brain and I need to go home and write them all down before my head bursts under the pressure.

"Hey."

"*Mmm*," I murmur. His voice is beautiful. Calming. But I'm drunk and convince myself I've imagined it.

"Are you okay?"

I feel like I'm floating as I turn around. When I see Theodore's stunning face staring back at me, I wonder if I've passed out and I'm dreaming about him. He looks concerned, his brow furrowed as he steps towards me.

He places a gentle hand on my shoulder and I press my lips to it, smiling against his flesh. His skin is cool, refreshing, and I rub my cheek over it. "Are you okay?" he repeats, his voice urgent.

"I will be if you let me fuck you," I say, pressing my chest to his and kissing along his jaw. He tries to push me away, but I'm insistent, grabbing at his dick through his pants.

"Stop!" he roars, wedging his hands between our bodies and forcing me away.

I trip over my own feet and smack my back on the wall. "Fuck you," I snap, glowering at him.

"What's wrong with you? I saw you in the club and… this, this isn't you."

"You don't fucking know me." My words are slurred but it doesn't stop me talking. "You don't know anything about me." *Nobody does.*

"I know you've had too much to drink. Let me get you to the taxi rank."

I stop listening, too fascinated by the ripples in the canal below me. I'm too hot. I bet that water is cool, though. It entices me. I want to feel it on my skin.

"What the…" I think Theodore is talking but I've lost interest in him. He doesn't want me to fuck him? Fine. There's no reason for him to still be here. "What the fuck are you doing?"

It feels like something is caught on my shirt but I push past the resistance and hitch a second foot onto the wall. I'm crouched down, balancing, about to stand when suddenly I feel pressure around my waist.

I fall backwards, landing with a thud onto the hard ground. My eyes are open but all I can see are lights and a blurred face. A shock of pain registers and I think it's coming from my wrist. Or maybe my neck. My back hurts, too. *Or is it my head?*

"What the hell are you playing at?" I know that voice. That's Theodore's voice. It makes me smile. I wonder if he's the fuzzy face hovering over me. I reach out to touch it but the figure disappears.

There's some kind of commotion occurring around me. I hear lots of different voices, but I focus on Theodore's. "Call an ambulance," he says. "I think he's taken something."

"I just wanted to cool down," I say, wondering what all the fuss is about.

The blurry face returns and I try to bring it into focus but I'm too tired. "Shit. You're bleeding."

Who's bleeding?

He can't mean *me* because I feel fine. To prove it, I scramble into a sitting position, or I *try* to, but the fuzzy face that sounds like Theodore lowers me back down.

"Help is coming. You've hurt your head. Don't move."

His unnecessary concern angers me and I push myself back up. "I'm fine." *Jesus. What's the big deal?* Defiant, I crawl up onto my knees, preparing to stand. Theodore's face becomes clear and I look him straight in the eye. "See?"

That's the last thing I remember before everything turns black.

* * *

I wake up in an ambulance. "What's going on?" I ask, scanning my surroundings. I spot Theodore sitting on a foldout chair beside me. "Why are you here?"

"You-"

"Damn. I forgot to call Helen to arrange a meeting on Monday. Where's my phone?" I try to lift my head but it's stuck. "I need my phone.

Theodore, give me your phone. Wait…is it Monday or Tuesday? I think I'm booked through Monday. Best make it Tuesday. Where are you taking me?"

"Mr Hol-"

"Theodore, *phone!*" I demand. *Why is no fucker listening to me?* I try to reach out but my arms are stuck, too. "I've got so many new ideas right now. I need to get home and draw up some plans. I'll email them to Helen as well. Where's my phone?"

"Mr Holden," a guy in a green uniform says, his voice deep and authoritative. I don't like him already. "I need you to tell me if you've taken anything."

I struggle against the restraints. "Why can't I move? Get these damn straps off me."

"Sir, I need you to calm down for me."

"Yeah? Well I need to get out of this fucking ambulance. I have work to do! Theodore, dammit, where's your fucking phone?"

I'm trying to kick, punch, wriggle… anything that will give me enough leverage to pull myself up. I'm too hot. I'm too cold. I'm fucking angry. *Why've they put me in here?*

The guy in green starts talking but I shout over his voice when I see him flicking a needle in front of his face. "What's that for?" He ignores me, and starts moving it towards my arm. "I don't need that!" My back is rigid, the veins in my neck bulging as I try to move. The sharp needle pinches my skin and I growl into the air. "Get the fuck awa…."

* * *

My eyes are still closed when I wake up again. I'm in a hospital. I can smell it. *What the fuck have I done this time?* I tell my eyes to open but only manage a small flicker. My mouth is dry, my mind foggy, and I know instantly that I've been sedated. The knowledge forces a groan to trickle from my throat and within seconds I'm being poked and prodded.

"Welcome back, Mr Holden," I hear, presumably from a doctor.

Patronising bastard.

"Can you open your eyes for me?"

I'm trying, dick. Breathing heavily through my nose, I concentrate. With each flicker they open a little wider, making me squint as the harsh, artificial light pierces my pupils. Blinking rapidly, I see four figures surrounding me, their faces a little hazy. I can make out the blue scrubs well enough to know that three of them are medical professionals, but the fourth…

Fuck.

The fourth is Theodore.

"Can you tell me your name?"

Here we go. I'm frustrated but I know the drill. If I don't answer they'll just keep me here longer. "James Holden."

"Date of birth?"

"Third of April, 1984."

"Ah, happy birthday."

Oh, fuck off. "Is it?"

"Who's the prime minister?"

"David Cameron."

"And what year are we in?"

"2015."

I almost forget Theodore is here until he takes a step towards me. "Get him out of here," I say, too disgusted with myself to look at him.

"You're going to need somebody to accompany you home once you've been assessed," the doctor informs me.

"Assessed for what?" Theodore asks, his voice low, timid.

"I said I want him *out* of here!" I demand. I don't want him to see me like this. It will be all over Holden House by Monday morning. "Get my brother. His number's in my phone."

"I'm sorry, sir, we didn't find a phone on you when you were brought in."

Shit. I hear a woman's voice telling Theodore he needs to leave but I raise my hand. "Wait. Theodore, give me your mobile."

I can see him clearly now but I refuse to look into his eyes. He steps as close as he needs to, leaving a generous space between us, and hands me his phone. I tap Max's number into it and pass it back. "Call him," I say. "And then *leave*." My tone is clipped. I'm ashamed, and I want him gone.

I don't watch as he walks out. I *can't*. I don't think I'll ever be able to look at him again. Instead, I close my eyes and continue to answer more inane questions while I wait for my psyche eval.

Chapter
Five

~Theo~

Outside, near the ambulance bays, my pulse thuds in my ears as I hit 'call'. I don't know what I'm supposed to say because I don't understand what's going on. I've seen people drunk a thousand times, but James wasn't just drunk, he was…hell I don't even know what he was.

"Hello?" a man answers, and I gather a deep breath.

Crap. I don't know your name. "Um, hi. Are you James Holden's brother?"

"Yes. Where is he?" His words are rushed, panicked, almost as if he knows something's happened.

"He's in A&E. I-I'm not entirely sure what's happened. I think he's taken somethi-"

"Is he okay?"

"Oh, yeah, sorry. He seems fine now. The doctor is with him. He fell and hit his head. His wrist is swollen, too, so they're sending him to X-ray soon."

"Shit," he mutters. "I can't get there for a few hours. I'm in Glasgow, but I'm getting back in my car right now."

"Okay," I say, nerves making the word crack on my lips. I haven't known James long but I know he's not a patient person and I dread passing on the news.

"Did they sedate him?"

Why would he ask that? I'm taken aback by how un-surprised he seems by this situation. "Yeah. At least, I think so. They gave him something in the ambulance. He was, um, kicking off a bit."

"Are you staying with him?"

"Um…"

"I assume you're one of the friends he was celebrating his birthday with?"

I had no idea it was his birthday until he gave his date of birth to the doctor. It made my chest ache with sadness. No one should spend their birthday alone. Where were his friends? His family? There's so much more to James Holden than he shows and I want to delve deeper as much as I want to run away.

"Actually, he's just my boss. I don't really know him that well." I never wanted to know him. I still don't. Only now it's for different reasons. Now, it's because I'm scared of what I'll find.

"I understand," he says. He sighs down the line, dejected.

"But I can stick around outside until you get here," I offer, immediately wondering why the hell I've said it. James doesn't want me here and, honestly, I don't think I want to be here either.

"I'd appreciate that. Thank you. I'm setting off now."

After telling him which hospital, we exchange goodbyes and I stare down at my phone. There are several texts from Ed wanting to know what's going on. I'm not sure I should tell him, even if I knew, so I ignore it and tuck the phone back into my pocket.

I walk gingerly back inside the hospital and over to James' cubicle. I hover outside his curtain for a few minutes, hoping a nurse will pass and I can give them his brother's message. They all look so busy, though, and I don't want to interrupt. Swallowing the lump in my throat, I give in and peel back the curtain, mentally bracing myself for James' anger.

I expect him to yell, but when his gaze meets mine he simply looks away, staring at the wall. The sleeves of his shirt are rolled up to his elbows and it's the first time I've seen his tattoos in any kind of detail. One forearm is decorated to the wrist with Japanese artwork, but the other is bare. I wonder if his tattooed arm extends into a full sleeve and a heaviness descends on my chest when I realise I might never find out.

"Your brother's on his way," I mutter, looking at the floor. "But he's in Glasgow and-"

"What the hell's he doing in Scotland? I only saw him this morning."

I don't know the answer, so I just shrug.

"Well I'm not waiting for him. I'll call a cab when they let me go."

"You shouldn't be on your own right now."

"Don't pretend to know what I need," he spits.

I shrink back a step. "The doctor said you might have a concussion, that's all."

"He shouldn't have told you anything without my permission."

"He didn't. I, um, I overheard."

I don't know why I'm putting up with his bullshit. He's right. I don't know what he needs. I shouldn't be here. I owe nothing to him or his brother. "I'll ride in the cab with you." Again, I don't know why I've said it. I didn't plan to. Things just keep toppling from my mouth without warning or prior thought. Just like when I agreed to ride in the ambulance with him. I should've left *then*.

"I promised your brother I'd stay with you." It's an excuse but it's not the reason. I don't *know* why I'm doing it. Right now, I don't know *anything*.

James sighs, appearing defeated. "Please yourself." He surprises me. He's never struck me as a man who relents to *anyone*. "But you can wait outside."

I nod weakly, even though he's not looking at me, and make my way to the waiting room. I stop by the triage office and peer through the open door. There's a male nurse inside, tapping away on his computer, and I knock on the door to bring attention to myself. I tell him who I am and who I'm with and ask if he'll let me know when James is discharged. He agrees, and I walk away to find a seat.

It's a busy night and there aren't any chairs available, so I pace up and down instead. I'm just glad we weren't brought to my brother's hospital. I don't think I could be arsed trying to explain what's happened, especially when I don't know myself.

I think back to my past relationships, but I'm not sure I can even class them as that. None of them lasted more than a few weeks and I always thought that was because we had nothing in common, yet James and I most definitely don't have anything in common and I can't stop thinking about him. You hear about people, some say soulmates, just *clicking*. You see it in movies, read it in books, but that's fiction, fantasy. It doesn't happen in real life. *Does it?*

Three and a half hours I wait for news. I keep myself alert by drinking copious amounts of coffee from the vending machine. It tastes worse than the cheap shit in my flat but it keeps me awake.

A few minutes after being told that James has been discharged he emerges from the double doors that lead to the A&E department. He looks at me just briefly and then stares at his feet as he starts walking to the exit. I jog lightly to catch up with him and ask if he's ready for me to call a taxi.

“Nurse already did it,” he says, his voice barely a whisper.

The car is waiting as we step outside. I’m glad because it’s the middle of the night and my arms are freezing. James slides in the back seat while I walk to the other side and get in next to him.

“Spinningfields,” James says to the driver.

Wow. My annual salary would probably only cover a single month’s rent in one of those apartments.

“How are you feeling?” I ask, my voice low, shaky.

“Fine.”

I nod slowly and leave it at that. Clearly, he doesn’t want me to talk to him, so I keep quiet the rest of the way. When we pull up outside his building James pats down his pockets and sighs. I already know he doesn’t have his wallet. The paramedics couldn’t find anything on his person to officially I.D. him.

“I’ve got it,” I say, pulling a twenty from my own wallet and handing it to the driver.

James is already out of the car, walking ahead. I don’t think he expects it, but I follow him anyway. I just want to make sure he reaches his apartment and then I’ll leave.

“I don’t need a babysitter,” he says, punching in a code that opens the main doors. He walks through them and I hover outside. “Are you coming or not?”

"Um..." I jog inside because the doors are about to close, not giving me enough time to make a decision.

I'm so confused. He told me to leave with one breath and asked if I was staying with the next. I'm in the building now so I might as well follow. That's what I tell myself anyway. Stuffing my hands into my pockets, I keep my head down as we ride the lift and my eyes wander to James' foot which is tapping incessantly against the floor.

When we reach the top floor, he steps out and I trail behind. He's managed to keep hold of his keys and he teases them out of his pocket, jangling them until he finds the right one. There's only one door up here, I notice. Surely he can't occupy the *entire* top floor? *How much money is he actually worth?* A fucking *lot*, I decide when I step into his home. I walk into one *huge* open plan living space. Every wall is painted brilliant white with the exception of one which is exposed brick. It's very modern – modular sofas, high-gloss kitchen, and a TV bigger than my bedroom mounted on the wall.

"You have a balcony?" It comes out like a question as I tread across the great room.

The far wall consists of floor-to-ceiling windows, the centre panel housing French doors that open up onto a terrace overlooking the city. Manchester looks pretty stunning from up here. Nestled under the dark sky, it's a sea of lights and artistic buildings. You don't see that during the day. When you're scurrying around trying to get from A to B, all you notice are swarms of people, littered pavements, and heavy traffic.

"You don't have to stay," James says. He joins me at the window, standing next to me, and I stare at his reflection in the glass.

"Do you want me to leave?"

"I don't care," he says, shrugging, but I don't believe him. I'm not sure why. Maybe it was the unusual crack in his voice. Maybe it's because he hasn't *ordered* me out yet. Maybe it's the way he's standing, shoulders slumped, head down. Or maybe…*maybe* it's because I don't *want* to leave yet.

"You got anything to drink?" I ask, clarifying straight after. "Pop, I mean."

"There're some cans of Coke in the fridge."

In the large U-shaped kitchen, I pluck two cans from the American style fridge-freezer. I also notice a selection of Sainsbury's branded food and I exhale a short, quiet laugh. Of course Mr Moneybags shops at Sainsbury's. When I turn around, I notice James is missing. My brow furrows, and suddenly I feel very strange standing, alone, in my boss' flashy penthouse. Feeling awkward, I walk over to the pristine white sofa and take a seat, setting the cans down on the glass table in front of me. I look around and find everything is so clinical. There are no clues to who James Holden is. Nothing personal. No photos, books, DVD's. It disappoints me.

Is he coming back? He's not on the balcony, and all the doors down the hall are closed. Briefly, I contemplate looking for him but I have a nervous feeling in my gut. It seems stupid to wait here indefinitely, so I decide to give him ten minutes to reappear and then I'll leave.

Just as I'm about to stand and walk out, I hear footsteps approaching. I turn my head and see James walking towards me. He looks freshly showered, his hair damp, and is dressed more casually than I've ever seen him before in track-pants and a white vest. The thin material clings to his muscles and it's the first time I've noticed just how fit he is. I try not to get hard, but my damn dick won't listen to me.

He sits right next to me and my gaze won't leave his sculpted arms. That Japanese art *does* extend right up to his shoulder, the swirling cherry blossoms winding around his defined biceps. The top of his other arm is inked, too, with some kind of mountain landscape, branches and floating leaves. He's stunning.

In an effort to get my errant dick to calm down, I look away and sip on my Coke. I can't see him, and we don't speak, but I can *feel* his presence throughout my whole body.

"How's your wrist?" I know it isn't broken because he's not wearing a cast, but I can't think of anything else to say.

He holds it up and flexes it around in a circle. "Just a little swollen."

I nod, but he doesn't see because he's staring at the coffee table. "And your head?"

He shrugs. "Couple of stitches."

I sigh with an emotion I don't even recognise. "What happened, James?"

He turns and looks at me through narrowed eyes, his gaze heavy with burden. "That's the first time you've ever said my name."

Is it? The intensity of his stare makes my breath hitch and I can't look away.

After what seems like forever but not nearly long enough, he turns his head away again. "I was drunk," he says.

"Where were your friends?"

He scoffs like I've said something amusing, but I'm certain I remember his brother saying he was celebrating his birthday with friends. "I don't *do* friends."

"Isn't that…" I trail off, searching for the right word. *Sad, boring…* "Lonely?"

"I prefer being alone. It's better that way."

He's always so cryptic, so confusing. I wonder if he does it on purpose, whether he *wants* me to probe further, or if it's his way of telling me to mind my own business.

"I think I'd go crazy being alone all the time. I'd be lost without Tess."

"She's the girl I saw you with in the village?"

"Yeah. She's my best friend."

"How stereotypical of you," he says, his tone the lightest I've heard all night.

"Not really. It's not like we sit up all night discussing fashion and guys' arses…not when she's more interested in football and girls."

"You don't like football?"

"I like the shorts. My interest stops there."

James smiles, only a little, but there's a glint in his eyes that makes me think it's genuine. "So, what do you like to do when you *are* alone?"

I say the first things that come into my head. "I listen to music, write, read, binge on Netflix."

"What kind of books do you enjoy?"

Wow. We appear to be having an actual, two sided conversation. Not just an exchange of innuendos and insults.

"Anything. Everything. I have my favourites – Andrea Moore, JD Simmons, Paul L McLean, but I like to try unknowns, too."

"You like JD Simmons?"

"Oh yeah. I've read every one of his. I have to say, when I handed you his contract I had a bit of a moment. Maybe I'll bump into him one day when he comes into the building." Not that I'd know who he was. I stalk *all* of my favourite authors online but if JD Simmons owns any social media accounts, I haven't been able to find them yet. Guess he doesn't need them. Self-promotion isn't necessary when your name alone is enough to propel you onto the bestseller lists.

"He never comes into the office," James says, making me sag in disappointment.

"But you've met him I assume?"

"Yes." A smug grin twists his lips and I suspect he's trying to make me jealous.

It works. "Well if you ever need an assistant next time you have a meeting, maybe give me a shout." Damn, just the idea makes me giddy. My favourite writers are like royalty to me. Rock stars. Although I know it's not likely to happen, the thought of getting to meet one of my idols was one of the many driving forces behind my application to Holden House.

"I'll bear that in mind," he replies, but something in his expression makes me think he's placating me. "So why marketing? With your passion for reading, I think you'd be better suited to submissions."

"It was the only opening you had."

A smile so small it's barely noticeable teases his lips. "Guess I should've known that."

"What about you? What do *you* like to do?"

I don't expect him to answer. Not honestly, at least. He's always so careful not to reveal too much about himself. Sometimes I get the feeling *nobody* really knows who James Holden is.

"I read, too. I work. I run. I surround myself with music as often as possible."

They're not life altering revelations but they're genuine, intriguing. Bizarrely, I almost feel a little closer to him. For the first time I admit to myself that I don't actually hate him. I never have. If anything, I hated *myself* for giving into him so easily the first time we met. Rightly or wrongly, I'm ashamed of the way I behaved that night, but I can't blame James, no matter how much I want to. He didn't force me into anything. He didn't even encourage me. He didn't need to. I wanted it. Wanted *him*. And as I sit here inhaling shallow breaths, goosebumps mottling my skin every time I look at him, I think I still do.

"Going off the playlist in your car, you have very eclectic taste."

His smile grows a little wider. It's mesmerising. He should do it more often. "I like different songs for different reasons, play certain songs for certain moods."

I want to ask for more details but I'm not confident enough. I don't know him, not the *real* him, but I possess a tiny flicker of hope that maybe I'm starting to. I don't know why I make my next move. That's a feeling I'm beginning to get used to. Maybe it's because he looks so lost, so alone, so in need of someone to touch him, connect with him. Maybe it's because he's so close but not close enough. Perhaps it's because I can barely breathe through the urge to feel his skin against mine, to absorb some of the hidden pain that haunts his beautiful face.

Or maybe, it's simply because I *want* to.

I start by placing a tentative palm on his thigh, slowly, carefully, smoothing it up and down. He stares down at my touch, his body frozen and expression beguiled. Warily, I move my hand upwards, gliding the pads of my fingers just barely under the hem of his vest, grazing his taut stomach.

Unexpectedly, he grabs my wrist, paralysing me. I wonder if I've gone too far, but he guides my hand lower and presses it over his hard cock through his pants. I grip it through the material and he arches his back against the sofa, groaning into the air. Feeling bold, I scoot closer and lean over him, hovering my lips just inches from his.

I look straight into his eyes, searching them, trying to discover who he is. I see confusion, lust, maybe even *fear*, then he closes them and fixes his mouth to mine. He drives his tongue between my lips, his designer beard scratching my face, and in an instant all traces of delicacy have gone. I'm back with the guy I met in the bathroom that night, now, as he grabs my shoulders and shoves me lower, breaking our kiss.

My mouth waters as he tugs on his pants, his prominent cock springing free, begging for attention, as he pushes them down his legs.

"Wow," the word falls out of my mouth when I see his strong, athletic legs, the flesh embracing his muscles adorned with more, exquisite artwork. I can't see an inch of bare skin as I scan them up and down. His tattoos are vibrant, captivating. They contain every shade and depth of colour. "They're…" *Stunning, beautiful, mesmerising…* "Magnificent."

I look up at him and he's watching me, his expression curious as he studies my face. I keep my gaze on him as I slip off the sofa and kneel on the floor. Idly, I wonder how many other men there have been, right here in this position, but I force the thought away. The only thing I care about is that *I'm* here, right now, my mouth so close to his twitching cock I can already taste it.

Curling my fingers around his thick base, I tug gently, retracting his foreskin before licking my way around the deep ridge. He has a cute little freckle on the end of his tip. I kiss it, then drag his whole length into my mouth.

"Fuck that feels good," he moans, and satisfaction balloons in my chest.

I kiss and lick up and down his shaft, finishing each teasing stroke by circling his moist tip with my tongue. Every gasp, every groan that drips from his mouth makes me feel like a god. Growing impatient, he grabs a fistful of my hair and pushes my head until I have no choice but to swallow him all the way to the back of my throat.

He's in control now. He directs the speed at which I take him in and out of my mouth over, and over again. He's too thick, too much, and it makes me gag and splutter but I don't stop. My mouth slams down on him repeatedly, so forceful I need to support myself by placing my hands on his open thighs.

"That's it," he practically growls. "Suck it, Theodore. Suck it *hard*."

After what feels like hours, James lifts my head, staring straight into my eyes. My jaw aches. I'm breathless. I miss the taste of his salty pre-cum on my tongue. He crooks his finger and I rise to him immediately, desperate to taste his mouth again. His pants are still hooked around his ankles and as I crawl up onto the sofa, he kicks them off.

"You're good at that," he whispers against my jaw, before kissing his way down my neck while he un-pops the buttons on my shirt.

My head tips back and I close my eyes, focusing on every touch, every lick of his warm tongue. My heart hammers fiercely in my chest and my breath comes in short, fast pants when his hand sneaks into my waistband and brushes against my dick. "Oh, God…"

"These need to come off," he says, kissing along the muscles of my chest.

I raise my arse off the sofa and push my jeans and boxers down, kicking them off and onto the floor. He uses both hands to roll my open shirt over my shoulders and I shrug all the way out of it before locking my lips onto his. His right hand flies to my cock and he wraps it in his fist, squeezing and relaxing his fingers as he strokes it roughly up and down.

His kiss is urgent, desperate, and I can't breathe through the intense pleasure ripping through my dick, so I pull away. I peck at his neck, digging my fingers into his broad back. I'm naked, but James is still wearing his vest. I want, *need* to feel his flesh against mine, so I pinch the hem of his top and start to pull.

He stops me, abandoning my aching cock and grabbing both of my hands. "Bend over the couch," he says, his tone firm, demanding.

I don't hesitate to do as he asks. I never do. I stand up and walk to the side of the sofa, using the arm to support my weight.

He leans over me from behind and kisses the back of my neck. "Don't move," he orders, so of course, I don't.

I stare after him as he strides across the room, admiring the way his glorious arse flexes with each step before he disappears through one of the pine doors. He returns a few seconds later with a pump-dispensing bottle of lube and as my eyes dart to his impressive erection, I notice it's already wrapped in a condom. He strokes it up and down a few times as he walks closer and I can't wait to feel him stretch me. He positions himself at my back, and I swallow hard when I hear him pump the bottle of lube.

"Wider," he says, wedging one hand between my legs.

My response is automatic. I adjust my feet and arch my back, completely exposing myself to him. Using his fingers, he spreads the cold lube along the crevice between my arse cheeks, making me gasp, and then he massages my hole before plunging two fingers straight inside.

"Holy *fuck*," I moan, my hips thrusting against his hand of their own accord.

"So tight," he whispers, his chest pressed to my back as he nuzzles my neck. "Has anyone been here since me?"

"N-no." The word stutters as he fucks me roughly with his skilled fingers.

Pulling his fingers out of my body, he speaks right into my ear. "Good answer."

I sag, breathless and already grieving the loss of him in my arse. I don't miss him for long. Seconds later, he pushes into me, slowly at first, and a throaty sigh escapes his throat.

"Oh yeah," he breathes, plunging all the way inside and hitting a spot that makes me cry out.

He doesn't allow me much time to acclimatise to the intrusion, and his deep, powerful thrusts burn in the most delicious of ways. "Fuck, don't stop," I say. "Don't ever fucking stop."

He pants and grunts with every buck of his hips. "You like that, huh? You like me pounding your tight arse?"

"Y-yes. Oh, *fuck*, yes."

"Take your dick, Theodore. Wank yourself off for me."

The way my name sounds on his tongue resonates through my entire body. I can't even begin to understand why but he has complete control over me and, I don't only allow it, I fucking *love* it.

Removing one of my hands from the arm of the sofa, I reach for my dick, gripping it firmly at the base. I've barely touched it but I already feel the pressure of an impending orgasm swelling in the base of my spine. As my fist tugs at my weeping cock, James' heavy balls slap against my flesh as he grinds into me. He uses so much force, my arm starts to tremble, struggling to support my weight.

"I've got you," he says, gripping both of my hips and holding me in place.

Three small words and yet they're enough to make my dick throb in my hand, my balls pulling up into my body as spurts of hot cum spill out over my fingers. "Ah *shit*," I hiss. "Fuck, James…."

He continues to pound me, not giving me a second to catch my breath. "Christ, I fucking *love* you saying my name as you come."

I massage my load into my cock and suck my bottom lip between my teeth. I know it's about to end, evident by the harsh growls erupting from James' throat, but I don't want it to. I wish I could stay here, relishing the feeling of his cock assaulting my hole, forever.

"I'm gonna come, Theodore," he spits. I didn't think it was possible but he rocks into me even faster, deeper, *harder*. "Gonna come so fucking hard."

And, fuck, he does. He slams into me one last time and collapses onto my back, his vest damp against my skin, and I lose my grip on the sofa and fall forward.

His breath is hot as it blankets the back of my neck and I crane my head to face him, reaching behind and stroking the side of his face with my fingers. "And *you're* good at that," I say, smiling.

He returns my smile, only his looks forced. He pulls out of me quickly, and then stalks off, to what I assume is the bathroom, without looking back.

I stand up, feeling somewhat deflated that he left without a single word, even though he's only in the fucking bathroom. How pathetic is that?

"Shit," I mutter to myself, noticing that a rogue droplet of spunk has dripped onto his sofa. Spitting onto my clean hand, I attempt to rub it off but only end up making it worse, so I hide the stain under a cushion instead and hope he doesn't notice until after I've left.

"All yours if you want to get cleaned up," James says as he re-enters the room. His voice is clipped and I can't prevent my lips twisting into a frown.

"Thanks," I say, my tone thick with awkwardness.

The twathole version of James Holden is back; the arrogant wanker side that makes me want to hate him. But I can't, dammit. Again, I'm more annoyed at myself than I am at him. I was foolish to believe I'd made some kind of connection with him.

Picking my clothes up off the floor, I walk to the bathroom naked, silently cursing myself along the way. *Jesus.* His bathroom is big enough to be an apartment in its own right. A large oval bathtub with chrome feet, easily spacious enough for three people, sits proudly in the centre of the room. There's a freestanding shower cubicle, mirrored cabinets, and one of those fancy toilets built into the wall.

I need a shower but I'm exhausted, confused, and I just want to go home, so I freshen up at the sink instead. I dress quickly after washing my hands and splashing my face, then, when I see my reflection in the mirror, I huff in frustration. I'm starting to get sick of my whining arse. *Talk to him, or don't, but for fuck's sake stop droning on about it.*

When I step back into the main living space I spot James outside, smoking a cigarette on his balcony, looking out over River Irwell. For a few seconds, I watch him from afar, trying to decide if I should say goodbye or just leave straight away. I *want* to leave, but of course that isn't what happens. Given that my body seems intent on disobeying my mind lately, I'm beginning to wonder if I should start telling myself I actually *like* him. Maybe *then* I'll be able to walk away.

I step up behind him, my hands tucked into my pockets. "I should get going," I say.

He doesn't even have the decency to turn around. "Sure."

"Will you be okay on your own?" I don't know why I ask. I refuse to believe it's because I care. "Your brother should be here any minute."

"I'm a big boy. I'll be just fine."

I nod, even though he can't see me as he puffs a plume of smoke into the black sky. "Okay. Guess I'll see you at work then."

"Yeah."

I turn to leave, my heart heavy with rejection. I'm barely off the balcony when I hear him speak.

"Theodore."

I spin around to the sound of his voice. He's still standing with his back to me, but I stare at him anyway. "Yeah?"

"Thank you." There was more sincerity in those two words than any he's ever spoken before. His voice is raw, honest, filled with sadness.

What's hurting you, James? "No problem." And then I leave, my thoughts and emotions in turmoil once again.

I don't know what I feel for James Holden, or *why* I feel anything at all. But I *do*, and seemingly, I'm powerless to stop it, so maybe I should stop trying.

When I get home, Tess is waiting for me. I toss my keys onto the kitchen counter and sigh. "You waited up?" I haven't checked the time in a while but I know morning can't be far away.

"Of course I did. I've rang you, like, thirty times. Where've you been? Is he okay?"

Tess and Ed were with me in the village when I spotted James acting strangely. Ed thought it was hilarious, seeing our usually formal and uptight boss dancing on a podium, and Tess was altogether uninterested. She thought I should leave him to it. But I couldn't. Something was wrong, though even now I can't explain *what*.

I've gotten to know the firm, self-assured bastard everyone else sees, but I've also seen glimpses of the man behind the mask he wears; the man who likes to sing, poke fun at me, talk about random nonsense. The man who wears a smile so dazzling it lights up his entire face. That wasn't the man on the podium. That was a whole new side of him I hadn't seen before. He was more than drunk. He was almost…*high*.

It surprised me to see him acting that way but I wasn't necessarily concerned. That only kicked in when I followed him outside. I went after him because, like always, I didn't have a choice. I've been drawn to James since the first time I saw him, for reasons completely unbeknown to me. I'm not sure I'll ever understand it and I'm getting tired of trying.

When he climbed up onto the wall it felt like my heart had leapt into my throat, choking me. It's not a *huge* drop to the Rochdale canal, but in his reckless state he could've banged his head, been unable to swim or not known how to get out…all kinds of scenarios sped through my mind. People turned, some staring, some laughing. I didn't know he'd completely lost his mind, all I knew is that he wasn't listening to me and I needed to get him down. So, I grabbed him and pulled, bringing us both crashing to the ground.

Unlike James, I was sober and had enough rational thought to save myself with my hands during the fall. He, however, went limp, lifeless, letting his head take the brunt of the impact. He didn't fall from a great height but, still, he's lucky to have come through it with only a couple of stitches.

"He's fine," I say, shrugging out of my shirt. I'm dirty, but exhausted, and plan to strip to my boxers and crawl straight into bed. "Few stitches, that's all."

"What a moron. He must've taken some seriously dodgy shit," Tess says, shaking her head.

"He said he didn't."

Clearly sceptical, she raises an eyebrow. "And you believe him?"

I can only shrug. I wasn't with him when he spoke to the doctor and, naturally, they didn't tell me anything because I'm not a relative. I'm not even a friend, really. I don't know what I am to him. I like to think I'm more than an employee, but who the fuck knows.

"So you've been at the hospital all this time?"

I consider lying but realise there's no point. Not to Tess. She knows me too well. "He was discharged a few hours ago. I went back to his place. Wanted to make sure he got home okay."

Her eyes narrow and, slowly, she tilts her head, studying my expression. "You've shagged him again, haven't you?"

I open my mouth to protest, but what's the fucking point? "Yeah." I sigh, dropping my head and staring at my foot as it draws invisible circles on the floor.

"Bloody hell, Theo," she grumbles. "Even if he wasn't your boss, you don't need to be getting involved with some kind of crack-head."

"He's not a crack-head. Christ, Tess."

"Oh, I'm sorry. I forgot you were his best friend."

"Don't be like that."

"What do you expect? You don't know anything about him, you've been walking around like someone killed your puppy since you met him, and yet you can't seem to stop yourself dropping your kecks every time he looks at you!"

"It's only happened twice," I counter, as if that makes it all better.

"Yeah, and look what happened after the first time. You've been a whiney bitch ever since."

I want to argue but I can't, because she's right. "I didn't know him then."

"You *still* don't."

"I do. Kind of. He's not a bad guy. Pretentious and arrogant, yes, but he's…I don't know, *more*."

"More?"

"He thanked me."

Tess scrunches her nose. "For having sex with him?"

"No! For…" I realise I don't actually know. "For helping him out, I guess."

"I'm sorry," Tess says, her tone softer as she rubs my arm. "I'm being a twat. Just…be careful, okay? I don't want you getting hurt."

"Right now, the only thing I'm feeling is tired." I start walking towards the bedroom. "You coming?"

"Only if I can sleep on the left. You've got a loose spring on the right. I swear, it nearly took out one of my ovaries last week."

Dramatic, much? "Whatever. I could sleep on a washing line right now."

No more than five seconds later, I'm in bed. Another five seconds, and I've fallen into a coma.

* * *

When I reach the office on Monday morning I walk over to Ed who's chatting to Stacey, and Katie from design.

"Told you he was a weirdo," Katie says.

Ed greets me with a nod before getting back to the conversation. "He was making a right tit of himself. Bet he doesn't show today. Probably too embarrassed."

"And, he was going to *jump*?" Stacey cuts in.

They're gossiping like high-schoolers and I feel utterly disgusted by it. Tugging on Ed's arm, I ask if I can have a word. Nodding, he follows me to my workstation.

"Mate, what the hell are you doing?" I ask, my tone baffled.

"How'd you mean?"

"Telling people about Saturday. This isn't Jeremy fucking Kyle. He doesn't need it publicising for your entertainment."

"Oh, come on. You have to admit it was funny seeing that he's not as smart and cocky as he makes out."

Funny? "No, actually, I fail to see anything *funny* about it. He could've really hurt himself." *Or worse.*

"Chill out, Theo. He was pissed, that's all. Just a regular nobhead who'd had too much to drink like the rest of us. He treats people like crap all the damn time. Thinks he's better than us. Won't kill him to get a taste of his own medicine for once."

I wave his stupid reasoning off with my hand. "Well, keep me out of it," I say. "I've no desire to get my kicks at the expense of someone else."

"Jesus, didn't realise you were his best bud."

"I'm not."

A sardonic grin tugs on one side of Ed's mouth and he glares at me, staring straight into my eyes. "You've fucked him haven't you?"

"No!" I deny it because the way he's smiling at me, amused, makes me feel embarrassed. Maybe even a little ashamed.

"It's written all over your face. Makes sense now, why you're sticking up for him."

"That's not why. Maybe I just don't get off on laughing at other people's misfortunes."

"Well trust me, just because he's fucked you doesn't mean he deserves your loyalty," he says, ignoring me. It pisses me off. "He won't return the favour."

"Oh yeah?" My tone is sarcastic. "And you say that from experience?"

I've suspected Ed is one of James' many conquests for a while but he's never confirmed it.

He simply shrugs, and I decide it's the closest to a *yes* I'm going to get. "He'll have forgotten about you already. He uses people. Only cares about himself."

I disagree but don't argue. I'm sick of discussing it. "By the way," I say. "Tess said you owe her a tenner."

"It was *five!*"

"Yeah, you'll soon learn not to borrow from Tess. She charges interest."

"Interest would be twenty pence," he grumbles. "That's extortion! I'm skint enough as it is."

Smirking, I shrug my shoulders.

"I'll nip to the hole in the wall at lunch."

I'm relieved when he walks away. He's annoyed me but I'm forced to wonder if I really would feel the same if his gossip centred around anyone else, or if it's because of my skewed, possibly imaginary, connection to James.

It's an unusually warm day for April and so I wriggle out of my suit jacket and drape it over the back of my chair. When I look back up, Stacey is by my side.

"If you've come to gossip I'm not interested," I snap.

Her eyes widen in response to my harsh tone. "Actually, I just came to say it's time for the weekly briefing in Mike's office."

"Oh," I mutter, feeling like a dick.

"But…I know we haven't known each other that long, but if you ever want to talk about anything, I'm here."

Huh? My eyebrows draw together in confusion.

She must notice. "I don't know what happened on Saturday, but from the look on your face, I think there's more to it than Ed's version of events."

"Not really," I say, because it's true. James *was* drunk, and he most certainly made an arse out of himself. There may well be more to it, I suspect as much, but I don't know for sure and probably never will. "Guess I just don't find it as amusing as he does."

"For the record, nor do I. I might've listened, but it won't go any further. Not from *my* mouth, anyway."

Offering a weak smile, I stand from my chair. I appreciate her words, but I don't want to talk about it anymore. The last thing I need is people wondering why it bothers me so much. It's stressful enough trying to figure that out for myself.

I walk into Mike's office wondering if James *will* show up today. Part of me hopes he doesn't. If Ed has anything to do with it the whole damn building will know about Saturday before lunch. The other part of me, the stronger and possibly foolish part, can't wait to see him again.

Chapter

Six

~James~

Pausing outside the revolving glass doors to Holden House, I clear my throat and straighten my tie. Max tried to convince me to take a few days off but I refuse. This is *my* company. It relies on me, and I won't let my people, or my father, down.

Offering my usual greeting to security, and then Jane on reception, I stride towards the lifts. People filter inside the lift as it stops on various floors and I'm sure I receive some questionable glances. Ignoring them, I look straight ahead until I reach the thirteenth floor.

I head straight to Mike Nolan's office, looking at my watch. I'm late for his weekly briefing and I consider skipping it, but I can't. Sitting in on every department meeting each Monday is not only a colossal waste of my time but also an increasing burden as the business continues to grow. But, it's how my father did things. He thought it vital to connect personally with all levels of staff, show his support. Communication builds trust, understanding, and work ethic, which are essential for a company to thrive. That's what he used to say anyway. I, however, think it eats into valuable time I could be spending on more important things.

The meeting has already begun by the time I reach his office. I'm glad, because it means I don't have to talk to him beforehand. Arms folded across my chest, I stand at the back of the room. A few people turn at my arrival but the only person I'm interested in is Theodore. He hasn't seen me yet, and he doesn't until the redhead nudges his shoulder and blatantly nods to where I stand.

Dick.

He looks almost amused, the redhead, and I wonder if he knows about Theodore and I, or maybe he's reliving what happened on my birthday. I think I remember seeing him there, but I can't trust my recollections of that night. Narrowing my eyes, I glower at him. He soon looks away.

My focus turns back to Theodore and I feel a stab of disappointment that he's not looking at me. I suspect he's thinking about me, however, because he's staring at his feet rather than Mike who's addressing the room.

I spent the whole of yesterday telling myself to leave him alone, to go back to a time when I didn't know he existed. He doesn't know what he's getting into with me and he deserves better.

Nobody should get close to me. I'm too much. Too broken. Life is better alone. I like it that way. Solitude is addictive. Once you discover how peaceful it is, you no longer want or need to deal with people anymore. It's why I keep my distance from Max, but unfortunately for him he's family and he *has* to love me. Theodore doesn't. He has a choice and he should choose to have nothing to do with me. He *has* to, because I'm not strong enough to push him away.

Maybe, after Saturday, he'll make the right decision. Perhaps he already has and that's why he won't look at me. But…what if…what if Saturday was just a blip? What if I'm not as sick as they think I am? I'm not crazy. It was the alcohol that caused me to behave like that. I'm not supposed to drink to excess and I *know* that.

These questions continue to burn a hole in my head throughout the meeting, contradicting everything I'm trying so hard to force myself to believe. I feel so much better lately. I can't tell anyone that of course because they'll accuse me of being manic. But they don't live in my head. They don't *know* how I'm feeling. Maybe it's *their* fault, the doctors, my brother, that I've never felt good enough for anyone. They're so intent on labelling me, insisting that I'm 'not well'. They don't want me to be happy. If I am, I'm sick. If I'm sad, I'm sick. They want me to live as a fucking robot and I've complied…until now.

What if they're wrong? What if I *do* have a right to be happy? What if I *can* be what Theodore deserves? I've never even contemplated a relationship before, not just because I've been convinced that I'm a burden to anyone who gets too close, but because it's never interested me.

But Theodore…

I can't stop thinking about him. Wanting him. *They* don't want me to *feel.* They've kept my system pumped with drugs, tablets that block all my emotions, for years. They don't want me to *live*, merely exist, and I've allowed it. But Theodore's broken through. He makes me *feel* again and…and I like it. I like the flickers of hope in my chest when he smiles, the bubbles of excitement in my stomach when he laughs, even the guilt I feel when I piss him off. They're emotions I haven't felt in such a long time and I crave more of them, crave *him*, crave *life*.

So when the meeting ends and his team disperse from the office, I do the very thing I've been telling myself not to since the early hours of Sunday morning. I step in front of Theodore, blocking his path. He tilts his head to the side, his expression quizzical as he looks up at me with caution.

"Can I have a word? In my office."

He hesitates and I watch his Adam's apple move slowly up and down his throat. My tongue itches to dart out and lick it, but I don't. "Sure."

Stepping aside, I extend my arm so he can pass. I walk behind him, admiring the way his grey pants hug his perfectly sculpted arse. I need to stop thinking about that so I overtake him, leading the way. We ride the lift alone and he keeps his gaze on the doors, while mine is fixed on him. He seems nervous. I thought we were past that. I thought he'd grown immune to my bullshit.

"I haven't said anything," Theodore rushes out as soon as we step into my office. I shut the door behind us and twist the blinds closed on the glass wall separating Helen's office from mine.

"Said anything?" I question, perching on the edge of my desk.

"About Saturday. Isn't that why I'm here? People are talking, but it didn't come from me."

"That's not why I want to talk to you." Although that *does* explain the strange looks I've been getting. "I asked you here so I could thank you, and apologise."

"Apologise?"

"You shouldn't have had to see me like that, and you certainly didn't have to stick around. But you did, and I want you to know I appreciate it."

Theodore looks uncertain. He assesses my face, his brow creased. "Are you trying to get me to have sex with you again?" He sounds almost annoyed.

"Is that all you think I see in you? A quick fuck?"

He shrugs and it riles me. "Isn't it? It seems as soon as you've got what you wanted from me you go straight back to being a jerk."

Ouch. That stings, but he's absolutely right and it makes me sigh. Maybe I can't do this after all.

I'm already hurting him and I didn't even realise. "I'm sorry. That's all I have to offer."

He stares at me with an expression I can't decipher. I don't know what I expect him to say but I want him to say *something*. Anything.

"I wish I could stay away from you."

Okay, maybe I didn't want him to say *that*.

Standing up, I walk tentatively towards him until our chests are just inches apart. "Why?" I breathe.

"You…you scare me."

Whoa. My head swims. My chest aches. "I don't want you to be afraid of me, Theodore."

He's so close I can feel his breath on my face. "I'm not. Not really. I just…" he trails off, closing his eyes while dragging in a deep breath. "I don't understand you. I think I *want* to sometimes, but…"

I move in on him, placing my hands on his hips. "But?"

"But…I sense a darkness in you. Danger. I don't know you. Not really. I think you're hiding, and I'm scared that if I find you, I won't be able to handle it."

My pulse thuds violently in my ears with each deep rise and fall of my chest. "You see all that?"

I stare into his vivid green eyes, my forehead pleated in bewilderment. He *sees* me. I've known it all along. I don't know how or why, but he *does*.

And he's still here.

"Am I right?" he asks, his lips so close to mine I can almost taste them. "Are you hiding, James?"

Yes. I'm not brave enough to say the word aloud so I kiss him instead. His face crumples as if he's in pain but he doesn't resist. I take it slow, gentle. Softly, I trace the edges of his lips with my tongue, my hands twisting into his short hair. He allows it, but doesn't reciprocate.

"Tell me to stop, and I will," I whisper into his mouth.

"Don't stop," he murmurs, his breath catching.

Smiling, I dip my tongue between his lips, grazing his teeth as I push him backwards until his back hits the door. Reaching behind him, I twist the lock and start unbuttoning his shirt with my other hand.

His hands clamp down on my shoulders and I break away from our kiss and start kissing and licking the exposed skin of his chest. His head falls back and he groans as my impatient fingers start tugging at the zip on his pants. Dropping to my knees, I pull his pants down with me, burying my face in his groin, his hard cock slapping my cheek.

I haven't tasted him before and I salivate at the thought. I don't tease him, don't take my time. I can't. I need him too badly. Moistening my lips, I wrap them around his tip, taking him straight to the back of my throat.

"Oh my God," he moans, arching his hips.

I'd smile, but my mouth is full and I don't want to empty it until I've swallowed everything he has to offer. Cupping his balls, I roll them between my fingers, tugging them gently as I drag my lips up and down his shaft over and over again.

Holy fuck. A burst of pre-cum dances on my tongue and I groan against his delicious dick, revelling in the fact the vibrations make him quiver. Desperate to feel him pulsate in my mouth, I add my hand, squeezing the base and dragging it up and down in rhythm with my lips. His cock starts to twitch and his hips thrust as he forces himself deeper.

"Ah shit, James."

My name on his lips ignites fireworks in my chest and I suck harder, stroke faster, until his legs start to wobble and he grabs my shoulders for support. With every withdraw, I flick his tip with my tongue and I feel him growing closer. His cock jerks, the taste of him intensifies, and his breaths are short, strained. His head knocks against the door at the exact moment he spills into my mouth. I keep sucking, swirling his warm load around in my mouth, savouring every drop before swallowing and slowly, reluctantly, easing my lips off him.

For a moment, I just stare at his swollen cock, admiring the glistening tip. A tiny drop of cum leaks from it and my tongue darts out, catching it before it falls.

Smiling proudly, I rise to my feet and palm his flushed cheek with my hand. Leaning in, I lick his lips, my dick throbbing at the knowledge he's tasting himself.

I kiss a trail up to his ear and whisper, "I have a meeting in an hour. I need you to pick up the relevant documents from accounts."

He angles his neck so he can see me, his brow furrowed in confusion. "You don't want anything?"

A sly grin creeps onto my face. "That was about *you.* I want you to know I don't just use you for my own pleasure. Well, maybe I did the first time, but I'm not as selfish as you think I am."

"I-I don't think that."

"Yes you do."

He opens his mouth to reply but I place my finger over his lips. "I need those documents."

"S-sure," he stutters, his expression stunned and oddly adorable. "I'll get right on it."

Still grinning, I turn for my desk. "You might want to pull up your pants first."

"R-right. Yeah."

Taking a seat behind my desk, I sit back in my chair, clasping my hands together as I watch Theodore straighten himself up. He dresses swiftly and offers a small, somewhat bemused, nod before unlocking the door and leaving my office.

I'm so fucking happy right now. It's an emotion I'd almost forgotten and I refuse to let it go.

* * *

Sliding my waning dick out of Theodore's mouth, I sigh. "I really need to get going," I say, grabbing the headrest of the backseat of my car to pull myself into a sitting position. "Max is expecting me."

Theodore wipes his mouth on the back of his hand while I fasten my pants and belt.

I smile, but he doesn't return it. "What's wrong?" I ask, reaching out to touch his arm.

He shrugs, staring down at the foot-well between the seats. "I don't know if this is what I want."

My breath catches in my throat and for a second it feels like my lungs are paralysed. "What do you mean?"

"What is this, James? What are we doing?"

I'm confused, and I'm sure it shows on my face. "I think they call it oral sex in the back of a car." I know that's not the answer he's looking for, but I just want the serious look on his face to disappear.

It doesn't. "It's not enough. For the last few days, all we've done is fuck in your office, in the car, in a bathroom at the village. I'm starting to feel like some kind of cheap fuck toy."

"Theodore…"

"I don't like it, James. I don't like the man I'm turning into. Sex used to mean something to me. I didn't just give myself to anyone who asked. But with you…"

His words fade and I don't know what to do, what to say. I want to reassure him but I don't know how. I've never done *this* before. Theodore's the first man I've ever fucked more than twice. Does that make this a relationship? I wouldn't know. Is that what he's even asking for? I wouldn't know that either.

All I know is that I'm not ready to stop being with him yet. He's a good man. He has values. He *cares*. He makes me wish I could be like him. He makes me want to be *better*.

"I know it's just sex," he continues. "And that for some people it doesn't need to involve emotion, but it does for me. I can't help it."

"Don't say that like it's a bad thing," I say. It's not a notion I particularly understand, but I admire it nonetheless. "I don't know if I can be who you want me to be, but…but I can try."

He shakes his head and it confuses me even more. I'm losing him and I don't know how to stop it.

"I'd never want or ask you to change. That's not how relationships work."

"Is that what you want? A relationship?"

Theodore sighs. "I just want to know you. *You*. Not just your dick."

He has no idea what he's asking for. If he did, I'm sure he wouldn't be sitting here right now.

"I'm really not that interesting," I say, forcing playfulness into my voice. I suppose it's my way of trying to dodge this whole, uncomfortable conversation.

"But I *am* interested. To everyone else you're an uptight, arrogant prick, but I've already seen deeper than that. And…and I want *more*."

More? "I don't know if I can give you that."

Sighing, Theodore pulls away from my touch. “Then I can’t do this anymore.”

“Wait!” I say, panicked as his fingers curl around the door handle. “I’ll try. I don’t know if I *can* do it but, please, let me try.”

“Why? I’m sure you’ll find a replacement in no time. In fact, for all the shit Ed talks about you, I’m pretty sure he’d jump at the chance to suck you off in your car. You wouldn’t even need to say please.”

“But I don’t want him, or anyone else. I want *you.*”

“Why?”

“I don’t know. I could come up with some cheesy bullshit but it would be a lie. You’re different. I haven’t been able to get you out of my head since the very first time I laid eyes on you. It makes no sense to me so, no, I can’t tell you why. But…I-I need you, Theodore.”

Closing his eyes, he exhales slowly through his nose. “I feel like I might be about to agree to the worst mistake of my life.”

“I can’t promise that you’re not,” I say, my heart pounding.

“But no more sex. I’m banning it.”

What! “For how long?” My balls ache at the thought.

“Until we know each other a little better.”

“So…you want to *date* first?”

“I know it’s old-fashioned but-”

"It is," I cut in. "But I also find the idea strangely fascinating. I can't say I'll be any good at it, but I'll give it a go."

"You will?"

"The concept of courting has-"

"Jesus, don't call it that. You make me feel like an old man."

I can't help but smile. "*Dating* has never appealed to me before, but for you…" *I think I'd do just about anything.* What the hell has this man done to me? "For you, I'll try."

"Okay then," he says, with what looks like a mixture of surprise and suspicion clouding his eyes. "Let's just hang out. See what happens."

Hang out? I don't think I've ever 'hung out' in my life. "I can still wank though, right?" I ask, my tone teasing.

Theodore rolls his eyes and offers a lopsided smile at the same time. "I want to get to know you, not control you. Wank away."

When I realise our time together is coming to an end, my smile fades. "Can I at least kiss you before you leave?"

He responds with actions, climbing into my lap and twisting his fingers into my hair. My lips part, eager to take his tongue, but it doesn't appear. Resting his forehead on mine, he pecks feather-light kisses across my top lip before sucking it gently between his teeth and releasing it again.

"I've gotta go," he breathes, pulling away from me.

My mouth is still open. I'm breathless. Excited. Confused. Hopeful. *Terrified.*

"And you're *sure* people can't see through this glass?" he adds, looking up at his block of flats through the tinted window.

"Bit late to be thinking about your modesty *now.*"

"That's not even funny. Tess is up there. Her seeing me suck your dick would be like fucking you in front of my grandma."

A small laugh trickles from my throat. "You're good. I promise. Nobody saw; not Tess, not your neighbours, nobody."

He nods, appeased. "I'll see you Monday?"

That's too long. "Or before."

"But not for sex."

"No sex." I salute him. "Scouts honour." But fuck if this isn't going to be hard. *Literally.*

Theodore smiles, opens the door and clambers awkwardly out of the car. "Goodbye, James."

The door is closed before I can reply. My head falls back on the window and I close my eyes, composing myself while praying to a god I don't even believe in that I'm doing the right thing.

Please. Please don't let me ruin this.

* * *

"Uckle James! Uckle James! Come and see!"

I've barely walked through the door to my brother's house when Isobel tugs on my hand and starts pulling me into the living room. "Look at what, princess?"

"YouTube!"

I turn my head towards Max, drawing my eyebrows together, and whisper, "Three year olds use YouTube?"

Max chuckles. "She knows her way around it better than I do. Drink?"

"Just water, please," I say, clapping his shoulder before joining Isobel on the plush three-seater.

Isobel is engrossed in the TV. I'm struggling to see the appeal. So far, all I've seen is a pair of hands opening two rows of Kinder eggs one by one.

Laura, Max's wife of six years, appears with my water and she bends down and pecks my cheek. "Good to see you," she says.

Smiling, I take my drink. "Thanks." I take a small sip and then flit my gaze between her and the TV. "How is this entertainment?"

Laura laughs, shrugging. "The voiceover woman makes my ears bleed."

"Whatever happened to Rosie and Jim? Tom and Jerry?"

"Uckle James!" Isobel calls for my attention, yanking the sleeve of my jacket. "Look! She got a paw patrol toy."

"Wow. That's awesome, princess."

"Paw patrol is well sick."

"Sick?"

"She spends a lot of time with my nephew," Laura explains. "He's twelve, and everything's either sick or peng."

Peng? I'm thirty-one and suddenly feel like a pensioner.

Laura disappears to finish dinner, leaving me alone with Isobel. For a while, I just stare at her. Her hair is longer since I last saw her and she's definitely taller. Kids grow *fast.* She looks a lot like me, or at least like I do in childhood photos. I don't like that. It makes me worry about what else I might've passed on to her. She's perfect. Sweet. Kind. Adorable.

Happy.

Every time I see her I hope she doesn't turn out like me. Sometimes I find myself analysing the things she says, her mannerisms, actively looking for similarities between us. If I'm honest with myself, I think that's the reason I don't come here too often. I love her so much, but the thought of *tainting* her somehow tortures my mind.

"When's Nanna coming?"

I've been so busy watching Isobel I didn't notice Max enter the room. He stands next to me, addressing Isobel. "She's on her way. Go and ask Mummy for a wipe for that mucky mush of yours."

Isobel licks the back of her hand and rubs it across her mouth instead.

"*Isobel,*" Max says her name sternly, making her huff. "Go to Mummy while I talk to Uncle James."

Here we go. I've managed to avoid him since he left my apartment after my birthday trip to the hospital.

"If I do can I have a zine when we go to the shop?"

"We'll see."

Appeased, Isobel jumps up and starts running out of the room. "Mummy! Daddy said I can have a zine!"

"She can't read, can she?" I ask. She's a bright girl, and I don't know much about kids, but surely three year olds can't read magazines.

"She likes them for the shitty toys stuck on the front. The kind that break after two hours and end up punching a hole in the sole of your foot when you least expect it."

I nod, though I'm not familiar enough with kids toys to really understand. "So, how's work? Did you go to Glasgow?"

Turned out, Max was asked, last minute, to travel to his firm's Glasgow branch to implement a new training method they've developed at his Manchester office.

"Stop trying to avoid the topic, James. I want to talk to you before Mum gets here."

My jaw tenses. I don't want to do this with him. I know he cares, and that I'm an arsehole, but it's uncomfortable and I want to run away.

"Has the cut on your head healed?"

"Almost. Still a little tender but the stitches are starting to dissolve."

"And how about *inside?* Are you sleeping okay?"

"Yes." My tone is clipped. I don't mean it to be but I can't seem to stop it.

"Have you made a doctor's appointment yet?"

I sigh, frustrated. "I don't need one. I've already told you, I drank too much that's all. I fucked up. It won't happen again."

"You shouldn't be drinking *at all.*" His voice is concerned rather than reprimanding and guilt pools in my stomach.

"I know. I don't usually, but lately…" I trail off, running a hand over my flustered face. "It's been tough getting to grips with the running of the company. I just slipped." I shrug. "But it won't happen again," I repeat, willing him to believe me.

"If you need help, why not look into selling a share? Finding another business partner?"

"No." The word is acidic as it rolls off my lips. How can he even suggest that? "Dad managed, and so will I."

"But Dad wasn't…"

He falls silent and anger bubbles in my veins. "Wasn't what?" I snap. "*Sick?* Mentally ill? Fucked in the head?"

"Stop it, James."

I don't *want* to stop. I want to defend myself, but when I hear my mother's voice in the hall, I clamp my mouth shut. She doesn't know the half of it, and she never will.

My mum knows I've taken antidepressants in the past but, beyond that, we've never really talked about it. I've never felt able, or even wanted, to discuss anything of any real emotional importance with my mother. I can't say for sure if it's *her* issue or *mine.*

She's a good mum. She loves me, of that I have no doubt. I had a good childhood, never went without. But like a lot of people, she can be judgemental. I don't think it's necessarily intentional. I actually think she sees herself as quite open-minded, but nevertheless I've grown up listening to her comment on the news, celebrity gossip, neighbourhood rumours, with phrases like, "Suicide is selfish." "They don't know how good they've got it." "How can they be depressed when there are children dying in the world?" And her personal, and most used, favourite, "He/she needs to snap out of it."

She's not a bad person, possibly all talk. I'm sure she'd never voice her views outside the family. Most people only air their honest opinions, judge things they've no experience with, to people they're close to. Would she react differently if she knew one of those 'selfish' strangers she mocks was her own son? Possibly, but I have no intentions of finding out.

I stand up to greet her. "Ah, so that's what my youngest son looks like," she says, pressing her hands to my cheeks.

"Sorry, Mum." I kiss her cheek. "I've been busy with the company."

Smiling, she releases me and bends down to Isobel who's just ran in from the kitchen.

"Nanna!" Isobel sings, wrapping her little arms around my mother's legs. "Did you bring chocolate?"

"Isobel!" Max scolds.

It doesn't faze her. "Nanna always brings chocolate."

Her vocabulary stuns me. It hasn't been *that* long since I last saw her but the development is remarkable. She's more fluent, clearer, than I remember.

My mother winks and reaches into her coat pocket, pulling out a bag of chocolate buttons. Isobel practically rips them from Mum's fingers and starts opening the packet.

"You can have them after dinner," Max says, taking the bag from her.

Isobel pouts. "But Nanna said!"

"Carry on and you won't get them at all."

"Oh, Max." Our mum tuts. "Don't be so hard on her. She's only three."

I witness the battle on Max's expression as he fights the urge to roll his eyes or, worse, tell her to stop being an interfering mare. It makes me smile.

"Yeah, Dad. I'm only three. God sake."

"Izzy!" Max is wearing his angry face and I have to turn away so he can't see me laughing. The kid is bloody adorable.

"Izzy, honey," my mum begins, taking her little hand in hers. "Why don't we go help Mummy in the kitchen?"

She does it to stop Max disciplining Isobel for her attitude, and when they're out of sight, he releases the eye roll he's been holding.

"Deep breaths," I say, snickering.

"Pisses me off," he whispers. "Last week she actually stormed out of the house, tears and everything, because I shouted and made Izzy cry. The little sod had a tantrum and threw a toy at the TV in our bedroom. Cracked the screen. What the hell did she expect me to do? Give her a cuddle and a pat on the bleedin' back?"

I can't help find the whole tale highly amusing.

"It was all an act for Mum's benefit too. She knows exactly how to play her nanna. I swear, she got over herself and started pretending to be a cat before Mum had even driven off the driveway."

"Mums are supposed to interfere," I say, still smiling. "Think it's the law."

"Dinner's ready!" Laura calls out, and so I turn around to make my way to the dining room.

"James," Max says, his voice low as he stops me with a hand on my shoulder. "This is the last time I'll mention it, I promise. I know you don't like talking about it, but you *would* if you were struggling, right?"

No. I force a smile. "Yes," I assure him, patting his hand. He removes it from my shoulder and nods. I can't quite tell if he believes me, but it doesn't really matter. I feel great. I've got this.

My stomach growls when the smell of shepherd's pie assaults my nose. I didn't realise I was hungry until Laura places a generous plateful in front of me. It's my first decent meal in, probably, a couple of weeks, and I tuck in eagerly.

"Mummy," Isobel says, half way through the meal, huffing like a stroppy teenager. "I've told you I don't like peas." She's a bossy little madam and she knows how to work it, putting her hands on her hips and making everyone laugh. The funniest part is she's already eaten half of them.

"Well if you don't eat your peas that must mean you're full," Max says. "And if you're full, you mustn't want your chocolate buttons."

"Oh, Max," Mum interrupts. "You should never force a child to eat something they don't like."

That statement would be less amusing if she hadn't done the exact same thing when we were kids. To this day, she gets in a bad mood if you don't clear your plate. I've lost count of the amount of times I've heard, "I don't know why I bother standing for hours making food when no bugger eats it."

"She *does* like them," Max says. "She's just acting up."

"I'm only three, Dad."

God help my brother when Isobel hits puberty. I daren't even imagine how big her attitude will be then.

We carry on eating and Isobel finishes her peas without another word. When Laura brings in apple pie and custard for dessert, Isobel starts telling us all what she wants for her birthday, which is eight whole months away.

"Spiderman?" I question. "I thought you like Hulk?"

"Spiderman's sick," she says, shooting imaginary webs from the palm of her hand.

"She reminds me so much of James," Mum says. It makes my smile fade. "He's never been able to make his mind up either. I've lost count of all the silly ideas he's come up with in his life."

I chuckle, because it's expected of me. I'm sure she doesn't mean to, but it's comments like that which have always made me feel small, stupid. It's why I stopped telling her things about my life when I hit my late teens. It took me a while to find a career I was passionate about. I get bored easily. Distracted. I *have* tried my hand at many things. Some I gave up on, some I failed at, but I'd rather have given them a go than die wondering 'what if?'

"Remember that time you wanted to write a book?" My mum asks, tipping her head back and giggling. She's mocking me and I don't even think she realises.

I catch Max watching me, and I think he notices that my smile is awkward, as I hope she moves onto something else. He changes the subject, and relief floods my veins. "So, how'd you do at Weight Watchers this week, Mum?"

"Ugh. Two on. It's all Marie's fault." Marie is the friend in London she stayed with last weekend. "She took me out to eat every night, and you can't eat out without having a pudding and a bottle of wine. I don't think the chippy I had when I got home helped either to be fair. Or the bag of Maltesers. Oh, and the bacon was going out of date so I had to eat the full pack or it would've gone to waste."

I find it remarkable she only put *two* pounds on this week. I daren't say as much of course. I don't actually feel like saying anything at all.

Not to the adults at least. Isobel is more on my wavelength. "Did you have a good day at nursery, princess?"

"No. I hate nursery."

Her answer pangs deep in my gut. *I* hated nursery, too. They say you don't remember much of your life before reaching four years old, but I remember sitting alone on the brown nursery carpet, littered with various stains and pieces of Lego, crying silently until my eyes ran dry, like it was this morning. Every. Single. Day.

"I'm so sorry, but I forgot to do something at the office. I need to go," I announce. I didn't plan to say it, to *lie*, but I need to get out of here. My mood is slipping. *Fast.*

Everyone seems to understand and Laura gets up first, kissing my cheek before starting to clear the table. My mother follows suit and makes me promise to call her in the week before kissing my other cheek. Isobel, however, clings to my leg.

I prize her off me and lift her up so her face meets mine. Holding her with one arm, I reach into my pocket and pull out the first note I lay my hand on.

Kissing her nose, I hand her the twenty. "That's for your magazine," I say, and then kiss her nose again. "And maybe some sweets, too."

Seemingly forgetting my existence, Isobel wriggles until I lower her onto the floor. "Mummy! Mummy!" she calls, running out of the room. "Look what Uckle James gave me!"

"I'll have to try and get that off her before she flushes it down the toilet," Max says as he walks me to the front door. "It's her latest thing."

Taking the handle, I open it, and Max follows me out to my car.

"Thanks for dinner," I say. "Sorry I can't stay longer."

"She hates nursery because another kid threw sand at her today. She'll have forgotten all about it tomorrow."

"Um…" I feel like this conversation has a deeper meaning but I can't figure out what it is.

"Kids have bad days like the rest of us. I saw your reaction. You're worried she feels the same way *you* did. But honestly, James, she's had an argument with another kid and she'll move on soon enough."

I'm not sure how he can read me so well but that's not important right now. Maybe 'normal' people, 'normal' kids, do have bad days. Maybe she *will* get over it, so to speak. Trouble is I only have my *own* experience of life to compare things with, so I can't help putting myself in other's situations and imagining how *I* would deal with them. I don't know any other way.

All I know is that life can be exhausting, soul destroying, *painful.* For me, growing up, *every* day was a bad day. Even when I laughed that tinge of sadness remained, tormenting me, mocking my happiness as it tried to force its way to the forefront. More often that not, it won.

It still does.

"Take care of yourself, James," Max says when I fail to respond.

"I'll call you." *Sometime. Maybe.*

I slide into my seat and Max pats the roof of my car as a goodbye. Driving off without looking back, I feel my happiness slipping away. I can't allow it. Not again. I need to get it back.

I just don't know how.

Chapter
Seven

~Theo~

In bed, I roll over and bang my head on Tess' elbow. I love her, but she's the *worst* person to sleep next to.

"I'm gonna buy you your own bed," I grumble, rubbing my forehead. "You practically live here anyway."

She's sat up against the headboard, reading a celebrity magazine. "Blame Naomi. It's like she thinks this new guy she's seeing is supplying her oxygen through his dick."

"Must be serious. What is it now, a month?"

"Almost two. She normally gets fed up after a week tops. She's in love apparently."

I laugh and stretch my arms above my head. "So what are your plans for today?"

"Same as every Saturday. Move as little as possible. You?"

I can't decide whether to reveal my plans, mainly because I don't know if they're stupid.

"Your silence tells me they involve David Gandy."

"There's a fair at Heaton Park this weekend. Thought I'd pick him up and take him."

Tess snorts. "A funfair? You really think a funfair is David Gandy's scene?"

Her reply makes me sigh. "Maybe you're right." I knew it was a stupid idea.

"Hey, I'm not saying don't do it. So what if it's not his scene? It's *yours*. Whatever you two have got going on together shouldn't be all about him."

What are *we doing together?* I don't know and I wonder if I ever will.

"Plus it's a public place so that'll aid your sex ban."

I'm not looking at her but I can hear her smile through her tone. "Stop sounding so amused by that."

"T, I don't know the guy so I shouldn't judge, but…"

"But you're going to anyway, right?"

"But you've hardly been bouncing off the ceiling with happiness since you met him. I can't say I understand what you see in him, he sounds like a tosser to me, but if you *are* going to keep seeing him, don't let it all be on his terms. You want to go to the fair? Then go to the fucking fair."

"But what if he doesn't want to go to the fair?"

She rolls her eyes at me but doesn't seem frustrated. I think she's just making a point. "Then come pick *me* up and I'll go to the bloody fair with you."

"Thanks, Tess. I think." Looks like I'm going to the fair one way or another today.

"But if I *do* go then you're paying for the food. I paid a fiver last time for a hot dog the size of a rat's dick."

She makes me laugh. "Not sure what rats you've seen but I'm pretty sure you've uncovered a new species."

"Whatever. Go brush your teeth. Your breath is knocking me sick."

Great. Kicked out of my own bed by a woman that doesn't even live here. "Yes, ma'am."

* * *

I'm nervous as hell when I approach James' apartment building. My hand stutters over the call button for the penthouse several times while I try to gather enough courage to press it. I even turn around a couple of times but then tell myself, out loud, to quit being a pussy.

When I eventually push it I wait several seconds for an answer and sigh when it doesn't come. I press it again and am about to give up when a man dressed in some kind of security uniform opens the door. Of course a place like this would have security. *Dumbarse.*

"I'm trying to reach the penthouse," I say, stuffing my fidgeting hands into my jeans pockets.

"Mr Holden only stays here during the week," he informs me.

"So…" *Oh just give up. This is clearly a sign that your idea is stupid.* "Where does he live at weekends?"

"I'm not his dad, kid. I have no idea."

I decide this guy is a twat. "Right. Thanks." I don't know what I'm thanking him for. He doesn't deserve the smile I can't stop myself offering.

Deflated, I head back to my car. Two options remain now. Give up and go home, or give in and call James. The choices make me huff in frustration. James has instigated *everything* we've ever done together, which really is just sex, and I wanted to take charge for once. Surprise him. The memory that I have his brother's number springs to the front of my mind and I contemplate dialling it for only a second before realising that would be weird.

Reluctantly, nerves bubbling in my throat, I call James.

"Hello, Theodore," he answers. His voice calms me instantly.

How does he do that? "Hi. It's, um, me."

"I know that. I greeted you with your name."

"Right. Yeah." Fucking hell I've turned into a babbling moron. *Pull yourself together.* "Where are you?"

"Home."

"No you're not. I'm there right now." I cringe when I've said it. I sound like a bloody stalker.

"I have more than one."

Of course you do. Flashy, magnificent bastard. "Oh. I thought we could meet." I sound nothing short of disappointed and I'm annoyed I've allowed it to filter into my tone.

"I'm not tagged, Theodore. I'm allowed to leave my house." His sarcasm is so damn infuriating, yet I can't get enough of him. Clearly, I'm a glutton for punishment. "Where would you like to meet?"

"I thought…" *Crap.* My idea feels even more stupid now I'm about to say it. "It's probably not your thing, but there's a fair at Heaton Park this weekend."

"A funfair?"

Why does everyone feel the need to repeat it like it's the most ludicrous thing they've ever heard?

"I like them," I mutter, feeling like a giant dick.

"I haven't been since I was a kid."

Great. He thinks I'm a child.

"Meet you there in an hour?"

Oh. "Sure," I agree. "Okay."

"And, Theodore?"

"Yeah?"

"Lose the nerves. We're getting to know each other, right? You like the fair. That's something new I've learned about you today. I'm looking forward to discovering more."

Well damn if words like that don't make me want to set fire to my no sex rule.

"See you in an hour," I say, ending the conversation with a smile so wide it makes my jaw ache.

I drive straight to the park, knowing I'll arrive way too early, and hope I find out something new about *him* today, too.

As expected, I'm early. I get out of the car but stay close to the entrance while I wait for James. Even though I'm alone, a wide smile tugs at my lips. Looking over to the rides, games, and candyfloss stalls, I'm ten years old again.

There's a light drizzle in the air but it doesn't dampen the atmosphere. There's laughter, happiness, everywhere. I feel like James and I need more of that. He's always so serious, and although that intrigues me, he needs to smile more because when he does he's fucking beautiful.

I walk around, my hands stuffed into my pockets, keeping an eye on the car park for around thirty minutes before I see him. There are strange flutters in my chest when he approaches. It sounds so cheesy but it's the truth. He excites me. He makes me nervous. He even scares me a little. He makes me feel a thousand different things at once.

He looks hot as hell. It's rare to see him out of a formal suit and a simple jeans and a black v-neck jumper make him look so much more...relaxed. He looks like he's been plucked straight off the cover of a glossy magazine and I have no doubt that he knows it, too. When he reaches me, he rests one hand on my hip and kisses my cheek. It makes me feel giddy and I hope the fact I've turned into a lovesick fool doesn't show on my face.

"That's almost romantic of you," I say, butterflies swimming in my gut. "I can't remember the last time you didn't greet me by grabbing my crotch." I can't remember because I don't think it's ever happened.

"That was before I started courting you."

A sly grin tickles one side of his mouth and I know he said *courting* just to annoy me. No matter how hard I fall for this man, I suspect he'll always piss me off.

"So," he begins. "Introduce me to the funfair experience."

Now he's here, I'm not sure what to do next. I actually feel a little lame, surrounded by families and children. "Let's just take a walk," I say.

James proffers his hand. "Lead the way."

James walks beside me as I head over to the crowded area. There's music playing, people laughing, children running. It's impossible not to feel uplifted yet when I look at James his face is void of expression.

"You've never been to a fair?"

"Sure. When I was a child. I never really liked them though."

Oh. It takes me a moment to figure out how I'm supposed to respond to that. "How can anyone *not* like the fair?"

A small smile flashes across his face for a brief second before his expression morphs into what looks like sadness. I'm curious, but I don't push.

"Guess my brain doesn't work the same way as everyone else's."

What does that mean? It feels like, in some small way, he's attempting to reveal something to me. As always, he's cryptic, but I think he's trying. There are so many layers to James Holden and I imagine it's going to take a lot of chipping to get to his centre. But I *want* to, despite the voice in my head screaming at me to run away.

"I come here to run pretty often, though."

"You run?"

"Every day, if I can."

"Me too. Well, not every day anymore, but as often as I can. My favourite place to run is Hollingworth Lake. I miss being able to do that every week."

"I've never been. You'll have to take me one day."

"You want to run with me?"

"I want to do *everything* with you."

I haven't felt butterflies like I'm experiencing now since I was in Year 9 at high school and Damien Kaye smiled at me. "I should warn you, I'm fast."

James sniggers, tightening his grip on my hand. "I'm faster."

"Is that a challenge?"

"No. Just a fact."

Laughing, I shake my head and bump his shoulder. "So, does this brain of yours allow you to like candyfloss?"

"Of course!" He smiles and it's magical. Infectious. My own lips twist into a grin and I start jogging to the nearest candyfloss stand.

We eat from our sticks as we walk. Then I spend fifteen quid trying to win a teddy at a stall and don't manage to knock a single can over with my beanbag. James, however, wins with his first pound coin. Of course he does. *Fucker.*

He chooses a giant Peppa Pig teddy and I wonder if he's going to give it to me, like they do in the movies, but he doesn't. Then I feel like a twat.

"This will keep me in Isobel's good books for at least a month."

"Isobel?"

"My niece. She's three, and the cutest person on the planet."

His love for her shows on his face. It makes me smile. I've never imagined James with a child. He has a natural hardness about him, and whether he meant to or not, he just showed me another of his mysterious layers.

"She sounds adorable."

"She is, but she's sassy too. She's the boss. Drives my brother crazy but I think she's so funny."

I could listen to him talk about this little girl I've never met forever. I love the calm that washes over him when he thinks about her, the softness, fondness, in his voice. We talk about his family for a little while longer. He tells me what his brother does for a living, tells me about his mum, albeit briefly, and I'm captivated by every word. I'm not naïve enough to think I've knocked down his iron walls, but I've made a dent and that's good enough, for now.

I convince him, eventually, to ride the carousel with me, He shakes his head as if he can't quite believe what he's doing, right up until our horses start to move. I don't take my eyes off him, Peppa Pig resting in his lap, as we go around. I can't. His eyes are wide, stunning, as he laughs. At one point he spins an imaginary lasso in the air and yells, "Yee haw!" and I feel like my lungs will explode from laughing so hard.

This is the side of him no one else sees. He looks so fun. Carefree. Young. The positive energy radiating from him is addictive and I want more. *Need* more. I can try to deny it but I know it's a lie. I'm falling for James Holden fast. *Too* fast. I sense danger ahead but I can't stop it.

I don't want to.

* * *

Dusk closes in when we reach the car park. My car is closest, and I lean against the driver door, missing James already even though he's standing right in front of me.

"I've had a really great day," he says, cupping my cheek in his palm. I nestle into his gentle touch and my insides feel like they're melting. "Thank you, Theodore."

The use of my full name makes me smile. He's the only person who's ever called me that. I've been Theo, or T, to everyone since the day I was born. "You know, I think you've earned the right to call me Theo."

His brilliant smile lightens his whole face. "I'm good with Theodore. I like the way it feels on my lips."

Oh dear God. He really isn't helping my struggle with the sex ban.

"Will I ever understand you, James?" *Shit! Where the hell did that come from? What a nobhead.*

His eyebrows pull together and his hand slowly slips from my face. "Probably not."

Ouch. His answer stings all the way to my core.

"I'm a very complicated man, Theodore."

I've known this since the first time we met but hearing it aloud almost destroys me. That alone baffles me. How has this happened? This connection. This pull. This *need* I feel for him. It's more than attraction. It's a craving. An addiction. I feel like he could be the best thing that ever happened to me, or the most damaging. No in between.

"But I want to," I say, the words cracking on my lips. "I want to understand you. *Know* you."

"You don't," he replies without hesitation, without emotion or expression.

"You said you'd try."

"And I will. I *am*. That doesn't mean I think I *should*."

Just when I think I'm breaking through he unravels it all with just one sentence.

"You don't trust me." It's an accusation as opposed to a question.

"It's not about trust," he counters, squeezing his eyes closed. I can't tell if he's frustrated or in some kind of emotional pain. "Dammit, Theodore!"

Whoa. He's angry. My neck jerks back in response. "I'm sorry," I say, but I don't know if I mean it. Maybe I shouldn't have pushed him, but maybe he shouldn't have reacted like a dick.

"No." James shakes his head, his annoyance dissolving into a sigh. "Don't apologise. Not to me. I shouldn't have snapped, and now I've ruined what's been a perfect day with you."

Taking his face in my hands, I kiss him. I kiss him because he needs it. I kiss him because *I* need it. I kiss him because it feels right.

"The day isn't over yet," I whisper against his lips.

He presses his cheek to mine and smiles, his trendy stubble scratching my skin, and once again everything is right with the world.

For now.

"Take me to your place."

I don't know why but his suggestion fills me with nerves. "Um…"

"I want to see where you live. Who you are. It's only fair. You've been to *my* apartment, *and* stained my couch."

Holy freaking shit. If my cheeks burn any hotter they will surely explode. "My flat isn't…well, I doubt it's up to your standard."

"I'm not a snob, Theodore." He sounds a little offended.

"And Tess is probably there, too."

James raises an eyebrow. "I know how to converse."

I feel oddly comforted by his sarcasm. It's easier to understand than when he's being cryptic.

"I'd like to meet your friend."

He would? James has never struck me as a people person.

"You look surprised."

"No. It's just, you're not the most sociable person I've ever met."

"She's important to you, and you're important to me. I want to meet her."

I swear James Holden is the only person I know who can flip between being a conceited prick to perfectly charming, several times, during a single conversation.

"Okay then," I agree, unsure of my decision.

"Your car or mine?"

"Yours." Not only is my car a rust bucket on wheels, the passenger footwell is currently filled with McDonald's wrappers and rubbish. "I'll pick mine up tomorrow."

Knowing they lock the park gates at night, James waits for me in his car while I move mine to the roadside of a neighbouring street. I make my way back to him, feeling inexplicably nauseous, and pray the whole way that Tess doesn't humiliate me.

I don't speak while we take the stairs up to my floor. James is what can only be described as fucking loaded and I can't help feeling embarrassed, not good enough. Twisting my key in the lock, I half-hope Tess isn't here, but I know she will be, and I'm right.

"I bought mince so you could-" She cuts herself off when she turns around and sees me, *us*. "Well fuck a duck."

I roll my eyes before shooting her a death glare. "This is Tess," I say to James.

Stepping forward, he offers a hand to shake. "Nice to meet you, Tess."

Please play nice.

"And you, David."

Bitch!

"Um, my name is James," he corrects, pursing his eyebrows in confusion.

Tess shrugs. "You'll always be David to me."

James looks to me for clarification but I ignore him. I'll tell him later. Maybe. Unless Tess gets there first. Right now, she's too busy ramming her nose into his neck.

"What are you doing?" James asks. He must regret coming here already. I sure as hell do.

"She's sniffing you. For a lesbian, she sure has a fascination with how men smell." My explanation sounds ridiculous, and that's because it is.

"A man's aftershave says a lot about them," she says, as if her weird behaviour makes complete sense. "Armani," she decides.

I've never tried to guess. I just know he smells delicious.

"You have a good nose," James says. "And what does that say about me?"

"That you're not cheap. You're driven, controlling, intelligent and cocky."

James smiles, shaking his head a little. "And you got all that from my aftershave?"

No. She got all that from me. I'm planning her murder as we speak.

"What were you saying about mince?" I ask Tess, diverting her attention away from James. He doesn't seem bothered, but *I* am.

"I fancied shepherd's pie, so I bought the ingredients for you."

Tess is more than capable of cooking, she just chooses not to.

"Do you like shepherd's pie?" I ask James. Crap I'm nervous. I haven't even got a sofa for him to sit on while he eats. He must think I'm a tramp.

"I do. I had it last night in fact."

Damn.

"Well you haven't had Theo's," Tess interrupts. "It's amazing."

I smile awkwardly while Tess plonks herself down on the living room floor in front of the forty-two inch smart TV. It's probably the most expensive thing in the whole flat and I only have it because my brother upgraded and usually gives me first refusal on his cast offs.

"You're not helping?"

She doesn't look back as she starts flicking through the channels. "David can help you."

I want to kill her.

Much to my surprise, James pushes his sleeves up to his elbows. "What can I do?"

I've never imagined him cooking, which on reflection seems stupid. He lives alone and, given the fact he's alive, clearly eats. But still, I feel like I can check off another box on the Getting to Know James Holden list.

"You could chop up and fry some onions while I peel the potatoes?" It comes out like a question.

Stepping up to the sink, James washes his hands. Such a simple, routine task and yet I can't stop staring as he lathers the soap between his fingers. I think I'm being inconspicuous with my ogling until, suddenly, his wet hands dart to my face.

They're freezing as he runs his palms down my cheeks, making me gasp. "You *arsehole!*" I yell in shock, my laughter betraying the annoyance I want to feel.

"It's water, not acid. Stop overreacting."

I adore his playful side and it always seems to appear when I least expect it. My nerves slip away with every word we exchange and by the time dinner is almost ready, I'm completely at ease with him being here.

"Wait, what are you…" James watches with a curious eye as I start opening a tin of baked beans. "You're putting *beans* in it?"

Grinning, I tip the contents of the tin into the mince. "Just trust me."

He looks unsure but doesn't argue. "So why did Tess call me David? Do you bring a lot of men up here?"

The smile I'm wearing evaporates immediately. "What? No!" Silently, I curse myself for being unable to prevent the blush invading my cheeks. "Obviously when we first, um, *met*, I didn't know your name. I described you as a younger looking David Gandy, and it kind of stuck. With Tess anyway."

I'm too embarrassed to look at him but I imagine he's smirking. "David Gandy, eh? I'm flattered."

"I don't see it so much anymore. Now, you just look like James. But because Tess is an arsehole intent on humiliating me, I doubt she'll ever use your real name again."

"Well, it *is* my middle name so she won't be entirely incorrect."

"You're kidding? Your name is James David Holden?"

"According to my bank statements."

Another box checked. "It's ready." I'm relieved to be able to utter those words and deflect from the whole David Gandy scenario.

"You're not grilling it?"

My nose scrunches. "I don't like crusty mash. I will if you prefer, though."

James raises his hands. "Nope. Fluffy mash sounds good to me."

I've made shepherd's pie a thousand times, but as I plate up I can't stop hoping it tastes okay. The kitchen is tiny and I can reach the counter holding our plates and the fridge behind me without taking a step. Pulling out the grated cheese, I sprinkle some on Tess' mash before asking James if he wants some too.

"Please," he says, nodding. He watches me scatter some onto his food and then raises an eyebrow when I return the pack to the fridge. "You don't like cheese?"

"Can't stand it, unless it's on pizza. I like pizza."

"And cheese and onion pie," Tess cuts in, joining us in the kitchen.

"That's not proper cheese," I argue.

"Well it's not fucking plastic."

Tutting, I grab her plate, shoving it into her chest. "Eat," I say. If her mouth is full, she can't bloody talk.

She struts away, laughing, and I realise I don't have anywhere for James to sit. He must've noticed my lack of sofa when he arrived but, still, it leaves me feeling awkward. "I, um, I don't have much furniture yet," I all but whisper.

Shrugging, James takes his plate, walks the few steps over to where Tess is sitting and joins her on the floor. The sight of them together makes me smile. Despite my embarrassment about living in an unfurnished box, I like him being here.

"You gonna treat us to cutlery or what, T?"

If she didn't have her back to me I'd flip her the middle finger. *Lazy bitch.*

Plucking three forks from the drawer, I make my way over to them, then pause and turn back to fetch some knives. James is a formal kind of man. I imagine he uses knives.

Sitting down, I pass out the cutlery and, true to form, Tess makes a snarky remark. "Knives too, eh? I didn't realise you were royalty, David."

Laughing, James starts tucking in using only his fork. I don't know if that's how he'd normally eat, or if it's a result of Tess' comment. More to the point, I don't know why I'm obsessing over fucking cutlery.

"I'm sure Theodore thinks I'm posher than I actually am," James teases, offering me a sideward glance.

Tess snorts, presumably at the use of my full name.

"But I grew up in a terraced house in Wythenshawe. My father's company didn't hit the big leagues until I was in college."

I can't take my eyes off his face, enthralled by everything he has to say, every layer he peels away from his guarded heart. He fascinates me.

"I went to a regular school, ate fish finger butties for tea, worked in a transport office when I dropped out of college after a couple of months..."

Wow. And here's me thinking he was born with a silver spoon in his mouth. I feel like a bit of a judgemental dick now.

"I'm just a regular guy," he tacks on, shrugging. "And on another note, this tastes amazing."

My lips twist into a proud smile. "It's the baked beans."

"I'll be sure to try it out. Where did you learn to cook?"

"My grandma. I used to stay with her a lot during the school holidays when I was little. She made everything from scratch. Meals, bread, cakes...I used to love watching her."

"If I ever get a chance to meet her, I must say thank you." He shovels his last forkful of food into his mouth.

"You'll have your work cut out," Tess pipes up. "Unless you can communicate with the dead."

"Damn, I'm sorry," James splutters.

I shoot Tess what must be the twentieth death glare of the night before focusing on James. "Don't be," I assure him. "It was seven years ago now. Lung cancer."

He nods slowly, his expression apologetic. An awkward silence follows, broken by Tess licking her plate. It makes James smile and, in turn, so do I.

"Are your grandparents still alive?" I ask, gaining confidence in asking him questions. Surprisingly, he seems more comfortable answering them, too.

"My grandfather on my mother's side is, but he doesn't recognise us anymore. Alzheimer's. He's in a care home in Warrington."

"I'm sorry. I imagine that's even worse than them being dead. To know who they are, to love them, and yet you're a stranger." My voice fades, my mind unable to conceive what that must feel like. "Sorry. That was insensitive," I add the second I realise I've practically just told him his granddad would be better off dead. *Fucking moron, Theo.*

"No need. You're right. It's been difficult for all of us." The rawness in his tone steals my breath for a moment.

"Do you visit him often?"

"As often as I can. At least once a month. Sometimes, if only for a few minutes, he remembers me. I see it on his face when it registers and…" Emotion causes a crack in his words and a lump forms in my throat. "I cherish those moments."

We stare at each other and, right now, he's the only person in the world.

"Well, I don't know about you two but this third wheel is gonna leave you to it." Tess' voice startles me back into reality.

"You don't have to leave," I tell her.

"I'm not." She jumps to her feet. "I'm going to bed. *Your* bed. At least with your sex ban I don't have to worry about fuck-grunts and banging furniture keeping me awake."

I'm too mortified to reply but in my head I'm wondering if you can buy arsenic on the internet.

"So she knows about your ban, huh?" James asks when the bedroom door closes behind Tess. He sounds amused.

"I tell her everything. Though I'm beginning to regret that after tonight."

James chuckles. "I like her. She seems fun."

"You do?" I don't mean to sound surprised but James and Tess are opposites in every possible way.

"She makes you smile," he says. "And you have a beautiful smile, Theodore."

Biting my bottom lip, my gaze wanders down his body until it lands on the laminate floor. I'm not sure whether I'm embarrassed, flattered, or turned the hell on. Probably a little of each.

After clearing the plates into the sink, I nip into my bedroom and grab a spare duvet, laughing quietly at the sound of Tess' snores. It's the closest to a sofa I can manage and I spread it out onto the living room floor for James and I to sit on.

Castle plays on the TV but we don't watch it. For hours we simply lie together, on our sides, face to face. Sometimes we talk, sometimes we just stare at each other, but we don't touch even once.

And it's perfect.

What sounds like a bomb detonating over my head startles me awake and I leap from the floor like a ninja on speed. "What the fuck, Tess?" I blast, silently grateful that I haven't shit my pants as I eye up the two pan lids in her hands. Unsurprisingly, James is sat up, too. I don't remember falling asleep with him.

"Ha! Your faces! That was even funnier than I planned."

Strangely enough, she's the only one laughing.

"Your mum called. She's doing dinner early today. Tom's bringing his new bird over."

Blinking the sleep from my eyes, I scratch my head. "Tom's got a girlfriend?"

My brother has *never* brought a woman home before. His idea of a relationship is sleeping with a girl for a second time before he ends it. *A bit like James*, my mind torments me. My gaze roams to him, still sitting on the floor, and I inwardly tell my thoughts to fuck off. He's here, that's all that matters.

"Your mum sounded equally shocked," Tess says. "Yet weirdly excited. Think she's picking out a wedding hat already."

"Tom's your brother?" James asks, standing up.

"Yeah. Sunday is family day at my mum's. I can't get out of it." It comes out like an apology, although I don't mean it to.

"And you shouldn't. Not all families are so close. Don't ever lose that."

Something hides in his words and I study his face. Envy, maybe? Is he not close to his family? The concern in his brother's voice when I called him from the hospital made me think they were tight. So did the sadness in James' eyes when he talked about his dad. Perhaps I'm reading too much into it, seeing things that aren't there. I just can't seem to shake the sense that there are some pretty dark demons lurking inside him and I wonder if his family know about them.

"Can I use your bathroom before I leave?"

"Course." I point to the relevant door. "It's the one on the right."

I smile as I watch him walk away and I know I look like a soppy fool. More to the point, I know Tess will pull me up on it.

"You look happy, T."

That certainly isn't the insult I expected. "I am." *I think.* Is that what this feeling is? The one that makes my chest tighten, my stomach flutter, when I'm with him, when I think of him? Is it happiness? "But don't mention him to my mum yet," I whisper.

"Um, *okay.*" She sounds confused.

"She'll want to meet him and I'm just not sure where things are heading between us yet."

James coughs, startling me. I wonder if he genuinely needed to cough or if it was his way of alerting us to the fact he could overhear.

Shit.

Tess disappears into the bedroom without a word and I swallow forcefully as James steps closer to me.

"Thank you," he breathes, before brushing my lips so softly with his I can't be sure I haven't imagined it. "I had a really great time yesterday."

"Me too." And I mean it. I've learned so much about him in the last twenty-four hours. Nothing monumental, but the little things that have moulded him into the man he is today. His tastes in music, films, books. The places he's worked, bits and pieces about his family, although the latter was brief. I don't think he feels comfortable discussing the people he's close to and I can't imagine why. It's just one of the many mysteries surrounding James Holden that I've yet to figure out.

"See you tomorrow," I whisper against his mouth.

"You can count on it."

He breaks away from me and I feel empty. Lost. I miss him already and he's barely reached the door. When it closes behind him, I run my tongue across my lips as if trying to taste him again. I can't, and it leaves me feeling deflated.

"That was sweet," Tess says, her smile beaming when she re-enters the room.

"You were spying on us?"

"Of course I was! I'm actually offended you think I wouldn't."

"Well, that's kinda weird, but whatever tickles your pickle."

"Watching two guys play tonsil tennis doesn't tickle *anything*, but seeing my best mate so happy does."

I smile because it makes me think about James and everything we did yesterday.

"And you know, he's not nearly as much of a twat as you made him out to be."

"I did *not*!"

"Whatever. It's not *that* long since you couldn't finish a sentence about him without saying how much you detested him."

She's right, yet that feels like a lifetime ago, not weeks. When I think back to the James I knew then he's like a stranger. I can't even remember what it feels like to hate him, which reaffirms my suspicion that I've never hated him at all. I just didn't want to love him.

Whoa. Did I just say…love? *What the fuck? Like. I meant like.*

"And he's hot, too. And that's coming from a lesbian. Bet he's got a rocking bod underneath those clothes, right?"

"I wouldn't know." It's never occurred to me how weird that is until I just said it aloud.

"What do you mean you don't know? You've had sex with the guy."

"It's always been, I don't know, rushed. He's never taken his shirt off before." Something about that sentence makes me feel uncomfortable, maybe a little embarrassed.

"Hmm. Okay." She looks as bewildered as I suddenly feel and I hope she leaves it at that. "By the way, you've got a bazillion Facebook notifications. Your phone was twinkling like a Christmas tree on acid when your mum called."

I've been neglecting my social media lately. With James and the new job, I've barely had time to take a piss.

"People are expecting updates on the new book." I sigh, frustrated that my writing mojo seems to have fallen out of the window and landed under a speeding bus.

"Then give them one. When we get back from your mum's tonight get in bed, open your laptop, and remind yourself why you do it."

"It's just not going the way I expected it to. Paul knows Rick is hiding something but he doesn't know what. He doesn't know what, because *I* don't know what yet. I'm struggling to get into my character's head with this one."

It's only when I say the words aloud I realise I don't need to get into their head anymore, I'm already there. I have been since the night I met James. Suddenly, I'm filled with ideas, words, and emotions. I'm excited, and I kiss Tess' forehead with a giant smile on my face.

"We need to pick up some decent coffee on the way to my mum's," I say. Tonight is going to be a late one as I pour my feelings into my laptop through my fingers. TS Roberts is officially back.

* * *

It's late afternoon and we're sitting on my mum's floral sofa, stuffed so far to the brim with chicken dinner I fear I might literally burst. Amused by the sight of my mum fussing over Jennifer, Tom's latest squeeze, I toss a sideways smirk Tess' way. I knew from the moment we arrived my mum was making an effort because she's wearing a skirt, something she only does for weddings, funerals, and when she's trying to impress people.

"Bakewell tart, Jennifer?" Mum offers, holding out a plateful of shop-bought cakes. I've no doubt she'll have pulled out all the stops and bought Mr Kipling's as opposed to Tesco's own brand.

Jennifer plucks one from the plate and smiles. "Thank you, Mrs Davenport."

So far, I approve. She's not one of the usual bright orange bimbos I've previously seen my brother with. She seems sweet and intelligent. She looks it too with her jaw length, brunette bob and thick, dark glasses. I like her.

Mum brings the plate to Tess and I and hovers it in front of my face. "Theo? Tess?"

Tess grabs one while I hold up my hand. "No thanks. I'm still full from dinner."

Mum tuts. "I've already taken the cherry off for you. Eat it."

Resisting the urge to huff, I take the one that has a little hole where the glace cherry should be and force myself to bite into it. If she brings out anything else I'll almost certainly spew all over her cream carpet.

"So, Theo," my mum begins, making herself comfortable on the armchair. "Are there any plans for *you* to settle down yet?"

Here we go. Tom's been with someone for a month and now I'm lagging behind. "When there is you'll be the first to know."

"You know gay people can marry these days. What are you waiting for?"

"I'm well aware of that, Mum." I can't stop myself from laughing. "But just like straight people, I need to find someone first."

"You need to get a move on. I won't live forever you know."

"I'll bear that in mind," I say, smiling and shaking my head.

"What about you, Tess? Any lady in your life I should know about?"

I'm laughing wickedly in my head, as I'm sure Tess was during my turn to be grilled.

"Still waiting for Angelina Jolie to call me back."

I love how my mum treats Tess like one of her own children. Tess' dad disappeared before she was born and her mum is an alcoholic scrote who lives off vodka and cigarettes paid for by the government. I guess you could say my mum has unofficially adopted her. Tess isn't just my best friend, she's family.

"You should grow your hair. Wear a little makeup. Make the most of that pretty face of yours." She sounds offensive, but she really isn't.

Like most mums, she just can't help being an interfering busybody.

"I'll bear that in mind." Tess steals my answer.

Cheater.

We stay another hour or so, Jennifer remaining the hot topic of conversation the entire time. My mum interrogates the poor girl, requesting her whole damn life story. She answers every question, but I feel a little sorry for her. My mum's great, but she can come across a little intimidating until you get to know her. She's fiercely protective of Tom and I and, although she makes a fuss of Jennifer, she makes her stance clear with not-so-subtle comments that imply if she hurts Tom, she'll hurt *her*.

That's a mother's blind spot right there. If anyone is going to fuck up their relationship it will be Tom and his overly sociable dick.

When Tom and Jennifer leave I decide Tess and I should head home, too, but now the centre of attention has gone, my mum's questions turn to me instead.

"Any luck pitching your books to that Holder place?"

"It's Holden House," I correct. "And no. That's not why I took the job," I repeat for what must be the hundredth time since I applied for the position.

"Oh I know, I know," she says with a dismissive wave of her hand. "I just want you to do well, baby boy."

Tess is used to the ridiculous nickname my mum calls me now, but I remember a time when she would rip the piss out of me for days at a time over it.

"I *am*," I counter. "I've got over two thousand likes on my Facebook page."

"Two thousand?" She presses a hand to her chest. "Two thousand people know my son's name?"

"Well, my pen name," I say, but I don't think she hears me. Either that or she doesn't care about the semantics.

"Wait until I tell Pauline!" Pauline is my aunty. She lives in Devon and I only see her at Christmas. "That's so exciting!"

"I think so," I agree, feeling proud from her enthusiasm.

"They must be good books then, eh?"

"They are," Tess chips in. "You should totally read one."

My mum shudders. "Oh no. I prefer to think my boy doesn't know anything about the kind of dirty stuff he writes about. The reviews are enough for me."

"You read my reviews?" I don't know why but that shocks me a little. I've always known she's proud of me but it's not something we often discuss.

"Some of them. I avoid the bad ones. They break my heart. Everyone should like you, and some of them are just plain nasty. Doesn't that upset you?"

I smile at her concern. "Not anymore," I answer honestly. "You can't please everyone."

"Yes you can. You're mine, and you're perfect."

"They're judging the story, not me."

Well, some of them judge *me*, but they're arseholes who I refuse to let blip on my radar. I don't add that to the conversation because it would only worry her.

"We need to head off now, Mum. Tess is working early in the morning." It's a white lie but I always feel bad leaving her since my dad died. It's been four years but she's all alone in an empty house. I'm pretty sure it doesn't bother her as much as it does me, but having an excuse makes it a little easier to leave.

She follows us to the front door and kisses first me, then Tess, on the cheek. "Call me when you get home safely."

"I will. Thanks for dinner. It was gorgeous, as always."

"Oh, wait there!" I hold the door open while she scurries away, returning a few seconds later with a plate wrapped in tinfoil. "Leftovers. You'll eat it won't you? I don't want it going to waste."

"Definitely." It's a lie. "I'll eat it for supper." I love my mum's cooking but reheating potatoes should be a criminal offence. They taste like shit when warmed up several hours later.

On the way home Tess and I discuss Tom's girlfriend and agree that she seems nice, but because we're twats, we also take bets on how long it'll last. My money is on two months. Tess, however, thinks two weeks tops. When we reach the flat I give my mum a quick call to let her know I haven't died in a horrific car accident, and then grab my laptop. For the first time in too long, I'm excited about writing and plan to get stuck in right away.

"I'm going to the bedroom," I say, assuming Tess is staying over again. "You coming?"

"Nah. I'm gonna watch TV for a bit, leave you alone to get in the zone." She laughs but I don't get the joke. "Hey, that rhymed! Maybe *I* should be a writer."

"Spell onomatopoeia."

"Fuck off."

Tess always spent occasional nights over at my old flat, but since I moved to Manchester it's become a regular thing. I don't mind, I like the company in fact, but as I settle into bed I wonder if I should ask her to move in permanently. It seems stupid to shell out rent on a place she's barely at and, in all honesty, I could do with a little extra cash to furnish my living room.

Once I'm propped up against the headboard, my laptop open on my knees, I push Tess out of my mind. Closing my eyes, I bring all the conflicting emotions I feel for James to the surface, reliving every moment with him, every thought I've had about him, and then put them into words.

Several hours later, feeling satisfied, and positive about my work tonight, I close the laptop and yawn. It's almost three AM and I feel bubbles dancing in my stomach knowing I get to see James again in just a few hours. Grinning to myself, I put the laptop on my bedside table, shuffle onto my side and drape one arm over Tess, who's been snoring like a foghorn next to me since midnight. Closing my eyes, I don't expect to get much sleep and decide I need to invest in some damn earplugs.

* * *

The next day, Stacey collars me in the cafeteria and asks to speak to me about an email I sent out last week. Leaving Ed, Katie, and another girl whose name I don't know at the lunch table, I follow Stacey to her office.

I don't understand why she wants to speak with me privately and I'm nervous as I take a seat at her desk. "Did I do something wrong?"

"There is no email."

Now I'm even more confused.

"Are you sleeping with James Holden?"

Whoa. I consider Stacey a friend but I don't feel like I've known her long enough to be so blunt. Evidently, she feels differently.

"*What?*"

"It's something Mike said last week. I thought nothing of it at first, but then there's the way you defended him to Ed. I've seen the way you look at each other, too."

I don't look at him like anything. *Do I?* "Mike's a bellend. He doesn't know what he's talking about."

"So you're *not* sleeping with him?"

I sweep a finger under my collar because it suddenly feels like it's choking me. Christ, I'm uncomfortable, but I'm not mad at her. She sounds concerned rather than nosey or interfering.

Still, her worry, if that's what it is, baffles me. "It's not how you think it is." I realise how lame that sounds as soon as I've said it. "He's a good guy, Stacey. I like him."

Stacey sighs. Her smile is small, sympathetic, almost like she feels sorry for me. "*Really?*" She sounds surprised. "He's a bit of a miserable sod don't you think?"

"I know how he comes across. I couldn't stand him at first." Just thinking about him makes me smile. "But he's fun underneath."

"*Fun?* James Holden is *fun*?" Giggling, she shakes her head.

"He is! He has an amazing laugh. Throaty. Genuine. He's smart, too. Quick-witted. And he sings like *all* the time."

"You're taking the piss."

"I'm not! I don't know why he doesn't show it more, but I'm telling you he's a great guy."

Tucking a lock of hair behind her ear, she chews on her lip as if she's concentrating, summoning more questions. "When…I mean how…Most people here have known him for years and he's just 'the boss' to us. He's never exchanged a friendly word with anyone. He's strictly business, unless he fucks you of course, but as soon as that's out the way he reverts straight back into conceited CEO mode."

I fight the scowl that wants to crawl onto my face. I know all about James' indiscretions, hell, everyone does. That doesn't mean I like being reminded.

"Even before he made CEO he was a pretentious arse. How do you know him so well? And after just a few weeks?"

"I literally have no idea." I start to chuckle because, honestly, nobody is more surprised than me. "Remember David Gandy that first night you went to the village?"

"The guy you saw in the bathroom?"

"Yeah. Well what you don't know is later that night, I kinda had sex with him. What you also don't know is that David Gandy is in fact James Holden."

"No!" Her jaw drops open, any further and it would smack the floor. "But oh my God you're right! I never saw it before but he does have a look of him."

"You can imagine my surprise when I saw him here the following Monday."

"Sooo," she begins, drawing out the word. "He remembered you and you just hit it off?"

"Well, my car broke down that same Monday. James saw me and offered to give me a lift home. Then somehow he ended up picking me up every morning while it was in for repair and every day I started to enjoy being with him a little more."

"You *drive* to work? In city traffic?"

"I hate public transport." I shake my head as if somehow it will unscramble my thoughts, help me make sense of things. "There's just something there. A connection. A spark. I can't explain it. I know it sounds stupid."

"It doesn't," she says. "It sounds…" she breaks off, looking to the ceiling as if she'll find the answer she's looking for written on it. "Kind of special. I just can't get my head around the fact it's James Holden you're talking about."

"I'm not doing it for a promotion," I feel obliged to say. That's what Mike thinks and, no doubt, so would a lot of others if they found out.

"Oh, Theo, I know that. We wouldn't be friends if I thought you were that kind of lad. Why do you think I don't talk to Mike unless my job requires it?"

Huh? Wait…

Stacey sucks both of her lips between her teeth like she wants to eat her own mouth rather than elaborate.

"Are you saying Mike and…*James*…" The words that should follow taste bitter on my tongue so I swallow them back down.

"I'm sorry, Theo. I didn't think. Me and my big gob. It's common knowledge around here. I forget you've not been here that long. You know Holden's reputation though. Don't you? Crap, you didn't, did you?"

"Stace-"

"Oh God I'm doing it again, aren't I?"

"Digging a giant hole?" An inexplicable heaviness descends on my stomach but I force a smile.

Of course I know about his reputation. Hell, even *Ed* has slept with him. But *Mike*? The image that won't leave my mind makes me feel a little sick. I don't just *want* to hate him like I did with James, I genuinely despise the smarmy bastard.

"Chill out, Stacey. I'm okay with it." At least I *will* be. This shouldn't be news to me. It's probably safer to assume James has slept with every man in Manchester and consider it a bonus if I discover otherwise.

"He's not a threat, I'm sure. I've never particularly thought of Holden as a man with many morals but he's not stupid. You're a good lad, Theo."

I smile, but I'm not sure it's convincing. Knowing about Mike doesn't sit well with me but I'm most definitely not threatened by him. The only person who remains a threat to our relationship, if that's even what we have, is James himself.

"Honestly, don't worry about it," I assure her, because I mean it. If it really is common knowledge, I'd have found out about it sooner or later.

"If it makes you feel any better, as far as I know, it was a couple of years ago when Holden first started working for his dad."

"You knew his dad?"

"Oh yeah. Eric Holden was a great boss. A real gent, you know? He was so involved, took the time to get to know everyone who worked here.

That's an exception rather than the norm in a business this size."

"So what you're saying is, he was the complete opposite of James?" A slight chuckle catches in my throat.

"He was just as driven, and could crack the whip when he needed to, but yeah. You wouldn't have known they were related unless you saw them together."

"They looked alike?"

"Not so much. It was more the look in Eric's eye when they were together. Pride, I suppose. I guess you're not the only person who sees another side of Holden. Although I believe it more coming from you, if that makes sense? Eric was his father, of course he saw the best in him."

It's interesting how she refers to his father as Eric and James as Holden. She does it automatically, unconsciously, and it's testament to how differently the two men are perceived.

"You know, James actually said something similar to me once, about how his dad saw something in him that no one else does. I didn't quite understand because *I* see it, too. I have from the beginning."

"I can't help find it strangely fascinating," Stacey says. "I've always found him so abrupt, so…"

"Arrogant?"

She smiles. "Yeah."

"He is. Absolutely. I've told him as much, too. But that's not all he is."

"Well you know what, Theo? I'm happy for you."

"I'd rather you didn't tell anyone." I feel awkward saying it and, really, I don't think she would anyway, but I need to make sure. "I know what it looks like, what people will think of me, what they *already* think of *him*. I'm not ready to deal with all that yet, not until I know where we're going."

Or if we're going anywhere at all.

"Of course I won't. I only asked you because I consider you my friend. I'm not into gossip, I promise you."

"I know." I smile. "And for the record I think of you as a friend, too. If I didn't, I would've denied it."

She grins and raises an eyebrow. "Like you did with Mike?"

"When Mike asked me there was genuinely nothing going on. Well, kind of. Ugh." Rolling my eyes, I sigh. Then I spend the rest of my lunch break telling her everything, starting with the night I turned into a raging slut after nothing more than a smile from my mysterious stranger.

Chapter
Eight

~James~

In my office, our kiss fades, but I can't bring myself to break away from Theodore. Resting my forehead on his, I breathe him in. His scent dances through my nose, uplifting me, intoxicating me.

"I have to leave soon," I whisper, but damn I don't want to let him go. "Mike and I have a lunch meeting with a client."

I feel Theodore's brow furrow against mine. "Why am I different?"

I take a step back, studying his face.

"To the others. To Ed, to…*Mike*."

"Don't do this," I say, sighing as I back away a couple of steps further. "You know who I am, Theodore. I can't take it back and not screw them." I wouldn't even if I could, though I don't add that part. At the time, any man I've ever fucked was because I *needed* them in that moment.

"I know that," he spits, huffing in frustration. "This isn't about your past, it's about *now*. The future."

The future. It's something I'm not comfortable thinking about.

"You said it yourself, the first time I was just an easy shag. I just want to know why that wasn't enough?"

"Do you wish it had been?" *Where is this coming from?*

"No!" His quick response reassures me. "You're so different with me. You have been from the start. I just wondered why that was, what makes me so special?"

"I don't know the answer to that." Sighing through my nose, I tuck my hands into my pockets and stare at him. "I feel comfortable around you. I don't get that with many people." With *anyone*. "Let's flip it. You made it clear the way we met was a mistake, a one off, so why are *you* still here? What do you see in me?"

"I dunno." Tilting his head to one side, Theodore smiles. "When you put it like that I see your point. Guess you don't really have a say in who you fall in love with."

All traces of expression fall from my face. My mouth dries and I stop breathing, though I know my heart still beats as it pounds like a jackhammer in my chest.

"I-I mean I'm not…I don't…shit." He doesn't look at me. He *can't*.

He doesn't know me. I'm trying so hard to be a man worthy of his time, his trust, but…*love*? That isn't possible. Not yet. Maybe, *probably*, not ever.

"James…"

I'm paralysed as he steps towards me, my feet welded to the floor.

Reaching out, he curls his fingers around my arm. "I'm sorry," he mutters. "Can we just forget I said that?"

Why? Did he not mean it? Was it merely a turn of phrase? My chest aches with disappointment which, in turn, makes me really fucking annoyed with myself.

Pressing my lips to his, I reassure him with a kiss because there are no words to describe the battle commencing in my mind right now. "I need to go. Mike will be waiting in the lobby."

The look of unease on his face when I mention Mike's name is subtle, but noticeable. I don't like it but there's nothing I can do. I can't un-fuck Mike and, as his boss, I *have* to work with him.

"We're okay, right?" he asks as I turn for the door.

"I'll pick you up at seven." I think my reply answers his question efficiently but just to be sure, I throw in a wink too.

After my meeting, I plan to go home and get my head straight. I need to be alone, with music as my only distraction, while I decide where my future is heading, and whether I'm taking Theodore with me.

* * *

I don't make it to my meeting. Instead, I tell Mike to deal with it alone, not bothering to conjure up an excuse. I don't need to. I'm the boss and he has no choice but to do as I say. He's not happy with me, but he never is, and I couldn't give a crap if I tried. If I wanted my staff to fill the air with love, I'd own a dating website.

So now I'm lying back in the bath at my detached house in Alderley Edge, my arms draped over the sides. I slept well last night for the first time since my father passed away, yet I'm still tired. Maybe that's why I'm having a hard time thinking about Theodore, trying to process what we mean to each other.

Love. Such a small, yet utterly terrifying, word. I'd convinced myself things were different now, that *I* was different, that I was better. And I am…I think. But what if I'm not? He might not love me, but he cares, and if I'm wrong, if I *haven't* changed, he doesn't deserve to have to care about someone like me.

Either way, whatever feelings we hold for each other are only going to multiply. I know that because they continue to do so every time I see him. If I let this go any further without being honest, I could end up destroying both of us. If he's going to leave me when he finds out the truth, and part of me still thinks he *should*, it's better if he does it now before the time comes when he might say that small, terrifying word and actually *mean* it.

Looking down at my chest, brushing away the soapy bubbles, I laugh, mocking my ridiculous thoughts.

He will never love you. How could he? Look at yourself.

I'm forced to listen to the voice in my head because it's telling the truth. How stupid of me to even *think* about that four letter word when I haven't got the courage to show Theodore my body, let alone the demons that lurk deep inside my fucked-up mind. Deep down I *know* there is no future for Theodore and I. How can there be when I don't even see one for myself? Theodore has fallen for an actor. An imposter. I tell myself I'm trying by revealing the parts of myself I know he wants to hear, but I've been playing the leading role in a movie about a *normal* person.

And I'm *not* normal.

I'm fucked-up.

Broken.

Irreparable.

And he needs to know. I can't be what he wants me to be but I can give him what he deserves. The truth. The freedom to walk away. I've been a coward. A fake. I've played the part so well I started believing it was real. But it's not. It's a lie. A fantasy. The proof is written all over my chest.

I'm so tired. I'm slipping. I can't bring Theodore with me. He means too much to me.

I need to let him go.

* * *

My decision is made, but the restaurant I've brought Theodore to for dinner isn't the right place to bring it up. So for now, I'm not acting, just enjoying what could be my last night with the man I've grown dangerously close to.

Both of our phones are laid out on the table and, although he ignores it, Theodore's continues to light up every few seconds.

"You're popular tonight," I tease, flipping my gaze between his eyes and his phone.

"It's just Facebook notifications," he says, turning his phone over so he can't see the screen.

"*Your* Facebook or TS Roberts'?"

His whole body freezes for a moment, his arm hovering mid air. "How'd you find that out?"

"When I read *The Beginning of Never.*"

He swallows slowly, his cheeks pinking. Damn, I've missed that adorable blush. "When? *How*?"

"When I stayed over, I saw it on your bookshelf. The only reason you'd have multiple copies of the same book is if you wrote it. I read it while you were sleeping."

"You didn't sleep?"

"No."

"And…you stayed?"

"Yes."

"*Why*?"

"Because I wasn't ready to leave you yet." *I'm still not. Dammit!* "You're a beautiful writer, Theodore."

"Of course you're going to say that."

His lack of confidence baffles me. I don't think he has any idea how amazing and genuine he is, not just as a writer, but as a person.

"I'm not a sugar-coating kind of man," I say, hovering my glass of sparkling water in front of my lips. "I thought you knew that already."

Using his fork, he rolls the last few spirals of pasta around on his plate. "With others, sure, but I never know what to expect when you're with me. I see a different side of you than everyone else."

You have no idea. "Do you want dessert?"

"I couldn't," he says, straightening his back and clamping one hand to his stomach. "I'm stuffed."

Nodding, I wave the waiter over with my hand and ask for the bill. Disappointment floods my stomach. I'm not ready to leave yet, not brave enough to take him home and have the conversation I've been planning all afternoon.

I don't object, as much as I want to, when Theodore pulls half of the bill from his wallet. Usually, I would, but it annoys him and I want to enjoy his smile for as long as possible.

"You're quite good at this dating thing," Theodore teases as we step outside the restaurant and start walking to my car. "I don't know why you waited so long."

"It took that long for me to find someone I *wanted* to date."

"Careful, James. You'll have me thinking you care about me in a minute."

"I *do* care." My voice is firm, my expression a deadly shade of serious.

His smile vanishes in an instant. "I was kidding. I wouldn't be here if I thought you didn't care."

"Come home with me." *Please say no.*

"I'll have to let Tess know. She'll be expecting me home soon. It's looking like she's moving in on a more permanent basis."

"Yeah?"

"I was going to ask her anyway, but then today her roommate said she wants to move her boyfriend in. On the plus side, they have two sofas and Tess is gonna bring one with her."

"It's only a one bedroom though, right?" I say as we slide into my car.

"She'll have to put a bed in the living room or something. She's annoying as shit to sleep with. She kicks, snores, *and* talks."

I smile, but it's filled with sadness. I've often wondered what it would be like to have a best friend, someone who you can share everything with, someone who loves you for who you are without the added complication of screwing them.

Theodore calls Tess while I drive. I'm taking him to my house in Alderley Edge, though I don't think he knows that. I consider it my home, my private space. I've never taken another man there before, but Theodore isn't just another man. He's a first for me in so many ways, and no matter what happens between us tonight, he'll be the last.

"Fuck me, this place is huge," Theodore says, standing in the centre of my open plan ground floor. "How many bedrooms is it?"

"Five."

"Don't you get lonely having all this space to yourself?"

Like you wouldn't believe. "Not really."

Theodore strolls slowly around the living room, analysing the artwork on the walls, the books on my shelves. "Wait," he says, stopping abruptly and staring at me. "Have you brought me here to have sex? Because the ban hasn't been lifted."

"No, Theodore. I brought you here to show you who I am."

"Rich? Because I sorta guessed that already."

I laugh, but it's forced. He thinks he's getting to know me but he has no idea who I really am and a rack of guilt lies heavy in my chest. "Can I get you a drink?"

"Let's just talk," he suggests, taking a seat on the burgundy leather couch and patting the spot next to him.

Shrugging out of my jacket, I hang it up on the rack by the door and then join him. "What do you want to talk about?"

"Anything. Everything." He falls silent for a moment, chewing his lip while he ponders. "School. What were you like in school?"

Depressed. Lonely. "Boring," I say with a fake smile. It's amazing how powerful a smile can be, even a forced one. It's all it takes to fool people into believing you're not falling apart inside. "I pretty much kept to myself."

"Did you like it though?"

"No."

His expression twists into surprise. I think he's going to ask me to elaborate but he doesn't. "Good grades?"

"In the subjects I was interested in, yes. The others, I didn't even bother turning up for the exams."

"And what were your favourite subjects?"

"English language and literature, history, and art. I got A stars in each of those."

"So you were a boffin, eh? The type that was too busy revising to hang out with friends."

"I didn't revise." I didn't socialise either. "I have what I think they call a photographic memory. Once something's in there…" I tap on the side of my head. "It never leaves."

"Wow. Lucky bastard."

It's more like a curse, I think to myself. If it were an option, I would pay to erase some of my memories. To have a mind which remembers everything so vividly, feels everything so deeply, can be agonising.

"I know you dropped out of college. Why?" Again, he looks surprised.

"It was too much like school. I thought with higher education being optional I'd have more freedom. I was wrong. I don't deal very well with authority."

"Now *that* doesn't surprise me." He grins and it's stunning.

Reaching out, I run my fingers through his short hair and settle them on the base of his neck.

"What was your favourite food as a kid?" he asks.

"Beans on crumpets."

"Your favourite toy?"

"Hmm. Either my Discman or my Tamagotchi."

"You had a Tamagotchi?"

"Didn't everyone?"

"*I* didn't. My mum got me a cheapo version from the market and it broke after two days. What's your best Christmas memory?"

A knot twists around my stomach. "I didn't like Christmas."

"What the hell? *All* kids like Christmas. What's wrong with you?" He's joking, but his smile fails to infect me.

Everything is wrong with me.

Christmas. It's such a *happy* time. Excitement, laughter, everywhere. At least that's how it's supposed to be. For me, it served as an amplifier for the sadness rooted deep inside my mind. One Christmas stands out in particular. I don't know why. It was Christmas Day, 1996, and I was thirteen years old.

As always, my grandparents were staying with us. Presents were open, dinner was over, and we sat in the living room swapping cracker jokes, with Top of the Pops playing on the square TV next to the tree. My nanna was slightly drunk, my granddad was checking out the TV listings in the bumper Christmas edition of the Radio Times, and my parents were digging through the annual tub of Cadbury's Roses.

Everyone looked so happy, chatting, laughing, and wearing their paper hats. Except Max, who was too old and cool to join in with the festivities, choosing instead to sit in the corner playing with his first ever mobile phone. That was a huge deal back then and he couldn't wait to tell all his friends at school, seeing as it was too expensive to text them.

I tried to emulate their joy, but I felt like I was dying inside and I didn't even know why.

I told everyone I was going to my room to play my new Now 35 cassette. Laughing, my mum called me a miserable sod and when I left the room I heard my dad tell her I was just a regular, antisocial teenager. My mum was right, maybe not in the playful way she meant, but I *was* miserable. I was breaking right in front of them and nobody knew.

When I reached my room, I switched on my small TV and lay down on my bed. As everyone predicted, *2 Become 1* by the Spice Girls made Christmas number one and I remember that video as if I'd watched it just an hour ago. Silent tears ran down my cheeks as Emma Bunton twirled around in her burgundy coat and purple boots, her blonde hair piled into a bun on the top of her head.

I cried for hours that night. I cried until I struggled to breathe, until the muscles in my arms ached from holding my knees to my chest. I cried because I hurt, because I was lost, exhausted, bursting with pain I didn't understand. There was no cause, no reason. I cried because I was broken, and I'd never felt so alone in my life.

"Guess I couldn't cope once I found out Santa wasn't real," I joke, but I know Theodore sees through my sarcasm. His eyes search mine, like he's looking for me, the *real* me. Part of me wants him to find me. The other wants me to run away to my bedroom and cry myself to sleep like I did on that Christmas Day.

"Okay next question. Where were you when you found out Princess Diana had died?"

"My bedroom. I remember falling asleep on the couch the night before and my mother waking me up in the small hours, telling me to go to bed. On my way up the stairs she told me about the crash, but I didn't think much of it. Then, the next morning I woke up to Max telling me she was dead and it was all over the news."

"Did you cry?"

"Yes."

"*Yes?*"

"Contrary to popular belief, I'm not made of stone, Theodore."

"I didn't cry, but Tom did. I caught him in his bedroom watching a special feature about her on the news. To this day he swears it was because he stubbed his toe on the wardrobe."

"So where were you when you heard?"

"I was on a plane flying back from Majorca. It had been our first holiday out of England and I was buzzing for months about going. Did you holiday a lot?"

"We went abroad once a year. I've been to most of the Greek and Spanish islands, as well as Turkey, and Paris a few times. Tenerife was my mother's destination of choice, though. I know Playa de Las Americas like the back of my hand."

"You'll have to take me on a tour one day."

"I need a smoke."

I'm stood up and walking to my back door before he can reply. Standing on the patio outside my French doors that overlook the large garden, I pull out my cigarettes and pluck one from the pack, bringing it eagerly to my lips. The movement sets off the security light as I spark up, flooding the dark air around me. I drag in the calming nicotine, admiring the soft plumes of smoke as they swirl into the floodlight.

"Did I say something wrong?"

Turning slightly, I notice Theodore standing in the doorway. "No, Theodore. You haven't done anything wrong."

Shoulders hunched, he stuffs his hands into his pockets. "Are you coming back inside?"

"In a minute," I say, holding my dwindling cigarette in the air. After I force a smile to reassure him, he wanders back off through the house.

Noticing my cigarette has burned to the filter, I toss it on the ground, stomp on it, and light up another. I'm nervous, maybe even scared, but I'm not entirely sure of what. Now that I'm alone with Theodore, my plan to tell him everything doesn't seem so certain anymore.

When I eventually head back inside I find him hovering by the stairs. "Where's your bathroom?" he asks.

"There are two upstairs, or you can use the toilet over there." I nod to the door down the hall, just past the kitchen.

He walks along the hall and I see him reach for the wrong door handle. I almost stop him, even take a step forward, but I don't. My father was the only other person who knew what I use my study for, and in about three seconds, Theodore will too.

Door open, he stops just inside, not moving even though it's obvious that isn't the toilet. Padding over to him, I step past his body and enter the room, studying his eyes as they dart from wall to wall. Confusion laces his expression as he weighs up the framed cover art hanging on the far wall above my desk. Gingerly, he walks a little further inside and stands in front of the floor-to-ceiling shelves that house my books. *My* books. Books that *I* have written.

"No fucking way," he mutters under his breath. I remain silent, nervously awaiting his reaction. "These aren't...I mean you're not..."

"JD Simmons? Yes. Yes I am."

"I-I don't understand," he says, blinking rapidly. "He…I mean *you*…You're really fucking famous. To *me* anyway. Why didn't you tell me? Why didn't *anyone* tell me?"

"Nobody else knows."

Theodore's gaze continues to travel down my bookshelves. "So that's why he only deals with you? Because he *is* you."

Nodding slowly, I stare at his face. His eyes are wide with what looks like excitement as he runs his index finger along the spines of my books.

"Why? Why aren't you shouting from the rooftops about it? You're letting an invisible man take the credit for all these amazing stories."

"I don't do it for the credit. I do it because I don't have enough room in my mind to keep the stories inside. I do it because I can't talk to people and I need to get my thoughts out. I do it because when my fingers are on that keyboard I can be someone else." *Someone better.*

"Wait…" he says, plucking one of the books from the shelf. "Into the Darkness. David Simon. This isn't yours."

I take the book from him and stroke the front cover. It's been a few years since I've looked at this one. "Sometimes I self-publish under that name."

"Why would you need to self-publish with your success?"

"Those are my gay romance stories. They're not mainstream."

"Surely you have the power to *make* them mainstream? You own a *huge* publishing house."

Half smiling, I exhale a short laugh. "It doesn't work like that, Theodore."

"So your dad knew? I guess he must have if Holden House is your publisher."

"He did. He encouraged me. I never planned on publishing anything, but he talked me into it. Holden House wasn't so big back then, but we took a chance and the rest, as they say, is history. I released a couple that didn't really go anywhere, then when *Secrets in Rome* made the New York Times bestsellers list, we were blown away. I'm sure it was pure luck."

Theodore shakes his head, taking the book from me and placing it back on the shelf. "It wasn't luck, James. You are a wonderful, inspiring, *powerful* writer. I-I'm struggling to get my head around the fact that you're…" he trails off, laughing to himself. "JD Simmons is my fucking superhero. I…this is insane."

Superhero. I'm no fucking superhero.

"Every time I think I'm getting to know you, something happens that makes me realise I don't know you at all. I wish you could just…" His words fade and he sighs heavily.

"Just what, Theodore?"

Reaching out, he palms my cheek. The contact makes my heart jump in my chest. "I wish you'd show me who you are. I feel like we're dancing in circles."

Show him.

Slowly, I reach for the top button on my shirt, my pulse hammering in my throat as I start unfastening it. I can't *tell* him who I am, my mouth is too dry, my tongue suddenly paralysed, but I can *show* him.

I have to.

Theodore's hand slips off my face as he shrinks back a step. "What are you doing?"

My nervous fingers tremble as they continue to open my buttons. Taking a deep breath, I fix my stare onto his puzzled face and shrug out of my shirt, rolling it down my arms before letting gravity take it to the floor. I study his eyes as they wander up and down my chest. His jaw drops slightly and for a moment I expect him to turn away in disgust, but he doesn't.

Straightening his arm, his gentle fingertip traces the jagged edge of one of my scars, just above my navel. A gasp of air catches in my throat and my instinctive reaction is to flinch, pull away, *run*…but I supress it.

"What happened?" he asks, his voice low, barely audible. "Who did this to you?"

"I did." Two tiny words, yet they've popped open the valve on a crushing tyre of pressure that's been bound around my heart for as long as I can remember.

Removing the pad of his finger, he replaces it with the palm of his hand, smoothing it over my mutilated skin, across the scars, over the burns.

"Why?"

"I'm broken, Theodore. I always have been. I always will be."

His other hand appears on the damaged flesh and I can't understand how he can bear to touch me.

"I was diagnosed with bipolar disorder four years ago. It isn't going to go away. I'm not going to get better. A life with me could destroy you, Theodore. My mind isn't fun. It's dark. Twisted. And if you're going to walk away, I need you to do it *now*."

His fingers travel up my body until they land on my neck. "I'm not going anywhere, James," he whispers, pressing his forehead against mine. "Take me to bed. Not to fuck. Not to sleep. Let me hold you. I need to hold you."

My heart hammers against the walls of my chest but I can't make sense of the emotions running through my body. I turn slowly, concentrating on every step as I lead Theodore upstairs. Crawling into my king-sized bed, I curl up on my side and watch with bewilderment as Theodore settles in next to me.

He scoots close, our clothed knees touching, and drapes an arm over my waist, anchoring me to him. "Why, James? Why did you hurt yourself?"

Sighing, I stare at his shoulder, too ashamed of myself to look him in the eye. "Physical pain is easier to deal with. The pain in my head, the ache in my chest, if I don't release it…transfer it, it feels like it could kill me."

"Do you still do it?" he asks, his voice strained.

I still can't look at him. "No. I stopped a long time ago."

"So…the pain in your head is gone?"

"No, Theodore. It never leaves. I just found other ways to transfer it."

"By?"

"Fucking. Smoking. Drinking. Distracting myself however I can."

My replacement techniques worked pretty well until I met Theodore. Now, the thought of drilling my dark thoughts into another man makes me feel sick. I couldn't do that to him. I couldn't bear to hurt those beautiful green eyes that are watching me right now with so much compassion, so much care.

So much *love.*

I'm not sure where this leaves me. The urge to take a blade to my chest, to stub a cigarette out on my skin, has tortured me for the last few days. But I'm winning. I won't give in. I refuse. Although dwindling, part of me still believes I can be good enough for Theodore. Maybe that's possible now I'm being honest with him. I've spent my whole life being a liar. Hiding. I thought being alone was for the best, but it hasn't made me happy. Perhaps that's where I've been going wrong all along. Maybe I don't need to be alone. Maybe I *should* trust someone enough to share my problems with. Maybe…maybe *that's* the key to being happy. Being *better.*

I want it so badly. A future. A life with Theodore.

"Does anybody know? Please tell me you haven't been alone through this?"

"Max, to an extent. He walked in on me changing when I was eighteen. Saw some fresh scars. Forced me to see a doctor."

"I thought you were only diagnosed four years ago?"

"At first, I was told I was simply depressed. They prescribed antidepressants. I took them for a few weeks, felt better, felt *amazing* in fact, then stopped. Then the cycle started again and continued for several years. At this point I still self-harmed, but I was an adult, I lived alone, and it was easier to hide. Max thought I stopped after he found out. So did the doctors."

"Why did it take so long to get diagnosed?" He sounds almost annoyed.

"I didn't talk. I didn't go to the doctor of my own accord, not once. It always took a push from Max when he noticed me slipping. I'd go purely to placate him because I felt guilty for causing the worry in his eyes. It didn't take long to learn how the system worked, what I needed to say to obtain a prescription and get sent on my merry way."

"So what changed?"

A voice in my head tells me to stop talking, but I can't. It feels too good. "Max caught me cutting again, saw the extent of the years of damage I'd caused to myself. That time he came with me to see the GP, a different one than I usually saw. He told her about the self-harm because he knew I wouldn't."

I stare up at the wall, struggling to make eye contact with him. "She referred me for a psychiatric assessment. Max came with me. According to the notes the guy had my GP had raised concerns about bipolar type two."

"There are different kinds?"

"Type two causes milder episodes of mania, but more intense periods of depression. The man who assessed me, however, said he didn't believe in that diagnosis, said it's a fad brought over from America."

"He actually said that?" Theodore sounds as disbelieving as Max did when he heard it straight from the mental health assessor's mouth.

"Then he went on to say bipolar diagnoses are only usually made when someone ends up being sectioned or brought in by the police. He made me feel like I was wasting his time, but I wasn't there through choice. I didn't *ask* to be referred. I only went for Max's sake. Anyway, he diagnosed me with chronic depression and off I went."

"But what about the self-harm? He helped you with that, right?"

"I was too old apparently. Their services are only available to under twenty-five's. I was twenty-six."

"So…they just *left* you?"

"Pretty much. Max got me another appointment with the GP, and by this point I was exhausted. I felt like a fool. Maybe even a hypochondriac. But I went. For Max. She sounded surprised by what we'd been told, but her hands were tied. Max did all the talking. I couldn't. I was so tired. Resigned. Hopeless. She referred me for cognitive behavioural therapy, switched my antidepressants, and that was that."

"Did it help? The therapy?"

"It made me feel stupid. Patronised. CBT is all about changing the way you think, teaching yourself alternative choices. But I already know what I'm *supposed* to do. I *know* if I feel low I should go for a walk, talk to someone. I *know* if I feel the urge to hurt myself I should wait for it to pass, take a bath or, again, talk to someone. I *know* all that, but I choose not to do it. So, no, it didn't work. I'm sure it does for some people, but not for me."

There is no help for me.

Silence follows, but it's not awkward. It's peaceful. Calming. It surprises me that I don't feel embarrassed. Judged. I feel completely at ease in Theodore's presence.

"What caused it?" Theodore asks, his eyebrows knitted together in concern, and maybe a little curiosity. "Did you have a bad childhood?"

Sometimes I wish that were true. If I could pinpoint an issue I could work through it. It would be easier than knowing I was born this way. "I had a good life, great parents. I was brought up exactly the same as Max. Some people might say I have a screw loose in my brain, but I think that screw is missing altogether. It can't be tightened. I can't be fixed. It was never there to begin with."

His thumb draws small circles on my back and I feel it all the way down to my toes. "You mean you've *always* felt this way? Even as a child?"

"I've been fucked in the head for as long as I can remember."

"Don't say that. You're not fucked in the head."

He can't say that. He doesn't *know*. "I'd fake being sick from six years old, just so I could stay home. Not so I could watch TV or play on my Nintendo…so I could wrap myself in my quilt and cry until I fell asleep. I saw my first psychiatrist when I was eleven. I-"

"I thought you said nobody knew?" he cuts in, confused.

"My mum cottoned on to the fact I was pretending to be sick. After that I would point blank refuse to go to school. Eventually, when I reached eleven and went to high school, she had the head teacher on her back. They thought she was allowing me to play truant and didn't care about my education. But she did. She *tried*. I pushed her to the end of her tether. I had this ability to switch off from the world, even then. At first, she tried talking to me. She'd cry. Beg me. But I couldn't hear her."

"Because you'd switched off?"

I love how he's trying to understand. It's almost therapeutic. On some level I feel like he's starting to heal me…but that thought is dangerous. "It was like I wasn't even inside my body anymore. I could see a hazy vision of her in front of me, but I wasn't there. She'd plead, she'd shout, she'd shake me. But I was gone. She sought advice from the family GP and it was decided I had some kind of school phobia. *That's* why they sent me to a psychiatrist."

"And what did they say?"

I shrug. "I don't know. I don't really remember what we talked about, and my mum's never spoken to me about it. All I *do* remember from those appointments is staring at a bookend shaped like a cat on the shelf behind my psychiatrist, closing down while she did all the talking. Sometimes my mum would be in the room with us, sometimes I'd be alone, and sometimes I'd be in the waiting room watching the younger kids play with the plastic doll house while my mum spoke to the doctor without me. They put me on a course of anti-depressants and the appointments stopped."

"At *eleven?*"

"Yes."

"So then what happened? Did you go back to the GP?"

"No. I learned to hide it better after that. I learned how to be more convincing about being sick. I taught myself how to vomit whenever I needed to. I found out which parts of my body bruised the easiest, and I'd hit myself and conjure up a believable 'accident' so I could stay home."

"Jesus, James. She *must've* known. She's your mum."

Again, I shrug. "If she did she never mentioned it. When I was twelve I tried to slit my wrist, but I wasn't brave enough to go deep." I rub over the tiny scar on my left wrist and, as I close my eyes, I'm back in that bathroom, hovering my arm over the turquoise sink.

"How did nobody notice that? You were just a *child*. How did no one see?"

"It didn't bleed much. It was easy to cover with a long-sleeved jumper."

There's so much pain, so much confusion on Theodore's face, and I hate myself for putting it there. But I can't stop. I need to get it out. I've never spoken about this time in my life with anyone, not even Max, and my heavy heart feels a little lighter with every word I speak.

"I tried again when I was thirteen, this time thinking pills would be easier. My grandmother used to take distalgesics for her arthritis. I took a strip and kept them hidden in my bedroom for weeks. I'd stare at them every night before I went to sleep but, for a while, I still had hope. Hope that it was just a phase, it wouldn't last forever, I'd get better."

Tears sting the back of my eyes. I'm in as much pain right now as I was all those years ago. "But I got so tired, Theodore. My mother was upset all the time because the school wouldn't leave her alone, berating her over my poor attendance. I *hated* myself for doing that to her but I *couldn't* face going to school. I couldn't keep pretending I was okay. I was exhausted."

I dare a glance at Theodore's face and the silent tear rolling down his cheek almost destroys me. "So I took them. I swallowed the whole strip, eight tablets, with a bottle of elderflower sparkling water."

To this day I can't drink that flavour of water. It takes me right back to that place. I can still taste it on my tongue all these years later.

"Oh God, James…"

"It didn't work, obviously. I passed out on my bed for a few hours then woke up feeling weak and sick and ran to the toilet. I threw up violently, bitter green bile pouring from my body over and over again. My mother found me. She yelled. Asked if I'd taken anything. I denied it and we never spoke about it again."

"How the…why the fuck didn't she help you? She's your goddamn mother! She can't have been that stupid!"

He sounds annoyed with her and it makes me feel uneasy. "She's not a bad person, Theodore." I feel a powerful urge to defend her. She isn't responsible. *I* am. "I don't know if she knew. Sometimes I think she *must* have, but I'm a good liar." *I still am.* "Maybe it hurt her too much. Maybe she just didn't know what to do."

"You could've…shit, James you could've died."

"That was the plan." I hadn't meant to say that out loud and I don't realise I have until I see the shock register on Theodore's face. "It wasn't lack of will that stopped me succeeding. It was pure naivety. I assumed one strip would be enough. They were prescription strength painkillers."

"Y-you don't still have these thoughts?" It comes out more like a plea than a question. He's hurting. *I'm* hurting him.

It kick starts my instinct to lie. "Not for a long time."

I've attempted suicide three times in my life, although seeing the grief in Theodore's eyes makes me unable to discuss the third. Each time I was just a kid, but it wasn't for attention. I didn't want to wake up. I wanted the pain to stop, my demons to die. But I was too young and stupid to get it right. I haven't completely lied to Theodore. Thoughts of ending my life have flickered in the back of my mind since my last unsuccessful attempt as a fifteen year old, but never as intense.

The truth which I can't admit to Theodore, to anyone, however, is that now I'm older, wiser, if that urge to free myself from this darkness ever descends on me again, I have absolutely no doubt I will succeed. I have pills hidden, unused prescriptions I've held onto over the years. I have a fool-proof plan. One that I hope I never have to use, and one which I know I shouldn't have, but it's there…just in case.

"I can't believe nobody knew," Theodore all but whispers. "How can you not notice somebody breaking right in front of you?"

"Like I said, I'm a good liar. A good actor."

"You shouldn't have to be."

I disagree. The only thing discussing my problems achieves is placing that burden on someone else. It doesn't take it away from me. It just means I have to watch somebody else suffer beside myself.

"What changed? How did you get your diagnosis?"

"Max wouldn't let it rest. He pushed for a referral direct to a psychiatrist without a general assessment first. It took him months, but he did it. I didn't want to go. Cancelled my appointment three times. I mean, I'd been told I was depressed. He was a professional. I took his word for it. Thought I'd just be wasting their time again."

"You shouldn't have been made to feel like that. Professional isn't the word I'd use for that tosser."

I smile. Not because it's amusing, but because I'm relieved, if not slightly baffled, that he's still here. "Eventually, I gave in, if only to appease Max. It was a completely different experience that time around. This guy knew what he was talking about. Knew what questions to ask. He…well he took me seriously."

"But…you're better now?" He shakes his head before correcting himself. "I mean, it's being managed?"

"Yes." It's not a lie as such. I *am* managing it, just on my own. The lithium slows me down, and when my father passed away I needed to be alert or the business he'd spent his whole life growing would've gone to shit if I'd continued living as a robot.

So, I weaned myself off the medication, and it worked. My energy levels peaked to the point I could work through the night and still deliver kick-arse management skills during the day. Not only that, I wrote a new book, which I've just signed the publishing contract for, in just two weeks.

I'm not stupid enough to think these levels of productivity will last. I can already feel it waning. The tiredness is setting in, the need for more sleep. So as soon as the new book has completed the editing and publication process, and my staff have adjusted to the changes I'm implementing for the magazine contract, I'll start taking my meds again.

I've got this.

Chapter *Nine*

~Theo~

I haven't been able to take my eyes off James' face the whole time we've been lying in his bed, although he's barely looked at me. The things he's just revealed leave me feeling quietly terrified, yet I'm also completely in awe of him. All I can think about is that broken teenage boy, alone in his room with no one to hold him, no one to help him.

How was that allowed to happen? He was a child. I don't care how good an actor he says he is, somebody should've seen.

"I'm sorry, Theodore." The sound of his gravelled voice makes me realise I've been silent for several minutes. "It's too much. I've said too much."

"It *is* too much. What you've been through is too much. The lack of support you've had is too much. But the fact you trust me enough to tell me everything you just did, that you let me in, showed me who you are…No, James. That's not too much."

"I'd convinced myself you'd leave," he says, palming my cheek. "Part of me still thinks you should."

Part of me *wants* to, but I'm bound too tightly to him, to every side of him, to the strong and assured CEO, and the vulnerable, breaking man hiding beneath the surface. But I have no experience with mental illness and, honestly, it petrifies me. What if he's dragged into that blackness again? How do I get him out? What if he really *is* a good liar and I don't notice his demons strangling him until it's too late?

Can I live with so much uncertainty? Will a relationship entail me scrutinising his every move, every expression? How sad is *too* sad? How happy is *too* happy?

Am I strong enough?

I have no idea. All I know is when I uttered the word *love* it was an accident, but it wasn't a lie.

I love him.

I'm *in* love with him.

And it scares the ever living hell out of me.

"I'm not going anywhere," I say, hitching myself closer to him and burying my face in his neck.

His stubble grates against my cheek as I kiss the throbbing vein in his throat before I inch lower, pressing my lips to his chest. His taut muscles are littered with scars. Most are faded, silvery lines. Some are thick, raised, and some are tiny circles that spark soul-destroying images of him extinguishing cigarettes on his flesh.

Tears sting like grains of salt in the back of my eyes as my lips travel across his skin, kissing each mark in turn. Angling my head, I look up at his face and his expression twists into curiosity, maybe even fear.

"How can you stand to do that?" he asks, his stare intense.

"Kiss you?"

"Kiss…*them*. They're hideous."

"*They* are part of you, and you're beautiful."

I peck feather-light kisses up to his neck before crawling onto my knees and straddling him, taking his face in my hands. "So let me kiss you," I whisper against his lips. "Let me love you."

A small gasp seeps from his mouth. "You don't know what that means, to love someone like me."

I run my tongue over his bottom lip. "Too late."

His warm breath covers my face like a blanket and for a second I pause, enjoying the closeness.

"I need to feel you inside me, James," I say, breathless. Curling my fingers around the base of his neck, I dip my tongue between his lips, kissing him, *loving* him.

Working my hands between our bodies, I tease open the button on his pants, reaching inside and closing my fingers around his perfectly hard cock.

"Fuck, Theodore," he groans against my jaw.

Breaking away from his face, I shuffle down the bed, un-popping the buttons on my shirt with one hand before shrugging out of it and tossing it to the floor. I release his cock just long enough to remove my pants, my dick springing to attention, and he raises his arse off the mattress and does the same.

The sight of him steals my breath for a moment. He's stunning. *All* of him. Even the parts he's ashamed of. To me, I see scars of courage. Inflicting them gave him the strength to survive the pain that's plagued him all his life. I'm grateful to every one of them because he's still here, with me.

Running my hands up his colourful thighs, I admire the Japanese artwork decorating his skin. Now I know his secrets, know *him*, I wonder if his ink is another way of transferring the pain. The thought makes my chest tighten.

Leaning forward, I grasp the base of his cock and it twitches in response. I'm eager to feel it buried inside me, but first I need to taste him. I pepper soft kisses along his balls, sporadically nipping the loose skin with my teeth, gently, but firm enough to make him moan.

His fingers land on the back of my head, stroking through my hair as I clamp my lips over his swollen head, swirling my tongue over the freckle on his tip.

"Christ, Theodore…"

"I love this little freckle," I tell him, kissing it once more. Keeping my lips moist, I slide them up and down his thick shaft, my hand caressing his balls. I suck, lick, and tease him until his hips grind into the mattress, revelling in every gasp, groan and strained breath that trickles from his throat. He asks for me to turn around so he can play with me at the same time, and I do, but I'm not giving him the power this time.

"Ah, yeah," I whisper, breathing heavily onto James' cock as his tongue draws circles around my hole.

He keeps one hand on my dick, squeezing and relaxing, driving me insane while he works on me with his mouth. His tongue dips inside, thrusting gently as I take his cock to the back of my throat over and over again. Then, when he starts fucking me with his fingers I almost lose my frigging mind.

I release him with a soft pop and flip myself around. Automatically, he reaches out to his bedside table and blindly fumbles for a condom and lube, knowing what I want, what I *need* from him.

Kneeling beside him, I watch, biting my lip as he rolls the condom onto himself.

"Turn over, Theodore."

Pressing my nose to his, I place a chaste kiss on his lips before stealing the lube from his hand. "No."

He looks surprised, a little confused even, as I drizzle a generous amount of lube onto his cock, massaging it in with my fingers. Slowly, I raise my leg and hitch it over his hips, straddling him. "You're going to look at me this time, James. I want to see your face when I make you come."

His expression is wary, and I wonder if he's ever had sex face-to-face before, if he's ever given up his control. His eyes are narrowed but he doesn't utter a word as I reach behind myself and guide his cock towards my puckered rim. Keeping my fingers curled around the base, I lower myself onto him slowly, gasping as he stretches me.

My body stills for a moment and I bring my hands to his chest, using him to support my weight as I start to move. Everything about this is different to anything I've ever felt before. I'm so deeply connected to him, in every way possible. I don't think I'll ever be one man again. He's part of me. He completes me. He's filled a void I didn't even know existed before I met him.

Our gazes interlocked, we don't take our eyes off each other as I work myself up and down on top of him. His hips roll in time with my own as I rub the light dusting of sweat glistening on his flawed chest into his muscles. He's so damn beautiful, inside and out, and my heart swells with awe, pride…with love.

Smoothing one palm up his chest, I grip his shoulder, steadying myself while I take my leaking cock in my free hand. James reaches out, stroking my balls, and I tighten my fist and start to tug.

"That's it, Theodore," he mutters through gritted teeth. "So fucking beautiful."

Moving faster, I slam myself down on him again and again, the loud slaps matching the speed of my hand. I fight the urge to close my eyes, to lose myself in the sensations taking over my body, as violent jolts of pleasure dart through my spine and into my aching balls.

"Fuck, James," I whisper, my stare piercing his. "I'm almost there."

His brow furrows as he rasps and pants into the air. "Do it, Theodore. Come all over my body."

My legs begin to tremble, my knees weakening, and James takes over, pounding his cock so deep into my arse it makes me cry out his name. "James!"

Angling my cock forwards, I pump hard and fast until I feel my release surging through my shaft, exploding in quick, intense spurts all over his stomach.

"Holy shit…" he breathes, slamming into me one last time, his entire body juddering below mine as my hole clenches around his pulsating cock.

Falling forward, I collapse onto his chest and kiss the heat that has gathered around his neck.

"Stay with me, Theodore," he murmurs. "No matter how hard I push, stay with me. Believe in me." His tone is so raw, so powerful, and I can't prevent the tear that leaks from the corner of my eye.

Hovering my face just inches from his, I cup his cheek, stroking softly with my thumb. "Always."

There isn't a choice. I belong to James Holden. I can try to fight it, but the truth is this beautiful, haunted man, has owned me since the first time I looked into his eyes.

* * *

The next morning, I find myself in James' home office again, picking up books I must have read a dozen times and analysing their covers as if it's the first time I've seen them.

Upon hearing James' footsteps creep up behind me, I place the book I'm holding back on the shelf and turn around. "My brain is still struggling to process the fact that JD Simmons and *you* are the same person. You're just a…man." I shake my head. "A normal guy."

James snickers. "*You're* a writer, too," he says, as if I should understand.

"No, I'm not. Not like you. You're like a…a star. I'm just a guy tapping out his random thoughts in my spare time."

"As am I," he says, wearing a smirk. "Simmons is my grandmother's maiden name," he explains. "Which one is your favourite?"

I blow a puff of air through pursed lips. "I don't even know how I'm supposed to choose," I say, scratching my head. "Maybe *Promises*, purely because it's the first one I read."

Smiling, James plucks a hardback copy of *Promises* from the middle shelf and strolls over to his desk. Bending, he picks up a pen and scribbles inside the jacket before snapping it closed and handing it back to me. I feel giddy, butterflies swarming my stomach as I start to open it.

Putting his hand on top of mine, he stops me. "Don't read it until you get home."

Bemused, I lift an eyebrow, but I nod in agreement.

"Breakfast?" he offers.

"I need to get going really. I've no clean clothes here."

He looks disappointed but forces a smile. "Have things changed between us, Theodore?"

Stepping forward, I rest my hands on his tense shoulders. He's already dressed for work, looking sophisticated and utterly fuckable in his sharp, black suit. "Yes," I breathe. "Things have absolutely changed."

His shoulders stiffen under my touch and I squeeze them gently. "I finally know who you are, James. You're brave. Strong. A survivor. Things have changed because, today, I have no doubts about us, about *you*. Last night, you gave me *all* of you. You trusted me beyond a level I doubt I'll ever deserve, and I'm going to make damn sure you never regret it."

Pressing my forehead to his, I sigh. "I'm scared, James. I'm scared I won't know how to support you, that I'll let you down, but if you let me I want to try."

"Fuck, Theodore," he whispers, squeezing his eyes closed. "I'm scared, too. I've never done this. Some of the things I told you have never left my lips before last night. I didn't think they ever would."

My heart breaks all over again. The level of loneliness this man has lived through is unimaginable, unbearable.

"I can't promise you anything," he adds. "I can't promise I won't hide from you...*lie* to you."

"Promise to *try*," I urge, pressing my lips to his before enfolding his strong body in my arms. "You don't have to be alone anymore."

"I...I'll try," he mutters, so quietly I wonder if I've imagined it.

"I love you, James." His lips part but I hover my finger over them. "I don't expect you to say it back. Not yet. Just know that I *do*. I love you. What I feel for you, how connected I am to you, it's too strong to be anything else."

In this moment, with his brow creased and his eyes closed, he looks like a man in fifty different types of pain. So I do the only thing I can think of. I kiss him, breathing deeply, and try to absorb some of the hurt in his heart.

"I'll see you at work."

Smiling softly, he strokes along my jaw. "You will."

* * *

Arriving home after an unusually busy day at work, I head straight to my bedroom and collapse onto the bed. I don't think I've ever been so exhausted in all my life. I'm physically and emotionally drained.

Lying back on the mattress, my hands tucked behind my head, I try to process everything I've learned about James. I accept it, but I can't even begin to understand. I've never felt anything like the feelings he expressed. Sure, I've been down, sad, lonely at times…but nothing has *ever* made me contemplate ending it all. I've always been able to see the other side, to know that nothing lasts forever. The things James described seem completely incomprehensible to me.

I have so many questions. Questions I'm not sure James will be able to answer. He's on a different side than I am. He's *living* with his illness, not looking at it through a window like me.

Figuring the best place to start is the internet, I shuffle into a sitting position and pull my laptop out of its carry-case next to my bed. The top hits are trusted sites like the NHS and Mind so I start there. The descriptions and symptoms are rather clinical and I keep searching until I find the support links for friends and relatives of people with mental illnesses.

Eventually, I end up on a forum, reading through other people's experiences and situations. Some of the stories fill my gut with sadness and fear and it makes me question, once again, if I'm strong enough to do this.

"Someone die?"

My gaze flits to the doorway and finds Tess standing there, shrugging out of her coat.

"Please tell me you're not killing off Sam's brother."

"What?" My brain is too frazzled to decipher riddles just now.

"You look like you do when you're murdering one of my favourite characters."

"I'm not writing."

After kicking off her shoes and leaving them where they land, she jumps on the bed, propping herself up next to me and staring at the screen. "Oh my God, who are you making crazy? Bet it's Natasha. She's screamed nutjob since book one."

Huffing, I snap the laptop closed. "I'm not researching for a book."

"Well who else do you know that's crazy?"

"Stop saying that," I snap, immediately relenting. "Sorry."

Her playful expression turns abruptly serious. "What's going on, T?"

"James told me he's bipolar last night."

"Holy shit," she mutters, then blows through puckered lips.

"Christ, Tess, some of the things he told me…it terrifies me."

"You think he could hurt you?"

"No, no." I shake my head. "I think he could hurt *himself*. Hell, he *is* hurting, in his mind. It worries me that I don't know what to do, how to help him."

"So, he's depressed?"

"Not right now. I don't *think* so anyway. But from what he told me he could go down that path again, and if he does, what do I do? We're not just talking about being a little down in the dumps. He's been to some really dark places and I don't know if I'm strong enough to deal with that if it happens again."

"Don't suppose you could just walk away?"

"No! Fucking hell, Tess, I'm not a heartless bastard."

"No, you're not, but you can't stay with him out of sympathy."

"That's not why and you damn well know it. I told *you* how I felt about James before I even told *him*. I can't just switch that off."

"How can you be certain? That he's 'the one' I mean. *Why* are you with him?"

"I just *know*." I don't know why James and I are together. We're not particularly similar, we lead different lives, have different interests. There's just something there. A spark. A *pull*. It's been there since the first time I saw his face. It's baffling, yet undeniable. "Does there need to be a reason?"

"I guess not, but I had to be sure, Theo. You're my best friend and it would kill me to see you get hurt, whether he means to or not."

"I don't know what to do. I don't mean whether to stay with him, I've made that decision, it's just…"

"You should talk to Tom."

"Seriously? You think my whore of a brother is the best person to get relationship advice from?"

"No, dickhead, I think your *doctor* of a brother is the best person to get mental health advice from."

Hmm. "I think he actually worked on a psychiatric ward during his second year."

"I'm not suggesting he's an expert in the field, but he'll be able to help you better than I can. All I can do is listen."

Smiling, I take her hand in mine. I don't think James has ever had anyone to just *listen*. The notion makes my chest ache and I appreciate Tess all the more.

"I don't think Tom and I have ever discussed anything serious before," I say, unsure of how I will broach the subject with him.

"Bullshit. You told him you were gay before anyone else."

How did I forget that? "Yeah, I did." And he was amazing. Maybe I'm underestimating his qualities as a brother. "He said he didn't care as long as I didn't eye-fuck his friends," I add, chuckling at the memory.

"And did you?"

"If you'd seen the friends he used to have you wouldn't need to ask me that. One of them, Nate I think he was called, had a lazy eye and enough grease in his hair to fry eggs."

"Wow. Hot."

Sighing, I put my laptop on the floor and shuffle down the bed, rolling onto my side to face Tess. Draping one arm over her waist, I pull her in for a hug.

"Don't get comfy," she says. "I need a wee."

Rolling my eyes, I jab her in the back with my finger. "Twat."

"Bellend."

* * *

The next morning while I'm getting ready for work, I notice the copy of *Promises* James gave to me sitting on the kitchen counter. I left it there last night in an exhausted daze. Stroking the glossy cover, I shake my head, still unable to believe that not only have I met its author, I've fallen in love with him.

Opening the cover, my eyes wash over his neat handwriting.

Theodore. I can't give you any promises, but I can give you my heart. Take care of it for me. JD Simmons.

I suck in a deep breath and hold it there, unintentionally, until I feel a little dizzy. "I'll do my best," I whisper to nobody. But knowing what I know now, this seems like such a huge responsibility. I hope I don't let him down.

This book seems too precious to stand with my others on the cheap pine shelves, so I take it to my bedroom and tuck it under my pillow, where it will stay until I figure out where to keep it. I haven't decided whether to tell Tess about James' secret author life yet, or rather, I haven't decided *when*. I tell her everything. James knows that, but I should probably ask him if he's okay with her knowing first.

Several minutes later, my phone rings while I'm jogging down the stairwell. It's Tom, returning my earlier call. We chat as I make my way to the car and he tells me he's working all evening so if I need to see him urgently, I'll need to meet him at the hospital. I agree because it *is* urgent. I need answers. Guidance. I need *hope.*

Driving to work, I'm unsure of everything, but certain of *one.* I can't wait to see James' face again.

Unfortunately, when I step out onto the marketing floor, the first face I see is Mike's. "You're in submissions today. They're short staffed and the coffee machine's packed in. You need to arrange a replacement."

I can tell by his smug expression that he thinks he's inconveniencing me, but in truth the thought of spending my day in submissions excites me. "No problem." My accompanying smile makes his eyes narrow and I turn back to the lifts with a shit-eating grin on my face. Clearly, his plan was to piss me off, show me who's boss.

He failed. *Wanker.*

The coffee machine issue is resolved within an hour but I stay where I am. I like it here. I like the people, the work they're doing. Anthony is the head of the department down here and it's refreshing to work under someone who isn't a complete arsehole. By the end of the day, I've built quite a rapport with Anthony and I manage to convince him to let me sift through the slush pile. The majority of submissions are processed electronically and come through literary agents, but we still receive several hundred unsolicited manuscripts through the post every month.

After searching through them for half an hour, I agree that the majority deserve to be here, but a couple catch my eye and I stuff them in a carrier bag so I can read them at home. I'm not stupid enough to think I have any say in what happens to them, but if I believe in any of them I can try my best to fight the author's corner.

"Theodore?"

I look up to the sound of my name. The floor is almost empty, with only myself, a woman whose name I've forgotten, and now James.

"What are you doing down here? I've been looking for you. I assumed you'd gone home."

Standing up, I walk over to him. "They were short staffed down here," I explain. "And Anthony said I could look through these." I hold up the carrier bag with an eager smile on my face.

James rubs his thumb over my lips. "I like that smile."

Coughing nervously, I take a step back. "What are you doing?" I whisper, tossing an inconspicuous nod towards the woman working at her desk in the corner of the large floor.

"People are going to find out eventually, Theodore."

A small frown forces its way onto my face. "Not yet. I don't want people getting the wrong idea."

"And that would be?"

"That I'm screwing the boss to get a promotion."

"I don't work like that. You'll get a promotion when you've *earned* one, just like everyone else."

"*I* know that, but they don't know that I know that, and they don't know that you know I know that."

James chuckles, tipping his head to the side. "You could repeat that three times and I'm still not sure I'd understand a word you just said."

Damn, the smile on his face dives straight into my soul. Chewing on my bottom lip, I stare at him, my cock growing a little bigger with each blink of my eyes.

"If you don't want people to know, I suggest you stop looking at me like you want to drop to your knees and suck my dick right here, right now."

I know my nameless colleague won't be able to hear from across the room but, regardless, my eyes dart to where she sits.

"Come home with me and maybe I'll let you do just that," James adds with a wicked glint in his eye.

"I can't. I'm meeting my brother to discuss-" *Shit.* "Stuff."

"To discuss *me*."

"No. Not really. I mean, well, I just…"

"It's okay, Theodore. I'm glad you have someone that you can talk to about this, because sometimes I won't be able to."

His words hit me like a punch to the stomach.

"He's a doctor. I'm sure he'll be able to address any questions you have." James knows all about Tom, my whole family in fact. Whenever we talk about *his* family, somehow he always manages to switch the attention back to mine. "Maybe call me when you get home? If you want to of course."

"I *will* want to," I say, missing the sound of his voice already.

"Can I at least walk you to your car? Or does that imply you're fucking your boss?"

"Fuck off," I spit, my smile betraying the impact of my insult. "I'll meet you at the lift."

First, I need to tidy away the files I've been digging through.

* * *

At the hospital, I wait in the staffroom for Tom after introducing myself to one of the nurses. I've been here for an hour so far. I've checked Facebook, Twitter, and Digital Spy for any interesting celebrity gossip, and now I'm comparing the length of my fingers on both hands to see if they match.

"Hey, Theo."

I look up to see Tom bustling through the door, his green scrubs smeared with blood. My inquisitive mind wonders whose blood it is, what caused it, if they survived.

"RTA," Tom says, opening one of the metal lockers at the other side of the room. He steps out of his dirty scrubs and tosses them in what looks like a bin on wheels.

"They okay?"

Plucking a clean set of scrubs out of the locker, he throws them on quickly. "He's in surgery. Doesn't look good though."

His answer stuns me a little, even though I don't know the poor guy. "How do you deal with it? Death, right in front of you every day. How do you just…switch off?"

"I don't," he says, pulling out a chair from under the white table I'm sitting at. Taking a seat, he runs a hand through his hair. It's the same shade of brown as mine. In fact, we look similar in a lot of ways, except I'm a couple of inches shorter and he has blue eyes. "It's never easy, but it's the job. And when you save someone, when you get to give their family the good news, it makes it all worthwhile."

I'm a little in awe of my brother right now. Of course I know what he does for a living, but it's not something we've ever really talked about before. It makes me realise we've never talked about anything significant. He's always just been my sleazy older brother who takes the piss out of me at every available opportunity. But here, he looks so professional and intelligent. Seeing the blood on his clothes makes it hit me that *my* brother saves fucking lives.

"I'm proud of you, Tom." The words fall from my mouth without permission from my brain.

"Steady on, T. I'm not sure I'm ready to take our brotherly bond to the next level."

"I'm serious. Your job…it's important. *You're* important. People literally put their lives in your hands."

"What's going on? Something's bothering you."

"I'm fine," I lie with the straightest face I can manage. "I just came to pick your doctor brain."

"About?"

"Bipolar disorder." His expression turns quizzical so I quickly tack on, "It's research."

"You're still writing?"

I'm not overly surprised by his question. As with most things, it's not something we usually discuss. "Never stopped."

"It's not my field, but I can try and answer any questions you have."

Right, okay. Where do I begin? "Is there a reason for it? I mean, does something trigger it?"

"Possibly." Tom shrugs. "The cause isn't fully understood. Genetics can play a part, as can chemical imbalances in the brain. But it's an illness, like cancer or epilepsy. It's no one's fault. Sometimes, it just…happens."

"So, if it's a chemical imbalance, they can fix it, right? With chemicals. Medication. Replace the ones that are missing?"

Looking unsure, Tom clicks his tongue. "Mood stabilisers do as the name says. They lower the highs, elevate the lows. It's important to find the right one. Everyone reacts differently. Then there's therapy, counselling, learning how to take care of yourself, lifestyle changes."

Does James see a therapist? I suppose he must.

"It can be an unpredictable illness. Manic or depressive relapses aren't uncommon, which is why therapy is so important. It enables someone to recognise the warning signs so they can seek help before things get out of control."

Nodding slowly, I absorb the information. "What are the warning signs?"

"I can't say, Theo. Everyone is different, and their warning signs might be unique to them."

"You can give me examples, surely?"

Tom pushes a puff of air through pursed lips while he thinks. I don't like the word unpredictable. I need to know what I'm dealing with, what *James* is dealing with.

"Signs of mania can include restlessness, often high levels of creativity or productivity, what seems like a rise in ego, self importance, invincibility, recklessness…"

He could well be describing James, but his illness is under control. Although, invincibility? When he climbed up on that wall he was fearless, stupidly so. "But a person can be like that without being ill though. Can't they?"

"Some people are arseholes regardless of their mental health if that's what you mean."

Yes, that's exactly what I mean. James is definitely an arsehole – cocky, arrogant, patronising…but I love him.

"Irritability, sometimes violence can be signs, too. It's not always a case of being off your tits happy."

"And what about the depression?"

Tom's expression confuses me. He looks almost concerned and, given that we're talking hypothetically, I can't figure out why.

"Lethargy, lack of interest in things they usually enjoy, feelings of hopelessness, becoming withdrawn-"

"And how would I-*someone* recognise that?"

"That depends on how good they are at hiding it. Some people will talk, get help, others will keep it all inside. It can be a very devious illness for some people. They either don't recognise they have a problem or they don't *want* to. That could be because they're ashamed, they think it'll go away on its own, or they feel worthless and like they don't deserve help." Tom shrugs. "Again, everyone is different, and everyone diagnosed should be treated as such."

"But lethargy. That's easy to spot. I mean you'd notice if someone looked tired all the time."

"Possibly. But if they don't want you to know they might disguise it with excuses. Being busy, headaches, the flu. I think ultimately, if you know the person well and have experience with their illness, you'll learn to recognise the signs."

Therein lies the problem. I *don't* have any experience. Do I know him well? Possibly. But what if I don't? Would James lie to me? I know he said he has in the past, to his brother, to doctors…but that's because he didn't think they'd understand, that they'd judge him.

"Like I said, it can be a conniving illness, but it *is* an illness. Whoever it is you're talking about isn't doing it to hurt you."

"W-what?" I stutter, straightening my back.

"You're my brother, Theo. I *know* you. This isn't research, this is your reality right now."

"I…" My brain freezes.

"You don't have to tell me who it is, just know that you *can*. You can trust me, T. Confidentiality is part of my job description."

I've never thought of it that way. Tom has always been the older brother who used to get me in trouble by grassing me up to our mum. I guess I didn't notice him becoming an adult, despite him being older than me. On reflection, that seems so stupid.

"I've been seeing someone," I admit. "He's only just told me about the bipolar. Some of the things he told me, the way his mind works, it frightens me a little."

"I take it things are pretty serious between you?"

Sighing, I drop my head. "I love him, Tom."

"Wow. When did my little bro grow up on me?"

"About twelve years before *you* did."

Tom's mouth turns up into a lopsided grin. "If he's as serious about you as you are of him, he needs to include you. Inform you. Talk to you."

"He's trying. I think."

"What about his family? Do they support him? This isn't something you should take on by yourself."

"I haven't met them yet, but I think his brother is there for him. I just feel so…nervous. I don't want to, but I do."

"Just remember he's *not* his illness. It's a part of him, but he's still the same guy you first met."

I'm unable to prevent the small laugh that spills from my mouth. "The guy I first met was a dick, but even then I saw something more in him."

"Hold onto that. The *more*. And you know if he's being treated, which I assume he is, there's no reason to spend your life worrying, waiting for him to slip, because it might not happen. You can't live like that, either of you. People hear the words mental illness and immediately think *crazy*. But he's not crazy, and there's no reason you can't have a happy and positive relationship like anyone else."

"You think so?"

"I think it's important to be aware, arm yourself with as many facts as possible, about not only bipolar in general, but *his* bipolar and how it affects him, but don't let it become the biggest part of your relationship. Don't let it overshadow the man you fell in love with."

"Thanks, Tom. I wasn't sure whether to talk to you about this or not, but I'm glad I did."

"I'm glad, too. You're my little brother. You've annoyed the crap out of me since the day you were born but I'm here for you. I've probably never said it, but I assumed you knew that."

"I do. I wouldn't be here otherwise. I guess I'm just not used to having a serious conversation with you."

"Works both ways, right?"

My eyebrows pull together in confusion. "Um, course, yeah."

Tom groans, wiping his forehead on the back of his hand. "Jennifer's pregnant."

"Holy shit…"

Flipping roles, I spend the next twenty minutes being Tom's confidante. Unlike during *his* turn, however, I don't have any advice to offer. All I can do is listen, so that's what I do. By the time his pager sounds, ending our conversation, I realise he doesn't need my advice anyway. Understandably, he's nervous, but he and Jennifer seem to have things figured out. I'm going to be an uncle. *Fucking hell.* Even more bizarre, my brother is going to be a *dad.*

"A good friend of mine is in psychiatry," Tom says, pausing by the door. "I'll try and find out all I can for you."

"Thanks. I'd appreciate that."

"Gotta run, but call me anytime if you need anything. Got it?"

"Got it. Thanks."

Tom leaves, holding the pager clipped to the waistband of his pants as he jogs down the corridor. Folding my jacket over my forearm, I feel better than when I arrived. Reassured. This is still so new to me, but Tom's made me realise I've been seeing the future as a time spent waiting for the worst to happen, and it might not. I need to stop focusing on the bipolar, and start concentrating on James again.

* * *

I plan to head home after leaving the hospital, but I've not even turned the key in the ignition when my phone vibrates in my pocket, alerting me to a text.

Tess: Any chance u can disappear 4 the night? X
Me: What do you mean?
Tess: Lucy's here. I was hoping, coz ur the best friend in the whole world, that we could have the place to ourselves xxx

Is she seriously trying to kick me out of my own bloody flat?

Me: Who's Lucy???
Tess: Someone important. Fill u in tomoz. Pretty plz??? Xxx

Huffing, I roll my eyes. I'm knackered, irritable, and I want to go to bed.

Tess: With a cherry on top? And sprinkles. And whipped cream. I'll even throw in a flake??? X

Wow. This *Lucy* must be important. Tess *never* begs. I start to wonder why she hasn't mentioned her before and, in turn, begin to feel a little offended. We tell each other everything, or so I thought.

```
Me: Fine. But you're on washing up duty
for a week.
Tess: T - I FLOVE YOU! X
```

Great. Guess I'm left with two options – James or my mum. I know which I'd prefer, so I bring up James' number and hope he's not busy as I hit call. If I have to stay at my mum's it would mean getting up ridiculously early tomorrow morning to avoid the rush-hour traffic on the way back into Manchester.

"Holden," James barks upon picking up my call.

"Hey. It's me," I say, wondering why he doesn't already know that. I'm assuming by his curt greeting that he didn't look at the caller I.D. "You okay?"

"Sure." He doesn't sound even marginally convincing.

"I wanted to ask if I could stay with you tonight, but if you're busy…"

"I'm never too busy for you, Theodore."

I smile, relieved by his softer tone. "Tess has kinda kicked me out for the night. Are you at your apartment or the house?"

"Apartment."

"Have you eaten?"

"No."

Christ, plaiting shit would be easier than trying to tease more than a single word answer out of James right now. "Do you like Chinese?"

"Yes."

"Okay, I'll bring food. Be there in half an hour or so."

"Sure."

Ending the call, I sigh with concern. Something must've happened during the few hours we've been apart because there's no denying he's in a bad mood. There's no way to figure out what could be wrong without seeing him so, starting the engine, I set off to pick up dinner before heading straight to Spinningfields.

Armed with bags of food, I'm grateful to the security guy who opens the doors to James' building for me. When I reach the penthouse, I use the tip of my shoe to lightly kick the door instead of knocking.

"Shit," I mutter, noticing my foot has left behind a small scuff on the door. I'd obsess over it a little longer but it starts to open. Stepping inside, I see James is already walking away from me. I push the door closed behind me with my elbow and walk to the kitchen, setting the food bags down on the counter.

"What's wrong?" I ask, my tone cautious as I make my way over to the balcony where James is stood.

Sighing, he rips his fingers through his dark hair. "I lost the magazine contract," he spits. "All that fucking work. Gone."

"James..." I trail off when I realise I don't know what to say.

I put my hand on his shoulder, surprised when he flinches, but then he reaches up and clamps his fingers on mine. "I've lost so much fucking money. So much time and effort."

"There'll be other magazines," I say, regretting it immediately when he pulls away from me.

"You don't get it, Theodore! I've fucking failed! I had all these ideas, things that would make my father so fucking proud."

"He *is* proud of you." How could he not be?

"You didn't even know him."

Ouch. "Don't do that. Don't push me away."

My gaze falls to the floor while James stalks across the room, slamming his palms down on the kitchen counter. I've never seen him this angry and I don't like it. Risking a glance in his direction, I watch as his restless fingers drum against the black granite. His jaw ticks, the vein in his neck throbs, and I walk tentatively closer to him.

I want to know how he's feeling, but I can't decide if I'm more afraid to ask, or of the answer he might give me. Will this send him on a downward spiral? Is this the result of him already being there?

"Stop looking at me like that," James says, staring me square in the eyes.

"Like what?" *Concerned?*

"Like you're wondering if I'm having some kind of depressive episode. I'm allowed to be pissed off sometimes, Theodore, just like everyone else."

"I know that. I'm sorry, I just…" Frustrated with myself, with *him*, with this whole fucking situation, I draw in a long breath. "This is new to me."

Tipping his head back, James sighs. He steps towards me, settling his hands on my waist. "I'm sorry."

"I guess we still have a lot to talk about."

"And we will, but let's eat first." Pressing his lips to mine, he smiles against my mouth.

When he steps back, I reach for the bags on the counter. "I wasn't sure what you liked, so I got a selection."

"Is that chicken fried rice?" he asks when I pull out the first tub. I nod in response. "That's mine."

Grinning, I hand him the tub and, after grabbing two forks, he takes it over to the sofa. I follow him with the rest of the food and sit down next to him before peeling the lid off my crispy beef.

"I want you to meet my brother."

My hand freezes, hovering the forkful of food just inches from my mouth.

"Besides *you*, Max is the person who knows me best. I think it would be beneficial for you to know each other."

"You make it sound like a business meeting."

"You'll like him. He's nothing like me."

"I like you."

"But you didn't at first," he says with a cheeky smile that makes my stomach flutter. "Max is a nice guy. He makes a better first impression than I do."

"You don't speak about your mum much." I didn't plan to say that, and I wonder if I've overstepped the mark. Then, defiantly, I decide there shouldn't be a mark. We're a couple. We should share.

"She's my mum, and I love her, but I've never found it easy to talk to her. I've always been afraid of her judging me, or thinking I'm weak."

No parent could think that. *Could they?* "She knows you're gay though, right?"

"Yes. She wasn't exactly thrilled but she accepted it…eventually."

"Eventually?" Of course I know some parents don't take the news well, but I can only imagine how that feels. When I told *my* parents, my mum patted my shoulder and my dad told me not to forget the milk on my way home from school.

"She asked me why, told me how disappointed she was, and then asked me what she did wrong. Now? We just don't talk about it."

"How does that work? Have you never introduced her to one of your boyfriends before?"

"You're my first." His words tickle something deep inside my chest. "You know, when I was thirteen I made a friend online. The internet was new back then, we were the first out of my friends to get it, and I was so grateful to it because I got to say things I couldn't say in person."

"You mean in, like, a chat room?"

"Yes. There weren't the same dangers associated with it then. I got chatting to another boy who also thought he was gay. We told each other everything. It was easier, I suppose, when you didn't have to look each other in the eye. One day he told me his parents were starting to monitor his internet access, so we exchanged addresses. I wrote to him a few times but never received a reply. Or so I thought."

"What do you mean?"

"I discovered years later, from my father, that my mum opened them and threw them away before I could read them."

"*Why?*"

"Because she didn't want me to be gay."

What kind of stupid reasoning is that? Clearly, her tactics didn't work. "So what happened when you found out?"

"I laughed it off. Inside, even though I was an adult, it kind of hurt to know she'd taken my only friend, my only confidant, away from me. But she stood by her actions, so, like I always do, I brushed it off."

It makes no sense to me. James doesn't strike me as a man who yields to anyone. He never has. He doesn't suffer fools and he's most certainly not afraid to speak his mind, especially if he's right.

"She's my mum," he adds, shrugging, as if that's a reasonable explanation.

I don't like her already. "Maybe, but that was wrong of her."

As was the fact she left a suicidal teenage boy to vomit his attempt at ending his life into the toilet alone.

"This is cold," I mutter around my first mouthful of crispy beef. I've been too busy talking to eat. Putting it on the coffee table in front of me, I pop the lid back on.

"I can put it in the microwave," James offers, reaching for the plastic tub.

I raise my hand. "I'm not that hungry anymore. I'll eat it tomorrow."

"Fancy a shower before bed?"

"Together?"

Grinning, James stands and takes my hand. His answer glistens in his eyes as he winks and pulls me toward the bathroom.

I've been hard since I heard the word shower.

Chapter Ten

~James~

Two months later…

Peeling my eyes open, my head on Theodore's chest, I find his arms wrapped around me and snuggle further into them.

"You awake?" he whispers, running his thumb up and down my colourful arm.

"Mmhmm."

Over the last couple of months, Theodore has spent most nights at my apartment, or house, but last night I stayed at his place. It's Sunday, and he's taking me to meet his family this afternoon. The thought leaves me with a heavy stomach, but apparently he can't put his mother off much longer. She wants to meet me. *Me.*

I'm sure her mind will soon change once she has.

"Coffee?" he asks, kissing the top of my head.

"In a minute. I'm comfortable."

A small sigh escapes his mouth. "I need the toilet," he says, prizing himself out from underneath me. "And if I don't wake Tess now we'll be late."

"Right. Your mum's."

"She'll love you." It's not until Theodore replies I realise I spoke my thoughts aloud.

"You don't know that. I'm not a likeable man, Theodore."

"She'll love you because *I* love you."

I still haven't uttered those three tiny words to him yet. I feel it, I think, but I can't quite bring myself to say it. If I do, it almost feels like I'm giving him false hope.

"Talk to her like you do to *me* rather than the way you treat everyone else, and you'll be fine." He finishes the sentence with a wink that does little to reassure me. "I was just as nervous when I met Max for the first time."

I can appreciate that. When he met my brother, two months ago, it was more than an introduction. They were meeting as the only two people who know about my mental illness, and I know they discussed me when I headed out to pick up a takeaway.

"That was different. There's no way anybody couldn't like you."

"That's not the impression I got, not straightaway."

"What are you talking about?" Max likes Theodore. He told me.

"Before he left, he pulled me to one side and told me that if I didn't think I could handle your worst, I should walk away."

Fucker! I'll be having words with him. "And? Do you think you could?"

"Yes," he answers without hesitation. I don't know how much he truly believes that, and I hope he never has to test his theory. But…some days, lately, I feel like that day is coming. "Now get up." He looks down at his watch. "My mum will already have the meat in the oven."

"I just don't want to mess it up," I add. "They're important to you."

"And *you're* important to *me*. I can't offer you any more reassurance because I *really* need to piss…" After blowing me a kiss, he's gone before I can reply.

Climbing out of Theodore's bed, I groan from the ache in my muscles. He owns the most uncomfortable mattress I've ever slept on and I decide I'm going to replace it. He doesn't accept things from me without protest but, this time, I have the perfect incentive. If he wants me to stay over again, he'll let me buy him a new bed.

Shrugging into one of his t-shirts, I wander into the main living space. Tess is awake, but still curled up on the mattress on the floor next to the TV.

"Coffee?" I ask her.

Nodding her head, she stretches her arms above her head. "Sleep well?"

"No."

She laughs, and I know further explanation isn't needed. "You nervous?"

I force a flippant laugh. "No."

"Liar."

"Excuse me?"

"*Everyone* gets nervous about meeting the parents. Unless you have a heart of steel, which for a while there I thought you did, but now I know better."

"Oh, you do, eh?"

"I saw the tear in your eye when we watched The Fault in Our Stars."

Reaching for the coffee in the cupboard, I shake my head. "There was no tear."

"There was a tear."

"What tear?"

Glancing up from the empty mugs, I see Theodore coming towards me. Snaking his arms around my waist, he moulds himself to my back, resting his head on my shoulder. Tess is right. My heart can't be made of steel because it started racing the second I heard Theodore's voice.

"Tess thinks she saw a tear on my face when we watched The Fault in Our Stars."

"Oh, there *was* a tear."

"Whose side are you on?" I say, shrugging out of his hold to grab the kettle.

"The side of the truth. Also, I'm not brave enough to disagree with Tess, especially when I want her to iron my top while I'm in the shower."

Holding his hands in the praying position, he looks to Tess with puppy-eyes. "Before you object, remember I'm leaving the flat for you and Lucy tonight."

Tess huffs. "Fine. Your favourite one?"

"Yeah."

"You have a favourite top?" I ask, handing him a cup of coffee.

"My Diesel one with the white stitching." I don't know which top he's referring to but it makes me smile nonetheless. It's only a small thing, but I love the fact we're still learning about each other.

When Theodore disappears into the bathroom with his mug, I join Tess in the living room and watch her iron Theodore's t-shirt on top of a towel on the living room floor. We talk about Lucy for a few minutes, who I've only met a couple of times, then she steers the conversation onto Theodore's mother, causing the nerves to flood back into my stomach.

* * *

The smell of lamb arouses my nose when Theodore leads me into his mother's house. It's a small terrace and the front door opens up straight into the living room. A man stands from the couch to greet us, and although we haven't met before, I know it's Tom, Theodore's brother. They're shockingly similar, even the way they walk, but when Tom shakes my hand I notice his eyes are a different colour.

"Tom, James. James, Tom," Theodore introduces us and I offer a small nod as Tom releases my hand. It's a little discomforting knowing this man, this stranger, knows *all* about me, things my own family have no idea about. Still, I'm glad Theodore has someone knowledgeable to discuss my illness with when he doesn't feel like he can talk to me.

"Nice to meet you, Tom."

"Likewise." Tom's gaze flips to his brother. "Mum's doing the gravy. Go in at your own risk."

"I'm not that stupid. I'll wait for her to come out here."

"Where's Tess?"

"She's making her own way. She should be here soon."

I hover awkwardly, with my hands in my pockets, while Theodore and Tom chat about their week, and Tom's new shoes. After several minutes, Tom turns to me and asks about Holden House. He's making polite conversation, but it isn't something I particularly want to discuss, so I'm relieved when we're interrupted by a woman too young to be their mother.

"I've been banished," she says before kissing Tom on the cheek. This must be Jennifer, Tom's girlfriend. "Hi!" she adds, her voice chirpy, looking at Theodore and I.

"This is James," Tom says. "Theo's boyfriend."

She offers her hand for me to shake. "I'm Jennifer."

"Jennifer!" the lady who I assume is Theodore's mother scolds, wiping her hands on her apron. She doesn't look like Theodore, so I assume he and Tom take after their father. "I told you and that little grandbaby of mine to sit down. You need to take care of yourself."

Jennifer smiles and rolls her eyes at the same time, before perching herself on the edge of the floral armchair. I'm finding all these unfamiliar faces a little overwhelming. I meet new people every day in my job, but this is different. This is informal and requires idle, friendly chitchat, which unfortunately has never been my forte. In business, I'm direct and authoritative. I'm not there to be liked. I'm there to be listened to. I say what needs to be said and nothing more. Talking in a social setting, however, necessitates a whole different skillset, which I don't possess.

"Mum, this is James," Theodore says.

Dropping the cushion she's fluffing behind Jennifer's back, Mrs Davenport spins immediately as if she didn't know we'd arrived. "Oh!" she sings, lunging towards me. Placing her hands on my shoulders, she kisses my cheek. "You're a smoker."

My smile falters as she steps away. "Yes," I reply, forcing the word through my suddenly narrowed throat.

"Did Theo tell you his grandma died of lung cancer?"

"Um, *yes*. He did."

The way she stares into my eyes makes me feel twelve years old again. "Hmm."

Great. She disapproves of me already.

"Go easy, Mum," Theodore says. The bastard is grinning.

"They'll be nothing easy about sitting on the edge of his deathbed." Theodore opens his mouth to respond, but Mrs Davenport carries on talking. "Now sit down in the dining room. I'm going to plate up."

Tom and Jennifer follow her out of the room and I turn to Theodore, combing my nervous fingers through my hair. "She hates me."

Theodore laughs, and for a second, I *really* dislike him. "She doesn't. She's just one of those really annoying reformed smokers. Just be yourself, and she'll fall in love with you."

My eyebrow lifts of its own accord.

"Okay, maybe not *completely* yourself," he teases. "Leave the arrogant arsehole version of you at the door."

I'd laugh if I wasn't so nervous. It's a strange feeling. I'm used to being the voice of authority, dismissing other people's opinions. I find situations like this awkward. It's one of the reasons I rarely visit my *own* family.

"Relax, James," Theodore says, squeezing my tense shoulder as he leads me into the dining room.

Taking a seat on one of the wooden chairs, I scan the floral wallpaper rather than make eye-contact with anyone. For a while, Theodore and Tom chatter amongst themselves, while I simply listen, admiring the *easy* relationship these brothers seem to have.

Tess arrives just as Mrs Davenport is bringing out our meals, bursting into the house shouting, "Sorry I'm late!" while wrestling out of her coat. Sitting opposite Theodore, she takes a plate from Mrs Davenport. "Ooo, beef! You're spoiling us, Angela."

"It's lamb," Mrs Davenport corrects.

"Well, whatever it is smells chuffing amazing."

Much to my surprise, I start to relax while we're eating. Conversation centres around Jennifer and the baby scan she had last week, and then it moves to Tess, who lies about where she's been. She was with Lucy, yet she tells Mrs Davenport she had to nip into work to discuss an error on her wage slip.

Naturally, being fresh meat at the table, questions eventually turn to me and I answer as politely as I can. I'm unintentionally vague, and I find myself dancing around personal questions and directing the attention towards Theodore.

"Any plans for your birthday, Theo?" Tom asks, making my ears prick up.

It's his birthday soon? I realise it's something we've never talked about and it makes me feel like a shitty boyfriend.

"It's four months away. I haven't thought about it."

"Twenty-eight," Mrs Davenport cuts in. "How did my babies get so old so fast?"

Turning my head, I notice Theodore grinning and shaking his head. *Game over*. His mother just revealed his age. I'm still waiting for him to tell me himself, but what he doesn't know is that Tess already told me weeks ago.

Mrs Davenport's intense stare, which continues to unnerve me, lands on my face. "Maybe you could surprise him with a ring, James?" Her statement comes out like a question, knocking the air from my lungs, and I start to wonder if this is what anaphylactic shock feels like.

"*Mum*," Theodore says, his tone low, scolding.

"Have you thought about settling down?" she continues, still looking at me. "What are your plans for the future?"

"Tess has got a girlfriend!" Theodore pipes up, and I want to kiss him until I can't feel my lips.

The scuffle under the table when Tess very obviously kicks Theodore's leg makes everyone, except Mrs Davenport, snicker.

"Ooo, what's her name? When are you bringing her for dinner?"

There's a look in Tess' eyes that makes me think she's plotting Theodore's murder as she speaks, but still, she goes on to tell Mrs Davenport all about Lucy – what she looks like, the dates they've been on.

I listen for a while, but then my mind reverts to her comment about settling down. Suddenly, it's all I can think about. I haven't given much thought to my future with Theodore, my future in general. Life is easier to deal with when you take one day at a time. But what if that isn't the way Theodore copes with life? Has *he* thought about settling down? Marriage? Is that what he wants? Is that what he expects from *me*? If it is, I'm just not sure I can give it to him.

So where does that leave us?

"…James?"

My name snaps me back into the room and I look up to Tom. "Sorry, what was that?" Feeling awkward, I feign a smile before popping my last piece of roast potato in my mouth.

"Tess was saying how she enjoys working with Lucy. Do you find Theodore working with you a good thing?"

"Theodore works *for*, not *with* me."

When Tom's eyes grow a little wider I realise *that* right there is the arsehole side of me Theodore talks about, and I immediately laugh in an attempt to brush it off as a joke. "We work in different parts of the building so we don't spend much of our time together but, yes, I enjoy *all* time spent with Theodore, both in *and* out of the office."

"Ugh, pass me a bucket," Tess says, pulling a face.

Mrs Davenport presses a hand to her chest and sighs. "That's lovely to hear, James."

It's the first time she's looked at me like I haven't been scraped off the bottom of her shoe and I smile with relief. "Your son is very important to me, Mrs Davenport." It's the best I have to offer.

"I'm glad to hear it," she says, with what looks like a genuine smile plastered on her weathered face.

The rest of the afternoon passes fairly smoothly. We eat lemon meringue pie for pudding, we listen to Tom talk about some of the more unusual cases he's had to deal with at the hospital, and somehow, I end up talking for over twenty minutes about my father and the good times we shared together.

My eyes rarely leave Theodore as he interacts with his family. The relationship between them is so natural, effortless. Everyone in the room, bar me, feels comfortable whining, laughing, or even poking fun at each other, and I find myself grieving for an atmosphere I've never experienced in my own life.

Being around *my* family has always felt forced and uneasy. I've always felt this need to *act,* pretend to be the man they *expect* me to be. The only exception to this was my father, and that was only during the last few years of his life. When Max and I were children, our father worked eighty-hour weeks, trying to compete with the bigger publishing houses. It was only when we became adults, the business grew and my father sought out a silent business partner and executives to share the workload, that he had time to really get to know his children.

My father understood me. He didn't fall for my bullshit attitude and, somehow, could always tell when something troubled me, if I was struggling, even when nobody else did. One Friday night he took me away on a golfing weekend to celebrate my third novel hitting the New York Times bestseller list, an achievement I owe completely to him, to his encouragement, his faith in me. I'm sure luck played a generous part, too. Publishing was different then. Until several years ago, before indie authors found success, the market was much less saturated, giving a good story an easier chance to shine.

I can't swing a club for shit, but I enjoyed spending time alone with him. That was the weekend I told him about my diagnosis. I expected him to be shocked, tell me I needed to tell my mother…but instead, he enveloped me in a bear-hug, patted my back, and took me straight back out onto the course.

We talked about it in more detail when we got home, but for that weekend I wasn't a writer or a businessman, I wasn't an actor, and I *wasn't* bipolar…I was just a boy hanging out with his dad.

I miss him.

* * *

Back at my house, I toss my keys into the glass bowl on the table in the long hallway. "You have a great family," I say to Theodore, who's making his way through to the kitchen. I overtake him and fill a glass with water at the sink. "Although I'm still not sure your mother likes me very much."

Theodore's body presses flush against my back, his chin resting on my shoulder. "She's just making sure you're good enough for her boy." I can hear the smile in his voice.

Resting my head against his, I close my eyes, the warmth of his skin travelling through my body. "And am I?" I whisper. "Am I good enough for you?"

You know you're not.

"How many times do I have to tell you? I wouldn't be here if you weren't."

He sounds almost frustrated and, honestly, I can't blame him. I'm not only fucked in the head, I'm insecure, too, and it's something I only learned about myself after meeting Theodore. I've never been afraid of losing anything before because I've never allowed myself to become attached. The funny thing is I didn't *allow* myself to get attached to Theodore. I was simply powerless to stop it.

"Are you okay, James?" he asks, gripping my waist and slowly turning me around. "You seem a little distracted lately."

Am I? I must try harder. "It's just the business. I need to let some people go."

"Why?" His eyes widen.

"The deal I lost has cost us. I've been left with no choice but to close the design department and sub-contract out to freelancers."

My explanation is partly true. The magazine deal *has* lost us money – something which Gerard, my father's, and subsequently *my*, business partner is *not* happy about. He's a silent partner who doesn't deal with the day-to-day running and decision making, but he owns forty percent, and so in situations like this, I'm forced to validate his opinion. But truthfully, my reckless spending is responsible for pushing Holden House to almost breaking point.

When I met with my accountant last week he presented me with a mountain of invoices and contracts that I don't even remember ordering, yet there's no denying the signatures on the documents are mine. Agreements for office furniture, building work, and a new Beemer, which is arriving next week, stared me in the face and I have no recollection whatsoever of arranging *any* of them. Worst of all, profit figures for the last quarter are the lowest we've seen in six years and I didn't even notice.

My personal accounts show I'm not poor, by any means, but the balance is no longer growing which means I need to make some drastic changes before I'm, eventually, left with nothing.

My father must be so disappointed with me.

"I had no idea," Theodore says.

I shrug. "It doesn't affect you. Your department is safe." *For now…*

"It affects *you*, and you affect me."

Silence follows and I start to feel nervous…or is it guilt? I can't decide. All I know is that I'm, suddenly, acutely aware of every breath I take.

My fringe, usually swept to the side and held in place with wax, has fallen slightly. Reaching up, Theodore combs it back into place with his fingers. "And this is what's getting you down?"

"I'm not down. A little stressed, but I'm fine. I promise." I'm a lying bastard and I hate myself for it. We've had a few similar conversations over the last couple of months, where Theodore asks how I'm feeling and I lie through my worthless fucking teeth. A relationship shouldn't be this way. He shouldn't be constantly worrying about me. It's a burden he doesn't deserve.

I miss his smile. It's radiant, it *heals* me, yet I've barely seen it in a couple of weeks. He's a fun person, positive, and I'm sucking it out of him. I *want* to romance him, take him to dinner, on adventures, repeat the magic of the funfair…but, right now, leaving the house, even to go to work, fills me with dread. The fact I can't do that for him is testament to how selfish I am.

It's time to see the doctor. You know it is.

I can beat this on my own. I'll start taking my meds again.

It's too late for that. Talk to someone. Max, Theodore…just open your mouth and be honest.

"I'm okay, Theodore," I say, *lie*, palming his cheek. "Come to bed with me. Help me forget about the real world for a few hours."

Smiling, he presses his lips to mine. "Lead the way."

* * *

Two weeks later…

"…uncertainty. I demand to know what your plans are!"

Mike has been chewing my arse off for half an hour now, and I switched off about twenty-five minutes ago. I'm rarely in the mood for Mike, but today my patience is wearing especially thin since my mother's impromptu visit this morning. Gerard, my business partner, has found out about the financial mistakes I've made and, instead of being an adult and discussing it with me, he tattletaled to my mother.

'Why are you so irresponsible?'

'Your father trusted you. What do you think he'd say?'

'If you're not cut out for this, then I'll get Gerard in full time.'

Those are just a snippet of the things she had to say while I did nothing but stare at the light switch over her shoulder and pretend to listen. On another day I might worry about the points she raised, especially the one about my father, but today…today I'm too tired to give a shit. She has no shares in this business, something I *know* pissed her off when my father decided to leave his entire stake to me, so it's none of her fucking business.

Briefly, I look up from the document I'm reading and make eye-contact with Mike. "You're not in a position to demand anything. You work *for* me, not with me. Your department is safe. That's all you need to know."

"That's not good enough."

"Well that's all you're getting. Now, is there anything else? I'm busy." I'm not, I just want him to fuck off. I want *everyone* to fuck off. I don't know how much longer I can *pretend* for. I've tried the breathing exercises that are supposed to quell anxiety…and they do nothing. They don't take away the boulder in my stomach, the nervous flutter in my chest, or the feeling that everyone can *see* that I'm losing it. All they do is make me feel fucking stupid.

I need to be alone.

"Fine, but I'll be seeing a union rep over this."

Shaking in my boots over here. Twat. "That's your right."

With a frustrated huff, Mike straightens his tie and stomps out of my office like a spoilt child. The door has barely closed before another knock sounds and I slam the pen I'm holding onto the desk in temper. "*What?*" I bark.

"Bad time?" Theodore asks, popping his head around the door.

I gesture toward the chair opposite my desk. "Not anymore."

He tries to be subtle, but I still notice him scan Helen's office to see if she's there before he walks past the chair and perches himself on the edge of my desk. We haven't officially announced our relationship, but I'm pretty certain most people here know regardless. I don't employ stupid people.

"Have you eaten yet? You missed breakfast again," he asks, stroking along my cheek with the back of his hand. I fake a smile and slowly shift in my seat, distancing myself. I don't want him to touch me. It takes all my effort to tolerate it when he does. We haven't had sex for over a week and it makes no sense because Theodore means so much to me…yet his touch feels like ants crawling over my skin.

"Yes," I lie. "I grabbed a sandwich earlier."

"Did you drink the Lemsip's I bought you?"

Right. I have a 'cold'. That's the excuse I gave Theodore for being a little withdrawn lately. I *hate* that he believed me so easily. Sometimes I think I *want* him to push me, force me to *talk* to him, but he doesn't. And why would he? He trusts me. He doesn't know what a lying piece of scum I am.

"Yes. I feel much better."

"You still look rough. I'll get you some energy drinks on my way home from work. You've lost weight." His fingers wander to my chin, stroking my thick stubble. "And you need to shave."

"Did you just come here to insult me?" I snap.

"I'm worried about you. Your eyes are dark. Didn't you sleep well?"

"I slept fine." If anything I slept for too long. I have no energy lately. My bones ache and my head hurts. Sleep is the only thing that takes it all away.

Until I wake up.

"Get to the point, Theodore."

"Tess called. She's just taken a delivery for a new bed and a sofa." He sounds angry instead of grateful.

"Oh good." I check my watch. "They were earlier than expected."

"You can't do this shit without consulting me, James. I don't need your charity."

My eyes roll dramatically into the back of my head. "Don't be ridiculous. We're a couple. I'm not *donating* them to you. I bought them for *us*."

"You don't even live there."

It's like he's flipped a switch in my brain, sending me from calm to pissed off as hell in a nanosecond. When he's in *my* home, I consider it *his* space, too. "Then send them back," I snap. "I've got bigger things to worry about than a hissy fit over fucking furniture."

"Right. Like the business failing. *More* reason why you shouldn't be wasting your money on stuff I don't need."

He *does* need it, but clearly it's not my place, as his fucking *partner*, to interfere. "It's not failing." My tone is acidic and I'm sure my expression isn't too friendly either. "And even if it was it's none of your concern."

"Of course it is. We're a couple."

"Only when it suits *you*, evidently."

Standing, Theodore huffs and strides over to the other side of the room. "Now *you're* being ridiculous."

"Am I? If I'm so ridiculous why don't you just leave?"

"Leave?"

"Yes. My office, my life…just *go*."

"Don't be so stupid."

"So I'm stupid now, too?"

"I didn't mean it like that and you know it. Stop being a dick, James."

I'm not sure how or why this argument occurred, but I'm vibrating with anger and I can't control it. I *know* I'm not being fair. I *know* I'm pushing him away. But I can't stop it.

"Look," he begins, his voice soft and gentle as he walks back towards me. "I'm sorry. I didn't come in here to argue with you."

When he closes in I stand from my chair, keeping distance between us. "Yes you did. You're angry with me and you wanted me to know it."

"I'm not angry with you."

"*Liar!*" I spit, closing the gap between our bodies. "You're angry and now you're backing down because you don't want to push me too far. You're pussyfooting around me just like you *always* do. You think I'm unstable and it scares you."

"James…" he tries to interrupt but I ignore him.

"What's the matter? Huh?" With the palms of my hands, I shove him in the chest. "Are you scared I'm going to break? Snap? *Hurt* you? Come on, Theodore, be a fucking man and give it to me straight!"

"Stop it."

"You're angry! *Be* fucking angry! Stop being afraid of me and tell me how you feel!" I jab him again and he stumbles back a step. "Tell me dammit! Shout. Yell. Be fucking mad at me for once!"

"*No.*" Turning his back and stalking away, he remains calm, which pisses me off even further. "I relented because I don't want to fight with you. I don't like arguing, not because your reaction scares me, but because I fucking *love* you. Don't start throwing your illness around because that's *no* excuse for talking to me like I'm a piece of shit, and I *won't* put up with that from you."

I knew this moment would come eventually.

You're overreacting. Apologise.

"Finally," I say, exhaling a sarcastic laugh. "I'll drop anything of yours from my house at your workstation tomorrow."

"*What?*"

"You're done, right? Good. Because so am I."

"Don't be-"

Enough now. Stop it. He's done nothing wrong.

"Stupid? Ridiculous? Come on, Theodore, tell me what you really think."

"I'm not leaving you. I never implied that."

"Yeah? Well I'm leaving *you*!"

Stomping to my office door, I unhook my jacket from the hook and toss it over my shoulder.

With my hand covering the doorknob, Theodore attempts to stop me but I drag myself out of his grip and yank the door open so forcefully it bangs into the wall.

Searing rage floods my veins as I storm out of the building. I don't know why I'm so angry, but I've lost charge of my emotions and I don't know how to get it back, or if I even can.

Twenty minutes later, I find myself in my apartment, not remembering how I got here. I head straight to the bathroom, hoping a bath will relax me enough to think clearly again. I sit in the steaming water for thirty minutes or so, my mind tormenting me the whole time. By the time I'm standing in the kitchen debating whether to make coffee, dressed only in a towel, I loathe myself, and my life.

Staring at my marred body in the bathtub disgusted me.

I'm ugly.

Selfish.

Unreasonable.

Theodore won't admit it but he *is* mad at me, and so he should be. Not over the furniture, but at the kind of person I am. Maybe he doesn't realise it yet but how I acted in the office is who I am. We simply haven't been together long enough for him to know there will be plenty more of that in our future. I'm unstable. I push people away. He deserves better than that, better than *me*.

Say Something by A Great Big World trickles from the speakers in my iPod dock and I crank up the volume in an effort to distract myself from the ballooning anger in my chest. At least, I tell myself it's a distraction, but I know damn well I'm purposely torturing myself. This playlist is a collection of trigger songs for me, songs that amplify the misery strangling my heart. These are the songs I used to listen to when I cut myself, or when life started getting good and I needed to bring myself down before I learned to enjoy it. These are the songs that remind me what a fucked-up bastard I am…and *that* is why I pressed play. I *need* reminding before I convince myself that I can be good enough for Theodore.

As the lyrics pour into my ears I can't help but smile at the irony. If only I *could* say something, maybe then I won't push him to the point where he has no choice but to walk away.

Because I *will.*

I don't plan to throw the mug I'm holding and the action doesn't register until I hear it smash against the wall. The balloon has burst and a powerful urge to destroy everything in sight overwhelms me. Flattening my forearm against the granite surface, I send everything on the counter crashing to the floor in one swift movement.

Spinning on my heels, I kick the fridge, pain shooting up my toes and into my foot. The pain is the least I deserve, so I do it again, and again, before ripping open the cupboards and dragging the contents out with my fist. Finally, my strength weakening, I punch several dents into the wall before sliding down against it and curling into a ball on top of the scene of destruction that mirrors the inside of my head.

"James?"

I think I hear my name but I'm sobbing so violently there's every possibility I imagined it.

"James?"

Arms wrap around my shivering body and I don't realise how cold I am until I feel the warmth of Theodore's skin penetrate mine. "James, talk to me."

I will my mouth to open, to explain that I'm so engulfed in pain I feel like I'm dying, but it won't. The sobs slowly wane as Theodore's hands smooth over my naked skin but silent tears continue to roll mournfully down my cheeks.

"It's okay," he whispers in my ear, his breath caressing my flesh like a blanket. "I'm here. You're okay."

"It hurts, Theodore," I croak, the words splitting on my lips. "Hurts so fucking much."

Palming my cheeks, he twists my face until I'm looking at him. "Where?" he asks, his expression contorted with concern and confusion. "Are you injured?"

"My head, my chest…it hurts." I'm not sure if I've said the words aloud and part of me hopes I haven't. I don't want him to know. He shouldn't be here, see me like this…but I can't seem to pull myself together and move.

He uncurls himself from my naked body, my towel is missing, and my skin mourns the loss of his warmth by shivering.

Linking my arm at the elbow, he tugs gently. "Can you stand?"

In my head, I nod, but the action doesn't materialise. Using his arm for support, I pull myself up until I'm standing, head down, eyes fixed on the littered floor.

Slowly, he leads me over to the living room, and every step I take is an effort. Being alive is an effort. Every minute feels like an hour, every day like a month.

I'm so tired.

Theodore stops by the couch. "Look at me, James," he says, his hands resting tentatively on my shoulders.

I don't. I *can't.*

"*Please,*" he adds, his voice a desperate whisper as he places one finger under my chin, encouraging my head to rise.

Reluctantly, my gaze lands on his face, my vision hazy through the cloud of tears. "Take it away, Theodore."

I don't realise what I'm begging for until his tender lips graze mine. "I don't know how."

Tracing the edge of his lips with my tongue, I plead with him. "Make me forget."

Unsure, he kisses me softly, absorbing my pain, distracting me. Initially, I'm frozen, but when his tongue dips between my lips I melt into him, moulding my hands to the back of his head.

Mouths fused together, I blindly unbutton his shirt and roll it over his shoulders, pulling him into me, skin to skin. I can feel his heart thumping against the walls of his chest, as fast and erratically as my own and I press my hand against it, losing myself in the rhythm.

My heart beats.

I'm alive.

"I-I'm sorry," Theodore murmurs, breaking our kiss.

"No," I beg, touching my nose to his. "Take it away. *Please*, if only for a little while. I need this. Need *you*."

A single tear balances on his cheek and I kiss it away before burying my nose in his neck, inhaling the unique scent of him that never fails to calm me. Reaching between our bodies, I smooth my palms down his chest until they land on his buckle and I unfasten it before starting on his pants.

Falling to my knees, I bring his trousers with me and hover my mouth in front of his hard cock, while rubbing my palms up and down the back of his thighs. The muscles in his legs are strong and sculpted, despite him neglecting his running of late, and I relish the firmness under my fingers as I wrap my mouth around his swollen head.

"God, James…"

Every word, every moan that leaves Theodore's lips heals my fractured soul a little more. It won't last, of course, as a voice in my head continues to remind me, but I don't stop trying to push those thoughts away. I focus on Theodore, the feel of him in my mouth, the taste on my tongue, the sounds trickling from his throat…

Until he pulls back and falls to his knees in front of me.

"I don't know how to help you," he whispers, pain creasing his forehead as he rests it on mine.

"Make love to me, Theodore."

Raising his head, eyes a little wider, he studies my face. "You mean…"

"Yes," I breathe. "I want to feel you inside me. I *need* you."

He replies with actions, cupping both sides of my neck and caressing my lips with the gentlest of kisses. His fingertips sear my flesh as he runs them down my chest, making me forget everything and everyone else in the world. His touch is all I can think about, and when he kisses his way down to my cock, I'm just a regular guy, a *normal* guy, aching to be taken by the man I love.

"I love you, Theodore," I admit for the first time, my voice a breathy whisper.

"James, you don't have to"-

"I mean it. I love that you're here, that you're trying to understand. I love your smile…" I run my finger across his lips. "Your laugh. I even love the little creases in your forehead when you're pissed off with me. Just an hour ago I was suffocating, and now, with your skin on mine, I can breathe."

"James," he murmurs.

Placing one finger over his lips, I hush him. "I *love* you." It's probably the most honest, yet also the most selfish, thing I've ever said.

Sensing his hesitancy, I lie down on the floor, the thick rug soft under my back, and guide his hand to my cock. Locking my fingers over his, I slide his grip up and down my shaft, our gazes never parting.

Bending, Theodore peppers kisses across my chest, over my scars, over my heart, and I let go of all the hurt I felt just minutes ago. My pulse pounds in my throat, my breath catches, and when his lips land on my balls I lose all sense of who I am.

And it's beautiful.

"I love you," I whisper, arching my back and forcing myself into his mouth. "I love you."

Now I've said it once, I can't seem to stop repeating it. I need him to know, to *believe*, to *feel* it.

His mouth is too full to reply, but he moans against my weeping head and I feel the vibrations throughout my whole body.

"Oh God, Theodore…" I rasp when he slides a finger between his lips because I know what's about to happen. My legs fall open a little wider and I stare at his curious expression as he gently pushes his finger inside me. My instinctive reaction is to tense, urge him away, but I fight it.

"Relax, James," he says, crawling onto his knees until he's nose-to-nose with me. "Focus on me. Just me. Let everything else go."

Closing my eyes, I flick out my tongue, licking his lips as he draws his finger in and out of my body before adding another. He's warm on my skin, his breath sweeps over my face, yet he still feels too far away.

"*Now,* Theodore. I need to feel you *now.*"

Easing his fingers out of me, he settles them on my balls, making me groan at the delicious heat encasing them. With one hand on my cheek, he smiles, and I'm mesmerised by the glisten in his vivid green eyes which are just inches away from my own. "Not yet."

Sagging with disappointment, my eyebrows knit together in confusion. Does he want me to beg? *Because I will.*

"Theod-" I trail off when, still grinning, he crawls lower, kneeling between my legs.

The heat of his mouth hits me just seconds later as he licks small circles around my hole before sinking inside, making my thighs clench in desperation.

"Holy shit," I whimper, fisting his hair.

Warmth. Moisture. Pleasure. *Love.*

My breaths trickle from my throat in long, deep sighs until I feel like I might literally combust if he doesn't fill the ache in my ass, the need in my heart, right fucking now.

"Please, Theodore…"

He draws a zigzag up the seam of my balls with the tip of his tongue, along the rigid shaft, before finishing with a gentle flick on my swollen tip. "Wait there."

I couldn't move even if I wanted to. Goosebumps mottle my skin, mourning the loss of him as I watch him dig into my jacket pocket on the hook by the door. He rips open the condom as he walks back to me, rolling it over his perfect erection before dropping to his knees in front of me.

Instinctively, I start to roll over, but he stops me, keeping me in place with a firm hand on my shoulder. "I want you here with me," he says. "I want to see you. *Watch* you."

Nodding weakly, I offer a nervous smile while Theodore rips open the sachet of lube he found in my jacket. He drizzles some onto his cock first before, unexpectedly, doing the same to mine. Taking my hand, he curls my fingers around my throbbing dick and encourages me to massage in the silky coolness before resting his chest on top of mine, my knuckles brushing his taut stomach with every stroke.

I draw up my knees and, reaching down, he positions his tip at my puckered entrance. I swallow down the small lump of anxiety in my throat. It's been years since I've let someone take me this way, and never once have I looked anyone in the eye when they did. But this is Theodore. I need him. I trust him. I *want* to look at him.

With his intense stare fixed on mine, he pushes inside, forcing a rush of emotion buried deep inside my mind to the surface. It burns a little as he stretches me and a silent tear seeps from the corner of my eye – not because of the discomfort, but from the fact I feel whole, complete, for the first time in my life. I realise, when he stills, allowing my body to mould to him, that we're connected more deeply than I ever thought possible. Body and soul. Heart to heart. He's the piece of me I never knew I was missing.

"Move, Theodore," I choke out, my ass pulsating around him, begging for his delicious friction.

He does. He slips in and out torturously slowly, wiping the tear that I didn't feel fall from my cheek. "I've got you," he whispers. "I'm here."

I don't speak. I can barely breathe as he cups the back of my neck, his other hand gripping my thigh as he plunges into me a little faster. The sting has disappeared, replaced with a craving for him to go harder, deeper…and as if he can read the demand in my expression, he does.

"Fuck, James," he pants, glowing heat crawling across his neck, spreading onto his pale chest.

Hand still on my cock, I start to tug, knowing it will be over in seconds. "I'm close, Theodore," I say through gritted teeth, pressure building in my balls as a violent quiver shoots down my spine.

"Let go," he says. "Let everything go."

"Ah…Th…" The words stutter in my throat as a bomb of pleasure detonates deep inside my belly. "Th…*fuck!*" My legs tighten, locking around Theodore's back as my cock twitches in my hand, coating his stomach with jets of hot cum.

Theodore smiles, drawing his plump bottom lip between his teeth. "Your face is stunning when you come," he whispers, palming my cheek. It's the calm before the storm. After brushing my lips with his, he straightens his back, grabbing both of my legs and using them as leverage as he starts pounding me so hard, so deep, the rug moves beneath us.

"Oh my God," he groans, drilling into me over and over again. His hips thrust relentlessly and I reach out, working the mixture of sweat and cum into his heated skin with the pads of my fingers.

"James I'm…oh…shit, yes…"

I feel the moment he comes. I see it on his face, hear it in his breath. It's exquisite.

"Fuck, I love you," I say again as he drops my legs and collapses onto my chest. "I'm so sorry, Theodore."

"No." Raising his head, he angles his face right in front of mine. "Don't do that. Don't you dare apologise for letting me know who you are. *All* of you. I told you I was here for you, through light and dark, and I meant it."

I never doubted him, I still don't, but that doesn't mean it's fair. A disagreement over furniture pushed me over the edge today. Fucking furniture. I live my life balancing on a set of scales, the slightest weight tipping me into darkness. The problem is each time that happens, they never quite rebalance. Theodore's presence is enough to keep me teetering in the middle, but if he leaves, if he jumps off that scale, my weight will break it, and I will plummet beyond salvation.

That's not a responsibility anyone should have to carry, especially someone I love more than anything in the world. My life is hard, dark, complicated. Theodore's isn't, and I don't want to take that from him, but I'm too weak to walk away. I'm not strong enough to live without him, or with the knowledge that I've caused him pain by pushing him away.

If I stay with him, I'll hurt him. If I leave him, I'll hurt him. But if I was to disappear altogether, he'll hurt for a little while and then move on. He'll learn to smile again.

I think I know what I have to do.

"What are you thinking about?"

His voice snaps me back into reality. "Hmm?"

"You look…lost."

Tell him. You know what you're considering is wrong. Irrational.

"No, Theodore."

Tell him how you feel. Ask for help.

"I'm not lost."

Be honest. Tell him!

"I actually think, for the first time, I know exactly where I'm heading."

You're lying. You're misleading him. You're a fucking coward.

He can help you.

I ignore the voice of my subconscious because it's wrong. People have spent years trying to help me and they've failed. They failed because it's impossible. I was born broken. There's nothing to restore. The time has finally arrived for me to accept that, and I think I have. Nobody else will of course, especially Theodore.

More talking therapy. More drugs. More support – that will be his answer.

But it's all bullshit. I'm back at rock bottom, *again*, and I'm too fucking tired to climb back to the top, knowing I'll only fall down again eventually.

"Have you thought about making a doctors appointment?" Theodore asks, his cheek resting over my heart, our bodies still intertwined.

"I will. I'll call them tomorrow." It's a lie part of me hopes I don't see through. I know I *should* see a doctor, and I'm going to try and talk myself out of giving up. I'm past caring about myself but, although I don't understand why or how, there are people who care about me and I need to find the energy to do this for them.

What's wrong with you?

Haven't got the balls to put these people out of their misery?

You can't do anything right.

Your mother is right; you don't see anything through.

Knowing Theodore will be able to feel it, I attempt to calm my racing heart by taking deep breaths through my nose. My mind is fucked, my thoughts, my subconscious, conflicted. I don't understand what my head wants me to do and I'm quickly losing touch with reality, with what I *should* do.

I'm so tired.

"Let's go to bed," Theodore suggests, rolling off me and peeling the condom from his softened cock. "Everything is always clearer after a good night's sleep."

It's early evening, not bedtime, but I don't have the energy to protest. "Look at this place." Taking his hand and pulling myself to my feet, I shake my head, utterly ashamed of myself and the mess I've created.

"We'll worry about that in the morning."

Lifting one side of my mouth into a half-smile that's flooded with regret, I follow him to the bedroom. As I settle down on the mattress, pressing my back against Theodore's chest as he holds me, I pray to whoever might be listening that Theodore's right, that after a sleep I'll know what I need to do.

* * *

I've been tidying up the kitchen for over an hour, picking things up, sweeping broken glass, and trying not to wake Theodore in the process. My muscles ache with the movement, so I've given up and decided to make coffee instead. It's only four AM but despite being exhausted, I haven't been able to fall asleep. For a few hours I lay, content, in Theodore's arms, finally getting up when I realised Theodore was holding me and I felt…nothing.

If anything I felt a little restricted, and definitely too hot. Since meeting him I've always found solace in his touch, but in that moment I couldn't feel him anymore. I can't feel anything. Comfort, love, even anger and sadness…it's all gone.

I'm numb.

Has my mind given up? Have I reached the destination I always knew I was travelling towards? Is this numbness my soul's way of preparing myself for the inevitable?

You need to end this.

You need to fight *this.*

I shake my head in a lame attempt to unscramble my opposing thoughts as I reach for the freshly boiled kettle. I hover it over the mug, ready to pour, but those damn voices in my subconscious won't stop interrupting my thought process.

A shock of pain will do it. Jumpstart your emotions. Un-paralyse you.

The back of my hand is over the mug and under the stream of boiling water before I've even made the decision to do it. Pain sears through my flesh and I force out a controlled hiss through gritted teeth, fighting the powerful impulse to pull away.

The bedroom door creaks and my instinct to lie, conjure an excuse, kicks in immediately. Purposely dropping the kettle, I cry out as I jump back, gripping my wrist as I dash to the sink.

"Oh my God, what happened?" Theodore fusses, scurrying towards me.

Switching the cold tap to full force, I stick my hand underneath the spray. "Dropped the kettle. No big deal." It doesn't surprise me that I'm able to lie so readily, but it *does* disgust me.

"Jesus," he mutters, wincing as he takes hold of my wrist, bending to get a closer look. "We should get you to A&E."

"It's fine." I dismiss him with a shake of my head.

"It's blistering already," he notes. "I'll drive. I just need to get dressed."

"I'm not going to fucking hospital." It was my intention to snap, to raise my voice, yet I remain frustratingly calm.

It didn't work. The physical pain is there, my hand feels like it's on fire, the skin leathered and beaming red…but I'm not that bothered about it. I'm not bothered about anything. I'm not even bothered that Theodore's hand is rubbing my shoulder. Angling my head, I stare at his fingers. I love him, I know I do, but I can't *feel* it.

Dammit!

"Fine," he relents. "At least go to the chemist on the way to work. They might have a cream or something you can put on it."

"Actually," I begin, shutting the water off. "I think I'll stay home today. I can work from here."

Theodore smiles, albeit weakly, and I'm grateful he's looking at my face so he can't see that my hand has started shaking. "And you'll make that doctors appointment?"

"Yes." Turns out it *is* a lie I'll be carrying through. "I'm going back to bed for a while first. I didn't sleep too well."

"Good idea. I won't get back to sleep now, so I'm going to get a bath and get ready for work."

I smile because *he* does and, as old-fashioned as it sounds, he looks so damn handsome, even with bed-hair and scruff on his face. "I really *do* love you, Theodore," I say, pulling him in at the waist. "Don't ever forget that." Bypassing my lips, he kisses my neck and I fold my arms around him, hugging him close. "I'm sorry."

"Don't ever apologise for struggling."

I'm not apologising for last night, but for all the nights to come.

I've made my decision, right down to how I'm going to do it. I know what will work best for me and I *won't* fail this time. It's time to stop pretending, stop giving the people around me false hope that I will get better.

Because I won't.

I'm too far gone.

I'm too tired.

Pulling back, a look of confusion twists his expression. His lips part, a small sound – maybe the beginning of a question – escaping, but then he closes them again. "Go sleep. Call me if you need anything." He cups my face. "*Anything*. Okay?"

"Okay," I agree with the fake conviction I've become a master at.

We exit the kitchen side-by-side, exchanging one last glance before he veers into the bathroom. When I climb into bed I close my eyes and picture that final glance again. I say goodbye to it, to his smile…

And hope that he'll forgive me.

* * *

Pain is inevitable, suffering is optional. I heard that somewhere once and it stuck in my mind, haunting me, ever since. I often toyed with its interpretation and, now, I have the answer.

The pain is there. It never leaves. Sometimes it's bearable, but it's *always* there. It's pecked away at my soul all my life and, finally, it's won.

I surrender.

It's taken everything. I am nothing more than a hollow shell. There are no more pieces left to try and put back together. I have nothing else to fight with.

I'm exhausted.

Pain is inevitable, suffering is optional.

Today, I opt to end the suffering. Today, I welcome the pain as it slices into my wrist, knowing it will be the last time. As I watch my tormented life seep from my body in thick, red spirals, a small smile crawls onto my lips.

It's over.

I'm free.

My body starts to tremble and I lie back in the bathtub, closing my eyes. A rush of peace, contentment, washes over my dying body, cleansing my soul as I drift into the serene darkness, embracing the shadow for the first time in my life.

Forgive me.

Chapter Eleven

~Theo~

Kneeling in front of his grave, I place my hand on the cool stone. "I miss you," I whisper, hoping somehow he can hear me. It never gets easier. Somehow, grief becomes a routine part of life. It never leaves, you simply learn to live around it.

Looking around, my heart feels heavy seeing so many abandoned, moss-covered headstones. Where are their families? Tom and I have taken it in turns to visit our dad, every fortnight since the day he was buried. We bring flowers, we talk to him, and once a month we'll bring a sponge and bottle of bleach to clean away any dirt nature has blown onto his stone.

"What are you doing here?" Tom's voice doesn't startle me. I heard his footsteps crunching the gravel as he approached.

"Do you ever just…miss him more some days?"

"Yeah. Yeah I do."

"I keep remembering his saying lately – what's meant to be won't pass you by. How do you know what's meant to be?"

"You don't," Tom says, shrugging. "I think it just means you're supposed to find solace in the fact everything is already planned out for you."

Hmm. I'm not sure I like that answer. I need to *know* what I'm facing in the future. "Thanks for coming." My car jittered and growled all the way here, finally cutting out just before I reached the car park. *Unreliable heap of shit.* "You're a lifesaver."

"That's always my aim."

Right. Doctor joke. Usually, I'd smile, but not today. Today, I have a knot in my stomach worrying about James, Mike's being an even bigger prick than usual, and now my car is fucked. *Again.*

"You need a new car."

"Gee, thanks, King of the Bleeding Obvious. I can't afford one."

"You need to write faster then. You haven't released anything this year."

"It's not…wait, how do you know that?"

"I'm your brother. I take an interest in your work."

Bullshit.

"That and Jennifer is obsessed with you."

"She's read my books?" I don't know if that makes me happy or terrified.

"Hell yeah. I mentioned it *once*. Next thing I know she's read all three and has banged on about them so much I feel like I know the stories better than *you*."

"Wow, I…uh…" I'm speechless, and quietly proud.

"So what's wrong? I know there's something, otherwise I'd have told you to get the damn bus. I was sleeping. I'm on a night-shift tonight."

Sighing, I say a silent goodbye to my dad and jump to my feet, accompanying Tom to his car. "I'm worried about James." I haven't got the time to beat around the bush. If I'm late back from my lunch hour, Mike will rip me a new arsehole. "He had some kind of meltdown yesterday, smashed up the kitchen."

Max has talked about this side of James before, but it always felt like he was referring to a stranger.

"He's not been right for a few weeks. Not eating properly, sleeping in too late to shave before work. Doesn't sound much, but it's not…*him*. Says he's fine but…"

"You don't believe him?"

"I don't know." I shrug. "This is what I've been worrying about, that I won't see the signs, know when he's struggling, or even if I'm reading too much into it."

We reach his car and I slip into the passenger seat. Tom joins me, fixes his seatbelt and starts the engine. "Have you talked to his brother about it?" he asks, pulling out of the car park.

"Not yet, but if James doesn't make an appointment with his GP today like he said he will, I might have to. It just feels, I don't know, like I'm betraying him or something, sneaking behind his back."

"T, you know that's not true. It's what James himself told you to do if you were worried. His brother…Mark?"

"Max."

"Max has known James, known his illness, longer than you. I'm sure he'll be able to put your mind at ease, or at least know what to do, how to handle things."

"Wait," I say, raising my hand. "Pull over here."

He does as I ask before looking to me for an explanation.

"I need to nip in the chemist. James spilled boiling water on his hand this morning."

"By accident?"

"Yeah. I'm going to see-" *Hold on.* It *was* an accident, right? That's what he said and I've no reason not to believe him. Except, suddenly, I don't know if I do. "I, um, I'm going to see if they have any cream or anything. It blistered instantly."

"No, no, don't put anything on it. Sounds like a partial thickness burn. He should get it checked out."

"He won't." Because he's a stubborn arsehole.

"Want me to take a look? Either way, definitely don't put anything on it. If the blisters burst, he can apply a sterile dressing, but nothing else."

"Right. I'll buy some dressings then."

"I have some in the boot. Take some of those."

"Oh, thanks."

"Where to next?"

I check my watch and note that I'm due back at work in twenty minutes. *Shit.* "There's a KFC on the way to James'." I'm not hungry but I want to make sure he eats something. Mike will just have to wait. Fuck the consequences. "I'm not sure he'll bother cooking for himself right now."

"You really need to talk to his brother," Tom reiterates, setting off again towards Spinningfields.

"Maybe you can, I dunno, assess him while you're checking his hand?"

Tom sighs, then clicks his tongue. "I can give you a general impression, but it isn't my field. Regardless of that, I don't really know him well enough to make an informed opinion."

"Sure. I'd appreciate your input anyway."

"Look, don't get mad…"

My fingers grip my knee a little tighter. I know what's coming.

"You've only been with him a few months. Are you sure it wouldn't be best to just…walk away? You need to think of your own wellbeing too, and, well, maybe he's not ready for something so serious right now. Sounds like he's got some issues he needs to deal with."

Surprisingly, I'm not angry like I was when Tess suggested the same thing. This time I simply picture James' face, the way I feel when he looks at me. It makes me smile. "I can't."

"Got it bad, eh?"

"Yeah." I blow out a humourless chuckle. "I've never felt this way before. Sometimes I wonder *why*, you know? We're so different. What made us click?"

Eyes on the road, Tom shrugs. "Love - one of life's great mysteries. Take Jennifer. Initially she seemed no different to any other woman I've chased. I planned to get in her knickers and move on to the next, but as soon as I started talking to her there was just…something. I didn't know what it was, just that I wanted more. I don't know how love works, but it's something you don't get to decide. It just…happens."

"Wow. Check us out. It's like we're real grown ups."

Tom laughs. "How's this for grown up? We bought a pram yesterday. It's at Mum's. Apparently it's bad luck to bring it in the house before the baby's born, or some shit like that."

"Yeah? I still can't imagine you with a baby."

"Me either. I'm hoping knowing how to keep it alive is another one of those things that just happens," he says with an equal mix of humour and nerves in his voice.

"You'll be fine. Your biggest challenge will be getting Mum to leave you alone."

Tom pulls into the KFC drive-through and I tell him to order a Boneless Bucket before handing him a twenty-pound note. We don't speak much on the way to James' apartment, and when we do it's about trivial stuff, like Tom's expectations of the latest Star Wars film. Personally, I couldn't give less of a shit if I tried. I haven't seen a single one of them. Star Trek, however, is another story. I grew up watching them every Sunday with my dad.

After getting us into James' building by tapping in the door-code, I tell Tom to wait in the hall when we reach his apartment. I just want to check on him, make sure he's not naked, and forewarn him I've brought Tom to look at his hand so he doesn't flip out.

He's not in the main living space when I walk inside so I check his office. When I don't find him there, I assume he must still be sleeping and head to the bedroom.

"James?" I call.

No answer. *Hmm.*

I'm about to leave, maybe call his mobile to see where he is, when I notice the bathroom door is slightly ajar. It doesn't sound like a big deal, but it's unusual. Everyone has little quirks, things they're a little anal over, and one of James' is making sure the door is always closed when the room's not in use.

I step forward, planning to close it, but not before peering inside in case he's there.

"Oh my God, *James!*"

Dropping the bag of food where I stand, I rush to the bathtub - the room, my whole world, suddenly spinning.

"*Tom!*" I yell, my hand stuttering over James' lifeless body, not knowing where to touch, what to do. "*Thomas!*"

James is lying in a pool of red water, his right arm limp, dangling over the edge of the bath. "Oh God, baby. What have you done?" I fall to my knees, the thick, dark pool of blood soaking into my pants.

His eyes are closed, his head flopped to one side. I raise it, cupping his cheeks and pressing my forehead to his. "No, no, no. James. Oh God, James. *Thomas!*"

"I'm here, I'm here-" Tom cuts himself off when he steps into the bathroom. He pauses for just a second before flying into autopilot, trying to pull me out of the way.

I shrug out of his grip, my hand trying to touch every part of James' body all at once.

"Theodore *move*. Let me help him."

Right. Help him. Yes.

Nodding slowly, I gently rest James' head back onto the ceramic lip of the bathtub before stumbling to my feet. As Tom swoops into my position, I try to wipe the tears from my damp cheeks, but my hands are wet, coated with bloody water.

"Call nine nine nine," Tom says, two fingers pressed against James' neck. There are several empty pill bottles and two boxes scattered on the floor and Tom picks them up, scanning the labels quickly, before throwing them back where he found them.

He took tablets, too? Oh, James…

"Is he…"

"The ambulance, Theo! *Now!* Put them on speaker."

With shaky hands, I do as I'm told, setting the phone down on the tiles surrounding the sink. I take a step back, watching the scene unfolding in front of me through cloudy vision, my heart so heavy it feels like it could drag me to the floor.

After requesting an ambulance, my ears tune out as Tom uses technical words and spouts random numbers. I don't know if he's alive, if I'll ever hear his voice again, and it feels like a piece of me is dying.

Blood. It's everywhere. It's so dark, so thick, and it's pouring out of his wrists in globular spurts. In parts, the slashes in his flesh are masked by tattoos, making it difficult to tell where the ink ends and the blood begins.

"Theo, I need you to lift his legs, help me get him onto the floor."

What have you done, James? What have you fucking done?

"*Theo!*" Tom is right in front of me, his hands on my shoulders, and I've no idea how he got there. All I can see is James, and blood. So much blood.

"Theodore, look at me."

Somehow, I manage to do as he asks.

"I need your help. *James* needs your help. Are you with me?"

I nod, I think.

My body starts moving automatically and, rubbing the tears from my eyes, I follow Tom's lead.

"Remember his skin is wet. Get a firm grip," Tom instructs as I anchor my hands under James' limp thighs. "On my count. One, two…*three*."

Water laps over the rim of the bath as we lift, splashing my legs before settling into a shallow pool on the tiled floor. We move him to a dry area and, once he's safely on the floor, I just stand, rubbing my arms, not knowing what to do. I don't know if James is breathing and I'm too terrified of the answer to ask Tom.

Kneeling beside James, Tom removes his t-shirt and starts ripping it open down the seams. For a brief second, I wonder why, but I can't ask because I can't speak. I can't move. I can barely breathe.

Once his t-shirt is in two pieces, he bounds one around James' left wrist, pulling it tightly around his wounds before tying a knot and repeating the process on the other side.

"Y-you'll hurt him," I croak, so quietly I'm not sure I've even said it. I mustn't have, because Tom ignores me, pressing two fingers against James' neck for what must be the tenth time since he arrived.

"Oh no you don't, buddy," Tom says, placing the heel of his hand on James' chest before locking his other hand on top of that.

Oh my God. No. Please.

On raised knees, Tom pushes down repeatedly, appearing to throw his whole body weight into each one. It's nothing like you see on TV. He seems to be jabbing into James' chest with so much force it looks almost brutal. *Painful.*

The whole thing terrifies me.

"James," I whisper, throwing my palm over my mouth.

After what feels like an eternity, Tom stops compressing and tilts James' head back a little before blowing into his mouth.

"Is he…is…" *Oh my God.*

He works his chest again. I don't know what's happening. I don't know what to do. I've never felt so useless, so fucking *scared* in my entire life.

Seconds later, two paramedics bustle into the room and I stumble back a few steps, idly wondering how they got in before deciding I don't care.

"I need paddles," Tom barks, the male paramedic already removing some kind of machine from a long, dark-green bag.

Tom starts rubbing down James' chest with a towel while the female paramedic pulls two rubbery, orange sheets from her rucksack, placing them on James' chest. Tom picks up the paddles while the other man fiddles with the machine, while I do *nothing*. I can't help him. I'm paralysed.

"Charge to two hundred," Tom calls. The machine buzzes, shortly followed by Tom yelling, "Clear!"

James' body jolts, making my throat tighten. My gaze flips repeatedly between Tom and James and it almost feels like I'm an extra in a petrifying movie, like I'm not really here, this isn't happening.

"Charge to three-hundred."

Spinning around, I face the wall, my eyes burning, my heart sinking. I hear the moment James is shocked again but I can't watch any longer. I'm losing him, and the pain is unbearable.

What have you done?

"We've got sinus rhythm," Tom announces, but I don't know what it means so I stay facing the wall, squeezing my eyes closed to trap the tears inside. I hear them shuffling, spouting numbers, making things rattle, but I can't look. I won't. I refuse to watch him slipping away from me.

"Theo." A nudge on my shoulder accompanies Tom's voice. "They're taking him now. Do you want to ride with him or follow in the car?"

Turning around, I see James strapped into a stretcher, his listless body cocooned in a thick, green blanket. "He's going to die, isn't he?" I ask, my stare fixed on the stretcher as it's pulled through the apartment.

"I don't know," Tom says, sighing. "They'll take him straight to surgery, get him started on intravenous meds to counteract the pills he's taken, but…you should prepare yourself."

His words hit me like a kick to the stomach, winding me, and I double over, supporting myself with my hands on my knees.

Prepare yourself. How? How do I prepare to receive the worst news of my life? Is there something I need to do? Words I need to tell myself? Do I imagine it happening over and over again until I get used to the idea?

"If you want to go with him, you need to go *now.*"

"Right. Yes. Um…what, um…"

"Just breathe, T. Come on."

Patting my back, Tom walks with me out of the apartment and into the lift. The paramedics are already out of the building and when we reach the lobby, I start to jog, hoping to catch up.

"Wait!" I call out when I hit the street and notice the female paramedic closing the ambulance doors. "Can I go with him?"

"Of course. Quickly."

She ushers me inside and points to a foldout chair opposite James. This isn't a new scenario. I've sat here once before, watching a paramedic fuss over him. Last time, however, I wasn't in love with him, or if I was I didn't know it yet. Last time, he wasn't dying. Last time, I wasn't about to lose my whole world.

We're moving, sirens wailing, within seconds of me fastening my seatbelt. The paramedic hovers over James throughout the whole journey, jotting things down on a clipboard. By the time we arrive at the hospital, James has tubes sticking out of his arm and some kind of mask attached to a bag, which the paramedic is squeezing, over his mouth and nose.

I don't know how I'm managing to walk, I don't know anything anymore, yet my legs carry me forward as I follow James into A&E. Again, numbers are exchanged, stats, medications, and words I've only heard before on the TV.

"I'm sorry, you can't go any further," a woman in pale-blue scrubs says, raising her hand in front of me.

I look over her shoulder, watching James as he's wheeled further and further away from me until he disappears completely through a set of double doors.

"I need you to go to reception and give them your friend's details."

"He's not my friend." *He's my everything.* The nurse puts her hand on my quivering forearm and, for a moment, I stare at it. "Someone will come and find you when we have some news."

Nodding, I make my way over to the large, oval reception desk in a daze. A woman in a navy chequered blouse asks me for the patient's name and I answer while staring at the blood dried into my shirt.

At least, I *thought* I answered.

"Sir? Patient's name please?"

"Oh. Sorry, um, James Holden. James David Holden." I go on to give her his date of birth, address, and GP practice, and then I feel a hand on my shoulder.

"Hey," Tom says. "I'm gonna see what I can find out. When you're done here, there's a family room you can wait in." He points to it across the waiting room. "I'll come and find you in there."

"Okay."

"Next of kin?" the woman behind the desk asks.

"Um…" *Shit. Max.* "M-max. Max Holden. His brother. I'll call him. I need to call him. I'll call him."

"We can do that if you prefer."

"N-no," I stutter, shaking my head. "No, I'll do it."

Questions over, she points me in the same direction Tom did. I amble over to it, scrolling through my contacts while trying to find the courage to call Max. My hands shake as I hit dial. What if he holds me responsible? Shit, what if I *am* responsible?

"Theo?" Max answers, speaking my name with urgency. We're hardly buddies, so the fact I'm ringing at all is enough to spark panic.

"It's James. He- I- He tried…we're at the hospital."

"Which one?"

"Saint Andrews. He's…I don't know if…They said something about surgery. I think he's in surgery."

"I'll be right there."

I sit down on one of the dusky pink chairs with rubber-covered cushions while I wait for news, or for Max to arrive, whichever comes first. My restless feet won't quit tapping against the shiny floor, so I stand up and pace the small room instead. When I check my watch for what must be the fourteenth time, I huff in frustration, noticing hardly any time has passed yet it feels like I've been here for hours.

Stupid thing must be broken.

I stare at the ceiling, then I look at the floor, and I keep doing it until I become lightheaded. The blood is all I can think about. The metallic taste still coats my tongue from when I clamped my hand over my mouth. I can still smell it, *feel* it, and when I look down it's all I see, dried onto my clothes, my skin.

I've just sat down again when the door opens and I jump straight back up. It's Max, dressed in his office suit, his tie half-undone, and he looks as terrified as I feel.

"I'm so sorry, Max. This is all my fault."

"What's happened? The woman out there wouldn't tell me shit."

"I knew. I *knew* he wasn't right and I didn't do anything. I didn't tell anyone. This is my fault."

"Dammit, Theo, tell me what the hell's happened!"

"The bath. I found him in the bath. He…blood. There was blood. He…"

"Oh God," Max barely whispers, tipping his head back.

"He cut his wrists, took pills. If we'd arrived just minutes later, he'd…" I can't bring myself to say the words aloud.

"*We*?"

"My brother was with me. He knew what to do. Christ, Max, if Tom hadn't been there…I couldn't have saved him. I froze. I…I…this is my fault."

"No. No, it isn't."

"But I *knew*, Max. He's been quiet. Distant. I just thought it was work. Then yesterday he had a meltdown and trashed the kitchen, but I didn't want to interfere or go behind his back and talk to *you*. If I had…"

"This isn't your fault, Theo. He's not well. Nobody's to blame here."

"When he told me about the last time he tried to kill himself, I couldn't believe *nobody* noticed."

"Last time? What do you mean *last time?*"

"I vowed not to let that happen again. I swore I'd notice and I failed. I let him down."

"Theo, what do you mean *last* time?" Max repeats, anger coating his words.

"W-when he was a teenager. He tried to overdose."

"That's not possible," Max says, stumbling back a step. "I would've known."

"He said he only passed out, threw up a few hours later. But, still, he was alone. Just like today. He was fucking alone! How could I leave him by himself?"

"I…I had no idea." Max walks backwards until the back of his legs hit a chair. He falls into the seat, letting his head drop into his hands.

We don't talk any more. We don't even move for what feels like hours. I'm not sure if he blames me, I sure as hell do, or if he blames himself. It doesn't really matter. The only thing that matters is the man lying unconscious on a table somewhere in this ginormous building.

What have you done, James? What have you fucking done?

When the wooden door starts to open for the first time in God knows how long, Max and I leap to our feet simultaneously.

"Tom," his name rushes from my mouth in a mixture of panic and anticipation.

He's with another doctor, who turns straight to Max. "Mr Holden?"

"Yes." The tiny word, filled with so much emotion, cracks on Max's lips.

The doctor holds out his hand to shake but Max doesn't seem to notice, keeping his fingers in his pockets. "I'm Doctor Garcia," he says. "I just finished performing your brother's surgery."

"How is he?"

"Stable, for now. I've repaired the vessels in his wrists but I'm afraid it's too early to tell if there'll be any permanent nerve damage. Given that he ingested a fairly large quantity of lithium we've performed a gastric lavage to remove as much as we could. We've also given him some activated charcoal through a tube in his nose to absorb the citalopram."

"Citalopram? Where'd he get his hands on citalopram?"

Doctor Garcia offers a small shrug, while I silently wonder what the hell citalopram is.

"He's being taken to the ICU. You should be able to see him in an hour or so, though we've induced a coma so he won't be able to talk to you."

"Why? Why can't you wake him up?"

"Right now, like I said, he's stable, but his battle is far from over. Currently, he can't breathe on his own. Until he can, without the support of a ventilator, we'll keep him sedated. Give his body time to heal."

"And it will, right? He's going to be okay?"

"I'm sorry, Mr Holden, it's too soon to make that call. The next twenty-four hours are crucial. Your brother has quite a fight on his hands. It's down to him now."

I feel sick. Stifled. I stare down at the floor but it looks like it's moving so I look at the pale yellow walls instead. "Come on, T," Tom says, squeezing my shoulder. "I'm taking you back to my place."

Blinking my eyes back into the room, I notice the other doctor isn't here anymore. Max is sitting, slumped forward with his head down. *How long was I staring at the fucking wall?*

"I'm not leaving him," I say, twisting out of Tom's grip.

"Theo, look at me."

Reluctantly, I do.

"You're a mess. You stink, you're covered in blood, and you're exhausted. Come back with me, take a shower, eat a sandwich, and I'll bring you right back."

"He's right," Max interrupts, rubbing his palms down his cheeks before sagging back in his chair. "Go freshen up. We've got a tough few days coming up, maybe longer. Take a breather. Prepare yourself. I'll call you if there's any change."

Weakly, I nod in hesitant agreement. "What about your mum? Is she on her way?"

"I haven't told her yet," Max says, sighing regretfully. "I rushed over here on autopilot. When I've seen James, know what we're dealing with, I'll call her."

"Okay," I mutter, though I don't understand his thought process. If the situation were reversed and it was *my* brother fighting for his life in the ICU, my mum would be the first person I'd want by my side. But their family dynamic is very different and, even if I had the energy, it's not my place to question it.

"I won't be gone long," I say, patting Max's shoulder as I walk past.

What have you done, James?

Following Tom out to his car, I consciously keep my gaze moving in different directions. If I look at the same spot for too long, the image of James lying unconscious and drowning in a tub of red water reappears. That image, that memory, alone has the power to completely break me. If I lose him…

"How did I not see this coming?" I ask, sliding into the passenger seat of Tom's car.

"Don't, Theo. Blaming yourself, blaming *anyone*, won't help James."

"After his meltdown I thought I could take care of him. I thought…I thought if I just made sure he ate, got some rest, if I just…*loved* him…"

"This isn't your fault. He's sick, Theo. He needs help only professionals can give him, and he'll get it now. And while he does, keep doing what you planned. *Love* him. He needs you."

But I'm not enough. If I was, I wouldn't be covered in his blood right now. He must've known *I'd* be the one to find him. Why would he do that to me?

Oh, James…

* * *

We're back at the hospital in just over an hour. Max is still waiting in the family room and, given the amount of time that has passed, it unnerves me. "Why are you still in here?" I ask instead of *hello*.

"Had to wait for the shift handover. A nurse has just been in. We can go up in ten minutes."

"So he's…"

"The same."

"Good. That's good." Or is it? I have no fucking idea. "Has the, um…" I click my fingers, trying to remember the word. "The coal thing worked?"

"Activated charcoal," Tom cuts in. "They'll administer more doses at regular intervals."

"Did you know he was taking citalopram?" Max questions.

"I don't even know what that is." My head hangs in shame. I *should* know what it is, what he's supposed to take and when. *I've let him down.*

"It's an SSRI," Tom answers on Max's behalf. "A type of antidepressant, and a drug which wouldn't usually be prescribed to someone with bipolar, especially not the strength found in his bathroom. Either he's been seeing a doctor who's unaware of his history, or he's got them from someone else. Maybe the internet."

"How long has the stupid bastard been planning this?" Max mutters to no one in particular. There's no anger or venom in his voice, just overwhelming sadness.

Planning it? He couldn't have *planned* this. Could he? The idea rolls around in my mind, heavy like a boulder, and my head starts to ache. He can't have made a conscious decision to put me, put his family, through this kind of pain.

Could he?

No. He wouldn't. This had to have been a snap decision, a moment of weakness and desperation. A cry for help perhaps. He didn't mean for it to go this far. He never intended to succeed, to leave me.

Did he?

When the door opens, interrupting my thoughts, the nurse that walks through instantly becomes the centre of our attention. "The ICU are expecting you. You can go up whenever you're ready."

Max is already by the door, waiting for the nurse to move. I, however, am frozen. Again.

"I'll take you through the service lift," Tom says, heading for the open door. "It's closer."

I'm scared, Tom. I think I've said it out loud until Tom turns around, cocking his head. "Come on, T."

"Right," I mumble, somehow getting my feet to cooperate.

Tom leads the way with Max by his side, while I lag behind a few steps. Nerves claw at my throat when I step out of the lift. My airway feels restricted, like something's pushing into my chest. Tugging on my collar, as if that will ease the imaginary pressure, I hover by the nurses station while Tom discusses more numbers and technical jargon with another doctor. They clearly know each other well. It's evident in their casual stance and the way the older doctor pats my brother's arm before walking away.

"What'd he say?" I ask Tom, the second he steps up to me and Max.

"Just a little more in depth version of what his surgeon told you. Look, guys, before you go inside, remember there will be a lot of machines. Don't be alarmed by all the beeps and wires. They're there to help him."

"Uh-huh," is the only sound I can summon. I start to move forward towards the room I assume James is in, the one Tom's doctor friend pointed to while they were talking, but Tom grabs my arm, stopping me.

"James has a tracheostomy. It means there's a tube attached to a ventilator, fed through a small incision in his trachea..." Tom points to his neck, just below his Adam's apple. "It can look a little scary but, again, it's there to help him, and I can assure you it doesn't hurt."

"Okay," I breathe, closing my eyes for a few seconds. "Okay."

What I don't realise until I walk into the large room is that no amount of reassurance from Tom would ever be enough to prepare me for what I'm seeing right now. It's a small ward with four beds, four patients, and an office behind a glass wall manned by three nurses and a doctor in green scrubs.

He's a young doctor, like Tom, and I wonder if they know each other. His stethoscope is cool – striped with all the colours of the rainbow.

"Theo?"

I've never seen one like it before. Maybe he works on the kid's ward.

"*Theo?*"

I bet she *doesn't work with kids,* I think, eyeing up the older nurse with grey hair and a sour expression. Her stethoscope is black. Ordinary. Her eyes are ordinary, too. I don't see a very exciting story behind them. I imagine her in a marriage of convenience, no kids, works overtime to avoid spending time with her equally boring husband.

"Theodore?" My full name snaps me from my musing and, for the briefest second, my heart flutters.

James?

It's not James of course. It's Tom, and he's holding my upper arm. "It's okay, T. Come on. He needs you."

But I don't want to look at James. I'm not sure I can handle it. My knees are already weak, and I'm scared that if I look at him, they will buckle altogether. Instead, I stare at the doctor's stethoscope again. Tom should get one like that. Maybe I could get him one for Christmas.

"Let's go outside," Tom suggests. "We'll come back in a little while."

He needs you. Be strong for him. Don't let him down again.

Sucking in a deep breath, I shake my head in defiance. "No. I-I'm okay."

Releasing my breath through pursed lips, I flex my clammy fingers and turn around. James is lying on the bed in the corner, and the second I see him, my head falls to one side as if my neck is no longer strong enough to support it. Max is sitting on a high-backed chair to James' right, so I amble to his left and hover my hand over James' arm, too afraid to touch it.

"God, James," I whisper, allowing my thumb to brush over the blue dragonfly tattooed onto his forearm. His skin is so much warmer than the last time I touched it. It's comforting, so, sitting down, I lower my hand and interlock my fingers with his.

The back of his hand is pink and blistered from the boiling water and when Max asks why, I tell him. He doesn't reply, simply looks down, closing his eyes.

My gaze travels up, over the bandages covering his wrist and I can't prevent the image of what's underneath from torturing my mind.

"I'll leave you alone for a while," Tom says, patting my back.

"Me too." Max stands from his chair. "I need to call my mum."

I hear them walk away but my eyes are trained on James. It looks like he's sleeping, which comforts me because it means he's not in pain. My gaze keeps wandering to the tube in his neck and it makes my stomach feel queasy and my chest ache. The sterile dressing around it doesn't do much to hide the incision and all I can think is, *why?* Why did he do this to himself? Why did he give up? Why wasn't I enough?

"Why didn't you talk to me?" I whisper, brushing the back of his hand, careful to avoid the cannula, with my thumb.

The machine next to me makes a whooshing sound every time it forces air into his lungs, and each whoosh stabs into my heart like a knife. There are several pieces of equipment, each emitting different beeps, displaying numbers I don't understand, and housing various wires and tubes attached to numerous parts of James' body. I don't know how they're helping him, I can only hope they *are*. I'm not prepared for any other outcome.

"Come back to me," I say, reaching out to palm his cheek. "Be the stubborn bastard I *know* you are and *fight.* Fight for me, James. I won't let you down again."

Tears roll freely down my face and I don't even attempt to stop them. People throw the term *heartbreak* around all the time, and until today I naively thought its definition was sadness. Only now, sitting here with my head pressed against the guardrail of James' bed, do I realise that it *literally* feels like my heart is breaking, splitting in two. It's not just sadness, it's a debilitating ache in my chest. It's struggling to breathe – consciously focusing on each breath I take because it feels like if I don't my lungs will collapse. It's suddenly having all my future dreams ripped from under my feet because all I can think about is getting through today, getting *James* through today.

Heartbreak is uncertainty.

Desolation.

Confusion.

Doubt.

Anger.

Fear.

Heartbreak feels like your entire world is crumbling above your head, and all you can do is sit back and wait for it to crush you.

This is our story. It's not supposed to end here.

"Don't give up, baby. Don't give up."

* * *

"Theo."

There's a nudge on my shoulder. I want it to go away.

"Theo. Come on, mate. Time to go."

"Huh?" Peeling my head off the back of the chair, I see Max standing over me. We're in hospital. *James*. For the briefest of seconds, I'd forgot. For just a moment, my life wasn't falling apart. "Sorry," I mutter, massaging the stiffness in my neck. "Must've nodded off."

"It's kicking out time. Tom's waiting for you downstairs."

Looking at James, I don't want to leave him. How am I supposed to say goodbye not knowing if it will be the last time I ever do? "You'll call me, right? If there's any change," I ask, knowing as James' next of kin, he'll be the person they contact.

"Of course I will."

Standing, I bend over James and lower my lips to his forehead. "You be here in the morning, You hear me? Don't you dare leave me." I stroke his cheek, whispering straight into his ear. "If you can hear me, James, know that if tomorrow never comes, I…I love you."

I walk out of the ICU with my gaze locked onto my feet. I left a piece of me behind with James and all I can do is pray he holds onto it. If he doesn't, I fear that part of me will be gone forever.

Max and I exchange quick goodbyes when we reach Tom and then I follow my brother to his car.

"You okay?" Tom asks, fixing his seatbelt.

"What part of today makes you think I'd be fucking *okay*, Tom?" I bark, relenting immediately. "Sorry. I didn't mean to snap."

Putting my seatbelt on, I realise I haven't seen James' mother yet. "Did James' mum visit? Did I sleep through it?"

"No. She can't face it just yet apparently."

Selfish bitch. "He's her fucking son."

I *hate* her. Maybe if she'd given a shit when James was a kid, got him some help, supported him, he wouldn't be fighting for his life right now.

"Do I know everything?" I question. Confusion forces Tom's eyebrows together, silently asking me to elaborate. "I know doctors gloss over details. You'd tell me if he wasn't going to make it, wouldn't you?"

"Theo, when they told you it was too early to give a prognosis they meant it. They're not hiding anything from you."

"So the surgery went well? I saw you talking to that doctor."

"Jason, Dr Garcia, is a friend of mine. James couldn't be in better hands. His heart stopped again during the surgery, but they got him back and gave him the best chance to fight this."

"He will. He'll fight." He *has* to.

"Theo…you know that's just the first step, right? Even if…*when*, he wakes up, his mind is going to take a *lot* longer to heal."

"I know that. I'll drag him to the GP surgery by his ear if I have to."

"James won't be going straight home, T. He'll be taken to a psychiatric unit."

"You mean…like sectioned? He's not a basketcase for Christ's sake."

"He's mentally ill, Theo. His mind is in a bad place. The likelihood is he's going to be disappointed he didn't succeed and if he's released he could try again. He needs specialist help, and you need to prepare yourself for the fact it could take a *long* time."

Disappointed? Try again? "No." I shake my head. "It was a mistake. When he wakes up he'll realise that. He just wants help. It was a flash of despair. Maybe he'd been drinking and didn't know what he was doing."

"There was no alcohol in his system."

"He wants to get better. I know he does," I carry on, ignoring Tom.

"This isn't about you, Theo."

"I know that!" I yell. "Do you think I'm that self ab-fucking-sorbed?"

Tom sighs, his lips melting into a concerned frown. "What I mean is this has nothing to do with his feelings for you. This isn't because he doesn't care about you, or because he thinks you don't care about him. You haven't caused this."

"I-I know that." The words don't sound as convincing as I'd hoped when they leave my lips.

"You need some rest. Do you want to stay at mine tonight?"

"No, I, uh…" *I need my mum.* "Can you take me to Mum's?"

Tom pats my knee and then twists the key in the ignition. "Sure."

Raw emotion bubbles in my chest when we pull into my mum's driveway. I know the pressure will burst the second I see her, but she always knows how to comfort me, what to advise.

"Does she know what's happened?"

Tom nods. "I called her while you were sleeping. I called Tess, too."

I must call Tess as well. "Will you pick me up in the morning? I understand if you're busy."

"I'm working early because I missed my shift tonight, but I'll leave the house early. I can take you home or you can ride in with me and wait in the staffroom until visiting time."

"Thanks," I say, opening the car door. "For everything."

"If you need me, whatever the time, I'm only a phone call away."

"Thanks, Tom."

Stepping up to my mum's front door, I fumble in my pocket for my keys, stopping when it starts to open in front of me. Standing to one side, my mum lets me in before closing the door and wrapping her arms around me, cradling my head to her shoulder.

"I'm so scared, Mum," I whimper, letting my tears soak into her shirt.

With her flattened hand, she rubs small circles on my back. "It's okay, baby boy. Everything's going to be okay."

For the next few minutes, my body shaking, all the pain, fear, guilt, and sadness pours out of me in violent sobs. I don't move an inch, clutching my mum so tightly my fingers start to ache as I fall apart in her arms.

Stay with me, James.

* * *

The next day I get Tom to take me home so I can change and update Tess. I've yet to speak to her and, after Tom's call last night, she must be worried sick. Heart in my throat, I ring Max on the way. There's been no change in James' condition overnight and I don't know whether that's good or bad.

"It's good," Tom assures me, and I believe him because I *have* to.

Back in my flat, I end up crying again the moment I see Tess. Through the haze of tears I don't notice Lucy sitting on the new sofa until I've relayed the last twenty-four hours to Tess.

"Oh…hi," I mumble, my gaze lingering on that damn sofa. The sight of it gives me a heavy feeling in my stomach. Maybe if I hadn't brought it up, started the argument in James' office, he wouldn't have broken down, he wouldn't have tried to k…

I can't even think the words.

"I'm gonna take a shower," I say, embarrassment from crying in front of someone I barely know heating my cheeks. That adds even more weight to the chain of guilt hanging from my neck. I hardly know Lucy and I *should.* She's important to Tess, Tess is important to *me*, and I haven't made enough effort.

How the hell did my life get to the point where I just keep screwing everything up?

Staring into the mirror after my shower, I still look like shit. My eyes are so dark and swollen I can't help wonder if they'll ever look normal again. I don't want to look at myself anymore so I dress quickly, brush my teeth, and then call work. Mike rang several times yesterday after I failed to return, and again this morning, but I don't have enough energy left in me to deal with him so I dial Stacey's extension instead.

I'm purposely vague, explaining that James has had an accident and I need to take a few days to be with him. There's a wariness in Stacey's voice that makes me think she doesn't quite believe me but that's the least of my problems right now so ignore it. I don't know what James will want people to know and it's not my decision to make. I also don't know what's going to happen 'at the top' of Holden House. James has a silent business partner and other higher management members that I've never met, but I assume Max is dealing with those.

"Lucy's nice," I say to Tess as I tie the laces on my shoes. "I'm sorry I haven't gotten to know her properly yet."

Tess smiles, and for a moment she looks lost in her own little world. "You know that 'click' you told me about when you started seeing James? The one that makes no sense, it's just…there? I felt that click. We just *get* each other, you know? I think…" she trails off, lowering her voice, presumably in case Lucy can hear us from the bathroom. "I think I love her."

Knowing how that feels, I smile. "I'm happy for you." And when James is better, because he *will* get better, I will get to know Lucy like I should've done already.

"Do you want me to come with you to the hospital?"

"No need. I'll probably have to hang around until visiting hours. I'll be fine on my own."

"Well if you change your mind, I'll be on the first bus over there."

"Thanks," I say, forcing a weak smile. "My taxi should be here any minute. I'll go wait outside."

"Do you want me to arrange for your car to be picked up from the cemetery?"

"Thanks, but Tom said he'll sort it."

When I stand from the sofa, she throws her arms around me. "I love you, T."

"Love you too, gorgeous," I whisper, fighting the urge to cry…again.

Drawing a deep breath, I head out of the flat to spend another day, flooded with worry, uncertainty, and hope, by James' side.

* * *

Day two: No change. I sit with James, alongside Max with Tom popping in whenever he can, for as long as the nurses will let me. At night, I don't sleep, my brain forcing me to relive everything that's happened over and over until it's time to get up and do it all again.

Day three: No change. I'm living in déjà vu hell as the day pans out exactly the same as the last.

Come on, James. Wake up for me.

Day four: Today, the doctor with the jazzy stethoscope attempts to wean James off his ventilator. It's unsuccessful, and the day remains the same as the previous two.

Day five: No change.

Day six: "Hello?" I answer Max's call in a panic, abandoning the task of making toast that I'll nibble at until I throw it in the bin.

"James is awake. The hospital just called."

When I exhale, it feels like fifty tonnes of pain pours out of my body. "Oh thank God."

"We can't see him just yet, but they'll let us in before visiting time. I'm going over now. Do you want a lift?"

"Yes. Absolutely. Yes. Please. Thank you." *Oh God thank you.*

"I'll be there in about twenty minutes."

"Thank you." *Thank you, thank you, thank you.*

After hanging up on Max, I call Tom. It goes straight to voicemail, he must be at work already, so I leave a message before ringing my mum, then Tess.

I'm already outside, my feet tapping anxiously against the pavement, when Max's car pulls up. I get in quickly, and he sets off again before I've even finished fixing my seatbelt. The drive seems to take forever, every traffic light working against us, and when we arrive we head straight up to the waiting room outside the ICU.

We've been waiting for almost an hour when Tom turns up, dressed in his scrubs. "Any news?" he asks.

Sighing, I shake my head.

"Let me see what I can find out."

Both Max and I stare after Tom as he walks away. He disappears into a room marked 'Staff Only' and returns after several minutes that feel like hours, with another doctor.

"You can go through," the other doctor, an older man with salt and pepper hair and an outdated moustache, says. "I'll join you in a few minutes to discuss any questions you might have."

Nodding, Max turns straight to the door of James' ward.

I start to follow, but I'm stopped by Tom's hand appearing on my chest. "I'm so sorry, Theo. He's not ready to see you just yet."

"What do you mean?" I argue, attempting to step past him. "The doctor just said…"

"He was talking to Max. James doesn't want to see you. His care team have to respect that."

"He…doesn't *want* to? Why? What…what have I done?"

"He's recovering from a major trauma. Physically *and* mentally. He just needs some time."

I feel like I've been kicked in the stomach. "But *why*? How much time?" This doesn't make sense. "If you just let me see him, he'll change his mind, I know he will."

"I can't let you do that. I'm sorry, T, really I am. You're going to have to be patient."

Patient? Time? How am I supposed to do that when I'm going out of my fucking mind?

"You should go home," Tom adds. "I'll keep checking in here and keep you updated."

"No," I spit. "I'll wait."

"Remember what I said about the long road ahead? He's in a bad place right now. He might not change his mind today."

"Then I'll come back tomorrow, and the next day, and the next. Whenever he changes his mind, because he *will*, he *has* to, I'll be here. I'm staying."

Tom's hand settles on my shoulder, squeezing gently. "I need to get back downstairs, but I'll come back when I get a minute. You know where to find me if you need anything."

"Thanks."

And so, I spend the rest of the day pacing the corridor, drinking disgusting vending machine coffee and feeling utterly fucking useless until Max reappears at kicking out time. He gives me a ride home, sounding almost guilty as he fills me in on James' progress. Apparently, James spent most of the day refusing to talk, rejecting his meds, and sleeping.

I want to see him so desperately. His refusal hurts. The worry and confusion are suffocating. Is he ashamed? Does he blame me? Is he pushing me away for his sake or mine? These are merely a fraction of the questions that race around my mind on a loop throughout the night, and when morning rolls around, I snuggle with Tess for a while before getting myself ready for another day pacing corridors.

Day seven: James' physical condition continues to improve. He still won't see me.

Day eight: James has two psychiatric assessments carried out by two different doctors. His blood pressure started fluctuating during the night, but by the afternoon they manage to stabilise it again. He still won't see me.

Day nine: His doctor puts in a request for a bed at the psychiatric unit. Since this news was broken to him, he hasn't spoken a single word to anyone. He still won't see me.

Day ten: As usual, I'm standing outside the ICU when Max tells me James is being transferred today.

"Will he see me before he leaves?" I ask, my voice weak with exhaustion.

Max shakes his head, looking anywhere but at me. "Maybe when he's settled in." He sounds as hopeless as I feel.

"Maybe."

"You should go home for now. I'll call you once he's at the unit."

He doesn't say it directly, but I know he's suggesting I leave so I don't see James on his way out. I don't have the strength to argue. I'm all out of fight. "Sure. Let him know…just tell him I love him."

Max smiles. It's a sad, sympathetic, smile, but I appreciate it nonetheless. "Will do."

Head bowed, I leave the hospital. I'm not sure why it pops into my head, maybe because James is about to take another step closer to home, but his apartment suddenly becomes all I can think about. I don't think anyone's been since it happened, Max hasn't mentioned it, and it needs cleaning. Part of me thinks it could destroy me going back there, but the other needs something to focus on. I need to keep busy. I can't handle another day of sitting, pacing, *waiting*.

I'm on the bus, thankful to have a seat to myself, when Tess calls. I automatically note the time on the screen when her name flashes up and assume she's on her lunch break. "Hey," I answer.

"How is he today?"

"Still won't see me."

She sighs down the line. "Oh, T. I'm sorry. Where are you now?"

"I'm on the bus on my way to James' apartment."

"Why?"

"I've not had time to get my car fixed."

"Not the bus, dickwad, why are you going to his apartment?"

"It needs cleaning. He can't come home to how it is now."

"You shouldn't do that on your own. Where does he live? I can be there in half an hour."

"I'll be fine. Let's face it, your boss doesn't need another reason to sack you."

"Pfft. He's not in today anyway. Besides, I can't help it if I get the shits. He wouldn't want me to spread it to the rest of the staff, I'm sure."

I'd laugh if that part of me hadn't died. "Thanks, Tess, but I'm good. Promise. Gotta go, mine's the next stop."

"Okay. Catch you later."

I told a tiny lie. My stop is ten minutes away but I can't face talking any longer. When I talk, I cry, and if I cry any more my head will burst.

The noise on the bus grates on my nerves – the harsh engine, people laughing, a baby that won't stop bleeding crying. On top of the already deafening thoughts running riot in my mind, it's too much, so I twist my earphones into my ears and hit *play* with the button on the cord.

Demons by Imagine Dragons penetrates my ears and, shit, if this song wasn't written for James. That's when it hits me. *Music.* There're hidden meanings and emotions in every song. I wonder if that's why James listens to it so often. He relates to it, maybe uses it as a way to express the things he can't say out loud. Perhaps I can get through to him that way.

My stop is nearing, so I'll revisit that thought later.

I miss you.

The five minutes deep breathing and trying to steel my emotions outside the door to James' apartment does shit to prepare me for what I'm about to see. When I walk inside, I'm right back to the day I found him, and I haven't even reached the bathroom yet.

I literally shake myself off, cranking my neck from side to side, before treading cautiously to the bathroom. My eyes close as I round the corner, silently hoping Max has already been here and forgotten to tell me.

He hasn't.

The stagnant water, coloured with James' blood, still fills the bathtub. The towels Tom used to dry him off, again stained with blood, remain on the floor where he left them. Pieces of fried chicken and shrivelled fries litter the tiles and as far as I can see, only the empty pill bottles are missing, presumably taken by the paramedics.

For a while, all I can do is stare. Stare…and remember. After who knows how long, the entry buzzer snaps me out of the trance I've slipped into, but I don't answer it straightaway. I can't let anyone in here until this mess is gone.

But it sounds again.

And again.

"Hello?" I answer, my voice curt after stomping over to the receiver.

"Let me up, bellend."

Tess. Her voice makes my lips curl into an almost-smile as I let her into the building. Hanging up the receiver, I open the door and wait for her. She appears from the lift opposite moments later in her work uniform – black joggers and a white t-shirt with the company logo sewn into it.

"How did you find me here?"

"I rang Tom. I'm not letting you do this alone."

"It's a mess in there," I warn. "There's b-bl-" Throat tight, I can't finish my sentence.

"All the more reason to have me here. We'll get it done in half the time."

"Thank you," is all my wobbly voice will allow me to say before I turn to the kitchen in search of a bucket. Some things are still out of place after James' destructive breakdown the day before...*it*...happened, so I rearrange as I go along. Eventually, I head into the bathroom armed with a washing up bowl filled with soapy water, a bin bag, and some sponges.

"Jesus," Tess mutters, following behind me. "God, Theo...I can't even imagine what finding him in here did to you."

"Would've been a whole lot worse if Tom hadn't been with me," I say, bile scratching at my throat as I roll up my sleeve and reach into the water, pulling the plug. "He knew just what to do. Didn't think I'd ever say this, but I'm so fucking glad my car broke down again, otherwise I'd have been on my own."

I watch the water swirling down the drain, relieved to see the back of it. It leaves pink-tinged, residual watermarks around the edges, so, dipping my sponge into the washing up bowl, I clean there first.

"Sometimes," I begin, detesting myself for what I'm about to say. "Sometimes I wish I'd never met him, just so I don't have to feel his pain. How selfish is that?"

"It's not selfish, T. Not even a saint would be able to go through what you are without having some doubts. You're not selfish, you're just hurting in a way I can't even imagine."

"He's hurting more."

"No, he isn't. He just didn't cope with it as well as you."

If I could summon the energy it would take, I would laugh. I'm not coping. I'm merely existing. Living in limbo. I can't see a future anymore. Everything I saw just a couple of weeks ago is *gone.*

"What a waste of KFC," Tess says, attempting to lighten the dense atmosphere as she tosses the rotting food into a black bag.

We work for a couple of hours, cleaning everything three times. Every stroke of the sponge makes my chest ache a little more, but by the time we've finished, there's no trace of the horror that occurred here.

"So," Tess begins. "What do you want to do now? We could grab a takeaway on the way home, catch up on Criminal Minds."

"Actually, I think I'm gonna stay here."

"All night?"

I nod. "I feel closer to him here. Besides, the kitchen still isn't perfect, and everything should be perfect for when he gets back, whether he wants me here or-" The word gets caught on the lump that's formed in my throat.

"He's not seeing things clearly, T. When he's had the help he needs, he'll come around."

"Maybe." Staring at the ceiling, I sigh. "But I have to learn to accept the fact he might not."

"And how are you going to do that?"

Dragging in a deep breath, I shrug. "I have no fucking idea."

When Tess leaves, I hit shuffle on James' iPod which is permanently sat in a square dock in the kitchen. A sense of calm washes over me the very second the music starts filling the lonely apartment. There's always music here, and when I close my eyes I can almost feel James sneaking up behind me, his hands settling on my hips as he breathes into my neck.

I miss you. Please miss me, too.

I potter around the kitchen for a while, reorganising cupboards and making notes of things I need to replace. Later in the evening, Max rings to tell me James has been moved to the psychiatric unit and that he's not only refusing to see *me* now, but him as well. Apparently the staff there are a lot stricter with visiting times. I'll no longer be able to wait outside his room, strolling their corridors, but they can't stop me waiting outside the building during every visiting hour available, and that's exactly what I'm going to do.

Exhausted, I go straight to bed after ending Max's call. Removing my clothes, I fold them neatly over the back of the plush chair in James' bedroom - because I know tossing them on the floor would annoy him - then I climb onto the mattress. Hugging a pillow, embedded with his scent, to my chest, I break down for the thousandth time since I found him…crying myself into a restless sleep.

I miss you.

Chapter

Twelve

~James~

"Morning, James," the chirpy nurse, who comes in every morning, says. "Time to wake up."

I am *awake*. I don't look at her. I don't look at anybody. I spend my days lying on my back with my head flopped to the side, staring at the magnolia wall until my spine starts to ache, then I turn over and look at the wooden cupboards with no doors instead.

"I have your meds. Are you going to take them for me today?"

No.

She asks again, and again she gets no response. I just want her to go away. I want it *all* to go away.

"The breakfast trolley will be coming around soon. Are you going to eat today?"

No.

"I'll be back in a little while to change your bandages."

When she leaves, I roll onto my side and continue staring at the wall. I shouldn't be here. I shouldn't be *anywhere*. I was so certain I wouldn't fuck it up this time, but I did. I fuck *everything* up. I'm a waste of a life.

* * *

For four days I haven't spoken to a single person. Sometimes I think I might. Sometimes I think I *should*. But those thoughts aren't strong enough to win over the only thing that plagues my mind every long minute of every long day.

I don't want to be here.

Perhaps if I ignore everyone long enough, pretend I don't exist, my body will eventually give up like I planned.

"Knock knock," Peter practically sings as he walks into my room. Peter Donovan is my therapist, a step above the nurses who won't quit fussing over me, and one below my psychiatrist, who I've only seen once. Peter, however, graces me with his annoying, unwanted presence twice a fucking day.

His visits pan out exactly the same every single day. He talks, I don't. Yesterday he told me if I carry on refusing my meds they will have no choice but to *force* me to take them. That shouldn't be allowed to happen. I'm a grown man. I should be able to make my own damn decisions. What difference does it make to their lives if I'm here or not? If anything, they should be grateful for the extra bed. No point wasting it, wasting their time, the government's money, on someone who doesn't fucking *want* it.

"Nurse Marie tells me you ate some breakfast this morning. That's great."

Patronising bastard.

"What made you start eating?"

"I was hungry." *Fucktard.*

Peter pulls up the chair next to my bed and sits down. "Talking, too? I'm honoured."

What the fuck? Aren't you supposed to mollycoddle me and ask about my feelings?

"So, how are you feeling today?"

Here we go. "Fine." Why am I talking? *Shut the hell up.*

"Now that's not strictly true, is it?"

"*What?*"

"I've been doing this job for seven years. Training for even longer. In my experience, people who feel *fine* don't try and take their own life."

I can't believe I'm here, listening to this shit. It was all supposed to end.

"So you've eaten, you've spoken, how about you take your meds for me?"

"There's no point."

"Why do you think that?"

Seriously. Stop talking, James. Stop talking, now. "They don't work."

"They do."

"No, they *don't*."

"Why not? How do they make you feel?"

"Like a robot. A useless robot." I don't want to talk to him. He's just such a sarcastic arsehole I can't seem to help myself.

"Okay, answer this honestly. Did you decide they make you feel like a robot while you were taking them, or after you stopped?"

"What's that got to do with it?"

"Answer it."

Huffing in frustration, I drag myself into a sitting position, dangling my legs off the edge of the bed. For the first time, I take in his appearance. He's wearing beige slacks and a white shirt with a lanyard hanging round his neck. He can't be much older than me, but he dresses like a grandfather. "After. I didn't notice while I was taking them because, like I said, I was a fucking robot."

I stopped taking them after my father died because I *needed* to. Suddenly, I was faced with a huge responsibility and a workload I wouldn't have been able to deal with without the extra energy, longer waking hours.

"Or maybe you didn't notice because while you were medicated you really did feel *fine*, as opposed to the *pretend* fine you're feeling now."

"You're wasting your time. Talking therapy doesn't work either."

"Well it won't...if you don't *talk*."

Go fuck yourself.

"Your brother has been by again today."

"I don't want-"

"And Theo is outside."

Theodore. His name makes my chest ache and my stomach swell with guilt. It's the first emotion I've felt since I got here and I don't like it. The only way I can fight those feelings, is with anger. "I don't want to see him."

He needs to forget about me, dammit!

"Why not? He cares about you, as does your brother."

"They shouldn't."

"Why not?"

"Because I cause them pain. They worry about me and they shouldn't. I'm not worth it."

My mental illness, my problems… they're infectious. They don't just affect *me*, they spread to other people, people I care about. It feels selfish to carry on living, to keep the pain of being close to me in their hearts.

"So you think they're stupid?"

"*What?* No! Of course not."

"But they waste their time caring about someone who isn't worth it. Doesn't sound too clever to me."

"Stop it," I spit, shaking my head in an effort to unscramble my thoughts. "You're twisting my words."

Where's the distant, note-taking, fake-sympathising professional I'm used to dealing with? Is this guy even qualified?

"James," he says, his voice low and serious. "If I'd come in here and started asking generic questions from a list, looking down my nose at you while scribbling down my thoughts, would you have answered me?"

Umm…

"I might not do things the conventional way, I might not pussyfoot around and relay everything I learned in the textbooks, but I *am* qualified and I *can* help you. You just need to let me."

Hmm, well that's different. It almost sounds like he's asking for my permission rather than ramming diagnoses and medications down my throat. I also can't help wondering if he has some kind of magical mind-reading powers.

"It never goes away. The sadness. This feeling that I'm broken." I stare at the floor as I talk. Telling him anything at all is hard enough. I've already spilled more information about myself than I ever have before to a professional and I don't have the courage to watch his reaction as I do.

"Even when I feel great, it's still there, taunting me, telling me it'll come back."

"You say it *tells* you. Is it a voice? A voice that's not yours?"

"No, no. It's not a nutjob kind of voice." I realise that probably isn't appropriate terminology when I'm stuck in a psychiatric ward and apologise immediately. "Sorry, I just mean…They're my *own* thoughts. You know, how you silently talk to yourself? They're my own thoughts talking to me. I'm not hearing voices. Am I making sense?"

"Perfect sense. So in your mind the depression makes you broken?"

"Yes."

"Maybe you are. That doesn't mean people shouldn't care about you. Value you. More importantly, it doesn't mean you shouldn't value *yourself.*"

"You don't understand what I'm trying to say. I *can't* be fixed."

I was *born* this way. I've been struggling with this darkness, this emptiness, for as long as I can remember.

"Neither can a three-legged puppy, but you can bet your backside someone will love it."

"That's not the same and you know it."

"I'll tell you what I know so far. I know two men ask about you every day, desperate to see you. They care about you, and no sane human being becomes emotionally attached to a robot, as you referred to yourself earlier. So, James, I think you're lying to me. I think you're not telling me about the *real* you, the James those men care so much about. Why is that?"

I shake my head. I know what he's trying to do and it's not going to work. "Max *has* to love me. I'm his brother. And Theodore…his heart is too big to see the bad things."

And there's so much bad. So much darkness. Emptiness. I'm…I'm too tired.

"Do you want to know what I think?"

Not particularly. "Go on."

"I think you're focusing on the bad because it's easy."

"*Easy?*" *What the fuck?* "You think what I'm feeling is *easy?*"

"I think it's easier to accept things are never going to improve than fight for them to get better."

"Are you even allowed to say things like that? Isn't it against some kind of Therapist Rulebook? It's not very professional."

"Have the other professionals you've seen helped you?"

"No."

"Then maybe it's time to try a different approach."

For the first time, I look him right in the eyes. His expression doesn't falter, as if he genuinely believes there's hope for me. I admire his optimism, but I can't summon it myself.

"I've fought all my life. It doesn't work." Tears sting the back of my eyes and I pray they don't fall. It's clear by the fact I'm in here – dirty, unshaven, with bandaged wrists – that I'm weak, that I'm a failure. I don't need to reinforce that knowledge by crying in front of him.

"*I've* being the operative word there. *Nobody* is capable of getting through this life alone, James. When your boat is drifting from the shore, it's okay to use an anchor for support. We *all* need an anchor. Without people to love us, we'd just drift further and further away."

"What if…" I want to stop talking now. I want to curl up on my side and go back to giving up. It hurts, and he's *right*. Giving up *is* easier than this. "What if I've already drifted too far to be saved?"

"You almost did, but your anchor, Theodore, held you in place. Now you need to make the journey back to shore. It's a long way, and it's *okay* to need help getting there. That's what *I'm* here for. That's what your medications are for. That's what the people you love are for. You do love them, right? Max, Theodore."

"Of course I do." Why would he ask that? I tried to leave them because I love them. I tried to *free* them.

"Robots can't love," he says with the smuggest grin on his face.

Suddenly, I'm laughing.

Laughing? Have you forgot where you are? What a mess you made of things? You have nothing to laugh about.

And so, the laughter fades, replaced with that damn knot of sadness, of *hatred* towards myself, bound tightly around my stomach.

"I think we'll leave it there for today," Peter says.

I feel an odd stab of disappointment. He can't leave yet. He said he'd help me and he hasn't. I'm not fixed yet, dammit!

"You did well today. Thank you for talking to me."

I still can't quite believe I actually did. All I've done since the second I woke up is silently curse the bastard who saved my life, and think of ways to make sure I succeed next time. For a while, I even considered talking, saying all the right things which I know they want to hear so they'll discharge me.

Then I could take myself away to a place where it would take someone days to find my body.

But that's *not* why I talked to Peter today. I talked because I couldn't help it. Peter asked the right questions, questions no one else has ever asked before. He treated me like a person instead of an illness and it caught me off guard, kicking my walls down. Maybe it won't continue. Maybe the darkness will set in again and remind me it's part of who I am, that it will never leave.

But for now…for now I feel a little…*okay*.

"Before I go," Peter mutters, pulling an envelope out of the file he's holding. "This is from Theo. Don't open it if you're not ready. It's *okay* to not be ready. But if you do, and you want to talk about what's inside, you know how to get hold of me."

Nodding once, I take the envelope. "Okay," I whisper, the word wobbly on my lips.

I run my thumb over the brown paper. There's something small and hard inside. It intrigues me, but not enough to open it, so I tuck it under my pillow.

"Oh, one more thing," he adds, spinning on his heels when he reaches the door. "If you want to listen to it you'll need to check out your earphones and charger from the office."

Right. There are rules here about any kind of cords, anything sharp, or anything small enough to be swallowed.

Now I'm even more scared to open it. Is it a phone? Has he recorded a message for me? I can't handle that. Not yet. Hearing his voice would literally strangle me with shame.

Why can't he just walk away? Can't he see it's for the best? That I'm not worth his pain?

Two minutes ago I was feeling okay. Now? Now I'm lying in a ball on my bed, tears seeping into my pillow, and cursing myself for not cutting deeper.

I'm a selfish, fucked-up bastard.

* * *

Three days later…

I took my meds today. I'm not sure why. I'm still not convinced they'll work but I downed them in one before I had chance to change my mind. After talking with my psychiatrist, he's decided to treat me with something different this time. So this morning, I took my first ever dose of quetiapine, an anti-psychotic, which apparently helps long-term bipolar depression.

We'll see.

My wrists are still bandaged, and they've stayed clean for twenty-four hours now so I assume the weeping has stopped. The scald on my hand is healing too; the blisters have burst, leaving loose white skin in their wake. I stare at it frequently, torturing myself, trying to force those feelings back to the surface, for no other reason than I'm fucked in the head.

My therapy is going well, I think. I've never told a professional about my suicide attempts as a teenager, or the depths of my self-harm before, but Peter manages to tease this kind of information out of me somehow. Usually by being a sarcastic arse. But I guess I can relate to a sarcastic arse better than a condescending twat who's walked straight out of a textbook. It's almost a battle of wills between us. I *need* to challenge him, raise the stakes in our bullshit-a-thon.

I don't have what you could call *hope* yet, but a tiny part of me wants to believe it's on its way. Theodore's envelope remains unopened under my pillow. I haven't been able to face it yet, but I'm getting there. Last night I briefly considered letting him see me when I realised I missed him.

God, I miss him.

But if I see him, I fear the guilt will overwhelm me and I'll be right back where I started.

* * *

One week later…

They removed my bandages yesterday. It's set my progress back a little because now I can't stop staring at the angry scars on my wrists. They're not neat and tidy. They're swollen, mangled and ugly. They won't hide easily. I also can't feel my left thumb. The worst part is, they're a reminder. Seeing them takes me back to that day, to those feelings, and I'm overcome with hurt, anger, regret, and selfishness.

Some days I regret putting the people I love through what I have, other days I regret that I didn't succeed.

I'm working on the latter.

A few hours later I'm sitting with Peter in my room. Some days he comes here, some days I see him in his office. Today, without the bandages, I feel more comfortable here.

"What do you feel when you look at them?"

Damn. I didn't realise I was staring at my wrists again and I quickly tug my long sleeves over them.

"Shame. Failure." I shrug.

"You could see them as a sign of strength."

I blow out a laugh, saturated with sarcasm. "I gave up. I see weakness, not strength."

"You survived those scars, James. You *fought.* You're *still* fighting. You've made good progress this last week. Do you think you'd be where you are now if those scars weren't there? Would you have sought help?"

Again, I shrug. The guy brings out my petulant teenager side.

"This isn't over when you walk out of here. You have an illness, James. A lifelong, *manageable* illness. The mind is life's most powerful tool…and also the most fragile. You need to take care of it. If you don't want to go back to that dark place you're going to do things right this time, do you hear me? You're going to utilise your support system. You're going to reach for that anchor whenever you need it."

I nod, because I'm not sure I can agree out loud. "I…I don't think I'm ready to leave yet," I admit. The thought of facing the real world, my colleagues, my family… I can't. *What must they think of me?* "I feel safe here."

"You have a way to go before you'll be ready for that."

"Oh yes. I have to make something." I laugh at the ridiculousness of it. I could make the best progress in the world but nobody gets out of here until they've socialised in the arts and crafts room upstairs. I swear, if you don't feel like a headcase before you come in here, they'll make damn sure you do before you leave. "I haven't painted a picture since I was five years fucking old."

"It's more about interacting with people. We've talked about this."

"Interacting with nutjobs? Perfect prep for the real world."

"Hey, remember you're one of those nutjobs before you judge," he says with a smirk. That right there is one of the things I like most about Peter. He's brutally honest and, when he's not being a dick, he also makes a lot of sense.

"You're not ready *now*," he continues. "But carry on like this, taking your meds, *talking*, and you *will* be."

"The meds make me feel like I've been chewing sand. I feel nauseous, too."

"That'll wear off. We've discussed that, too. Quit complaining."

"You shouldn't talk to a mental patient like that you know. You could tip me over the edge."

"Then I would feel smug that you can't do anything about it because we're watching you too closely." The smartarse actually winks at me.

"Thank you, Peter."

He raises a curious eyebrow.

"For making this…*easier*. I've never had a therapist like you before. It feels like…like you 'get it'."

"Sure I do. I've read the textbooks."

Shaking my head, I smile. "I think I'm going to open the envelope today."

"Yeah? Do you want me to check out the earphones for you?"

"Before you do…is it his voice? Has he recorded a message for me?"

"I've no idea. He's not *my* boyfriend."

"Right," I mumble, chuckling with nerves.

"So…earphones?"

"Yes, thanks."

"Back in five."

With an anxious heart, I tease Theodore's envelope out from under my pillow and smooth the creases that have formed around the edges with the pads of my fingers. I do nothing but stare at it until Peter returns, and by the time he hands me the earphones, I'm not sure I'm ready to open it after all.

"I'll be around for another hour or so if you need me," Peter says, patting my shoulder.

"Does he call often?" Once the words are out, I don't even know why I've said it. I'm tormenting myself. Part of me wants Theodore to move on and forget about me, but the other part would be crushed if he did.

"He's here every day."

"Here? In person?"

Peter nods. "Come visiting time he sits right outside. Brings your clothes, toiletries."

"That's not Max?"

"No, but your brother rings every morning to see how you are."

For days after I arrived here all I thought about was myself – how tired I was, how angry, lost. I refused to think about anyone else because it was too painful. Thinking about Theodore or my family had the power to weaken my resolve, my determination to escape, to *die*…so if they popped into my mind I would shove them right back out.

Knowing that they didn't do the same, weighs me down with the most intense feeling of selfishness. It feels like I'm drowning just off shore but no one can see me struggling to stay afloat. I've been sinking my whole life, occasionally managing to bob to the surface until the current of misery drags me back under. I don't want to fight for air anymore. I want to get out. Swim to shore. Live on dry land and accept the fact I might have to dip my toe back into the water every once in a while.

I want…I want to *fight*.

When I look up, Peter is gone, leaving me alone with whatever Theodore wants to tell me. Am I ready to hear it? I'm not sure, but I owe it to him to try.

Sliding my finger under the tab, I break the seal on the envelope and pluck out an iPod, *my* iPod I think, and a letter. Chewing my bottom lip, I suck in what feels like my first breath in hours and start to read.

James,

You're a stupid fucking idiot and I'm mad with you…but I also love you. I LOVE YOU. *I don't understand what's going on in your head. I've tried, but no, I don't get it. But I'm here. I can't understand what you're going thorough but know I'll be by your side while you do. Know that I'm close, even if you don't want me to be. I'm not going anywhere. Unfortunately for you, you're not the boss here, so you're just going to have to suck it up.*

I'm forced to look up for a moment, blinking the tears away. If I close my eyes I can see the expression on his face as he wrote that last sentence. He's cute when he tries to be authoritative.

I hope you're not being too much of an arse to the nurses. I can imagine them talking about what a pompous twat you are in the staff room. At least I hope they are. If you're pissing them off it means you're coming back to me. I'm sure they can handle you. I've met your therapist. He's certainly unique, I'll give him that. He seems as stubborn as you, which is good. You need someone who won't stand for your bullshit.

I miss your bullshit, James. I miss your attitude. I miss the feel of your skin. I miss the way your jaw ticks when someone, usually me, annoys you. I even miss your freckle.

I miss you.

I'm staying in your apartment. I hope you don't mind. Not that I care if you do...I'm not leaving. I can be a stubborn bastard too. I learned from the best. It's not very tidy I'm afraid. Right now there's two day old, half-eaten Chinese food all over your coffee table. Oh and the fridge is filled with cheap food instead of your fancy Sainsbury's shit. If you want to change that you better hurry up and get better so you can come home.

Okay, I've rambled long enough. I'm putting your iPod in the envelope. You must be missing your music. I've not touched your songs but you'll find a playlist with just three songs on it. They're songs that say everything I want to tell you, but I can't because you're being a dickface.

You'll be Okay by A Great Big World – I need you to listen to every single lyric and BELIEVE them.

Here Without You by 3 Doors Down – I'm here. I'm with you.

Maybe Tomorrow by the Stereophonics – Just...because.

Get better, James. Choose to keep going. Choose US. I'll be here whenever you're ready.

Theodore

PS: The halogen lights in your kitchen have blown and I don't know how to get them out to replace them.

When I finish reading there's a smile etched onto my lips. A real, genuine smile that I can feel tugging at the skin around my eyes. Lying down, I roll onto my side and read the whole thing again, then I twist my earphones into my ears and scroll for the playlist he's created. I laugh when I find the playlist titled *Get the Fuck Better.* I start from the bottom because *You'll be Okay* is the only song I'm not familiar with. I also think it might be the hardest to listen to.

Maybe Tomorrow sparks memories that keep the smile on my face. I'm taken back to the night I first saw him, belting it out of tune, to playing it in my car for no other reason than I wanted to see him squirm. I was happy in those moments. I *have* known happiness. My brain has been lying to me and I believed it so easily.

When *Here Without You* dances into my ears I start to sink again, but I fight it. I kick and struggle, and vow to make it to shore so I can be with him. Right now, I don't want to be here without *him*, either.

The last song is as difficult to hear as I expected. I try *so* hard to believe the lyrics like he asked me to but I just…*can't.* Not yet. Will I be okay? I don't know. But I *want* to be.

Without giving myself time to think, I get up and walk out of my room. I have only left the safety of my room a couple of times and I feel self-conscious, as if everyone is watching me, as I make my way to the staff office.

The door is open and Peter stands from his chair, walking over to me as soon as he spies me coming.

Dragging in a deep breath and holding it there, I mutter, "When Theodore comes inside today…I want to see him."

* * *

One of my nurses is due soon to watch over me while I shave. In front of the mirror, after showering and changing, I rub at the thick stubble coating my face. I look like shit. I've lost weight, my hair needs cutting, my skin is pale. I can't help wondering how Theodore will react to me. I look nothing like the man he fell in love with.

He loves you, I remind myself. I need to hold onto that, to believe it even when my mind is telling me not to.

When my nurse arrives, I make the effort, for the first time, to read her ID badge that's pinned to her shirt. "Thank you, Jackie," I say, taking the disposable razor and shaving foam from her. I'm grateful she lets me go into the bathroom alone, although she asks that I keep the door ajar.

It takes me a while to remove the hair that I've allowed to build up over the last few weeks, made more difficult by my thumb that refuses to cooperate, and when I'm done, I barely recognise myself. It's been years since I've been clean-shaven, usually opting to run over my beard with the clippers. Again, I wonder what Theodore will think. Having smooth skin definitely accentuates the gauntness of my cheeks, but I look marginally more acceptable than I did fifteen minutes ago.

Stepping back into my room, I pass the used razor back to Jackie. "Thanks."

"Looking good," she says, smiling. "Doors open in ten minutes. You'll need to wait in the day room for your visitor."

"Okay." I nod. "Thanks."

My courage starts to wane when she leaves, so I read over Theodore's letter again to remind myself why I'm doing this. I'm doing it because I miss him, because I need him, because I *love* him.

I haven't been in the day room before and as I soon as I get there I don't like it. There are several couches dotted around, and a stack of plastic chairs either side of the door. In the corner, there's a desk with a nurse sitting at it, *watching* us. Someone is *always* watching us.

There's a woman, younger than me, sitting in one of the large armchairs. She's clutching a teddy bear which is tatty and worn, and nodding her head like she's having a conversation with someone who isn't there. When I sit down, a man who's so young he might well be a teenager, walks over to me, wearing an eye-patch and fidgeting with the zip on his jacket. "I didn't do it, you know. They say I did, but I didn't."

I offer an awkward smile, not knowing what he's talking about or how to respond. I feel like I don't belong here with these people. I'm not insane, just…sad. I'm not judging them, intentionally at least, but they make me feel nervous. I don't know how to interact with them.

"He's harmless," says a woman, a patient I think, as she sits down beside me. She's probably a few years older than me, smartly dressed with her auburn, flecked with grey, hair tied up into a neat bun. "That's Jimmy. Schizophrenic. He thinks he's in here for stealing his neighbour's wheelie bin."

"Oh. Okay."

"I'm Nancy," she says, holding out her hand for me to shake. "Depression, borderline personality disorder, and attempted suicide…for the third time. What are you here for?"

Wow. Blunt much? "Bipolar and attempted suicide. I'm James."

"It gets easier. Once you're past the refusing to leave your room stage, you'll soon get to know everyone. Over there…" She points to the woman with the teddy. "That's Suzy. She sits in here every day but I've never seen her with a visitor. The guy over there, folding paper, that's Gary. He's bipolar and OCD. He's a great guy, funny, but don't touch his stuff or you'll see the not-so-funny side of him. Have you got a visitor today?"

"Yes. My partner, Theodore."

"Like the chipmunk?"

I laugh, the memory of his 'I want to hate you almost as much as I want to fuck you' face, still fresh in my mind. "That's what I said when I met him. Didn't go down too well."

"I'm waiting for my husband."

"You're married?"

"You don't need to sound so surprised. Even us crazies can fall in love."

"Sorry," I mutter, flustered and feeling like a gigantic dick. "I didn't mean-"

"I'm just teasing. Honestly? When I'm on a spiral it surprises me, too. Three times I've been in here, yet he's still out there, waiting for me."

"Don't you feel…*selfish?*" For some reason I can't fathom, I feel completely at ease talking so frankly to this stranger. It's her eyes. There's something lurking behind them that I can relate to.

"Yes. I still feel that way. But you know, I think people, especially people like us, forget how powerful love can be."

"How do you keep going? I mean, *three* times…I don't think I have the strength to come back from this again."

"Hope, I suppose. I don't really have an answer for you. Every time I feel the same way. Exhausted. Numb. But somehow, at some point, that hope kicks in. It's all you can do. Hope you'll get through it, hope you can be good enough for the people who love you, hope that it's the last time you'll ever feel that way."

"What if hope hadn't kicked in? Or what if you'd succeeded?"

"A month ago that was all I wanted, for it to end. When I got here for the third bloody time I decided I'd stop trying with the pills, talk my way out of here and take a leap off the motorway bridge instead."

That's exactly what I thought, too.

"Now? I'm ready to keep going. Keep *trying.* It's all I can do."

"And if you spiral again?"

Nancy shrugs. "I have to believe that I won't. So do *you.*"

"But you can't guarantee it."

"No, but you can't guarantee you won't be living the happiest day of your life and get hit by a bus either. We can't live on what ifs."

"You know, for someone in the loony bin, you talk a lot of sense. You seem so…so *normal.*"

Nancy laughs, patting my knee. It surprises me that I'm not bothered by the contact. "I doubt you'd have said that if you'd met me a month ago. We *are* normal, James. A little different to most, perhaps, but we're still people all the same."

"You've been here a *month*?" I can't decide if the idea of being here that long fills me with fear or relief.

"Well, just under. What level section are you on?"

"Two."

"That means they can keep you here for up to twenty-eight days. But if you're a good boy they might let you out early," she says, winking. "Hasn't anyone discussed that with you?"

"My therapist might have but, well, sometimes I'm guilty of switching off."

During an absentminded glance across the room, I spot Theodore hovering in the doorway. I stare at him, my heart hammering in my chest. He's even more beautiful than my mind's memory of him. His hair is a little longer, the subtle highlights grown out at the roots.

He walks gingerly over to me, his hands tucked into the pockets of his jeans, and for a moment I forget how to breathe.

"I'll leave you two alone," Nancy says, reminding me she even exists.

"Th-thanks," I stutter, my gaze locked on Theodore. Standing up, my legs feel like jelly, and I consciously tug on the sleeves of my shirt. He seems as afraid to start the conversation as I am, and for a few long seconds, we just…stand.

And then his chest crashes into mine, throwing his arms around my back.

"I'm sorry," I whimper, holding on to his body like I'll collapse if I don't.

"Don't you dare," he whispers. "Don't you dare apologise for what you've been through." Pulling back, he cups my cheek, stroking the freshly smooth skin with his thumb. "I'm just so happy to hear your voice. And you smell good. I'm guessing you haven't smoked since you've been here."

Right until he said that, I haven't craved for a cigarette. Now, I suddenly miss the taste. "Don't suppose you've brought any with you?"

"No, and I'm not going to either." He sounds so bossy. I adore it when he tries to act all alpha-male on me. It never works, but I'll let him have his moment.

"There's a tool in the drawer under the microwave," I tell him as we settle into our seats, opposite one another. "For the lights. It's like a small suction cup."

"You can show me when you get out of here."

I nod, attempting to smile, but the muscles in my face aren't working. "How are things going at work?"

"I haven't been in so I don't really know. Max has it covered though. You don't need to worry about that."

"But…you won't get paid." A sigh escapes from my mouth. He shouldn't lose money because of *me*. "If you need anything, you can use my credit card. You know that, right?"

"My mum's been helping me out, and I have my royalties. I'm doing fine."

"I'm glad you've had people to support you." It gets me thinking. "Did, um, my mother visit while I was in hospital?"

Theodore's expression drops, and I already know the answer. "Um, no. No, she didn't."

The knowledge stings, but I'm not mad with her. I can't imagine how hard it must be to see your child in that position. I let her down.

"Is it hard?" Theodore asks, changing the subject. He doesn't need to admit it aloud for me to know he doesn't like my mother. "Being in here?"

"I've been on nicer holidays," I tease.

He rolls his eyes at me. "And…how are you feeling?" His voice is quiet, cautious.

"Are you asking if I still want to kill myself?"

"No! Well…"

"I don't think so," is the best I can offer. "I still have a long way to go."

"But you think being in here is helping?"

"I hope so."

He looks disappointed, but I can't lie to him to make him feel better. That's what landed me in here in the first place.

"What about you? How have *you* been?"

"Terrified."

Reaching out, I take his hand in mine. The warmth of his skin, the way his fingers fit perfectly in mine, makes all my problems disappear…for now, at least.

"Why wouldn't you see me?" he asks, his voice low, hesitant.

"Shame. Anger…"

"You were angry with me?"

"I was angry that you saved my life. I was angry that you were still here, that you didn't move on. I was angry at *myself* for hurting you, for not doing the job properly. I was angry at *everything*."

"God, James," he breathes, closing his eyes while he comprehends what I'm saying. "I wish you'd felt like you could tell me these things."

"I'm working on that."

"With Peter?"

"Yes."

"You like him?" He looks surprised.

"Some of the time. He gets me to talk. I've no idea how."

"I do. You won't let *anyone* be a bigger arsehole than *you*. He's making you fight for dominance."

Blowing out a chuckle, I nod. "You might be onto something there."

For the rest of our time together we talk about casual things – Tess and her girlfriend, his brother and impending fatherhood, the fact the walls in this room are painted vomit-yellow. The conversation is light, easy, and he doesn't push me for anything more.

At one point his gaze lands on my wrist, and I stop him when he reaches out to touch it. "Not yet," I whisper, tugging on my sleeve.

He nods faintly, immediately focusing on my face. "Can I come back tomorrow?" he asks after the nurses rings the time-up bell.

Cupping the back of his neck, I press my forehead to his. "I'd like that."

He's so close, yet I don't feel the urge to kiss him. Holding him, inhaling his scent, feeling the warmth of his breath on my face, is all I need. When he finally breaks away I feel like I've healed just a tiny bit more.

"And Max? I know he's desperate to see you."

Blowing steadily through pursed lips, I try to quell the anxiety taking over my body. "Sure."

He's your brother. You can do this.

"Is he…" I cough to clear the lump of nerves that's appeared in my throat. "Is he mad at me?"

Theodore sighs through his nose, squeezing me a little tighter. "Nobody is mad at you, James. *Nobody.*"

I bet my mother is. I don't think she means it to, but worry has always come out as anger ever since I can remember.

That damn bell rings again and, after laying a chaste kiss on Theodore's lips, I reluctantly unpeel myself from his body. "I love you."

Theodore smiles, wrapping his arms around me for a final time and crushing me to his chest. "Thank you," he mouths. "I love you, too. Always."

Theodore gave me a bigger gift than he could ever realise today. He gave me that inkling of hope I've been searching for. Back in my room I figure out just how to tell him so, too. The song he chose for me by A Great Big World has been playing on a loop in my head since the first time I listened to it, and I know the perfect song of theirs to reply with. *One Step Ahead.* So, pulling out my iPod, I create a new playlist titled *Thank you* and add just that song. I will give it back to him tomorrow.

When dinner rolls around, filled with a newfound sense of determination, I refuse to eat alone in my room again. Heading out into the communal dining room, I suck in a deep, preparing breath, and pull out a chair next to Nancy. I know I'm being watched, and that this will be marked down as progress in my file, and it fills me with a small sense of pride. I *am* making progress. I *will* make more. I *will* get better.

For Theodore.

For my family.

For *me.*

Chapter

Thirteen

~Theo~

Naively, I thought the knot of worry tangled around my stomach would loosen once I saw James. It hasn't. The poised and confidant man I knew just isn't there anymore. The James I visited yesterday was timid and nervous. His back was hunched, his fingers fidgeted, and his eyes were so…lost. I don't know how to help him and I feel so damn useless.

After yet another bus ride, I wait for Max outside the hospital unit. When I see him arrive, his mum by his side, my stomach flips in anger. *So she's decided she can be arsed seeing him now, has she?*

Swallowing down my frustration, I decide I need to give her the benefit of the doubt for James' sake, and offer a weak smile.

"Hey, mate," Max greets me with a pat on the shoulder.

"Hey."

Julia, James and Max's mother, doesn't acknowledge me, so neither do I. After pressing the buzzer to be let inside, we walk through to reception and Max signs us into the visitor's book. There are so many buzzers and locked doors here. It's like a prison they've tried to disguise with pots of plastic flowers and landscape paintings.

"Do you mind if I go in alone for a couple of minutes first?" I ask, turning to Max.

"Ye-" Julia tries to answer, but Max over-talks her.

"Of course," he agrees, making the childish side of me feel a little smug when I see the scowl on his mother's face.

James is waiting in the same spot as yesterday, talking to a guy wearing an eye-patch.

"I didn't do it," the guy says, twisting his fingers together in front of his chest. "Don't let them tell you I did."

Nervous, I smile awkwardly, and step past him to get to James.

"Hey," James says, standing to hug me. His touch melts my anxiety instantly. I miss this.

When we sit down, he tugs at his sleeves like he did yesterday. I try not to stare because clearly he's self-conscious, but I hope, in time, he learns that he doesn't need to hide. Not from *me*.

"Don't look so nervous," he says, clamping his hand on top of mine. "They won't hurt you."

Is it so obvious that this place, these people, make me feel uncomfortable? I can't help it. I'm not judging on purpose, but they frighten me a little. "Sorry. I don't mean to."

"It takes a while to get used to, but they're just people who aren't well. Like *me*."

The difference is James is *my* person, and I feel at ease with him whatever he's going through.

"Have you taken your meds today?"

"Yes. I'm being a good boy," he replies, wearing a sarcastic smirk that calms my racing heart.

There you are.

"Oh, I have good news. JD Simmons hit the New York Times bestsellers again. Number twelve."

"Yeah?"

"Yeah." Leaning forward, I whisper in his ear. "I'm so proud of you."

When I pull back, I expect to see a look of excitement on his face, but it's not there. "Aren't you happy about it?"

"I am." He shrugs. "It's just that release feels like a lifetime ago."

Yeah. Yeah it does. "Max is outside." I draw a deep breath. "So is your mum."

"Oh," he mutters, his solemn gaze sweeping the floor.

"You don't want to see them?"

"No, I do. I'm just a little nervous. Embarrassed, I suppose."

"You have *nothing* to be embarrassed about. They're your family. They love you."

He looks unsure and my heart aches for him. "You'd better go get them. My mum doesn't like to be kept waiting."

Your mum can kiss my arse. "Okay. Back in a sec," I say, keeping my true thoughts to myself before squeezing his hand and fetching his family.

James is standing when I return with his mum and brother, running his fingers through his hair as if trying to make himself look presentable. He's thinner, his hair has grown out of style, but he's still beautiful. He's still my James.

Julia sits straight down in the chair I can't help thinking of as *mine*, whereas Max puts his arms around his brother and claps his back.

"When are they letting you out?" Julia asks as James and Max sit down.

When he's better, you selfish old cow. Maybe it was an innocent enough question, but because I dislike her, everything she does pisses me off. Like the fact I need to pull up another chair because she's sitting in *mine.*

"Not yet," James answers. "A couple of weeks, maybe."

"You should've told me you were struggling," she says, and I genuinely hope she's about to prove my opinion of her wrong. "I'd have called Gerard in sooner. Maybe we wouldn't have lost so much money."

Yeah…my opinion hasn't changed.

"It was more than the business," James says, his voice timid as he stares over her shoulder.

"Well, what else is bothering you?"

"Nothing. It's…it's not like that."

"You have a nice home, *two* nice homes, a good car, a great career," she continues, ignoring him completely. "Do you know my friend Maggie? She was diagnosed with breast cancer last month. She has *real* problems and she'd do anything to survive."

"I'm sorry," he whispers, barely audible.

"What were you thinking?"

"I-I'm sorry."

"To just…*give up* on life like that? When you're perfectly healthy?"

But he's not *healthy. He's sick. Bitch.*

"Mum," Max interrupts, his voice scolding. "You're not helping."

"He knows what I'm trying to say," she dismisses with a wave of her hand. "Don't you, James? Everybody gets depressed now and again but not everyone chooses to put their family through this. You see that, don't you, James?"

"Y-yes," James mouths, agreeing with her like a scared child.

"Everyone gets a little *down* sometimes," I cut in. "Not depressed."

She looks at me like I'm something she wants to squish under her boot and it takes purposeful effort not to snap.

As if sensing the tension, Max changes the subject. "Isobel got in trouble at nursery yesterday. She flushed a kid's drawing down the toilet."

James laughs, and it's magical. "Why?"

"He called her a baby."

"Good for Izzy. That'll teach him for messing with our girl."

"That's what I thought. I couldn't tell her that of course. She's lost her tablet for two days."

"Her tablet? She's only three!"

"It's a special kiddy one," Max clarifies. "She's been asking about you."

"She has?" The brightest, most genuine smile illuminates James' face.

"She's been making her birthday list. You're down for a Paw Patrol Pup Pad."

"I have no idea what that is."

"Oh, she'll tell you. She had me circle it in the toy catalogue so she could show you."

"I can't wait to see her," James says, and there's a sincerity in his smile that makes me believe him.

"What's the food like?" I ask, keeping the conversation light…at least until his mother's gone.

"Edible," he replies with a smile. He's still tugging at his sleeves and I wonder if Max notices, too. I doubt his mum does. She's too self-absorbed to pay attention to what her own son is doing. "I'll ask if I'm allowed to bring you some sushi in from the place you like tomorrow."

"Ew. Do you like that stuff?" Julia asks with a shudder. It might well be the only thing we agree on.

"I'd love that," James says. "Thank you."

Awkward conversation and uncomfortable silences continue throughout visiting time. Julia is the cause of the tense atmosphere, though I'm sure she's too conceited to know it. I also expect I'm alone in that thought. She's their mother and they love her, but that doesn't mean *I* have to.

"I'm sorry," James mutters, unnecessarily, for what must be the twentieth time as he hugs his mum goodbye with one arm.

"Just cheer up and get out of here. We'll discuss your position in the business when you're home. It might be time to make Gerard an active partner."

She looks at me briefly when she let's go of James and I force a smile, hoping its insincerity shines bright. *I hate you.*

When Max and Julia leave, I linger behind for a minute to say goodbye. "It was good to see you smile today," I tell him, clasping the top of his arm.

"It *felt* good."

"Whatever you're doing, keep going. I can't wait to lie with you. *Hold* you…" Leaning in, I hover my lips next to his ear and whisper, "…without eye-patch guy watching us."

James chuckles. "I want that, too."

Smiling, I let go of his arm, my fingers mourning his warmth. "See you tomorrow?"

"You will."

I turn to leave, stopping when his hand appears on my shoulder. "Thank you, Theodore." Reaching into his pocket, he pulls out his iPod, handing it to me.

I raise an eyebrow, confused. "For what?"

"Staying."

My lips curl and I drop my head to the side, resting my cheek on his hand. "Always."

* * *

The next day, I'm taking the bus into town to pick up James' sushi when I receive a call from Max. "Hey," I answer, my mood upbeat.

It's quashed immediately. "The hospital just rang. James had a bit of a meltdown this morning. He can't have visitors today."

My heart slowly slithers into my stomach. "What kind of meltdown? Is he okay?"

"He got upset after his therapy session." Max sighs. "Smashed up his room."

Oh, James. What are you doing?

"The nurse I spoke to said it's normal, that we should expect setbacks like this."

But I wasn't. He seemed so positive yesterday. A little quiet, perhaps, but more like himself.

"Right. Okay. Can I go tomorrow?"

"I don't know. I'll call in the morning and see how he is."

"Okay. Thanks for letting me know."

Disheartened, my hand falls into my lap after ending the call. I'm beyond gutted, knowing James is struggling and, once again, I'm not with him. All I have to offer is my arms, my love, and I'd do anything to give that to him right now.

There's no point in continuing my journey, so I get off the bus at the next stop and wait for one that will take me back to my flat, where I plan to wait for Tess…and probably cry.

* * *

It takes three days for James to be ready to see me again, and I spend those days listening to the song he chose for me over and over again. At first, it filled me with faith, now I just feel sad. Has he stopped believing the lyrics?

Keep going, James. Keep believing.

After the last time he refused to see me, I needed to distract myself somehow before I fell apart entirely, so yesterday I went into work, quickly wishing I hadn't bothered. From the second I stepped onto the marketing floor I had Mike up my arse, threatening disciplinary action over my absence. Stacey corrected him after lunch, stating that I'd been approved for unpaid leave. I think she might have made that up, but I'm grateful regardless.

I expected Stacey to quiz me for details about James but, to her credit, she didn't. Ed, on the other hand, pushed me for gossip at every available opportunity, so I avoided him by making myself look busy even when I wasn't.

When I got home, I finally started reading through the manuscripts I rescued from the slush pile to take my mind off things. It worked for a while, and I put one that intrigued me to one side in the hope I can convince submissions to take another look. It consisted only of the first three chapters, but I want more, so there must be something worth investigating.

I went back in this morning. As much as I hated yesterday, it's a necessary evil. The curiosity surrounding James' absence won't subside until things return to normal, whatever *normal* may be.

Now, I'm at the hospital, sushi in hand, waiting for visiting time to start. Max thought it best I come alone so James' doesn't feel overwhelmed and I appreciate that, knowing he wants to see him just as much as I do.

When I'm let inside along with a handful of other visitors, I find James sitting in a different spot today, by a window overlooking a garden area. Walking over to him, I raise an eyebrow and hand him the paper takeaway bag.

"So what happened?" I ask, feigning a scolding expression.

"I'm sor-"

"I didn't ask you to apologise. I asked what happened."

"You're cute when you're mad. Do you know that?" He smiles, but I don't return it, as much as I want to.

"What happened?"

"Peter asked me some difficult questions. The answers made me feel selfish, which in turn made me angry…then ashamed. I lost it. They increased my meds the other day. Peter said that may have contributed to it, but…it's no excuse."

"No, it's not. I almost wasted a fortune on raw fish that would've gone straight in the bin."

He smiles again, and I'm glad he can hear the humour in my voice.

"No more diva strops, you hear? I missed you."

"Yes, sir." He salutes me.

"I've been to work the last couple of days." I go on to tell him all about it. He laughs a couple of times while I rant about Moron Mike, so I keep going just to see the smile on his face a little longer. "Have you thought about going back? What you'll tell people?"

I hope I'm not pushing him, but it's a subject that must've crossed his mind.

"It's none of their business," he says, his voice commanding and authoritative. I've missed that. "But my mother's mistaken if she thinks Gerard is taking charge. She doesn't have the authority to make those kind of decisions."

But will you tell her that? I hope he does.

"I know where things went wrong and I know how to fix them. My father trusted me for a reason. I'll be talking to her about it when I leave here."

"Yeah?" I don't intend to sound so surprised.

"Peter and I have been discussing my relationship with my mother these past few days. He's made me realise that I'm not disrespecting her by disagreeing, by putting myself first sometimes."

I'm not sure what to say without sounding like an 'I told you so' arsehole, so I keep quiet.

"I know you agree with him. It's written all over your face."

"*You're* my concern, not your mother."

James shrugs nervously. "She's the only person I've never had the balls to stand up to. I don't know why that is, or if it will change, but I have to try. When I get out of here, things need to be different."

A proud grin creeps onto my face. "It's good to hear you talk like that. Positive."

"I'm trying." He sneaks his fingers into the paper bag and pulls out the tub of sushi. "This looks delicious." Taking the two disposable chopsticks, he picks up a piece of fish and tosses it in his mouth.

"I've never been able to figure those things out."

"Chopsticks?"

I nod.

"Here," he says, taking my hand. "Hold this one like a pencil." He guides my fingers into position. "Then rest this one here, and move this one up and down with your thumb and index finger."

I practice the movement for a few seconds, then dip them into the tub, picking up a piece of food. My mouth opens, as if that will somehow keep it in place, and I'm pleased with myself for managing to lift the food successfully out of the tub.

And then it falls on the floor. "Shit," I mutter, picking it up with my fingers and throwing it in the paper bag. Heat rushes to my cheeks, knowing that someone, somewhere, is always watching us in this place. "I'll stick with knives and forks."

We talk about all kind of things for the rest of my visit – some serious, some light-hearted, and some random nonsense. When it's time for me to leave I feel more optimistic than ever that he's coming back to me, and so, when I say goodbye, I tell him to keep it up or I'll shred his favourite ties.

* * *

One week later…

At Heaton Park, James and I stand side by side, preparing to set off into a sprint. He's been released on a trial day, supposedly to help him adjust to the outside world. We worked out a plan yesterday, together with Peter, on how to spend our four hours together today. So…we're running.

"Don't go getting all suicidal on me again when you lose, will you?" I tease. I don't say it to trivialise what he's been through. I say it because I don't want it to be a dirty little secret. I don't want him to feel ashamed. It needs to be out there in the open, discussed, if only between *us*. He needs to know that I'm not angry or hurt, that it's *okay* to talk about, that he doesn't have to hide from me.

I say it because this is who we are. Nothing has changed. We're the same people we were before and I have no intention of treating him any differently.

"I appreciate that you can say things like that to me," he says, his voice serious. "You make me feel normal."

"You *are* normal." I brush his cheek in a small moment of tenderness before I set off into run. "But you're also a loser!" I call over my shoulder.

He's on my tail within seconds, but I pick up my speed, determined to beat him. He's out of practice, but so am I, and given that my legs are a couple of inches shorter than his, I have to keep pushing myself until my muscles feel like they're bleeding. As my lungs start to burn I inwardly curse myself for slacking over recent months. I'm surprised how unfit I've become in such a short time.

When he's home to stay, we need to do this every day.

"Come on, slacker!" James shouts, overtaking me.

Bastard. He doesn't even look warm, whereas I'm breaking a frigging sweat, too exhausted to breathe, never mind reply. I can't let him win, even if it feels like it will kill me, so I summon every ounce of strength my body possesses and push forward until I'm by his side and jerk my foot out in front of him.

His fall is hilarious as he tumbles onto the grass. He rolls onto his side, clutching his knee dramatically, and I can't stop laughing.

"Cheater!"

"Don't blame others for your downfalls. Don't they teach you that in therapy?"

Scrambling to his feet, James laughs. "I think I preferred it when you used to hate me. You were far less irritating."

"I irritate you?" I smirk at him.

Palming my cheek, he stares straight into my eyes. "Like you wouldn't believe."

"I'm glad you know how it feels." I peck his lips with mine, then spin on my heels and run. "Come on, slow coach! We haven't got all day!"

We run for just over an hour, competition remaining in place the entire time. I won. Did I cheat? Absolutely. But I still won. It's not my fault he didn't have the initiative to trip me over first. We go back to my flat, because it's closer, and shower and change separately. James isn't ready to be intimate with me yet, and I know that's because he's paranoid about his scars. Honestly, I'm not ready either. The next time I'm with James in that way, I want to spend the whole night holding him, loving him.

With two hours to go before he needs to be back at the hospital, we go out for dinner. Nothing fancy, just pizza and conversation without eyes boring into the back of heads. It's nice. *Normal.* I don't want it to end, but of course it has to.

Saying goodbye at the hospital later feels even harder than usual, but I have to hold onto the fact that what we shared today will soon be *every* day. Peter is waiting for James when we reach reception, no doubt to discuss James' day and how he feels about being in the 'real' world. I can only hope he feels as exhilarated as I do, and that it will put him that one step closer to coming home for good.

"See you tomorrow," I say, releasing his hand slowly, brushing his fingers until they disappear.

Love you, he mouths silently, before turning his back and following Peter down the hall.

Love you, too.

* * *

One week later…

James is coming home today, and I set off to pick him up in his Mercedes, because mine is in the garage, finally. I've never driven anything so fancy before and I find myself driving like an eighty-year-old, terrified I'm going to break it. My insurance would only cover third party damage and I'm guessing if I've had to save for almost a month to get my crapheap fixed, I'd have to sell my soul to repair *this* car.

James is waiting outside, along with his therapist, when I arrive and as I pull up in *his* car, his eyes widen a little.

"Eager to leave, eh?" I call after winding the passenger window down.

"No," Peter cuts in. "*We're* eager to get rid of him."

James tosses his holdall into the back seat before sliding in next to me and, reaching over, squeezing my knee. My gaze lingers on his hand and all I can think about is him touching me with it, skin on skin. I can't wait to feel him again, not sexually, just *close*.

"You'll need to see your GP this week to arrange repeat prescriptions," Peter says, holding onto the roof while he bends to the window, passing James a white paper bag containing his medications. "They'll have a letter from Dr Calder on record, so they'll be expecting you." His eyebrows wiggle as if to tell James to not even think about ignoring his instruction.

"Your outpatients appointment card is in there, too," he continues. "And so is my number if you need anything, *anything* before then."

"Got it," James agrees. "Thank you."

"No need to thank me. My wages do that." Peter winks. "Now go on. Get the hell outta here."

And then he's free. He's coming home. I'm not foolish enough to think he's *better*. In fact, according to Peter, he'll *never* be *better*...but he *can* manage his illness. He *can* enjoy life. He can be happy. And if he falls? I'll be right there to catch him.

For most of our journey back to his apartment, James stares out of the window, his expression contemplative. It must be strange, heading back to normality after being held hostage, in a sense, for just over a month. I can't pretend to understand so I stay quiet, letting James lead the conversation when, and if, he wants to.

He's with me. That's all that matters.

When we reach his front door I pause, twisting the key in the lock. "Don't freak out. I'll have it tidied in no time."

James raises an eyebrow, oblivious to the scene he's about to walk into. He keeps his homes pristine and orderly, like show-houses, and so when he walks inside and his eyes meet clothes on the floor, dirty dishes piled high in the sink, and crumbs scattered all over his centrepiece rug, his mouth falls open.

"I was going to do it this morning, but Mike wouldn't give me the morning off," I say, scurrying around the living room and picking up the dirty washing. Mike didn't actually *need* me. He could've asked anyone with a brain cell and two fingers to send out blanket rejection letters to literary agents. As usual, he was being an awkward arse, knowing I can't afford to take the chance of undergoing a disciplinary after my recent absence. *Twat.*

Clothes in a pile by the washing machine, I start running the hot tap, ready to clean three days worth of pots.

Creeping up behind me, James reaches out and shuts off the tap. "Leave it. The mess will still be here after."

I lift a dubious eyebrow, my pulse quickening. "After what?"

"After I've held you for a little while."

My heart melts in my chest as I take his proffered hand. He leads me to the bedroom and crawls, fully clothed, onto the mattress. I join him, lying on my side so we're facing each other, draping my arm over his waist. "You're here," I whisper my thoughts aloud, rubbing small circles on his back. "I've waited so long for this moment. This bed is too big for one person."

"You stayed here the entire time?"

"Beats being at home with the loved-up lesbians. Seriously, I thought *one* woman nagging me about the toilet seat was bad enough."

"Sounds like things are getting serious with Lucy."

"She's there *all* the time, so I reckon so, yes. And Tess is, I don't know, different. She smiles more than rolls her eyes these days."

"Wow. Can't wait to see that."

"I felt closer to you here," I explain. "But now you're home, I'll leave whenever you're ready."

"What if I don't want to be ready?"

Huh?

"What if I don't want you to leave?"

"You mean…*ever?*"

"Yes."

Whoa. "Are you asking me to move in with you?"

"Yes."

"But I make a mess."

"Then you'll clean it up," he says, a sly wink pinching his eye.

"I'm unorganised. I eat cheap food. I dance naked to Taylor Swift when I get out of the shower."

"I like Taylor Swift." James grins. "And I like seeing you naked, too."

Tiny bubbles, filled with a mixture of nerves and excitement, swell and pop in my belly. "I can't pay you much."

"I don't want your money, Theodore."

"Well I'm not living here for nothing. I didn't sign up for a sugar daddy. This is a partnership, and I want to pay my way."

"You make it sound like a business deal. Where would you like me to sign?"

Jerking my leg, I kick him in the shin. "Stop being a wanker. I'm serious."

"Serious about moving in with me?" There's a glimmer of hope in his rich brown eyes. It's infectious, and as much as I want to keep a straight face, my smile betrays me. "I'll need to talk to Tess. See if she can manage the rent on her own."

"Theodore, is it a yes?"

"Yes," I breathe, enthusiasm fizzing in my chest. "It's a yes!"

James' lips crash into mine, stealing my breath for a moment. *Oh my God…*The feel of him, the taste… "Fuck I've missed you," I say into his mouth, gripping the back of his head, keeping him close.

Our tongues dance together, our lips brushing, stubble grating, in a slow, savouring kiss. This is where I'm meant to be, with James, forever.

Wriggling my hips, I adjust my body, trying to loosen the tight denim straining against my hard cock. I want him so badly. I *need* to feel his skin on mine. Walking my fingers down to the hem of his shirt, I start to lift, my knuckles skimming the faint trail of hair on his stomach.

"Wait," he urges, grabbing my wrist. His grip is weak, his nerves damaged, but I pull back immediately, concern flooding my veins when I see the look of fear on his face. After pulling his t-shirt back down, he tugs on his sleeve, unwittingly revealing the cause of his anxiety.

I haven't seen his scars yet. I haven't pushed him to show me, but, "It's time, James," I say, kneeling up and pushing him onto his back. Lifting my leg, I straddle his hips, pinching the bottom of his shirt between my fingers.

Slowly, I tease the white material upwards. The unwarranted shame pouring from James is palpable as I guide it over his head and it breaks my heart. I don't look at his wrists straightaway, feeling as terrified as he does about my reaction. First, I toss his shirt behind me and kiss his lips, lingering there for a moment before moving onto his chest.

His old scars are familiar. They no longer fill me with sadness. They're a part of him, and he's beautiful, but after kissing each one, my palm smoothing the soft flesh hugging his faded muscles, I know it's time to see, and *accept*, the new ones.

"You don't ever need to hide from me, James," I say, my eyes trained on his as I run my fingers down his colourful arm.

He gapes at me with curiosity through hooded eyes as I trace the raised lines with the pad of my thumb. "I'm going to look now, okay?"

He nods once, so slightly it almost wasn't there.

Conscious of each deep breath I take, I let my gaze travel down his arm, over the delicate cherry blossoms inked onto his skin, and to his wrist.

Oh, James…

I follow the angry, crisscrossed scars that rip into the lilac peony with my fingers before lowering my head and resting my lips on them. I do the same to his other arm, the scars more pronounced there without tattoos to hide behind, and then lay my cheek against his chest.

"Do they make you angry with me?" James whispers with a tremor in his voice. "You can be honest with me."

"No," I breathe. "I'm grateful."

"*Grateful?*"

"Grateful that I'm able to see them, see *you*, like this. Healing."

Closing my eyes, I kiss them again, before pressing my chest to his and nuzzling his neck. The scar on his throat from the tracheostomy is small, but red and puckered, and I kiss there too before whispering, "I love you, James. Inside *and* out. I'm sorry for not making you see that sooner."

"It was never about my feelings for you," he murmurs, twiddling a strand of my hair around his finger. "You do know that, right? You didn't let me down, Theodore. There's nothing you could've done."

I *want* to believe that.

"Sometimes I wish we could've met at a different point in our lives. Talking to Peter made me realise that this has been building since my father's death. That was my trigger. I was slipping long before I met you. You've only ever known me during the worst part of my life, and I wish I could change that."

"I don't," I say, my words oozing conviction. I lift my head, looking at him. "I fell in love with you at your worst. I've had some of the best times of my life with you at, as you say, your worst. So I can't even imagine how special life will be when I get to experience your *best*."

James smiles, cupping my cheeks with his hands. "How do you do that?" he asks with a mesmerising glint of wonder in his eyes. "See the positive in everything?"

"Well, it's easier when you're not a whack-job."

Laughing, James smacks my arse, hard enough to smart even through the denim.

"We're going to be okay, James. *You're* going to be okay."

He half-smiles, but it's awkward, like he doesn't quite know how to believe that yet.

Touching my nose to his, I whisper, "We'll take it one breath, one moment…" I brush his lips with mine. "…One *kiss* at a time."

"Sounds like a plan."

"I have lots of plans. Like now, I plan to kiss your neck…" I whisper straight into his ear. "Then I plan to lick a trail down your chest." I wedge my hand between our bodies, undoing the button on his pants.

"Oh yeah? Then what?" he asks, arching his hips while I tug at his waistband, guiding his pants and boxers down his legs. He kicks them from his ankles while I rip off my t-shirt.

"Then…" I continue, kissing and nibbling my way down his body. "I plan to do this…" Hovering my mouth above his cock, my tongue darts out, flicking his swollen head.

"Christ, Theodore," he moans, the words muffled from biting his bottom lip.

Lowering my head, I take him all the way to the back of my mouth, sucking him deep until he hits my throat. For a few seconds, I hold him there, the tip of my tongue tracing the thick vein that travels along the centre of his rigid shaft.

"Mmm," I groan, knowing the vibrations from my lips will drive him insane as I slowly drag my mouth up and down.

Releasing his cock, I blow softly, the sensation causing James to moan, fisting the sheets by his side. "You like that, huh?" I say, grinning proudly, fully aware of the answer.

Shifting a little lower down the mattress, I pry his legs further apart, my hands on the inside of his thighs, and run my tongue down the seam of his balls, stopping when I reach his tight hole. Moistening my lips, I kiss the puckered rim before dipping the tip of my tongue just barely inside.

"Oh *fuck*," he breathes, gripping my hair. Then he yanks my head away, leaving me bewildered and panting for air.

"*You're* the one getting fucked tonight, Theodore." His voice is firm, demanding, and it makes every nerve ending in my body tingle with excitement.

In less than a second, he's pinned me on my back, my jeans halfway down my legs. I hardly have time to take a breath before his hot mouth is clamped around my cock. He's not gentle, doesn't take his time. He's urgent, *fast*, in complete control.

"S-stop." My tone is weak, yet begging. It's been too long, he feels too good, and if he doesn't slow down the moment I've been anticipating for weeks will be over in seconds.

James looks up, his lips curled into a mischievous grin…then he goes back for more.

"Oh my God," I whimper, my hips bucking of their own accord, pushing my throbbing cock further into his mouth.

As if he knows when I'm about to enter the point of no return, he releases me and moves between my cheeks. He sucks, licks, and kisses in between fucking me with his fingers. Then he lands back on my cock and starts all over again.

"P-please, James," I urge. "I can't hold off much longer." I'm writhing and panting under his assault, my balls heavy, aching for release.

Offering me a moment of mercy while I remember how to breathe, James crawls onto his knees and nestles himself between my legs.

Stretching, I fumble in the bedside table drawer, plucking out a condom and a bottle of lube. James takes them from me, twiddling the condom between his fingers as he lowers his lips to my ear. "Let me feel you *properly*," he whispers. "I haven't been with anyone but you since I was last tested."

Neither have I.

"I want to feel you around me, nothing between us, just me and you."

"Yes," I breathe, taking the condom from his fingers and tossing it over the edge of the bed.

Falling back on his heels, our gazes interlocked, James drizzles some lube onto his fingers before wrapping them around his cock and massaging it up and down. He rubs the excess around my hole, working his fingers in and out a couple more times, before nudging the entrance with his cock and falling forward onto my chest.

One hand around the nape of my neck, the other gripping the back of my thigh, he speaks into my ear. "I love you, Theodore," he murmurs, pushing into me slowly.

The pressure is exquisite, and I palm his neck, never taking my eyes off him. "James…" I sigh his name, the feeling of him inside me, stretching, *filling* me, almost too much to handle. A rush of emotion overwhelms me, tears pricking the back of my eyes as he slides gently, leisurely, in and out of my body.

As if sensing the intensity, the significance of this moment, he kisses my lips, his tongue softly tickling mine. "You feel incredible this way."

My hips move in rhythm with his, my cock rubbing against his stomach. I grip his back, the pads of my fingers digging into his shoulder blades. "Oh, yeah…right there. Feels…so good," I choke out, his pace increasing steadily.

We're connected, body and soul, *nothing* between us, and it's perfect. *He's* perfect. "I love you so much, James."

He kisses me again, soft and gentle, and when he pulls away, straightening his back and grabbing my other thigh, I know he's about to switch gear.

"Take your dick, Theodore. I want to watch you while I pound the fuck out of you."

Swallowing, my heart rate quickening in anticipation, I reach for my cock, curling my fingers around the base.

"Ready?" he asks with a wicked spark in his dark eyes.

Too breathless to speak, I start to nod…but he rocks into me with so much force my head smacks the headboard before I've finished. "*Fuck,*" I hiss, hammering my cock with my hand.

His deep thrusts come hard and fast, the effort creating glistening beads of sweat on his chest. Pressure builds in my stomach and tingles shoot down my spine as he hits a spot I didn't even know existed, over and over again.

"I'm gonna…I'm com…oh…*fuuuuck.*" My whole body judders, the muscles in my legs clench, as jets of creamy, hot cum spurt from the tip of my cock, coating James' stomach.

"So fucking beautiful," he spits through gritted teeth, red heat crawling across his collarbones as he drives into me one last time, his cock pulsating inside me. "Fuck, yes."

I give him a moment to come down from the high, for his body to stop quivering, then I pull him onto my chest. "I've missed you."

"I'm not sure where we go from here."

Stroking his flushed cheek, I smile. A simple action, yet one filled with so much love, so much hope…so many promises. "Forward," I whisper, running my fingers through his damp hair. "One breath," I kiss his lips again. "One *kiss*…at a time."

Going forward won't be easy, especially for James. He has a lot to work through, a lot of demons to face and healing to do, but while he does I will be here. Right by his side. Always.

"You'll be okay."

Nodding, just slightly, he kisses my cheek. "I'll be okay."

Epilogue

~James~

One year later…

"Come in," I bark to whoever just knocked on my office door. I'm using my lunch break to polish my latest novel, a story loosely based on my life and experiences with mental health. It was Peter's idea. At first, I laughed in his face, then started writing it purely to prove him wrong. But, much to my annoyance, he was right.

The characters are fictional, and only Theodore and I would be able to see just how much truth there is to their story, but I'm not writing a confession to the world. I'm doing it because it's therapeutic. Writing this book has been a life altering process, allowing the thoughts and feelings I've suppressed for so many years to bleed onto the page without fear of shame or judgement…because it's 'fiction.'

So, yes, Peter was right, and he took a disgusting amount of pleasure from hearing those words slip from my mouth. When he's not pissing me off, Peter and I get on great. I gave up hope many years ago of ever being 'normal', but working with Peter has made me realise I don't have to be 'normal' to be happy. So what if my brain is wired wrong? It hasn't stopped me being successful. It hasn't stopped me forming relationships, loving people, letting them love *me*. And if my fuse trips, I have faith in the people around me to help me fix it back in place.

As Peter must've said a thousand times, broken crayons can still colour.

I've learned to *talk*, recognise my triggers, ask for help when I need it. I've also told a handful of trusted colleagues about my illness, built up a support system in case things spiral again. That doesn't make me weak. It makes me *determined.* I know what it's like to walk along the shore, and I won't risk drowning in the black waters again. I have too much to fight for, to *live* for.

Looking up briefly from the manuscript I'm working on, I see Mike striding towards my desk. "What can I help you with?" I ask, frustrated by his interruption.

"I've drawn up the contract for Patricia Dennis."

"She's a gay fiction writer."

"I know, but-"

"Then present it to Theodore."

Huffing, Mike slaps his file closed. Three months ago we opened a new division dedicated to gay fiction and LGBT romance. Theodore manages the department, not because we live together, but because he fucking *earned* it. The concept was his idea, he drew up the plans, worked out the finances, and brought Stacey on board to help him bring it all together.

I'm not sure how this affects Mike in the slightest, and he knows better than to voice his disapproval to my face, but it's glaringly obvious that it pisses him the hell off to have Theodore on a level playing field.

I returned to work a month after being discharged from hospital last year and the business was struggling for the first time in years. With support from Theodore and guidance from my financial advisor, we closed down three departments and started contracting out to freelancers. It was a difficult stage, one which I was only marginally strong enough to cope with at the time, but I got through it, the business got through it, and now we're almost back to where we were when my father died.

That is, in part, credit to Theodore's enthusiasm, hard work, and determination to make our expansion into LGBT fiction a success. He still writes, and is about to release his first book through the company, but his main focus is on Holden House. On a professional level, I have nothing but praise and the utmost respect for Theodore. On a personal level, I love him with all my heart. He saved my life. He continues to save it every single day. He's my hope, my strength, my reason to carry on. He's the best friend I always imagined having.

He's my everything.

"I just thought," Mike replies. "Your office is closer."

"I'm the CEO, Mike, not your errand boy. Anything else?"

"No," he says, head down as he turns away.

"Oh and, Mike?"

"Yes?"

"When you get back, black – two sugars." I'm not even thirsty, but the cocky bastard brings out my petulant side.

"No problem," he agrees, in a tone laced with copious amounts of *fuck you*. It makes me smile.

Once alone, I call Max to double-check the time Isobel finishes school. Theodore and I are picking her up and taking her home for dinner. It's become a regular Friday routine since Laura, Max's wife, began an evening floristry course at the local college two months ago. Two months, and I still can't remember what time she finishes school.

We have lots of routines these days. Every night, bar Friday's, after work, we jog together – sometimes around the block, others at the park. It *always* ends in a competition and *I* always win. My legs are longer, but I tell Theodore it's simply because I'm fitter than him.

We spend Sunday's in Rochdale with Theodore's mother, and once a month we take her out for lunch. It took a while to convince her that it was *okay* to take a day off from the kitchen once in a while, but she refuses to go anywhere flashier than a pub. She's a great woman who I have nothing but respect and admiration for, and dare I say, I think she might actually like *me,* too – especially since I stopped smoking.

On Saturday's we visit my grandfather in the nursing home. He doesn't know who either of us are and often refers to Theodore as the 'pansy nurse' who keeps hiding the whiskey, that he doesn't even own. It doesn't matter that he doesn't know who I am, he's my relative, and I now realise just how important family is.

Max and I have grown so much closer over the last twelve months, and that's because *now*, I'm ready to let that happen. I spent my whole life keeping people at arms length, foolishly believing I was protecting both them *and* myself. The scars on my wrists, still raised, but fading, are a daily reminder, however, that my methods didn't turn out too great, so I decided to embrace being open, allowing myself to love, *be* loved, in the hope it would ease the weight of the pain that's suffocated me since I was a child.

It did.

The darkness still looms over my head, threatening to rain down on me. Some days it does, only now I have people there to help me dry off before it seeps into my bones. I'd like one of those people to be my mother, but we don't talk much these days. She didn't take it well when I stood up to her over the business, when I reiterated the fact my father left his share to *me* and *only* me. She's disappointed in me, and dare I say, a little ashamed. We have a civil as opposed to loving relationship, and I'm okay with that.

I'm okay, just like Theodore, just like the song, said I would be.

~Theo~

"Did you buy mince?" I ask James as we stand outside Isobel's school gates. I'm planning to cook my renowned shepherd's pie with baked beans in for tea; a meal which earned instant approval from Izzy the first time she tried it.

"I thought *you* were buying it."

"*No.* I asked *you.*"

"Well I didn't." He shrugs. "Sorry."

"No you're not."

"You're right. I'm not." He looks hot as hell wearing his grey suit and a delicious smirk. Images of ripping them from his body take over my mind…and then I remember where we are and want to slap myself across the face for thinking inappropriate thoughts.

"We'll take her to McDonald's. Kids love McDonald's."

"Shepherd's pie is healthier."

"We're the cool uncles. Let her parents worry about her vegetable intake."

I can't help but smile. We *are* the cool uncles, and I love it. Children bring a refreshing, carefree quality with them, one that is too easy to forget when you're an adult with pressures and responsibilities. Isobel reminds us of the important things in life, like taking time out to ignore the stresses of the world and just…laugh. She doesn't care that we have deadlines or bills to pay, and while she's with us, neither do we.

My nephew, William, on the other hand, is a whole different level of scary. We had him for the first time last week and it was terrifying. He can't talk, so I have to guess what he wants when he starts bawling the freaking house down, and unfortunately for him, Baby isn't a language I've mastered yet.

He's on the move, too, using his tiny arms to drag himself along on his stomach. Eighteen times I had to pull him away from danger – electrical sockets, low cupboards, doors – in just *one* hour. By the time Tom picked him up, I was exhausted.

That's the *best* part of being a cool uncle – you get to send them home again.

"At least tell me you posted the passport forms?" I say. We're going to Tenerife in two months. James is going to show me the places he saw as a child and I can't wait. I've only been out of England twice in my life but that isn't the main reason I'm looking forward to it. For two whole weeks James and I will be completely alone, away from all sources of stress and monotony. I can't wait to relax with him, laugh with him, *love* him…all while trying to get a spot of colour on my pasty white skin.

"I got Helen to do it."

Typical. At least the job is done so I can't grumble.

"How's my princess?" James sings, bending down to Isobel's level as she runs towards him. The look on his face, the radiant smile, when he's with this precious girl is priceless. I never tire of seeing it.

"Harley got in trouble for snapping Freya's pencil today," Izzy says, ever the busybody. "*I* dint. I *never* get in trouble."

"*Didn't.* And I should hope not, young lady." James picks at an orange stain splattered across her white polo-shirt. "What did you have for dinner, little lady?"

"Pasta, and it was embarrassing," she says, pulling a face.

"Do you mean disgusting?"

"Yeah. It was 'orrible. I dint like it."

"*Didn't*, not *dint.*"

She literally rolls her eyes at him and turns to me. "Thedor," she says. She struggles with my name, but refuses to call me Theo since James told her I was named after the chipmunk. *Arsehole.* "Can I play on your gotchi when we get home?"

After mentioning, just *once*, not long after we met, that I always envied kids with *official* Tamagotchi's when I was little, James made it his secret mission to find me one, presenting it to me on my birthday. I've no idea how he got it – an original, boxed, nineties edition – but I assume he paid a fuck-tonne for it on eBay. It's a crappy toy, but one of the most cherished things I own.

For *James'* birthday, I bought him some solid gold, anchor cufflinks. He told me about the analogy Peter used while he was in hospital and it resonates with me to this day. I'm proud to be his anchor, grateful he trusts me enough to let me support him. When he opened the gift, I told him to look at them whenever he feels like he's drifting away from me and *believe*. Believe in *me*. Believe in *us*.

It was the first birthday in a long time that he didn't spend alone and we celebrated by staying in, being naked, and simply enjoying each other. He'll never be alone again.

"You better," I reply to Isobel. "He's not been fed today. But first, how does a chicken nugget Happy Meal sound?"

"Yeah!" she shouts, her smile beaming. "Is Tess coming too?"

Tess joins us for tea sometimes, on the occasions Lucy is working the late-shift in her new job at a call centre. When she's *not* working, they'd rather be on Canal Street than watching Ben and Holly's Little Kingdom. Maybe I'm ageing prematurely, but after a day dealing with twatwaffles like Mike, I'd much rather chill out on the sofa playing Who Can Fit the Biggest Scoop of Ice Cream in Their Mouth, than getting wasted.

"Sorry, darlin' she's out with Lucy tonight."

Isobel pouts, but quickly forgets about it. "When I'm olderer I want purple hair like Tess."

"You do, eh?" I take one of her hands, James takes the other, and we swing her up and down on the way to the car. "And an earring in my tongue like her, too."

Max and Laura must curse me daily for bringing Tess into Isobel's life, especially when she got home last week and said some kid in her class was an arsewipe.

Stopping in his tracks, James drops Isobel's hand. "Race you to the car?"

Isobel takes off without replying and James swiftly overtakes her before slowing down and letting her win. "Ah, you beat me!"

He's so happy, right now. *We're* so happy. Every moment like this is precious. There are times when he falls, moments when he relapses and gives into the darkness that's tormented him all his life. But it's okay, because I'm here. I've learned to recognise his silent cries for help and I offer my hand, guide him back.

I know when he's sitting in the dark of an evening, with no light or music, that he's feeling numb. I know when he lets dishes pile up in the sink rather than putting them in the dishwasher that he's tired, mentally *and* physically. I know that when he refuses to look into my eyes when he tells me he's fine that he's *not* fine. They're such little things, things he doesn't even realise he's doing. Things that nobody else would notice because to another person such habits are their norm…but I notice because I *know* him. They're just a few of the 'unique to James' signs and symptoms Tom told me I would learn to recognise, and he was right.

When you're living with mental illness, there is no happily ever after, like the kind we write about every day. Instead, we look forward to future days spent basking in the most dazzling light, followed by ones drowning in the deepest depths of darkness. There is only one constant, one guarantee, no matter which day we face.

Love.

A love so powerful it will carry us through. We will survive. Together. And when we're old and grey and the time comes for me to leave this world, I will do so knowing I was the luckiest man ever to live, for I got to call James Holden mine. An extraordinary man who showed me joy, sadness, and the greatest strength.

I will love him beyond forever.

The End.

Acknowledgements

This story and these characters hold a special place in my heart, so if you've got this far, thank you from the bottom of my heart for reading, for sticking with my boys throughout their journey. I love you.

As always, thank you to Reese Dante for another stunning cover. I am in awe of you!

Next I feel my friend Emma needs a mention, even though she's shit. She is my sounding board, my bitching partner, co-owner of our 'shit list'. She listens to me whining and offers the obligatory 'Aww Princess' whenever I need it and is possibly the only person I've ever had a complete conversation with using only memes. Emma, you're awesome, and it *almost* makes up for how shit you are. Don't tell anyone, but I kinda love you.

Denise, my bellend, I love you HARD! Thank you for your support and encouragement, and for embracing me as a princess. Thank you for letting me vent to you, for listening, for being there. If you hadn't have forced me to eat something green, I might just think you were pretty damn perfect!

Ooo Janie. Once again I feel incredibly lucky to have, not just a reader, but a friend like Janie. She never fails to amaze me with her enthusiasm and support. She also puts up with me whining and bitching whenever I need to, too! Janie, YOU ROCK!

Sanna Solin. Thank you for all the hard work you do for your favourite authors – for pimping, encouraging, and providing tips and tricks. You are a wonderful asset to this genre. Thank you!

TRACY McKAY! Since my last release I have acquired a new friend who is all kinds of FUCKING AWESOME! I swear, we are the *same* person. You're an ear to rant to, a brain to bounce ideas off and I have lots to thank you for, but really, it's all about the porn. Keep it coming!

Now for my beta readers! I have the best in the whole damn world. Emma, Tracy, Keeley, Denise, Theresa, Janie, Jackie, Danni, Laura, Lisa, Melanie and Karen. THANK YOU! Thank you for lending me your keen eyes, for loving my stories, for being there. I love you all to the moon and back and I'm insanely grateful to each and every one of you. I feel lucky to know you guys, and relieved I don't have to send my baby out into the world without having your approval first!

Thank you to the whole MM genre, and all the fantabulous people in it. I've never experienced a community like it. I have made some very special, lifelong friends in this genre. The support from readers, fellow authors, and bloggers is incredible and I feel insanely privileged to be a part of it.

Bloggers. Yes, I'm a copout because I won't name any specifically, and that's because I just know I will forget to mention someone important. But know that I love and appreciate everything you do for me, and the book world in general. I would be nowhere without your support. Thank you for everything you do.

Again, it has been a pleasure working with Ena and Amanda from Enticing Journey Book Promotions. Thank you for all the hard work you dedicate to the authors who work with you. You're freakin' awesome!

Finally, my readers. Thanks to you, I get to live my dream, doing something I *love*, every single day. Thank you for reading, for supporting me, for interacting with me. I love each and every one of you.

About the Author

Nicola lives in Rochdale, UK, with her husband and four little shi- children. She is addicted to tattoos and Pepsi Max, hates even numbers and metal spoons, and is altogether a little bit weird. She's also really crap at referring to herself in third person and making herself sound interesting.

If you want to keep up with my crazy world, you can do that by following me here:

www.nicolahaken.net

www.facebook.com/nicolahaken

www.twitter.com/NicolaHaken

www.goodreads.com/author/show/7094294.Nicola_Haken

www.pinterest.com/nicolahaken/

Instagram - @nicolahaken

Other titles by Nicola Haken

Counting Daisies

Being Sawyer Knight (Souls of the Knight #1)

Taming Ryder (Souls of the Knight #2)

The Making of Matt (Souls of the Knight #3)